Frank Cham

Misconception

This is a work of fiction. Names, characters, businesses, places, events, locales, and incidents are either the products of the author's imagination or used in a fictitious manner. Any resemblance to actual persons, living or dead, or actual events is purely coincidental.

This book is dedicated to my wife who has been there for every word.

Chapter One

Justine woke up tucked tightly into an unfamiliar bed with an awful noise whistling around inside her skull. Her right hand slowly climbed up soft hemmed cloth and over her tiny waist feeling along a line of three buttons and a breast pocket. Eventually the fingers spidered out and tugged at the edge of a dusty odored candlewick bedspread. This created a small divot where she could breath more deeply and her long lashes fluttered open revealing slightly bloodshot slate grey eyes, which ventured around the room and took in the surroundings.

Although the curtains were closed there was strong daylight beyond, which seeped in to vaguely illuminate a lightly furnished bedroom. Everything seemed plain, dull and painted in a magnolia monochrome. Eventually she gazed back down at her fingers to study the scraped varnish and a broken nail on her grazed hand.

'Marvellous,' she hissed, the "M" cracking her dry lips and the "arvelous" releasing the taste of rust and sour breath. Justine lifted her head off the pillow, but the sudden movement sent flashes of vivid colour to accompany the cacophony behind her eyes as she blacked out.

In what felt like just a moment, she was awoken again by the sounds of digging outside and the dulled tones of "God bless the child" coming from a gramophone somewhere beneath the room. Justine took a moment to breath deeply then paused and listened to the final words, *"Here just don't worry about nothing cause he's got his own. Yes, he's got his own"*.

The song was something familiar and she clung to the fading words. Her lover Harry had sung it badly, over and over, ever since she'd given him the disk two weeks ago. Not wanting to waste another moment of what ever it was that was happening, Justine forcefully flung back the covers, swung both legs out of the bed, stood up and called out his name.

The popping in her nose and ears made her think of fizzy water pouring through the void as she swooned back down. It lasted for two sparkly seconds, during which, the only thing that actually passed through her head was this thought; *'These aren't my pyjamas.'*

Ten minutes later the young girl became semi-conscious again and found herself tucked back into the bed. The digging was still there, but the music and her internal whistle had gone. Justine turned her head and opened just one eye this time, and slowly. The curtains had been drawn so that bright white light silhouetted three blurry figures burnt against a bulging oblong of sash window. On the left was a short, thin body slouched against a much taller rotund figure, which cradled the former in a long flabby arm. The third shape was wearing a hat, she was medium height, beautifully voluptuous and stood a foot or so apart from the other two. They all seemed to be facing away from the bed.

One of them spoke quietly, 'I don't think there's any long-term worry. Nothing a good meal and a bit of quiet won't cure.' Justine vaguely recognised the voice of Nurse Heather Jones, the local Doctor's younger wife. 'How old is she?' it continued.

'Twenty,' the other two shapes quickly agreed. Their voices were in perfect harmony, but with opposing pitch and tempo.

'Well she's young enough to cope with anything and old enough to know better,' the nurse stated. 'Get some sweet tea down her scrawny neck, then see if she'll take something more filling.'

Justine opened her other eye and tried to get it to cooperate.

'I got some soup on already and the tea's in the pot.' This, the sharper voice was definitely Harry's mother Margaret Clark. 'Have you heard owt from Doctor Jones yet?'

'I spoke to an ambulance driver this morning and she swore she'd seen him treating the injured men coming in from Kings Hill.' Nurse Jones was clearly trying to sound confident, but there was a wobble in her tone as she added, 'I imagine he's still doing his job, somewhere.'

'And do you *honestly* think our Harry will be alright?' Margaret asked urgently as her petite shape slowly peeled away from the larger one and leaned on the window frame to look outside. 'I mean there are a few still missing and he was likely to be hanging around with most of them.'

'Oh Marge,' the unmistakeable deep voice of Fat Florence cut in. She was Margaret's neighbour and a notorious gossip. 'You know my old man said he'd seen your Harry before the raid. He told you they were all goin' off in that scruffy old truck, away to the hills. They'll be sat up at Croft farm right now, working out how to make a few bob in salvage from all this mayhem you mark my words.' Florence quickly snapped from useful gossip mode into a more vinegar proclamation, 'I mean let's face it, he's gonna need a few extra pennies if Nurse Jones is right about you know what,' she turned away from the window and continued, 'inside of you know who.' Then she did a strange pointing motion, gesturing toward the bed by leaning her head and rubbing her pointed finger under her nose.

Heather followed the fingers line of fire, noticed that her patient was watching them and quickly interjected, 'So they're all fine then, just waiting for the roads to clear and the bridge to reopen.' The nurse approached the bed and asked tenderly, 'Now then little miss, can you tell me your full name?'

'You know my name,' Justine said with a sideways look of confusion, 'It's Justine Page.'

'And what year is it?'

'Nineteen forty bloody one,' Justine croaked out. 'Is there something wrong with your memory Nurse Jones?'

'No, and hopefully yours is fine too,' Heather smiled. 'So, what were you doing out in an air raid with nowt more than a brolly and your strawberry blond Betty Grable curls to protect you?'

'Raid?' Justine attempted to concentrate; 'I don't really remember that much and it sort of hurts to think.' As her brain laboured to process again she became deeply worried about the overheard conversation. She took a long slow breath of air then exhaled and asked impatiently, 'what happened to all my friends, where's my Harry?'

'He'll be fine.' Florence stepped closer and folded her ample arms, sending blobs of doughy bicep and bosom in every direction. She spoke excitedly and smiled like a woman who knew her own business and everyone else's too. 'You had quite a knock. The policeman said your umbrella must've saved you, but he didn't know what from? Quite the mystery you are.' Florence winked theatrically at the pale girl.

As Justine tried to sit up again, the three onlookers dived in to help, but mostly ended up in each other's way.

Heather was the voice of reason, trained to disperse unnecessary bodies in useful ways. 'Go and get that tea Margaret and you can do what you do best Florence, find out what's happening round the town.' As Florence turned away with a broad grin, Heather cautioned her, 'Florence Fairchild, don't you go spreading any more rumours. I expect you to come back with real information for once and no tittle tattle.'

By the time Florence left the room her smile had melted into a sorrowful and jowly recognition of her own weaknesses.

Heather put a hand on Justine's rosy cheek, soothing her while also covertly checking the skins temperature. 'So Miss Page, how are you feeling today?' she asked kindly.

'Quite groggy and a bit sick if I'm honest.' Justine fumbled around at the back of her head where the throbbing pains were regrouping. It felt as if someone had glued her hair up. 'Where is Harry?' she asked again.

'It will get better, don't worry.' Heather moved her soft hand to poke an errant spiral of hair behind Justine's ear then continued down to the girl's slim neck and started silently counting off the beats of her pulse.

With a jingle of crockery Mrs Clark's slippers shuffled back in. From what Harry had told her, Justine presumed Margaret was in her late fifties. Her body paused occasionally between rapid little jolts of motion, like a nervous sparrow in a housecoat. Short greying hair, wrinkles and chewed fingernails hovered around a tray, which contained a steaming cup of tea with two plain biscuits on the saucer. There was also a small brown teapot in a colourful knitted cosy and a glass milk jug next to a huge bowl of undistinguishable beige soup.

Margaret smiled, 'Got no sugar, but there's a big blob of honey in the pot, from the farm.'

Heather picked up the cup and saucer then ushered the rest away to a nearby nightstand.

'Can I have a cigarette please, where's my handbag?' Justine looked around the room too quickly and little golden sparks shot across her view again, but the bubbles and ringing in her ears had almost gone now. 'Is Harry alright?' she persisted with more vigour this time.

Margaret tried to sidestep the question. 'You didn't have a bag dear. PC Grogan wanted to get you some things from your flat, but…' Harry's mother stopped talking and looked to the nurse for assistance before adding, 'Your dress is washed now anyway and your, under garments.' She blushed.

'So what bits do you recall?' Heather asked again after briefly dunking one of the biscuits and handing it over. 'Tell you what,' Heather waved a hand in front of Justine's blank face. 'If you can eat that and drink the tea, I might find a cigarette to go with the second cup.'

Justine ate the biscuit with determined chomps then washed it down with the tea.

In response, Heather stood up to fish out a packet of Woodbines and some matches from her uniform's side pocket. 'Fresh air to start with my girl,' the nurse insisted as she placed the cigarettes on the tray then moved away.

In the strong light near the window the nurse looked fairly young, late twenties or early thirties with firm muscle tone on her smooth arms and legs. With a hefty tug she shuddered the glazed frame up a few inches, allowing the amplified outside noise to surge in. You could hear what the men in the street were shouting now. It was mainly deconstruction instructions, accompanied by a percussive gouging of shovels. Heather immediately decided it was probably a tad too vivid for the time being and slid the window back down with a clunk.

'So is it coming back, what happened to you yesterday in the raid?' Margaret asked before Justine could start to quiz them about Harry again.

The patient pondered the question and everything that she had seen and heard since waking up. There was a whooshing feeling as jelly memories flooded back and soaked into the sponges of her brain, but without the custard and cream there was still only half a trifle.

'I sort of remember, a fuzzy version of what happened yesterday.' Justine bit her lip then tried to sit up higher in the bed and look out beyond the nurse. 'I had an awful day at work, that's for sure. I was late to start with, I remember that and I was so tired. I must have fallen asleep at my desk in the afternoon. Then the sirens woke me up I think, or, or the storm. There was a big storm, right?'

Margaret and Heather nodded together.

Justine concentrated on that thought, 'So I tried to leave, but everyone was crowding at the front of the town hall. It was raining hard and I wanted to grab my umbrella before someone else did, so I went out the back way.'

The other two women looked at each other, questioning why raindrops would be more worrying than bombs. Margaret shrugged and raised an eyebrow to Heather then tilted her head toward the bed, confirming that she didn't understand young folks either.

'Every time I put something down at work some sod swipes it, you see?' Justine tried to explain. 'Make-up, nail varnish, sunglasses, it's terrible really because these things are so hard to come by and they,' her voice trailed off as she struggled to keep on track and got distracted by the scratched paint on her nails. *It was Harry who got her all these little luxuries,* she thought.

'Yes dear, but what happened next? You were getting the umbrella, remember?' Mrs Clark had taken her turn sitting on the edge of the bed now. She passed over the second biscuit then topped up the tea.

'I think Susan was there?' Justine closed her eyes for a second. 'Yes and I tried to tag along with her, down the back passage and out of council chambers. It was like a blackout, but it can't have been night. I thought we were both heading for the staff shelter outside, it's in the old records vault.'

'Anyway,' Nurse Jones urged.

'Well I couldn't see very well, just brief glimpses in the flickering lights and between the lightening flashes and it just made sense to follow in Susan's footsteps, but she was moving so fast it was difficult to keep up.'

'Hang about, who is this Susan?' Margaret asked impatiently. 'One of the other girls from your office right, another typist?'

Justine thought it through, trying to tidy the montage of information flopping back into her brain from the day before. After a few more seconds she replied, 'My supervisor, Mrs Hill, I found out her name is Susan.'

'Is it now, well I never?' Margaret moved closer and patted the covers for Heather to sit down behind her. 'I knew it began with an "S", but I thought it stood for sour, stuck-up or possibly, sadistic!'

Justine blinked then carried on, 'When I got to the shelter, Susan had vanished. There were some girls from the typing pool and the canteen and a few clerks having a brew. All the councillors from planning were down there too, drinking brandy and playing cards. I know it was silly, but I wanted to make sure Susan was alright, so I went back up to look for her.'

'Back up?' Margaret asked, wide eyed.

'Into an air raid?' Heather added. 'Didn't anyone try and stop you?'

'Yes, I think so, but not with any real effort.'

Margaret shook her head and sighed.

Justine passed back the cup and reached for the Woodbines. 'So, I went back up and things had gotten *really* noisy. The sky was still so dark, thick with storm clouds, almost black.'

Justine managed to light a match and Margaret helped her hold it steady to the tip of the cigarette. The young girl took a long drag then blew a cloud of blue smoke above the bed. It obviously made her slightly dizzy, but she soon recovered and tried to recall some more of the previous day.

'There were little orange pom-pom explosions inside the clouds, high up, but no sun, no stars or moon. When I looked back down, I thought I saw Susan ducking around the corner, towards the street. I was stood there getting soaked, so I popped my umbrella open and called after her to come back to the shelter.'

'And did she stop?' Heather asked.

Justine gingerly shook her head. 'Maybe she couldn't hear me? As I headed for the gate, there were people running and shouting in the distance, bigger explosions and bells, then...'

Something big crashed down noisily in the street outside. The reverberations rattled the window, juddered through the floorboards and thrummed across the bed frame.

'Go on love,' Heather insisted.

'Well, then I woke up here, in someone else's pyjamas.' Justine pulled at the blue and white striped fabric distractedly. 'These aren't Harry's are they?'

There was a long pause as if the others were hoping she would suddenly remember more.

Justine decided to fill the silence with a few more questions of her own. 'So where's Harry and all my stuff and why couldn't PC Grogan get anything from my flat?'

Margaret didn't have all the answers and the ones she had would surely earn her a far sterner look from Nurse Jones than the one she was currently caught up in. 'Constable Grogan said they found you just after the raid, in a sandbagged archway near the town hall. Yer brolly was all busted up and you had no shoes on. There was a faint trail of blood in the puddles leading back to the street, but he couldn't work out what'd hit you. He tied a soggy bandage from his pack around your noggin and bought you here in a car with WPC Birch. There were too many bodies up at the hospital and, well you should see the damage at Doctor Jones's surgery, it's shocking.'

Heather cut her off, 'Oh Margaret it's only broken glass and plaster, which can be swept up and replaced.'

Harry's mother dodged Heather's new glare by looking down to flatten out her pinafore.

'Margaret washed you and I came over to patch you up properly with a stitch or two. The umbrella took the worst of it, probably saved your lives,' Heather paused abruptly; worried that she'd let the cat out of the bag.

Justine looked confused for a moment as if she had misheard her, but blamed it on the foggy head and continued her questions regardless. 'How long have I been asleep?'

Heather checked the watch hanging upside down on her uniform. 'They got you here late last night. Margaret says you were semi-conscious and mumbling about all sorts of nonsense. You were spark out when I arrived, so you've been out for the count for nearly a day. It's as much to do with exhaustion and lack of nourishment as anything else my girl, that's why we let you sleep. You need some good food and rest, that's all.'

Justine looked shocked. She had suddenly recalled something else from yesterday, a fuzzy half memory of a conversation with a town hall receptionist about meeting Harry in the bar at the Bull and Bladder tomorrow, which was now today. 'So what time is it?' she asked insistently.

Heather shrugged, 'Just after five.'

'I have to go and meet Harry at the Bull.' Justine tried to get up and out of the bed, only managing to lift herself half way, before falling back and dropping the end of the cigarette into the sheets.

Mrs Clark dived in, grabbing the butt before it did any real damage. When she opened the window again to get rid of it, the sash jammed half way up.

'What is all that noise?' Justine croakily begged to know.

Heather held the girls hand. 'Look sweetheart, you do fully understand there was a lot of bombs last night don't you?'

'Yes well, obviously. There were the sirens and the big booming bangs just before I got laid out. Was there a lot of damage, was someone hurt?'

'Calm down sweetheart, there have been a few, *hurt* yes, but no one close to you,' Heather stroked Justine's arm.

'Well there was old Mrs Adams, over the road,' Margaret grumbled, turning to look out at the exploded street. She watched the workmen drop their shovels and dig with bare hands like rats in rubbish. When they pulled out a small lifeless body, she added, 'and her dog.'

'There are some very poorly folk up at the hospital, but I think we've all been lucky,' Heather insisted reassuringly.

'But is Harry alright, has he been hurt?' Justine pleaded.

'We don't know luv,' Margaret turned her head away from the window. 'Everyone's being very kind, telling me to *soldier on* and all that.' She took a moment to reflect. 'But I ain't seen him since he dropped off the motorbike yesterday morning and if I'm honest, I am quite worried.'

'Margaret you know they're all going to be fine, they just haven't got back here yet, that's all.' Heather was trying to keep calm and carry on, but it wasn't as easy as it looked on paper.

'I played a few of his records when I got sad earlier,' Margaret croaked. 'People keeps popping in to reassure me, but there's no sign of Minnie or any of Harry's pals.' She walked back over to the bed and shivered, trying not to let it show. 'So anyway, I am pretty sure they must 'ave stayed out of town. Probably helping out some poor souls who's worse off than us, don't you think?'

'Once the road blocks go we can all get back to normal, whatever that is?' Heather looked at her watch again. 'I must go and you should take it slow for at least another night love.'

'What can I do?' Margaret asked.

'You make sure she stays in bed. Home is the first place Harry will come, soon as he can get back into town.' Heather nodded Margaret towards the door.

When the women had left her alone, Justine sighed and lay back in the bed, trying to listen to the sounds of their voices as they trailed away.

'See you later then,' Margaret said when they got to the bottom of the stairs.

Nurse Jones opened the door and stepped over some bricks. 'And don't be telling her stuff she don't need to know till she's stronger,' she waved a finger and was gone.

After showing Heather out, Margaret decided to go up and get the patient to at least consider eating some soup. However, when Justine spotted the congealed skin on top, she turned her head away and vomited tea and biscuits onto a rubber backed floor rug.

'Well, I was warned that might happen,' Margaret cooed softly as she crouched down and scooped up the rugs corners to form a makeshift bowl.

Justine apologised between breaths then managed a second discharge of bile. 'Is it the concussion, only, well, I was feeling sick before?' she asked then added, 'Before yesterday I mean.'

'Yes dear that's what it'll be, the concussion and because you never flipping eat enough.' The old lady lied and tried to contain the mess, bundling it up as best she could. 'Don't you worry dear, I'll get a cloth and probably a mop too, but you must eat something more.' She looked at the floor again then added, 'An maybe you should leave them cigarettes alone too, just for the time being, eh?'

When Margaret had cleaned up properly, she offered to cook Justine the two tiny rashes of bacon and an egg she'd kept back for Harry's breakfast, as an alternative to the soup. She was surprised when the girl gingerly accepted. Worried that it might bring on more mayhem, Harry's mother propped her mop in the hallway then went back down to make the sandwich and a fresh pot of tea.

The smell of disinfectant and cooking grew very strong, but Justine was hungrier than she'd ever been and determined not to miss out this time. Alone in the room she buttoned up the top of the nightclothes, heaved at the covers and very slowly slid herself out.

Using the bedside table she managed to wobble upright then leaned on the wall to shuffle over to the open window. As her angle and proximity changed she noticed that several of its taped panes were cracked. At least the air there was cooler, tainted with bonfire odours, damp plaster and brick dust, but less stuffy than the old bedspread. Each lung full made her feel surprisingly better, but still feeling a little unusual, she looked for a more comfortable position. There was a wooden chair next to her, which still had a pair of Harry's oil stained work trousers folded over the back. Justine collapsed into it then leaned on the sill to take in the swaying scene outside. As her vision slurred back into a sharper reality, she was stunned.

It looked like a giant spade had dug up half the street then flipped over to let the bits fall back in roughly coordinated heaps. A mountain of bricks here, another made from broken furniture and windows there. Justine took a deeper breath and whispered bitterly, 'So this is what organised chaos looks like.'

The corner shop which should have been to her right had gone. A whirlwind of brick and plaster had burst from inside it, folding the house next to it in half. Her own little bedsit had been in the old Post Office building next door to that. Most of it was still there, but the roof was holed in places and smoke was drifting up through the distorted walls, windows and relocated tiles. Beneath the rubble, curved ridges of displaced cobblestones fanned out from the missing corner shop like frozen ripples on a pond. It was early evening now, but there were still people scurrying around with wheelbarrows, trying to clear the carnage. Men in shirts and braces were making safe what was left of the structures while dumbstruck women and children picked through the bric-a-brac of broken belongings.

Opposite the Post Office, where there had been nothing to absorb the blast, it had crossed the road and hammered on the doors of several old terraced cottages. Justine hoped there had been few at home to answer, because the doors were now buried beneath the crumpled roofs and walls.

Justine felt sick with anger and loss, a cold finger ran down her spine as a hot flush flared in her cheeks. She slumped in the chair gripped hard on the rotting sill and mourned the defeat of this tiny corner of her little world. Times were hard and for her to start again with nothing would be near to impossible. *And what of all the little treasured items she'd bought from her parent's home, many miles away to the North? What was the fate of all her pictures, memories, postcards and family trinkets? Were they all gone?*

Before there had been any particular man in Justine's life, she'd started to save for what her mother had called "The bottom drawer". In reality it had began as a couple of old lemon crates under the bed. Now that she *did have* a man, it seemed there would be nothing to share with him. She had no idea where he was anyway. 'God forbid,' she sobbed quietly, 'if he's even still alive?'

So this was what war felt like for all those people in the queues at the town hall. It had been going on for two years, yet this was the first time she had truly understood what it meant. Everything had been predictable and organised until now. The rationing, the rent and the working week, it had all felt as comfy to her as an old glove. Now that glove had come undone and hit her smack in the face. It felt awful.

Had she been half asleep, or half awake since war broke out? She felt like she had somehow missed the point until now. *How could anyone do this to another person? How could they have permission to remove other peoples loved ones, destroy their homes and leave everyone living with nothing to live for?*

A feeling of guilt suddenly spread through Justine for thinking about material possessions when there had been human losses too. Watching the mothers as they witnessed their ruptured homes being pulled further apart, Justine found clarity and she felt strangely more alive. The sheets, table covers, cutlery and knick-knacks she had put in that *bottom drawer* of lemon crates, they had really meant nothing. *Only one thing mattered now and that was life. She would find Harry, she would tell him that she loved him and that would somehow make everything normal again. Wouldn't it?*

Turning away, Justine pushed out beyond the windowsill to get a better view of the other side of town. In the far distance were the hills and she hoped, somewhere amongst them were Harry and his best friend Edward up on Croft farm. She held on to the thought of Edward and his family and how happy she had been spending time with them and Harry. Between the hills and town there was a wide wooded area with two big empty clefts that lined up with the other devastation outside. She prayed that they merely marked the site of bombs dropping on trees instead of people.

The badly drooped roofline of the terraces opposite, allowed her a better view of the mid distance. On this side of the railway sidings there was an unusual pint sized, sandy coloured canvas backed army lorry. It was parked out by the gates of the allotments, on the nearside of the woodland.

Justine could just make out a young soldier in a peaked cap standing at the truck's rear, kicking dirt. She guessed he was in charge of the four regular soldiers wandering amongst the rows of cabbages and fruit bushes nearby. Three of them wore funny little helmets with no brims; the other one had a floppy hat like a cowboy. They were all in pale desert fatigues. The tiny men stopped occasionally to search sheds and structures, looking very serious as they pointed scrawny little black machine guns inside.

Justine started to feel feint again and let herself slide back inside, slumping onto the chair. When she felt better she was intrigued to study her new interior surroundings in more detail, having never been in Harry's bedroom before.

He had very few possessions on show. Above the bed she saw a box brownie picture of herself, which was slotted into the side of a larger portrait of Harry as a boy with Mrs and the late Mr Clark. There was a stout wardrobe and matching tallboy cabinet on either side of the door. The top of the cabinet held a washbowl with some shaving kit laid out along side. A pocketknife and several books that were held upright by matching glass ornaments, sat on a simple shelf next to the window.

Justine got up slowly and discovered the books were a bible, a Bedford catalogue of vehicle parts and an oily manual for Harry's Brough Superior motorcycle. Hanging on a nail above the shelf there was a damp, curled and innocuous buff coloured calendar from nineteen thirty seven.

'That's a curious thing to have kept this long,' she said to herself while reaching out to take it down.

At that moment Margaret returned with a fresh cup of tea and a doorstep sandwich containing a well done egg stacked between Harry's ration of rashes.

'Did you say something luv?' Margaret asked.

'I was just thinking out loud that's all. I found this out of date calendar.' Justine put it back on the nail, sat down again and began consuming the food like a woman possessed.

Margaret looked at the mop and bucket through the open doorway, but it seemed it was not needed this time.

Between cheek swelling mouthfuls, Justine pointed outside with the remaining corner of sandwich and asked, 'What are those soldiers doing? Did one of the bombs not go off?'

'Well there's been all sorts of rumours, even talk of a full on invasion by parachutists. The bells was a ringing for ages, bonging out across the whole blooming valley.' Margaret moved closer and leaned out of the window. 'Then them nice troops turned up in droves and calmed things down. They arrived last night as the storm departed an' the sun came out again for a bit, that sort of helped,' she shrugged. Then looking down at the men still working on the wrecked buildings across the street, Margaret added, 'The bombs had done so much damage you see, people were trapped all over and it was a race to get 'em out before the proper darkness came back. Those soldier boys were very helpful last night and well organised. Best of all, they're all tanned and muscular with nice teeth.' She grinned and showed her own yellowing dentures as if to make the point.

'Have you been *looking after them* Mrs Clark?' Justine asked sarcastically.

'We had you to take our minds off of it all didn't we?' Margaret huffed.

Justine managed a tiny laugh at this. Mrs Clark giggled too.

'Well I mean, not *too* many people were hurt round here, considering all the damage. It could have been a lot worse couldn't it? An' the hoards of parachutists turned out to be just a handful of German flyers, bailing out after the big guns shot 'em down. Their bomber landed on St Mary's Chapel and by all accounts there ain't much left of that neither.' She made the sign of the cross and looked skywards

Justine passed back the empty plate and leaned out to look over the treetops and beyond the two points of smashed woodland. In the low hills she could just make out a small plume of smoke still drifting near the chapel's location amongst the distant forest canopy.

Margaret was the first to notice more soldiers heading back towards their vehicle near the allotments. At first it was just a movement near the tree line, then slowly they began to pop out into the clearing two and three at a time.

These soldiers had found something, or more precisely someone. As the last few figures cleared the trees you could see that one man was being held up between two squaddies. He was limping badly, dressed in black and with his hands behind his back. Several riflemen were covering him with their weapons as he struggled to keep upright.

'Germans,' Mrs Clark gasped, but her voice was hushed as if she thought she might provoke the brute, even from this great distance.

The two women looked at each other and leaned out a little further to get a better view of the action. The last two men to break tree cover were carrying what could have been the remains of parachutes.

The peak capped officer walked over to the injured man and spoke to him. The German looked like he was thinking of an answer then he spat in the officer's face. The gesture of defiance was clear. A rifleman behind the prisoner struck out at a kidney with the butt of his gun, which chopped the dark figure down onto one knee. The man in charge was not happy about either event. While another soldier helped the German up, the officer wiped away the spittle then rebuked the rifleman who'd struck out.

'Australians,' Margaret confirmed with excitement. 'Bloody loads of 'em, an' they're everywhere now. They says we're all gonna 'ave to put a few of 'em up if they hangs around. I saw one brute out front earlier that I fancy for a lodger and no mistake. Fat Florence says one of 'em is a little black boy in shorts.'

Justine looked puzzled. She took a moment to put the last few thoughts in her head back together, then turned to Margaret and said, 'I have to go, I need to find Harry.' It was not a request; it was a statement of fact.

'Yes, dear I know. I was thinking downstairs and I already considered trying to stop you, because,' she shrugged smirking again. 'You know I'll catch hell off of Nurse Jones don't you? But, well, what can *I* do to hold you back, I'm just a little old lady ain't I?' She passed over the cup, 'I knew as you would help me find him, soon as you got some scram down your gob an' had time to collect yourself.'

'I do feel much better now.' Justine slurped up the drink, passed the cup back and patted at her tummy. 'The sleep and the sandwich really helped.'

Mrs Clark looked down at Justine's hand with a massive grin across her face. 'Listen, there's summat I 'ave to tell you before you go.'

'What, what is it?' Justine tilted her head and awaited an answer.

'I wanted to tell you that,' in that moment Margaret saw the old family portrait on the wall and decided to wait until Harry was home before spilling the beans. 'I wanted to tell you that, that I've filled you a quick bath downstairs and you're not going till you've been in it.'

Justine stretched and rummaged at her bloodied and tangled hair again. 'Alright then and I need an alternative to pyjamas.'

'Already run over your dress with the iron and bought it up, it's on the cupboard in the hallway, them frilly undies too. My winter boots are the only ones that'll fit you I'm afraid. There's a small jacket what belonged to my old man or you can look through Harry's stuff.'

Justine stood up, surprised and reassured that she did not feel quite so faint this time. She took Mrs Clark's hand then decided to give her an enormous kiss and a hug instead.

'Good luck sweetheart.' Margaret said with a wobble in her voice and they both blushed

To escape quickly, Justine acted-out remembering the hot bath and went off to find her clothes. When she had bathed and washed her hair, the feel of the cool cotton dress sliding over her damp tummy and thighs bought back other memories. Memories of how happy she had been in Harry's embrace, only one day ago.

Chapter Two

In the early morning of that day before, Justine had been returning from a night out with Harry. She had been snuggled in behind with her arms tight around him while he'd throttled out the Brough Superior motorcycle and together they sliced the warm summer morning in two.

She was happy there; content to float through space until his pointy elbow burst the bubble and the motorbike came to an abrupt halt. With three words at the tip of her tongue Justine reluctantly swung away and stood at the kerbside, eyes closed, pouting for a kiss. When the bike immediately roared off again trailing fumes and dust, she coughed out her backup three words instead, 'You're an arse!'

Justine huffed as she pulled off a headscarf, brushed her self down and fumbled a key into the bedsit's front door. Upstairs, standing bare foot and half dressed at the bathroom mirror she was a little less than six foot tall. Her eyes stared into a slightly older face than she could recollect seeing before. It made her think of her mother for a moment until one tired eye winked back with a promise to her body of an earlier night, soon.

She skipped breakfast as usual and scurried toward work through a tic-tac-toe of taped up windows, backed by blackout blinds still half drawn. Along the route almost every surface had been adorned with patriotic bunting, sandbags or propaganda posters, just to remind her that there was still a war on. It was something Justine constantly tried to forget.

It had been two years since Chamberlain's broadcast had crackled out of her father's prized radio and infected their home sweet home. Two long years, but Justine could still feel the emotions bubbling up inside. That vision of her parents Sophie and Norman frozen in time, staring deep into each other's frightened eyes as everything changed around them. The three of them sitting there listening at the kitchen table, a daisy chain of squeezed hands. Justine's own concentration had drifted to the illuminated screen of the wireless. Those black on taupe highlighted cities; Vienna, Luxembourg, Paris and London had glowed and dimmed menacingly in time with the dialogue.

Back then Justine had never seen the world outside of her parents tiny village even though her mother was French. The way Norman told it,

Sophie had arrived with a suitcase full of Gitanes and when she'd smouldered her way through all of them she had given up. From that day on she had not smoked, not talked about France and never even spoken in her native tongue. It seemed to Justine that her mother had hidden away, had a baby and created a one-dimensional world around it.

As the Prime Minister droned on, Justine had focussed so hard on the illuminated dial that the words began to blur out and slipped away. It felt like she would never get to experience the world as it was in the here and now, unless she escaped soon. That broadcast had awoken questions deep inside her, questions that had gnawed away at her senses for years, looking for a release. *Why hadn't Sophie ever gone back and shown her daughter all the wonders of life in France? Why had they never left the stupid little English village that Norman had bought her back to after the first war?*

Back then in thirty-nine Justine had been very naive and frightened. Despite all of that, when Norman turned off the radio she had gone upstairs, packed a small case of belongings and simply waited.

When the call up had eventually come, she leapt at the chance of war work. Her only criteria were; that it had to be far away from the village and in a much bigger and faster location. She didn't want to be safe with mum and dad any more. She wanted to get out, to get away and to feel alive.

Since moving Justine had spent her time having fun, ignoring the growing shadow of conflict and reaping the benefits of breaking away. Benefits like regular wages, freedom, independence and more recently a lover.

Justine tried again to ignore all the tokens of war around her and thought instead of Harry making jokes last night at their friend's farm. As her hollow stomach lurched, the thought slid into a more graphic flashback from the dew covered wheat field they'd parked the motorbike in on the way back to town. This vivid image was of Harry pulling his shirt off to reveal those muscles in the dawn sun and it had taken her breath away, then and now.

She smirked and daydreamed on while walking the wrong way around the next corner. As soon as she stepped out a burst of low sunshine blinded her. It melted through the images inside her head in the same way a bulb can burn out a celluloid film. Confused, she had stopped and looked around then done that thing people do when they take a wrong turn. Looking down at an imaginary watch, she sucked her teeth, shrugged and turned back in the right direction.

Three roads away from Justine's wrong-turn, Harry Clark stepped out of the tobacconists and continued his journey to the end of the old High street. He had dropped the bike off in his mothers shed to save petrol and avoid the growing gaggles of women and children queuing up for the half empty shops to open. They were all holding empty baskets and wearing long faces, until they saw him.

The younger women's eyes flirtatiously followed him and smiled. It was a natural unconscious reaction because Harry represented the pinnacle of the few young and healthy looking men still left around the town. He was acutely handsome with a movie star appearance and a sportsman's physique. Most women would turn their heads and dreamily follow his over six-foot form as it undulated around them. He had short golden-brown hair, with a side parted quiff of sun kissed curls. His sharp dark brown eyes set above strong cheekbones, flicked left and right as he politely nodded good morning to them all with a dip of his head. It didn't matter that he looked a little unkempt. The open collarless shirt, the unshaven stubble and the grime embedded in his knuckles and nail beds just added to the effect.

The children stared because they thought he looked like a warrior and a true British bulldog fighter. They also watched their older sisters and mothers reactions to him and they wondered why he was not fighting at the front. Why this man mountain mechanic was not in the army or air force along with their own fathers or brothers and every one else who was fit enough to go to war.

Ahead of Harry's destination a bigger group of older men and women blocked half the road, spilling down the town hall steps and into the gutter. They did not look back at Harry; they had more important things to worry about.

Harry reached a set of big wooden doors and rummaged through his pockets for the key to the garage's smaller Judas gate. As one of the best Bedford mechanics in the area, he had been kept back in a reserved occupation. That's what his papers said anyway. He still felt young and strong at twenty-five and yet everyone kept telling him he had an old head. Living with a mother who'd had him late in life could have been to blame.

Harry had heard the stories, worked the dates and guessed he'd been conceived on leave. That his father's parting shot in the first war had been fired towards his mother's womb in the hope of hitting some kind of pseudo immortality. Then while heading for the front in the final few weeks of fighting he'd been blown out of his mother's life before Harry was even born. Mr Clark's brief thirty-six years had been signed off by the even briefer contents of a telegram. Caught there for a moment in those precious few words from an unknown official, then with a *"STOP"* he was neatly folded away and despatched to the sideboard.

Harry tried to cheer himself up with a glance sideways at one of his favourite girls, but she had gone. All summer long a fading sun toned woman in a striped bikini had beamed out at him from behind the petrol pumps. Her bosom enhanced slogan urging him to "TELL HER NOTHING" as "She might be an agent". Ironically, it was those last few words, beneath her undulating form that always made Harry smile the most.

Now a crude image of a car overflowing with passengers had been hastily pasted over her. The new cartoon car's occupants were singing the words, "Hi ho, hi ho, it's off to work we go." Below that a bolder caption read, "Help with the War and squeeze in one more!"

'Well that's not good for business,' Harry muttered to himself before realising the workshop door was already unlocked. This meant that his boss Albert Croft had beaten him to work yet again. Harry went inside, paused near his little shelf of personal belongings and felt around for a delicate bottle, hidden at the back. After spraying enough aftershave to mask the scent of two days spent without a proper wash. He put the bottle back, side stepped the atomised cloud and cautiously lit a cigarette. Thus began the general daily work routine.

New jobs and old invoices were held on a heavy brass spike resting on a tool bench beneath the shelving. Harry picked the paperwork up and began to lift off the top most sheets as a large furniture van endeavoured to pull up outside and finally stopped on the kerb next door. The mechanic in Harry recognised the sound of Captain Cooke's worn out Dennis truck shuddering into silence amongst the shrieks and curses of several nearby shoppers. He sighed heavily, pinched out the half smoked cigarette's tip and stepped gingerly back out onto the hot street.

A gentleman in his early sixties jumped down from the van's passenger door, dressed in the olive green officer uniform of the Home Guard. It was tailored cloth, not the cheap denim version the lower ranks like Albert had been issued with. The bulbous officer arched his back and hoisted up his gun belt and trousers, which although hand cut and well measured, could not be made to properly fit such a vast and heaving belly.

'Clark,' the captain snapped nasally through a thick grey moustache. 'My sergeant tells me you are the chap I need to speak to about softening the van's suspension.' The officer took a step closer and surveyed the garage frontage to confirm that they were almost in the right place.

Harry strolled over to the vehicle and crouched down with the top few note papers and receipts still in his hand. Looking in at the solid wheels and limp leafed spring suspension he nodded, 'You could be in luck sir, we might 'ave some parts that'll still fit this old flapper.' He got on well with most of the men in the Home Guard, but not their captain. His retired headmaster, turned antique dealer, was not the kind of man Harry wanted to wear a uniform for again, or drink a pint with, *ever*.

Looking back along the kerb to where the old truck should have stopped, Harry advised, 'You might need to sort them brakes out too. If you drop the old girl off later, I'll have a look under the petticoats and strip down her layers. See what's wrong with her undercarriage.'

'Very well, but not today,' Cooke huffed. He hated bad grammar and especially despised sexual innuendo of any kind. This was primarily because he didn't understand it.

'I had a word to Sergeant Sanderson, the other day at the pub.' Harry spoke slowly as if the captain was somehow impaired then gestured over at the van's driver. 'I think we're already square on what needs doing.'

Sergeant Sanderson was sitting at the wheel rolling a cigarette and trying hard not to roll his eyes or smile.

The captain played nervously with his moustache for a moment before saying, 'We need a big top up too boy, but I only have coupons for a gallon or so. I'm still awaiting this month's Home Guard allowance you see?'

'I can only give you what you have papers for,' Harry insisted.

Cooke raised his cap to wipe away some sweat then looked around furtively and whispered, 'I have been doing some extra mileage this week. Removal work for, for some official associates of mine.' The captain moved further from the eyes and ears of the nearby grocer's queue before he continued, 'They promised they would sort out the fuel vouchers with Albert. Has he not mentioned it to you?'

'No he hasn't,' Harry said firmly, but looked through the notes in his hand just in case. 'Hang on there's something here,' he mumbled while unfolding a perforated document from a fan of receipts, 'but these are municipal vouchers sir, for council vehicles only.' He counted them up and exclaimed, 'Blimey, that's a lot of fuel. Sorry, I just can't do it.'

'Look lad this is a bit hush-hush. I have been doing my bit to help out you see?' Captain Cooke leant over to view the note. 'The Council have requisitioned my assistance several times recently, but all for the benefit of the town I assure you.' Cooke waited a second. 'It is all there and signed for and official, you see? And there, Councillor Burdock has given his authority on the back.' He tapped on the note with a manicured finger, 'No one will question your work.'

'I dunno, I mean I can't even make out the signature.' Harry squinted at the docket then tried to hold it up to the light.

The Captain grabbed at Harry's wrist, 'I have the money too boy, don't worry and as you say, it is the paper work that counts and you have that in your hands.'

Harry shook off the grip and sighed. 'All right then, I'll do you half for now,' He agreed reluctantly. 'Back up carefully mind,' he called back to Sanderson who was struggling to change gear in the cab's tight confines.

Ten minutes later when the vast fuel tank was half full and capped, the captain patted the side of his van and Sanderson started her up. 'Well then, we had better be off, important business and all that.' Cooke walked away heading back around to the cab, then stopped and turned back to say, 'On another matter...'

'Here we go,' Harry muttered discreetly, expecting the "Your Country Needs You" lecture, but he was wrong.

'I presume Albert, I mean Corporal Croft, is free for his duties this afternoon? It is very important that every man attends. We will be out all night for a bit of, well anyway, can he come?'

Harry laughed. It was comical to him that anyone thought that he was in control of Albert's movements. Albert Croft was the boss and Harry his apprentice. Mutual respect stopped the roles from ever being reversed, although everyone else in town knew it should. Albert Croft was a tinkerer not an engineer, but he just about held in there as the one in charge.

'I would think he'd love a day out from all this grease and grit. Should I tell him to pack his best underpants?' Harry asked sarcastically.

There was no reply from Cooke, just more nervous moustache twiddling. The captain was deep in thought again and not listening to a word.

Harry looked at his watch and tried again. 'Albert is normally busy about now. You can wait in the yard if you like? He'll be out when he's finished the news-sheet,' he smirked, 'unless he uses the toilet papers I got for him instead.'

After more facial hair twiddling Cooke popped out of his trance. 'That should be fine then. Well if you could remind Corporal Croft about this afternoon, I will expect him here in full uniform at fifteen hundred hours, sharp.' The captain struggled to climb back into the cab, huffing all the way.

Harry waved a vague farewell and returned to reviewing his paperwork inside the garage. The front façade of the building had been there since the days of the blacksmith. It still had several iron rings on the sidewall for horses to be tethered to. Half the storeroom held a dozen dusty shelves filled with out-dated spare parts for carts and steam vehicles that no longer came in. The main building's newer corrugated roof had enough space beneath it for two medium sized trucks to sit side by side. It currently contained two such municipal garbage hulks that had seen better days, but Harry had the skills to keep them going for many more years. At the rear of these vehicles there was a little brown car belonging to Doctor Jones that Albert had been working on for several days.

After checking carefully around the garage Harry pushed the Judas door half closed with his boot. Quickly he pulled all of the remaining papers off the note spike in his hand to expose an embossed Bedford badge. Twisting and pressing it made the brass plate mechanism spring open, revealing a hidden compartment in the base. He removed a sheet of paper from within, then unfolded and read the note. In one movement all the other dockets were pushed back on the spike and the compartment clicked shut. The block was then repositioned back in the same relatively dust free square it had sat in for years.

Harry moved quickly to the very rear of the establishment, took out a lighter and lit the paper message. It dropped, burning end over end into a rusting hubcap on the floor as he relit his cigarette to disguise the smell.

'I worry about all this going up in flames,' came a voice from behind him as the small door creaked fully open again. He peered around the old garbage trucks to where Justine's contorted form was framed by the small doorway and bright sunlight. Strands of her short reddish hair lit up in the brilliance, which also made her dress a bit transparent.

Harry tried to ignore some of these facts as he walked nonchalantly towards her. '*I don't want to set the world on fire. I just want to start a flame in your heart*,' he crooned cornily with a big smiling finale.

Justine was unimpressed by the singing, but when Harry produced a packet, reached out and deftly flicked a single cigarette up, it was hard not to return the smile. 'I don't have time. I'm late thanks to you,' she smirked, then climbed inside, took the cigarette anyway and put it in her handbag for later. It was clear to her that Harry was up to something, but she decided against her better judgement that it was probably something nice.

Harry watched amazed as she sprang into a new stance and balanced awkwardly adjusting the line of her stocking with one hand while tousling her hair with the other.

'You should be in the circus with that act,' he joked. 'And don't draw too much attention to those posh socks neither or everyone will want a pair.' He quickly reached out to steady her, gripping gently on her bare arms with his strong hands.

She leaned herself against his hold, replying sternly, 'Oh yes, I could drive your silly clown wagon around the big top, honking the horn and all in my Sunday best.'

'She's not a clown wagon, I love Minnie more than you know,' he fired back.

'Oh I know Harry. I just wish you showed me half as much attention as you do that old wreck. Every Sunday you and your pals go off to tinker with her and I'm left all alone.'

'You know I love tinkering with you just as much as that truck.'

'Oh, thanks.'

Harry gave her a wink and stepped forward to embrace her shoulders with two grubby hands extended outwards.

She dodged him by stepping further inside the gloomy garage, then flattened the material down and asked, 'What do you think of the new dress then?'

'Nice, it looks familiar.'

'I should blooming well hope not. I made it from one of the old bed sheets that mother posted to me last week.' Justine moved in close, trying not to touch anything in the grimy entrance. After tilting her head she whispered in his ear, 'I told you all about it last night, remember?'

He could feel her warmth as a fragrance of floral soap gently pushed past his over powering aftershave. 'Course I do,' Harry nodded lamely as she stepped away again.

'I made the pockets and collar from a tea towel, they're not part of the new ration you see?' She retreated back outside into the sunshine and pirouetted so that Harry could take in the complete design.

Harry poked his head out and admired her and the dress. He really liked the sky blue colour, which made his brain start considering it for the final paint job on Minnie. As Justine continued to model he remembered the hidden note and all the other things he needed to get done today. Worried that commitments were spreading him a bit thin lately, he decided the lads would have to help out.

'Are you even listening to me?' Justine snapped, hoisting him outside and pulling at his wrist to check the time.

'Every word,' Harry lied as his big body tripped over the door's sill and into the light. 'I like that blue, it suits you.' He turned away, hands in pockets and leaned around the side of the garage to where Minnie was parked, lurking in the shadows.

The truck was less coordinated than the dress. The cab was navy blue, the bonnet a lighter RAF shade with one red door and one olive green.

The old Bedford banger did indeed have the look if not the style, of a big multi-coloured clown transporter, ready to fall apart at the push of a big red button.

Justine frowned at Harry. 'Hey dreamer,' she scorned, poking him in the ribs. 'I can meet you for lunch, if you can tear yourself away from fiddling with Albert's greasy nuts.'

'Well,' Harry grinned as he struggled to think of an excuse that would put him and his wagon in the right place at the right time. 'I need to take Minnie and service some wagons out of town. I might be back.'

Justine carried on regardless, 'Try and get back for lunch though, please. There's a big meeting this morning and Mrs Hill will be working me to the bone. I won't be invited to the lunch buffet, so I'll need someone to moan at.' She paused, awaiting some sympathy then pointed out, 'and that would be you Harry.'

'Good, for us I mean, not you or the food. We could get some chips?' Harry felt guilty, hating all the broken promises and lies that made his impossible life work. 'You wait by Mary's café, if I ain't there on time you can moan at her instead.' He always tried to believe that Justine *would* understand, if only he *could* be honest. As he leaned in to kiss her long pale neck she brushed him away and began to walk off briskly towards the town hall.

'You stink,' she said without looking back.

'But I'm wearing the scent you picked out,' Harry looked puzzled and sniffed at his armpit.

'Too much,' Justine called back at him. 'Use less, useless,' she laughed, stopping a few yards away and turning back to watch him trying to smell the cologne. 'See you later then, at one o'clock,' she smiled, shook her head and blew a very fake starlet kiss then walked away.

Harry stood and watched her legs shimmy away through the crowd, around the sandbags and up the curved steps of the civic buildings. 'No you won't sweetheart,' he admitted quietly and ducked back inside.

Chapter Three

It was quiet and much cooler beyond the heavy spinning doors at the entrance of the town hall. Justine felt goose bumps rising on her arms and calves as she pushed through the long, silent lines of people moving with her into reception.

She had noticed that the longer the war went on, the bigger the queues here became. Every week the faces seemed to grow more desperate, sullen and older. The building was a hub for the bureaucracy that war inevitably threw up for every household. Paperwork created a free flowing and unfathomable headache on both sides of the shiny wooden counters. She knew that even if these hopefuls had the current and correct forms, the rules would often change before fruition and they might all have to start over again.

She wondered if the men who planned this war ever considered these little lines of people who fed the war machine with *their* husbands, wives, sons and daughters. Her mind was still pondering this question when her body crashed through into chambers. She looked sideways and made a mental note to take her umbrella home tonight, before someone else adopted it. Next to it along a normally empty row of hooks was a neat line of identical dark grey raincoats.

Justine flicked a smile at the others in the room as she sat down and removed the cover from her typewriter. Two distinct groups of men leaned over a large oak table of plans and documents in front of her workstation. Half of them were familiar chubby old men in tweed; the rest were younger dark suited men with slender, well cut outlines.

None of them returned her smile, but her supervisor Mrs Hill managed to fire off a look, which was in every way the complete opposite of a grin. She had noticed the young girls tardy arrival and was unimpressed. Hill was better known around town as "The Widow". Always wearing mostly black in memory of her dead husband, complemented with a locket of his hair hung beneath a constant frown. She pulled out Justine's time sheet and marked down the lateness with a swift and heavy pencil stroke.

Lowering her glasses and looking sideways at the girl, Mrs Hill stated, 'I believe we are all here now Mr Burdock.'

Justine had only worked directly with the Widow for a month or so, but from day one she'd felt like a badly behaved puppy in the company of this sour woman who never praised her.

Councillor Burdock was balding, middle aged and had the blotchy skin, expensive old-fashioned clothing and large paunch of a man who clearly had more money and luxury than genuine style or sense. He stepped back from the other men and aligned his notes on a nearby lectern. 'Please take your seats gentlemen and my secretary will run through the minutes of our last meeting.' He beckoned Mrs Hill forward with a wobble of the head.

She pushed her glasses back up and began reading off points of interest as the men found seats around the main table, 'The *very satisfactory* report of the Air Raid Precaution Committee was presented by Councillor Hyde at our last meeting. It revealed the shelters in Church Street and Moor Street accommodating up to two hundred and forty people were practically complete. We are awaiting another delivery and accumulators for lighting and the laying on of water. When installed these two shelters will be fully equipped...'

Someone yawned loudly from a dark corner behind the seated men.

In the silence that followed Justine looked up from typing to try and see who had made the interruption. She realised quickly that no one else was looking around and was about to ask what was happening when Mrs Hill coughed, cleared her throat and carried on.

'A final point bought up by Councillor Moor was evidence of public shelters being misused elsewhere. Consequently solid doors have recently been fitted to ours and these are now locked at all times.'

This time there was a small snort of disapproval from the same spot on the far side of the room.

'Thank you.' Burdock waved her away. 'As a further point of order I welcome back Mr Jarvis and his colleagues from the Ministry of Works and Supplies.' He looked down at his notes and then scanned the room's darkest corner, looking for the new face. 'Can I also take this opportunity to introduce to my fellow councillors a Mr Stevens?'

'Stevenson,' corrected Mrs Hill.

'Not important,' Stevenson waved at them dismissively and leaned forward in his chair.

'Ah there he is, Mr Stevenson from the Ministry of, or Department of, what was it?' Burdock regretted not listening when Mrs Hill had tried to prepare him earlier.

She graciously passed him her neatly written bullet point notes and went back to preparing papers for the ministry men to sign later.

Burdock pushed on, 'Mr Stevenson is here to see what the committee have accomplished thus far. With special interest towards the acquisition of further land for future development.'

This final statement caught the interest of the other local councillors. Between them, the grinning and well-fed faces owned most of the surrounding area. They wanted as much of it as possible to be used for the war effort, so long as this was done at the right price. As one, the tweed side of the table swivelled in their seats to see what they hoped would be a new friend smiling back. The ministry men pretended to be a row of statues. All of them facing away from their higher-ranking official, whom they knew enough about to stay out of his radar.

Not aware of any threat, Burdock and the other councillors began a long round of welcoming applause from their side of the room.

Mrs Hill had watched the gaggle of grey suited Westminster officials arrive half an hour ago, all smiles and slick hair. Mr Stevenson had travelled in his own car though, clearly not sharing a stuffy train with the others. From every angle attempted so far, all that she had seen of this mysterious figure was his large fedora. Its wide brim dipped over one eye casting a shadow, which blocked most of the face from view.

When the applause had faltered away, Stevenson slipped a note pad into a briefcase at his feet and got up. With the hat still firmly in place he wondered over to the table and helped himself to coffee.

'Gentlemen, ladies,' he began. 'I am not here to cause alarm. We are happy with the progress in this region. Your efforts in production and fulfilling the requirements of the government are noted as being,' He paused to stir and tapped the spoon on the side of his cup, 'satisfactory.'

Justine did her job, taking down every word until Mr Stevenson walked over to her workstation and placed a leather-gloved hand on her pale fingers. She shivered.

'My dear,' he oozed the words in a calm and controlling voice. 'I am not technically here, no more than a fly on the wall shall we say?' Taking a shiny black pen from his jacket pocket he struck out several words on the page protruding from her typewriter. Then he sighed deeply, picked up her short hand pad and crossed out a few more scribbles from that too.

Justine glanced up at his right side and saw some grey beneath the hat's rim. He looked in shape and reasonably handsome from this angle. Slight wrinkles and crow's feet denoted to her that he was probably in his very late forties, about the same age as her father.

Then the cold glove was back on her skin, making a connection again as he said, 'I will let you know if I want you to document anything I have said. As I am not here, that probably won't happen though, will it?'

He smiled at her, which unnerved everyone else in the room. All of them were pleading with their eyes for her to reply. She looked to Mrs Hill who in turn looked to Mr Burdock for confirmation that all this *was* above board. Burdock nodded back over a chorus of stifled coughs.

Stevenson began to move around the table again. 'I only wish to see if there is anything more that *we* can do to help you. However, there could also be something you can do to help me.' Placing his cup in the corner of a map on the table, he slowly leaned in for a closer inspection of the area. Then in silence he picked up another ground plan and returned to his seat in the corner. When no one else moved or spoke he looked up from the document and said, 'Please go on about your business.'

Burdock spluttered back the attention of his team and outlined his requirements. 'Well ahem, yes, today's meeting is about acquiring the final signatures on our amended requisition and completion forms.'

As she cautiously took down notes, Justine thought about what a relief it would be to see all of the big public shelters finally functioning. Hundreds of cramped Anderson Shelters and dozens of large and crudely covered trenches had been constructed to satisfy ministry quotas since the outbreak of war. These were no longer enough for the industrial towns growing population, which had doubled with the need for more war workers.

Burdock regained his composure. 'Our citizens might grumble now, but soon they will see what we have achieved.' He beamed at his friends on the committee.

The councillors all smiled back, unashamed to profit from the conversion of their previously owned or recently acquired land and property. Some of the underground vaults and caverns they held in hand had already been used to make money for several generations of their powerful families. Now the huge subterranean storage areas had been rented, vented and cleared out, wired up and made profitable again and all at someone else's expense.

'We require more benches for the space beneath the old brewery. It will now accommodate two hundred residents from the houses and Gas Works surrounding the site.' Burdock took a breath, surveyed the room and ploughed on, 'We also need more toilet units and plumbing equipment for this site now. First aid centres, canteens and sleeping areas have already begun being installed in some of the other locations.'

Mr Jarvis and his dark suited colleagues nodded their approval as Burdock span through his list of similar requirements.

While Burdock droned on, Mrs Hill passed a large wad of papers along the table for Councillor Moor to sign. Moor was horrendously overweight and had the very complexion of the tinned meat his factories sold. The most legendary underground excavation in town was his. It allowed six hundred pigs each day to be stealthily moved beneath the streets, from the train yards to his slaughter cellars at the heart of town.

Justine had heard stories of the pig tunnel, but never wanted to see it for herself and was pleased to note that its conversion was not on the shelter meeting agenda. Instead Moor had finally agreed to share the use of a submerged passage beneath the river that had previously coupled his old and new factories together. His newer metal pressing factory had also been converted to make more profitable components for aircraft this year, alongside a still healthy sideline of tin cans. Every aircraft part produced was paid for on a government Cost-Plus contract. Which meant that Mr Moor's exaggerated costs of manufacture were being fully covered and then a buoyant percentage of profit paid on top.

Councillor Burdock was thankfully rushing things now, 'New street entrances have been constructed across the town. There will be an opportunity to examine one of these shortly.' Burdock checked his watch one last time and folded over the final sheet of Mrs Hill's notes before hesitantly adding, 'I am sorry to say we will not be able to enter any of the other underground spaces just yet.'

'But we need to view *all* of the excavations today, before fully signing off.' Mr Jarvis interrupted and pulled at his collar and tie with a curled finger. As the head of the ministry men and with the hat watching him from the corner, he was clearly agitated.

'As you know Mr Jarvis, the final stages require the installation of electrical and plumbing components. It would be far too dangerous for us to enter most of the unfinished shelters right now.' Mr Burdock looked deep into their doubtful faces, 'I wouldn't want to hold up progress by stopping our men from working at this critical stage. We do have one completed shelter prepared for your viewing gentlemen.' He grinned at the room, held out an expectant hand to Mrs Hill and clicked his fingers; 'My secretary will facilitate you with reports on all the shelters already *technically* signed off by your engineers weeks ago.'

Eventually the reports and matching legal documents were laid out on the big table, the majority of them ready to be witnessed and countersigned for the final time. Every autograph meant on-going expenses and money in the bank for the greedy, tweedy suits. Mr Jarvis seemed a little more contented to have many a box ticked for his department. It meant he could focus on the more difficult towns near the top of his ever-growing snag list.

As the last pages were passed along, a splinter group emerged to discuss their own plans. As soon as Mr Jarvis had put down his pen, Councillors Humble, Smith and Moor triangulated and cornered him.

'Mr Jarvis, regarding your recent notice of works requirements for industry,' Moor began.

'We think there is potential for military storage at these three new locations,' Smith stepped forward with a map and continued the presentation. He was much thinner and about ten years younger than the other councillors, but still had time to catch up. 'These old mills, the quarry and the mine, could easily be converted,' he pointed out the locations then rested a hand on Mr Jarvis's shoulder to keep him seated.

Moor and Humble pulled a card table nearer, unfolded the lid and produced from beneath it something draped in light fabric. Councillor Smith conjured away the cloth to reveal a detailed balsa wood concept for a large underground factory. Every visible face surrounding it wore a broad smile.

Mr Stevenson was not happy though. Moving over to the main table he unfolded his own vast geological map and placed it over all the others to obliterate them from view. 'These shelters in town are fine.' Using his fat black pen he circled several areas on the map. 'The land here in the woods and here on the hills will not be investigated further for any military or civilian use.'

Councillor Moor spoke up for his cohorts, 'But we have invested considerable time in our proposal for the industrialisation of these areas and we all...'

'You have invested nothing more than brandy, cigars and club membership fees.' Stevenson was showing a tinge of anger now, his shell of calmness slightly dissolved. He was also showing his face, full on for the first time.

Councillor Moor froze, staring into the strange darting eyes that flickered in front of him. He wished for them to go away and hide back under the hat where they belonged. They were bright green and piercing yet not identical. The left one seemed a lighter hue, more bloodshot near the nose with a wobbling retina. A thin scar jutted down across that cheek like a three-inch fleshy tick.

'I could have all these areas requisitioned in a flash and cut your whole syndicate off at the neck, just like one of your pigs,' Stevenson spat the words then paused. He took a deep breath, pressed a finger to his left temple and contained his exasperation. Then using all his skills to stay on track, he slowly exhaled and the hat's brim tilted generously back down again. 'Don't worry, you're factory *is* a good idea, I just want to put it over the other side of town, it would still be on your land.' Mr Stevenson bent down and chuckled as he toyed with some of the moving parts on the scale model and a large section broke off. 'When we became aware of your proposals, well we decided to do our own research, that is all. Better to be one step ahead of the proverbial herd.' He handed the broken components to Councillor Moor with an apologetic grin.

'But, this is the first time we have shown anyone our ideas?' Mr Moor looked at his two colleagues who seemed to be just as confused.

'Gentlemen,' Stevenson said abruptly with a trace of bitterness, as if the word tasted sour when addressed to them. Then he tried again with a huge crocodile smile. '*Gentlemen*, I just think you should concentrate on this main idea for now,' he leaned gently on the card table with both hands. His fingers gripped the edges and began to ever so slowly lift the sides up, folding it away. There was the faintest of cracks to be heard as the fragile model lost its support and began to feel the crush of the winged lid.

The three-headed cooperative was confused, but more than willing to tread carefully. So long as there was *something* in it for them. 'We agree,' they all conceded rapidly, one after the other. Then in the same sequence held out their hands to shake a deal. They all knew the gravy train had to stop somewhere, but if their first class tickets remained valid for the rest of the war, they were happy.

Stevenson rejected the handshakes without a care and walked around the table pointing out coloured shapes on his large map. 'We would like to take care to block any use of these old excavations. I have arranged for them to be filled in by my own team of specialist engineers in the next few days.'

Mr Burdock took the opportunity to join in. 'May we at least be informed as to why?' he mumbled while chewing on the end of a pencil.

'The threat of invasion is always a good one, I find. Also bootleggers and profiteers have used similar locations to hide contraband and illegal produce,' Stevenson replied matter-of-factly. The words floated on the air as he took the time to look each man in the eye.

Burdock bit through his pencil while the other councillors shuffled about uneasily.

'Good, so you understand the importance of stopping such black market corruption,' Mr Stevenson continued. 'And I would hate to hear about someone trespassing and getting hurt, or disappearing for ever into a dangerous hole in the ground.'

Mr Burdock bobbed around like a schoolboy wanting attention from the master and Stevenson allowed him time to speak. 'I just wondered,' the councillor said nervously, 'if we actually need to destroy them? I mean these places have real family and historical value to...'

Stevenson put up his hand as if stopping traffic. 'I am sure Mr Jarvis will contact you shortly about a *moderate* compensatory reimbursement.'

While the small audience soaked up his words, Stevenson turned to Mr Jarvis who had remained seated, silent and muddled for the whole confrontation. Jarvis was the most grey haired of the ministry men. His suit looked a bit more Saville Row than the others and he wore thick spectacles. It took him a moment to realise the attention was on him again. He felt bewildered by the whole affair, but was further confused when he found himself involuntarily stood to a preprogramed attention as his superior turned his full glare on him. Stevenson leant in close to his underling and spoke a stream of unheard words directly from steady mouth to twitching ear. Stepping back Stevenson reached into his coat and began to pull out a fat white envelope. Jarvis nervously waved the gesture away and swallowed hard. What ever was in that official letter, he didn't need to see it to believe it.

Mr Stevenson nodded graciously, returned the package to his jacket pocket and spun on his heals. He drifted back to the table, folded up his map concertina style and slid it under an arm before drinking his coffee and stating clearly, 'Any documents relating to the unsafe areas will be put together and passed to me, today.'

Justine sat watching him with her arms folded. The last thing he said before returning to his seat struck a chord with everyone in the room, including her.

'You know, you have done a splendid job of managing all this. You should get a pat on the back, you really should,' Stevenson predicted, as he considered how hard he would like to pat them and what with. Then the hat sat, bent down and returned the map to his briefcase.

Some of the slower men in the chamber began to congratulate each other expecting more admiration to follow.

Stevenson suddenly looked up and asked sharply, 'But, don't you think it's time you pulled your fat little fingers out of each others backsides and opened up your shelters?'

There was some argument and reproach from the councillors; none of it mattered to Stevenson. He was looking at his watch now and as the room continued to complain and rebuff his statement at some volume, he got up to leave.

35

Instead of responding to their anger Stevenson simply stated, 'I need to make some calls Mr Burdock. Your office will suffice. Please have all the relevant documents ready for me on my return.'

'But, well yes, of course.' Burdock spluttered.

Chapter Four

If you needed something and Edward Croft had it to spare, it was yours. Everyone liked the tall strong and intelligent hill farmer. Government initiatives had dictated the use of the big arable fields surrounding the Croft family farmstead since thirty-nine. Two years of following the rules of farming in wartime had made it quite profitable again, compared to the rag tag methods his father Albert had used in the past. Contract workers and Land Girls tilled the hills now and Edward left the majority of the farm in the capable hands of the estate manager, Mr Gibbs.

Unlike the neighbouring homesteads, Croft Farm grew more wheat and beets than meat. The little oasis around the farmhouse did shelter some animals, but of a kind that could sustain you while also remaining alive. Edward had goats, chickens, ducks, bees and even a few cows. His wife Victoria and their teenage children Cassia and Berty cared for the little petting zoo very well and shared any excess produce with anyone locally in need.

Edward had been a part time husband and sailed in the merchants until he was thirty and Albert had asked him to come home. Old war wounds and time had slowed his father down during the depression and the grandchildren had totally outgrown granddad's vintage style of jurisdiction. The opportunity for Albert to buy and run the town's garage seemed like the best solution for everyone and he'd happily stepped aside to beckon his son ashore.

The farm had always been Edward's anchor, a safe harbour where he could remain at bay. He had sailed the world, but came home because he knew what was coming and decided he'd rather die with two feet sunk deep in the mud back here on the family farm.

It was really hot in the yard today so he'd gone out to help check the livestock's water levels. Before making much progress the familiar rumble and honk of Minnie rattled up the lane. The old Bedford that Harry and he had built from spare parts was a big, hard working old girl. They'd carried all sorts on her in their time, most recently the kinds of things that you should only move in the dark and with the headlamps off.

Edward strolled out and opened a gate on the near side of a little concrete culvert bridge, which allowed passage over the stream and into the main yard. Having spent the previous evening drinking homebrew in Harry and Justine's company, Edward was not expecting to be reunited so soon, he was even more surprised to see two other friends perched inside the cab.

An almost matching pair of eighteen-year-old faces grinned out through the fly ridden windscreen. Edward didn't return their smiles. He was worried and annoyed. The twin farming brothers Elijah and Finn from down the valley, would not in normal circumstances have been allowed behind precious Minnie's controls.

Elijah lined up the wide wheels with the unforgiving narrow bridge and barrelled into the yard, skidding to a halt in front of a highly agitated mallard.

The ginger twins dismounted full of life and muscles, reminding Edward of two Orang-utans he'd seen caged on a dockside in Malaysia many years before. He closed the gate and took a quick look around as the three men came together to crushingly shake hands behind the truck.

'How goes it then Ted?' Finn asked, as if there was nothing to explain. Finn was a little shorter and thinner than his brother, which was how unfamiliar people remembered which one was which.

'I thought it were going well, but I weren't expecting to see you two young thugs today.' Edward examined Minnie for fresh damage then asked, 'Did you steal her off Harry, or is he hiding somewhere underneath?'

Finn shook his head, 'Copped us heading back from the market an' said he was too busy for all this nonsense today.'

'Told us to drive up here after picking up a special delivery for you.' Elijah pointed to an oblong mound strapped to the truck's cargo hooks. 'Said he had to make room for summat else.' The big lad reached over and pulled back a corner of tarpaulin, revealing two crates. 'Wants you to make 'em disappear,' Elijah whispered as he unlashed some of the ropes. 'Said you was to take us out for some practice after that.'

'Stop!' Edward ordered. 'We was s'posed to be meeting tomorrow. I is busy and I don't like change, unsettles me it does.' He moved closer to examine the load. The crates were three feet long with rope handles and red letters painted on each side. 'Is this stuff even safe?'

'Well there's safe, then there's *safe*,' Finn smiled.

'No sorry,' Edward shook his head. 'If I stash this lot in the shed it'll sink below the watermark see?'

The only watermark the twins knew of was the mucky one their mother kept angrily pointing out around her enamelled bath. They both looked at Edward as if he were speaking in some foreign tongue.

Edward tried to explain, 'Dad still thinks he owns the place see? He's got all sorts stowed away for his daft projects and scams.' The farmer removed his flat cap and rubbed away a line of sweat. His auburn hair was trimmed short in a practical crew cut. 'There just ain't no more room at the inn.'

'At the end of the day, orders is orders. So where we gonna stick em?' Finn asked.

'You can leave 'em right there sunshine. I ain't trying to be awkward, but this stuff can't go nowhere near 'ere.' Edward thought about the problem for a few seconds. 'I might have a place. You pull the tarp back an' tie it all up, then load all that junk on top.' He directed their eyes to some twisted angle iron over near the chicken pens. 'Chuck those old tyres and wire on too. I'll do what I'm supposed to be doing, then get our Victoria to sort some tea.' He looked at their gawping faces and suggested, 'Just act normally, if you can?'

Over a late breakfast of eggs and fried slices, the men discreetly discussed the merits of changing the schedule.

Victoria didn't care *when* her husband did the rook shoot he'd been planning or the fence work he'd promised Mr Gibbs. Today, tomorrow, it made no difference to her, so long as it got done. She did a thousand yard stare out of the window and said nothing. If all the chores were sorted and they got that dirty great wagon full of scrap out of the yard, she'd stay happy.

After breakfast the men loaded three shotgun bags into the wooden tool chest behind Minnie's cab and Edward turned her around. With a plume of dust the wagon trundled off along the lane, climbing further up the hill then down again into the lower slopes. Soon up to speed and hurtling down the long straight Chapel road, Edward tooted the horn at some land girls in the fields. Ahead of the truck a shower of rooks flew up into the sky then swooped back down into the tree line behind.

'Remind me to do summat about them big evil buggers later,' Edward insisted as he watched the last of the jagged shapes fly over the cab. 'Or the missus will be shooting at us.'

Eventually Minnie slowed down, dropping through her gears before turning off to vanish along a rough side lane. In seconds she had faded away into overgrowing bushes and was gone. Ten minutes later the colourful wagon rumbled back into view through a broken Victorian gateway on a parched field with a rough cliff at one end. An old quarry sank away on the other side and a rubbish dump sat untidily in the middle.

The quarry was not sophisticated, just a very big reddish hole bitten out of the slope. Its sheer sides were so steep that you would not want to keep any livestock near by. Which is why the rest of the fenced off area had become a tip for rotten oil drums and redundant farming relics instead. Minnie followed a couple of rutted tracks in the dry mud leading to a tall mound of red earth piled high above the cliff. It gave the vehicle good cover from anyone looking up the hill from town.

Edward turned off the engine and sat back with his hands on his knees. 'This is it then lads, start unpacking.'

'But this is rubbish!' Finn exclaimed, scanning the area.

'Well it is a bit of a dump,' Edward agreed with a smirk.

Finn turned to him unimpressed, 'You cant hide this kinda stuff in the quarry, everyone comes this way. I've done a bit of bird spotting up 'ere my self.'

The others chuckled, knowing exactly what kind of birds he'd been up here with.

'I ain't planning to sling them boxes down that big hole an' hope as no one trips over 'em. Just grab the crates and meet me by that rusty trailer, quick as you can.' Edward grumbled with feigned exasperation as he jumped down from Minnie and slammed the cab door.

Once on the ground he crouched to tie his boots and scanned around the area at waist level before bolting up the mound of earth for a better view of the whole valley. From that perch the town looked like a small industrial grey and brick red scar on an otherwise green landscape. It nestled hundred's of feet below, near the widening bottom of the river valley. Behind it, along the narrower banks, several of the smaller mills were back in production and coughing smoke again. A couple of churches dotted the patchwork landscape acting as hubs for the tiny villages near by. Various farms swept up from these white and slate blobs, filling the slopes on every side.

Edward could make out his family's land, high up on the far hilltop and stretching down to the long line of the big valley road. A rugged highland formed a protective horseshoe around all of this. Which was something that had always made Edward feel safe, before the war. His eyes followed a sparkling vein down as it spread into town and eventually, miles down stream and almost out of sight, opened out to form a broad river mouth.

Assured no one was nearby, Edward ran back down and landed on the abandoned old trailer with a thump. The ancient cart was more of a platform now, its wheels having rotted away leaving stumps of red oxide. He rummaged around for a length of metal pipe that was crushed at one end. He had just jammed it under the frame as the boys arrived with the first crate.

'Right you two put that down, *gently.* Then help me hoist this away.' Edward levered up the first few inches, creating a gap for their fingers.

The big oblong platform swung up, hinged by a furrow in the cracked mud. It leaned against an old broken down wall and revealed more misshaped junk squished into the dirt beneath.

The patch of flattened debris reminded Finn of the dried flowers his mother kept crushed in a thick scrapbook by the fire.

Edward got down and used his fingertips to brush away some of the dust. Eventually he found a loop of old rope in the dirt and pulled it up. With a twitch of his head he directed Elijah and Finn to find the other rope pull at the opposite end. 'Now lift together,' he said.

A large table sized tray of rubble and debris rose up, revealing a deep cavity beneath. They all heaved the heavy section over and lay it on the ground. Stone steps led down but there was no room for feet amongst the boxes and odd shapes stored upon them.

'You should be able to squeeze 'em in. Might need a bit of rearranging mind.' Edward stepped well away from the hole, partly to keep a look out and also just in case the lads got butter fingers.

The brothers whistled their astonishment and appreciation of the impressive hiding space. After grabbing the other crate from Minnie and rearranging the stores, everything fitted neatly into place.

Edward used the new tarpaulin to cover the top layer of boxes and crates before they replaced the hatch. Then he knelt down and expertly filled any cracks with gravel and bent bits of rubbish until you couldn't see a gap. Finally they lowered the redundant cart down slowly, trying not to disturb the loose earth. The addition of the old tyres and ironwork from the truck finished it off like the icing on a very manly cake.

It was time to have a sit down with cigarettes and a swig from the big earthenware bottle that Finn had stowed away in the cab. Edward had already anticipated the contents would be the twins strong home made cider, but still choked a little as it hit the spot. Wiping the sweat and drink from his chin, he looked around and mulled over the rest of the their day. Any shooting practice would have to go on somewhere else, so as not to draw too much attention here. The rooks would make a good moving target, but not with the kind of weapons they'd bought along. Edward twitched and turned an ear to the undergrowth near the gate behind them. 'You two wait 'ere and don't drink too much cider,' he gasped as he got up stiffly and shook out the bottom of his trousers creating a cloud of dust. He watched to see which way it drifted on the breeze then added, 'Look, I'm going to use the head in them bushes by the truck.'

As Edward walked away, Finn turned to his brother and interpreted, 'It means toilet.'

'What does?' Elijah frowned, taking another quick swig from the jar.

'The "Head", it's Navy talk for a toilet.' Finn nodded over at the shrubbery as he took the jar away from his brother and replaced the cork.

'I thought he meant the end of his knob,' laughed Elijah, spraying tiny amber pellets of alcohol into the scorched air.

The twins tried not to pay much attention as Edward rustled off into the shrubs ten yards away. Five minutes later they were a little concerned that he hadn't returned. Looking at each other to confirm they were thinking the same thing, Finn nodded.

Slowly at first, they began to cross over to the gap through which Edward had disappeared. Creeping up to the bushes, both brothers poked around while very quietly calling their friends name. When a screaming Edward burst out from the undergrowth faraway behind them, they nearly went to the toilet themselves.

As the twins swung around in fright they saw it was not just Edward emerging, he was wrestling a dark masked figure to the ground. The shapes rolled over each other, blurring into one as the dust kicked up around their bodies.

The twins ran back over to the centre of the angry mass and heaved the hooded man off their friend. But the stranger was too fast; he jerked free and swung his legs around swiping theirs away. In a flash he had winded Finn and got Elijah into a strangle hold, ready to snap his neck.

'Now,' said the muffled figure breathlessly. 'What happened to that cider you were all chugging down?'

It was Harry. He released his grip, rolled away and landed on his feet.

'I heard you coming before we even sat down,' Edward protested as he got up, walked back over to the cider jar and added, 'I was circling.' He had nearly ten years on Harry and was really feeling it right now. 'Sounded like that brown Austin, the reg is er, OK3540, or near enough.' Edward coughed the words out after taking a big swig to clear the orange dust from his throat. 'Doctors car right?' He raised an eyebrow towards the covered lane and passed the bottle across. 'Gears sound even more clacked than usual mind.'

'Albert's been "working" on it,' Harry nodded his approval of Edward's summing up.

'You been sneaking about, watching us from that bush by the gate for a few minutes and I'll bet you didn't hear *me* coming,' Edward insisted as he folded his arms smugly. 'Besides, I can smell you a mile off down wind, with that stink you've got on.'

'Well I was distracted by the heat and the chance of a cold drink.' Harry took off the balaclava and thumped down on the ground sweating profusely. 'Decided to try and stroll over an' take a swig without you noticing. Then I admit, I got a bit dizzy an' me brain stopped working for a bit.'

'A lesson to be learned there then,' Edward pointed to the woolly balaclava then mimed taking notes with an invisible pencil.

'You can tick off the goodies you ordered last week while you're at it.' Harry pretended to take something from his pocket; it was a joke they often shared. 'This is the receipt for all the money you owe the government. I took what equipment I could fit in the car and stashed it near the viaduct. It's looking pretty sharp up there now.'

Edward took the imaginary invoice and whistled at the cost. He sat down next to his friend as they shared the bottle with a good laugh.

Finn came over bashing the dirt out of Edwards crushed cap. 'I thought you was too busy for all this today Harry?' he asked, dropping the hat into Edwards outstretched hand.

'I was, but I managed to cut a few corners like. What with borrowing the car and you three doing one of my many jobs.' Harry tried to sound sarcastic, but it didn't come across. 'I was on my way back, figured you might be somewhere up this way and the land girls loose lips done the rest.'

'Easy life,' Edward insisted as they both lay back and giggled.

Elijah and Finn weren't as happy; they looked at each other and then at their feet. Finn spoke first to break the silence, 'I guess we need a bit more experience?'

'We thought it was just dump the crates and do some shooting,' Elijah continued.

'You should constantly keep an eye out for trouble, be alert,' Edward prompted sitting back up.

'Yes be a Lert, Britain needs Lerts. I read that in the bog at the Bull and Bladder,' Harry quipped, stretching out with his hands behind his head.

The twins were not in the mood. They were too hot and a bit bruised in both body and pride.

'Just stay on the ball and we won't get caught out,' Harry sounded friendlier now he'd got his breath back.

'Sorry,' was the best the twins could manage.

'Lets try a little job in town then shall we, see what you boys *have* learnt so far?' Edward proposed.

'They need to do more observation,' Harry pointed out while getting up to pat himself down. 'Self defence could do with a fair bit of tweaking too.'

Edward nodded with a smile.

'Right then, Ted, you know what needs setting up in town and the next stage with these two youngsters education, right?' Harry was clearly keen to get away again as he held out a squishy paper parcel. 'You might need this boys,' he winked, slapping it into Finn's hand. 'I have to go and meet some one.'

'You going to see a man about a dog Harry?' Elijah asked.

'No son, you are,' Harry replied with a sinister grin.

Chapter Five

Harry pushed the doctor's Austin back inside the garage then removed a small cardboard package from the glove box and climbed out as quickly as possible.

'What do you think you're doing with my motor car young man?' It was a good impression of the Doc, but the tone was wrong.

'Edward and the twins borrowed Minnie and I needed to get somewhere,' he hastily protested to Albert while palming the box into a pocket.

'You checking up on my work then?' Albert said crossly as he threw down a spanner.

Harry considered that Albert's explanation actually worked better. 'Yes, sorry, you're right. I wanted to feel how those new brakes was.' With a childlike innocence he added, 'You done a proper job.'

Albert folded his arms and looked at Harry with suspicion. 'Ask next time. I was about to drain the sump and sort the gears. Five minutes later and it would 'ave been a disaster.'

'Sorry, boss.' Harry did a sad face and moved off toward the front of the garage.

'I am the boss sunshine and don't you bleedin' forget it,' Albert yelled after him down the gap between the council trucks. 'Which is why I'm going off on guard duty later and you'll be on your tod till lunch tomorrow.'

'Yeh, that's fine.' Harry moved out of sight to check the contents of the cardboard box.

'Sort that delivery in the morning and get these wagons finished so as we can have some space back.' Albert leaned into the Austin's open window and sounded its horn before shouting, 'You listening lad?'

'No problem, I got it,' Harry confirmed as he tucked the package away again and looked for movement on the message spike.

'No more gallivanting, right?' Albert made it sound more like a question than a demand. He was old school, well past middle aged and had had just about enough of young people lately.

Harry checked his watch, 'I need to pop out again, just for a tick, sorry.'

'Bloody Norah, where you off to now?' Albert groaned, looking around for his sump spanner.

'Maybe I'm hungry, or I might be gallivanting. Am I wearing the right shoes for that?' Harry waltzed his way back, bumping down the narrow gap to the Austin and pointed into a toolbox where Albert's spanner had landed.

Bert retrieved the wrench and waved it in front of his apprentice. 'Gallivanting don't mean dancin', it means prating about all over the place without a care, looking for fun.'

Harry deflated and then said with sincerity, 'I do care Bert, I really do.'

Albert grumbled on while Harry checked his appearance in a large mirror shard and went to leave again via the front of the garage.

'What you got in that little box then?' Albert called after him.

'Chocolates,' Harry lied as he patted his pocket.

'Bollocks more like,' Albert snorted before sneaking after him.

He watched through a gap in a shutter as the lad crossed the street and ducked down a passage opposite. Albert skilfully rolled a cigarette without taking his eye off the road and waited for Harry to reappear. Sure enough seconds later he popped out of the next entry along and scampered back over toward the café. On the pavement outside, the café's young waitress Mary appeared from an archway. She looked up and down the street then pulled him away out of view.

'Bloody scallywag,' Albert tutted, then lit up his fag and went back to work.

Half a mile away Edward rolled Minnie into a space outside the train station and reached behind the drivers seat to tap on the glass partition. 'Come on you two shake a leg,' he announced. When nothing happened he turned to discover the twins had already scarpered.

'Little buggers,' Edward mused, pleased that the boys had shown some gumption.

Ten minutes later a breathless Harry jogged around the corner and pulled open the cab door. 'Started without you?' he frowned.

'Shows initiative,' Edward insisted.

'It shows you up more like, you old fart. One of us is supposed to keep an eye on them.'

'Better take a short cut then?' Edward suggested, throwing his friend the wagon's keys.

Harry checked his watch for what felt like the hundredth time today. 'You go and I'll meet you on top, if they make it that far?'

As Edward climbed down he asked in a whisper, 'Have you sorted Mary yet?'

Harry only winked in reply.

'So who you meeting now then?' Edward persisted.

Harry got in, closed the door and started the engine to end the conversation.

Two streets away from the station and shoulder-to-shoulder, Elijah and Finn surveyed the builders yard ahead of them. They had already strolled around and checked out the entire perimeter. There were no houses on this side of it and the Gas Works filled the skyline behind. The yard's head high panelled fence meant no one could see in from street level and the numerous stacks of festering construction materials would give them more cover once inside.

Old "Dunc the drunk" owned the yard. He had previously been a committed parent since Mrs Greene had died on the night their son Ian was born. The boy had grown up happily, becoming big and strong around the yard then joined the army during peacetime at the tender age of sixteen. A year ago he had been lost in action somewhere near Cappelle-la-Grande on his way back to Dunkirk.

It had damaged Duncan; he had broken down one morning and never crawled back up. The yard was always closed now. Instead of working, the owner chose to spend most days in the office with his new friend, her name was Gin and she lived in a bottle.

From most vantage points the decrepit yard did indeed offer many a hiding place. In one of these voids a hot and grumpy dog lay outstretched avoiding the strong sun. Etched into its collar there was one word, "ADOLF". The name was embellished with a swastika, but inscribed the wrong way around so that it actually depicted the Buddhist symbol of auspiciousness.

Adolf was *mostly* a very big German Shepherd; a breed that had become much less popular in recent times. Which is one reason why he had been so cheap to buy. When a few crates of plumbing and pipework had gone missing one bank holiday, Duncan had forced himself to purchase a box of new padlocks, a fresh case of gin and the biggest dog he could afford. Since then he'd shut the gates and left the beast to patrol unsupervised.

The chap who'd sold this monster had warned it was a killer, but at the time that was more or less exactly what Duncan had wanted. The old drunk fed Adolf better than he fed himself and occasionally cleaned up after the mutt. In return Adolf devoured rodents and allowed Duncan to live out his life in the office, generally undisturbed.

Finn crouched near the yard's chain linked gates and felt the heat radiating out from a topaz-enamelled sign in front of him. It had once proudly been emblazoned with the now fading words "D Greene and Son - Builders Merchants".

Elijah nodded at Finn who spat a giant lug onto the rusty gate bolt then almost silently slid it aside. The padlocked chain left enough slack to open the gate a few inches and spread further at the base by the pressure of the boys squeezing through. Once inside, Finn tucked away the parcel Harry had given them and the twins rolled out of sight to wait motionless in the shade, listening and tuning into their new surroundings.

The disembodied newsman on Duncan's radio was replaced by a more familiar voice, which said, 'And now I would like to sing you a song that I wrote a very long time ago, and far away...'

'Wish I was far away from those dog turds,' Finn whispered.

The voice on the radio continued, 'It's called Mad Dogs and Englishmen.'

'Bloody typical,' Elijah sniggered as they got up and began creeping along in the shadow of the fence.

Eventually they had to move out down the rotting rows of lumber and sand, towards their goal, which loomed ahead poking out above everything else. The huge set of ladders leaned precariously against a shed full of bitumen and roof felt. Up close the asphyxiating smell of hot tar and dog mess made the boys feel sick.

Finn gagged then gulped and held his breath. Quickly he untied a rotting hemp rope and guided the heavy, triple tiered ladders forward, allowing his brother to take up the weight. When the whole apparatus was almost horizontal Finn heaved up his end to waist level and gripped it tight. Unfortunately an iron nameplate set into the wooden leg had slowly been gathering heat all morning. Immediately and feverishly it branded a ridge into his forearm. Finn had been holding his breath for so long that when he cried out in pain, it was huge.

'Can you at least try and be quiet,' Elijah hushed as he flipped his grip around the ladders and turned to face his twin.

Finn looked up to swear in reply, then decided to stay silent. Twenty yards behind his brother, he could see Adolf casually walking out from behind a group of tumbled chimney pots. The shaggy animal yawned, shook his coat and sat down to scratch an ear. It had already decided whom to kill first.

'Have you trodden in something?' Elijah sniffed the air and looked down to check his own boots.

Finn shook his head while gently placing his end of the ladder back on the ground. A graceful arm then reversed its swing up to waist level and slid Harry's parcel out.

Elijah could be quite sharp sometimes. On this occasion he got it quick and snarled, 'Adolf?'

The dog was patient, he preferred a running target, and there was no hurry. Once in sight, the next move was *always* down to the prey. He liked to match the pace of his quarry, mostly rats, sometimes fat bailiffs and occasionally athletic postmen. It was the only entertainment the lonely brute had, and he didn't like to rush things.

Finn looked down nervously at the unravelling package in his hands and pointed out, 'There's a fair bit of meat in 'ere Lige, I don't wanna waste it.'

'It ain't no good to us, just throw the bloody lot,' Elijah screeched, shoving the ladder into his brother's shins.

After the package had been thrown hand grenade style, landing with an inviting slap, Adolf immediately tore into the starter and forgot about the main course, for now. Knowing this would only buy them a few seconds; Finn hoisted up the ladder and began to run away toward the rear of the yard.

'What did Harry drug it with?' Elijah shouted, hoping it was something quick acting and strong.

'Nothing,' Finn gasped, 'Ted said to 'ave some for us supper if we didn't use it all.'

After fifteen seconds the dog realised it had been duped by its own stomach and gave chase. By the time the twins were approaching the back fence Adolf was gaining ground fast.

Finn chose not to listen to either the barrage of swear words or the barking that followed him. His body just kept going, pumping away at full pelt, running at the fence as if it wasn't there. At the last moment he twisted around and heaved upward, skimming the ladder over the barrier as he in turn, crashed sidelong into it. Elijah kept a loose grip as it twisted then pushed forward until the steps were about half way over. At which point he simply used them as a ramp and clambered away at full pelt.

Before the snarling teeth finally caught up, Finn had hauled his body on board too, as high up as he could reach. Elijah stepped beyond the balance point so that the weight of him moving forward bought the bottom end up just in time.

Adolf made a leap for Finn's flailing ankles only to be rewarded with a hard smack in the windpipe under the chin. The lad continued to be levered up into the air until he was sliding head first down onto the street. The brothers lay there choking out snot as Edward ran over to help and the ladder clattered down onto the kerb.

Drawing air deeply into his lungs, Edward tried to speak, 'Stealing, is supposed to be, a stealthy and often a silent occupation you know?'

Adolf was still snarling and jumping up to claw at the rough interior fence. Duncan heard a commotion, but stayed in the office and hoped that what ever the mutt had discovered on the far side of his yard had deserved to die. He leaned forward to release a slatted office blind, which was tethered to a bent nail on his desk. The shutter clattered down onto a collection of dead flies, sending a few months worth of dust cartwheeling through the still air. Duncan stretched a little further forward to turn up the radio then poured

51

another drink. For once there were nice thoughts in his head as he settled back to watch a thousand tiny fairies float to earth.

Some local residents had begun to pay attention as Edward heaved up the first twin. 'All fine folks,' he called out to the small pockets of people standing in doorways, 'we got permission from Duncan, to borrow them.' He pointed down at the ladder. 'Bloody dog.'

'Nothing to see here,' Finn added.

Edward quickly directed the lads down a shaded alley and out of sight. Inside the dark maze the group travelled incognito, unless they reached a tight corner. At such junctions the ladder would rise above wall height and swing around to face the new direction causing minor casualties to plant pots and cats. Then it would submarine back down and not appear again for several blocks.

At one point they emerged into a group of children playing football in a wide cobbled passage. One skinny child picked up the ball and scornfully urged, 'Come on mister, hurry up, there's a bleeding match going on here.'

'HAND BALL,' all the other children shouted.

'Up yours!' the first child retorted, kicking the ball high and going back to the game. As the men apologised and nipped up the next entry, they could hear a heated argument breaking out behind.

Five minutes later the trio had almost reached the ladders new home. Edward stuck his neck out of the exit point and took a quick peek left and right.

Opposite them was a wide crossroads with an expanse of three story Georgian shops. These were wrapped around the corner of the main road leading up hill toward the town's market square. The shops were quiet, their windows empty. Especially the butcher's frontage, where local shoppers had spent the morning clearing the sparse shelves, one morsel at a time.

Edward and the boys still had to choose their moment well. They walked casually over into a side entrance between the shops, as if three men and a ladder was an everyday thing.

The narrow entry was impressively tall with an arched roof and brightly painted walls that dulled with each forward step. After ten yards of gloom Edward stepped out into a triangular courtyard, which was essentially a dead end. There *were* plenty of clouds and sky high above, but everything down here was black, partly in shadow and covered with decades of filth.

Grubby chainmail and ribbons hung motionless over what must have been the butchers back entrance. In the corner directly opposite was a toilet with no door or seat. It was possible the butcher still used it occasionally, but you would hope not, for so many reasons. The rest of the rear exits looked like they had not been used for years. Some were padlocked and forgotten, others bricked up completely. Though it had not rained properly for two weeks, water still dripped down dark beard like growths on the walls. A spiral curtain of wild plants and green algae clung to the masonry, marking the limited path of the sun.

'Right then lads,' Edward hissed quietly as he looked up at the cliff like buildings. 'Harry wants it up there. Wedge 'em up near the shape sticking out, above that old doorway at the top.'

The twins looked up, nodded and started to upright the ladder. The top reached up to a point just above the high door.

Elijah went up first to investigate. At the top he pulled on a rotted shroud revealing an old pulley beneath. After a few testing tugs he shouted down, 'Its fine, bit rusty, but sound enough.'

Finn shook his head in disagreement.

'If it takes my weight it'll take you two runts,' Elijah insisted and pulled himself further up, gripping the crossbar, testing the weight. Then in the same way you heave yourself from a pool or riverbank, he made the last bit of the journey and was on the roof. The pulley creaked a little, but stayed where it was.

Edward took the opportunity to give Finn the bad news, 'You need to stay down here and hold the ladder while I shimmy up.'

Finn nodded then did a double take, looked around and queried, 'And who holds it for me?'

'Sorry you're not going up.' Edward handed Finn a tightly folded sheet of paper, 'Take this, it's a sort of treasure map.'

Finn protested, 'But I always work with Elijah.'

'Not this circuit, it's time you both did summat on your own. Hold on while I go up, then walk the ladder over into the shadows and off you trot.'

Finn held the ladders with the paper clasped between his fingers and used his mouth to unfold it. A coin fell out and dinged off a stave before landing in the sludge near his boots. He struggled to read the first few bouncing lines as Edward climbed. There was a final wobble as his brother hauled their friend over the top.

'You and me are going that way,' Edward pointed over the shallow sloping roof and strode away.

Behind him Elijah leaned out into the weird perspective of the courtyard where his brother folded a sheet of paper away and bent down to pick something shiny up. Ultimately Finn pulled the ladder back, walked it into the nearest dark corner and vanished.

'Ted, why is Finn hiding the escape route, an' how're we gonna get down?' Elijah turned around sharply demanding an answer, but Edward had gone too.

He caught up as they reached the outer edge of the corner shops and started to demand answers again, but Edward insisted on silence. The buildings backed onto several flat square rooftops ascending the hill. Sometimes there were steps or rungs had been bolted in. Where there was nothing, they could easily climb the walls. With one last push they reached the highest platform where a hand signal from Edward warned Elijah to crouch down.

At the front of this final building a huge Hollywood style sign stated in reverse the name of the department store below. The letters created good cover to peer through with two conveniently abandoned scaffold planks along the sticky tar edged floor. Elijah saw a fantastic view of the market square stretched out below as he settled down on one knee. Directly opposite were the police station and its neighbouring courthouse. Two overloaded police cars were departing with their bells resounding echoes along the route. It was hot up there, so much so that the smell of melting roof tar took Elijah right back to Duncan's yard. 'Where's Finn?' he pleaded.

'What are you shouting off your big gob about?' Harry asked.

Tumbling over his own legs, Elijah twisted around and hissed, 'How'd you get up here?'

Obligingly Harry pointed out one of two square brick structures on the far side of the flat roof. 'Well I had two choices; there's the service building for the lift over there,' he smiled then pointed to the other block, 'but I decided to just use the stairs.'

'What? So why all that ladder daftness then?' Elijah puzzled loudly.

Harry held a finger to his lips and said quietly, 'We need an occasional route, for when things go tits up.' He knelt down between them to monitor the square.

'Or if it's night time, or a bank holiday,' Edward added.

'As long as we don't have to take 'em back to Dunc's yard, that'll be fine by me,' Elijah stated with relief. 'What are we doing here and what about Finn?'

'These buildings are the highest thing in town that's not yet being used by the ARP,' Harry stated with authority.

Edward continued to explain, 'You have to see it as it could be. One day soon that lot over there will most likely be our primary target.' He thumbed at the courthouse and police station then smiled.

'You need to get a feel for what goes on in the streets and learn to travel without spending too much time on them,' Harry chipped in. 'Go on, tell us what you see down there.'

'Just a load of windows, the tops of some striped market stalls, and a bloke selling cabbages from a cart in the big arcade entrance.' Elijah turned back, but the others urged him on. He tried again, 'There are some women talking about shopping on the corner. Can't see nowt else.'

'This is what *we* see,' Harry sighed. 'For starters there are more people buying cabbages than anything else. Under the barrow is a crate filled with boxes and cartons that you *won't* find much of in any ration book. Those women chatting are divvying up their black market treasure.'

'Either that or a bag of cabbage is more exciting than we ever thought possible?' Edward laughed. 'Hang on, is that Monkey bringing down extra stock?'

He pointed out a scruffy man struggling towards the arcade with a heavy suitcase. The little scarecrow disappeared from view for a minute then re-emerged empty handed to chat with the street vendor before accepting a small brown paper bag and walking away.

'There has been a flood of goods in town this week,' Edward recalled. 'Word is it was like some sort of fire sale going on.'

'Look there Elijah. Those big boots and the posh brogues under the courthouse porch belong to Patrick and that lawyer, Mr Walton,' Harry continued. 'He is trying to get Pat off some assault charges, which is why he ain't up here with us.'

'Mr Walton's one of us?' Elijah whistled, 'He seems a bit posh and feeble for all this.'

'No you clot, Patrick is one of us and hopefully he'll be free to join us later?' Harry's scrunched up face suggested he wasn't sure.

'Our old man says to stay away from that Patrick Tremayne,' Elijah pointed out nervously. 'Told us the bloke's a proper loony.'

Harry took a moment to stare scornfully at Elijah before rearranging himself in a shadow between the giant letters of the sign. 'The police station looks pretty vacant right now,' he noted without surprise as a trill bell started to ring out from across the road.

'Hang on a minute?' Elijah's attention slipped downward to a corner window on the bottom floor. 'That's our Finn, what's the daft bugger doing?'

Harry peered over the top, 'Thing is, we need to procure a bit of fancy dress and a few important passes. You can't just walk up to a copper and ask for his clothes and a copy of all the latest paperwork can you?'

Elijah was going into a flap, 'But you can't just walk into a police station and take stuff neither.'

'It ain't the first time is it?' Harry waved a finger at the boy. 'Don't forget I've seen your arrest records.'

'That was different, we was just taking back what they'd confiscated from us earlier. We were only school boys then, it's not the same.' Elijah's protests fell on deaf ears.

'We made it easier this time, told Finn to phone in and report a warehouse full of contraband first.' Edward put a calming hand on him, 'They might be too busy to see what goes on under their noses, but if you stuff something smelly up them big nostrils, they're off like whippets.'

Harry filled in the blanks, 'Then you cross wire the fire alarm and go inside while the admin folk exit neatly out the back.'

'But they are gonna be right mad,' Elijah suggested, 'once they see there's no contraband.'

'Who said they wouldn't find anything?' Edward asked with a little wink. 'We can always kill two birds with one copper, if it helps grease the wheels.'

'Finn will never get away with it, he's in over his head.' Elijah went to get up.

'No, look,' Edward grabbed his arm.

Elijah peered over the wall in time to see a black helmet exit via the front doors. The word on top of the tin hat read "POLICE". Its wearer swung a yellow messenger bag over one shoulder and looked up. The farmer's dusty trousers and boots did not match perfectly, but the little face in the chinstrap was all that his brother needed to see.

Patting the wall Harry said, 'Right then, we're off.'

Elijah remained where he was, staring out into space.

Edward nudged the boy, 'We need to go and pick Finn up, come on.'

Cautiously they crossed over, creaked open the roof door and headed down the stairwell within. At the bottom was the empty restaurant floor of "Rallies Department Store". On the other side of the tables and chairs there were more stairs and a lift. Before going down the three men made sure there were no marks on clothes and tucked a few bits in. Edward loaned them both his comb and took the inevitable ribbing from them about him being the one with the least hair.

'So where next?' Elijah asked as he put his finger out to press the lift call button. Harry batted the boy's hand away and pointed to the main stairs.

Edward whispered an answer as they descended, 'We are all gonna walk out, casual like. After that we pick up Finn, check on Pat and head off into them there hills.'

Chapter Six

After the morning meeting Justine was tasked with compiling two piles of documents and maps on the big oak table. One stack would go back to records and the rest would be handed over to Mr Stevenson who was waiting impatiently, checking his watch nearby.

The pre-lunch site visit had gone well and agreements had been made to complete the works over the next few weeks. All of the councillors were very keen to be available to receive the town's praise, as soon as the shelters were actually ready. Mrs Hill had checked their diaries and started to work on planning several events surrounding the opening ceremonies. Everything was sewn up neatly with time for some lunch. The only problem being, it was already a quarter to two.

Mrs Hill seemed to blank her assistant as soon as the shelter meeting had properly finished. 'Can I go when I've done this, please?' Justine asked as she added a folder to Mr Stevenson's pile and gently aligned the maps to stop them rolling away.

Mrs Hill looked through her, picked up a heavy phone receiver and tapped furiously at the two chrome buds that stuck out of its cradle. Once connected she said two words, 'Food now,' then she plonked the phone back down with a ping that seemed to echo on forever.

'I have to meet a friend, and I'm late,' Justine pleaded, waiting for a flicker of response from her superior.

Only a few moments later, several canteen staff with trolleys appeared to set out the buffet for everyone, except for Justine. Unless cold shoulder was on the menu, she was clearly expected to find her own sustenance as usual.

Deciding to just go for it, she turned to Mr Stevenson. 'This is all the material you requested sir,' she nodded and then walked over to her desk. In one fluid motion she picked up her bag and continued toward the exit hoping that no one had noticed her. She was wrong.

'I will expect you back promptly at half past, in my office,' Mrs Hill ordered, looking over and entering a note into the book of time sheets.

The young typist was not the only one withdrawing from the chamber. At the exit Mr Stevenson was already trying to push through the heavy wood and brass doors. He was overburdened with a well-stuffed briefcase and the large plans to the point where he could not escape single-handed. Justine stepped in and held the exit open, just to hurry things up.

'Thank you Miss Page.' Stevenson looked back at the others grabbing plates and cutlery. 'Not sticking around for the feast?' he asked bluntly as the doors flapped shut behind them.

'Not invited,' she replied simply. 'I am sure they have a seat for you, you should stay.'

Mr Stevenson peered through the door windows. 'I am not impressed by their filched food and culinary bribes. I only returned to secure these documents.' He patted the bundles in his arms. 'Thank you for preparing them so, efficiently,' he smirked.

'Records department sorted most of it, I just tidied things up,' Justine nodded vaguely, distracted by the clock behind him. It was pointing past ten to. She tried to get going with a quick departing smile, but he was in her way again.

'It seems we both have more pressing meetings to attend and in similar directions. Can you help me with the other portals please?' Mr Stevenson crooned, even managing a genuine smile.

Justine pushed past the ends of the rolled up documents and hurried to the next set of double doors. 'And will you actually *be* at those meetings?' she said without thinking.

Mr Stevenson uncomfortably broadened his smile and asked, 'Can I give you a lift anywhere Miss Page? My driver is waiting for us just outside. We can chat a little on the way.'

No matter how nice he was being, Justine was sure she did not want to chat. 'No thank you sir,' she replied smartly. 'I am just going a short distance.'

'Ah yes, you were meeting a *friend?*'

She did not answer. As they walked together towards reception nothing more was said.

As soon as they were outside he tried again, 'Before you go, might I have just the quickest of words? Please.'

'I really don't have much time, sorry.' Justine stressed her need to go, more than the apology.

Stevenson's burly driver was standing guard nearby. He opened the car's huge rear door to gently block Justine's path, then firmly encouraged her to get inside. After closing it behind her he opened the boot, relieved his master of the maps and waited on the kerb.

The saloon was luxuriously simple, its leather smelt new and the abundant chrome reflected fanned shards of light around the interior. Justine nervously pulled at her skirt to cover as much stocking as possible.

Stevenson climbed in on the other side, took a moment to settle and then continued their conversation. 'I came here because Mr Burdock's friends have ideas which, well they overlap with my own departmental remit.' He paused again, taking his time as if suddenly unaware that his passenger was in a rush. 'This particular location is a rabbit warren of hiding holes and, well, I needed to set some boundaries before we all clashed.'

'I just take notes sir, when I'm allowed to anyway,' Justine tilted her head and did the brightest of grins.

'Yes indeed, I am sorry about that.' Stevenson brushed something absent-mindedly from his knee and did a little huff. 'I wanted to tell you specifically, that after coming here today, well it has confirmed that I don't trust Burdock or his pals as far as I can spit.' Stevenson looked at her eye to eye before adding, 'and believe me, I never spit.'

'They're all right, some of them. Look I have to go now; I don't understand any of this. I just do my job.' She moved to open the door.

'I just do my job too. I am a man of the people and that is my role in government,' he injected suddenly. 'I would like to confide in you and for you to confide in me.'

Justine stopped and allowed him another few seconds of her precious time.

'I protect you all, even from yourselves. Now I need to look deeper into all of this, but something clearly stinks in your chambers and it is not Mr Moors pigs.'

'I am just a, a nobody,' Justine shrugged.

'You are a good egg in a tray of egg shaped chicken manure Miss Page. I will telephone you soon and you will answer my questions honestly. I will ask for you in person Justine. I will call my self the "Caretaker". No one will question the planning committee's secretary taking a call from a caretaker will they?' He clasped his hands and leaned forward excitedly encouraging a reply.

'Is that it?' she asked while pulling down the door handle.

'There was one more thing.' Mr Stevenson reached across and pushed the door open. 'Have a nice day.'

As Justine walked away she could clearly see that no one was waiting in the distance near the café. When she knocked on the garage door Harry was not there either.

Albert came out instead, wiping his oily hands and wondering what to say. He was suspicious of Harry's recent activities, but didn't want to make any accusations.

'Hello Bert,' Justine said, glancing over nervously as Stevenson's black saloon glided slowly past them. 'Did Harry come back from that job he was on this morning?'

'Er, yes?' Albert confirmed, unsure if Harry had done any actual work today or not. 'Said he were going for lunch ages ago. You might still *catch* him, if your quick.' Albert said with a wry smile.' He could see she was upset and decided not to push it further. 'Are you feeling alright luv, you look a bit pale?'

'Oh yes, I'm fine. Just been a long night and day so far, that's all,' she replied reassuringly and walked away.

The windows of the café were not steamed up, which normally meant no hot food on the menu either. It would be limp lettuce sandwiches and cold, virtually meatless pies instead.

Flies buzzed around the open door trying to navigate its chain-mail curtain. Inside, amongst the wafts of cigarette smoke Justine could see no shape or shadow that resembled her man. She popped open her clutch bag and found the little brass lighter Harry had made from a bullet case. Some more careful rummaging found the cigarette he'd given her earlier.

Mary the cafe owners daughter and only waitress, immediately popped her head through the mesh curtain and asked with a broad Irish accent, 'Can you spare one of those hon?' She was the same age as Justine and they had got to know each other quite well since Harry had properly introduced them to each other months ago.

Justine lit the end and dropped the lighter back into her bag. 'Last one sorry,' she said taking a long drag then offering it across anyway.

'Thanks a million.' Mary drew in her own lung full and passed it back. 'What's up Jus?' she chimed with a neat little smoky smile.

'Have you seen Harry in there today?'

Mary shook her head and exhaled the smoke, which drifted away down the street. 'Nah, he ain't been in.'

'Albert thought he'd come this way?' questioned Justine as she passed back the burning tube.

'Nah,' said Mary refusing the cigarette, 'Sure, it's *your* lunch girl, finish it yourself.'

'Have you seen him go past then?' Justine persisted.

'Not seen him, full stop. Our Patrick was away from here real early, asking after your man like a lost sheep so he was. I'm guessing Harry's not back at his garage then?'

'No,' Justine said while stubbing out the cigarette on the wall.

Mary held out her hand and offered to put the butt in the bin.

'If you see him tell him, I'm sorry I was late. I have to go back early, so I'll catch up with him later. Got it?'

'Okeydokey. You gotta get back for that awful boss of yours then?' Mary frowned as two old ladies pushed their way past her and out of the café.

'Mr Burdock, he's not that bad. Why doesn't anyone like him?' Justine asked.

'Nah, I mean that old battle-axe Susan Hill,' Mary said slipping back inside to pick up plates and cups from the tea stained tables near the door.

Justine had never before known, or considered a need to know Mrs Hill's first name. 'Well yes, she told me to be back by half past and no doubt she'll be there to check. Does she come in here a lot then?' Justine asked through the swaying curtain.

Mary took a moment to deposit the crockery on the counter then stepped back outside, wiping her hands on a tea towel tucked into her narrow belt. 'Nah, she would never come in here. Stuck up old prune. She prefers her own company to anyone else's, believe me.'

'I do hate working for her, the job's fine, but she's awful,' Justine confided, checking through the window to make sure no one was listening.

'Don't you let her grind you down with all her snooty looks and criticism. I mean it darling.' Mary put on a very English accent for a moment, 'Stiff upper lip and all that old bean.' She winked and returned inside.

Justine was slightly confused and stood there thinking for a few seconds before Mary popped her head back through the curtain.

Back in full Irish mode Mary snapped with a grin, 'Now feck off, or you'll be late yer arse.'

Stopping briefly at the garage, Justine walked through and found Albert's legs protruding from beneath a car.

'Can you tell Harry I need to see him please Bert?' she said crouching down to floor level.

There was a clunk as Bert bumped his head on the sump. Followed by a string of expletives, mumbled for her benefit. Then a clearer voice said impatiently, 'As soon as the little sod turns up, I'll send him off again to find you.' Albert exhaled and looked out from under the car. 'Sorry, I just need to get this done by three. What time is it now?'

Justine looked over at a cracked clock next to the broken mirror and sprang back up. 'Twenty five past.' she croaked. Her voice trailing off as her body bolted back out onto the street.

'Flaming young ones today,' Albert cursed in frustration as he got back to work.

As Justine crossed the town hall's entrance foyer a receptionist called her back, 'Miss Page, excuse me.'

Justine ducked past a man carrying a large hamper and headed back to see what was wrong.

'Oh Miss Page, Harry dropped these off earlier and said he would catch up with you in the Bull and Bladder tomorrow.' The receptionist held out a small, limp bunch of flowers.

'Brilliant,' sighed Justine shaking her head. 'What time?'

'He just said after work I think, or maybe it was six? Sorry.'

'No, what time did he drop them off?'

'Oh, just before lunch.' The girl shrugged and tried to pass over the flowers again.

'Can you put them in something?' Justine asked.

The receptionist ducked down and grabbed something from a shelf, 'Will this vase do, it has a chip, but...?'

Justine looked at the half dead bouquet, 'Actually I meant the bin,' she said, then disappeared as quickly as her heals would go on the polished floor.

Bursting into Mrs Hill's office, she almost stumbled over a familiar abandoned hamper. On closer examination it was not entirely empty and contained soiled plates, cups, wine bottles and assorted wrappers. Sadly they had all been drained or scraped clean. Justine felt like Cinderella as she set about cleaning everything before repacking the crockery into the basket.

The office had a tiny kitchen area with some shelves; a kettle and a medium sized Belfast sink behind a frosted glass partition. Feeling faint she poured a glass of water and drank it down in one long cascade.

Mrs Hill arrived with a flurry of paperwork as Justine gulped down the final mouthful and took a long silent breath. The phone rang making her stiffen a little behind the partition.

Mrs Hill answered it immediately. 'Hello. Yes? Of course I am here, where else would I be, well put them through...' She dumped the wad of documents on Justine's desk and stretched a little, waiting for the receptionist to connect the call. 'Is that you, don't do that silly voice, do you have the new equipment?' Mrs Hill listened, checking a chipped nail on her index finger. 'Can you install those today and test it again?' Susan looked briefly out of the window. 'Well let's hope it works this time. I will take a look tomorrow. Don't call me here unless it is very important.' Mrs Hill put down the phone and picked up her diary but wrote nothing in it.

Justine coughed and stepped out from the small kitchen area, which made Mrs Hill jump, not realising the tardy girl had for once got in on time.

'Ah, Miss Page I hope you're doing something useful back there and not just eavesdropping?' She snapped the diary shut and spun around.

'I have repacked the hamper ma'am.' Justine stuttered, subconsciously wanting to call her Susan. 'It looks like you all had a nice lunch?'

'Yes we did and I have put some bits and pieces aside in the canteen pantry.' Mrs Hill remarked distantly as she rolled through the previous phone conversation inside her head.

'Oh my word, don't tell me you saved something for me?' Justine thought, but said nothing.

'I want you to make the changes I have outlined here and type everything up again.' Mrs Hill pointed down at an inch thick wad of documents from the morning meeting.

Justine tried her luck. 'I didn't manage to get any lunch myself.'

There was no response, not even a flicker of interest.

'I went to the café and saw Mary Tremayne, but I didn't have time to get anything to eat.' Justine looked up as she said this, but there was no expression of surprise or recognition on Susan's face.

Mrs Hill avoided looking at the phone and mulled over what Justine had just said to her. 'I am taking the spare food home with me. It is not for you, silly girl. You should manage your time better in the future.'

'I just meant, well, can I go and get a bun from the trolley, please?' Justine begged.

'I know exactly what you meant.' Susan folded her arms and stared at the young girl as if sizing her up. 'You are here to work. I had to work through my lunch hour taking care of the gentlemen and editing these notes.' She looked at her watch. 'In fact I think I deserve to pop home right now. I wouldn't want anyone stealing my parcel from the cooler would I?'

As Susan opened the door and left, Justine could hear the refreshment trolley rounding the corner in the corridor outside. Her hopes rose for a few seconds until she heard her snappy supervisor call out and usher the tea lady away.

Justine dabbed at a teardrop in the corner of one eye before it could smudge her make up. Then she took a deep breath and decided to make a cup of tea to try and fill the void.

Chapter Seven

Albert had very recently realised it was a big mistake to have waited on the hot kerbside, reading a folded newspaper in his itchy denim uniform. Truckloads of high-spirited soldiers had been leaving town all day, following their weeks of training and preparation around the local hills. From slow-moving open backed processions these men had plenty of time to prepare their abuse.

'Wake up Granddad, look after the place will you.'

'Gonna swat 'em with your paper eh old man.'

'Take care of the drill sergeants missus for me.'

As they laughed mockingly someone tossed a bottle cap that pinged off Albert's forehead and rolled around on the floor.

'Quick the Germans are coming, fetch a broom pal.'

Albert carried on reading and gave himself a Victory V sign. The men returned his two fingered salute and cheered boisterously as they bumped away down the cobbled street and out of earshot.

The funniest thing about the Home Guard, considered Albert, *was the fact that it existed at all.* Made up of old men no longer wanted at the front and youngsters with no concept of what the front was. All of them thrown together back here, at the rear. If you were fit and the country could spare you from more important tasks, then you were in the *real* services.

'So what's that make you then?' Albert asked himself, looking down at the already worn cuffs of his cheap tunic.

At almost exactly twenty-three minutes past the hour the furniture van arrived and attempted to kill Albert for the first time today. Neither on time nor on target, it braked outside the garage and eventually stopped a lot further down the road. The old girl clumsily reversed and shuddered to a halt in front of Albert's still nervously upraised feet.

'And here are the rest of the left overs,' Albert muttered. It was a phrase he'd overheard around town whenever the Home Guard showed up.

The vintage veteran used the side of the van to haul himself upright then crammed his paper into the flap of an old army issue bag. Albert's faded green messenger satchel had seen him through adulthood. He still remembered writing his serial number under that flap on the day of issue.

That number had been re-inscribed many times over, but you could still make out fragments of the original numerals in blue ballpoint, bleeding out beneath.

Sergeant Sanderson met Albert at the back of the van and raised an eyebrow of apology for his tardy and somewhat frightening arrival. He opened the doors and helped Corporal Croft up without saying a word. Albert shoved himself in as best he could and the door closed, blocking out most of the light.

'Budge up,' Albert called out to anyone who was listening.

'We can't Corporal. Got my feet on a load of big crates up ere, taking up half the van they are.' The voice sounded like the young student, William Duffy who was only eighteen.

'Hang about, it could be ammo?' This was definitely the cheeky tone of Tim Walsh a twenty-year-old cockney. After a comedic pause filled with the sound of him banging on the crates he added, 'Nah, must be German ammunition boys, coz there's a bullet 'ere with Bert's name on.'

Albert grumbled a few swear words and made do with what little room he had.

'My arse is stuck on a creaky chair with wood worm down one leg,' shouted the disembodied voice of Fred, another impertinent young man in his early twenties who should have gone to art college, but had ended up as a factory supervisor. 'Unless I've sat on old Terry's lap by mistake?'

Everyone laughed except Terry who was already feeling achingly ancient at fifty-two. He waited for the immature laughter to die down then said, 'That is a chair Fred and if you don't shut your gob, you'll need a better doctor than me to remove it from your other orifice.'

Everyone cheered.

Fred retorted instantly, 'I thought all doctors were better than you Terry?'

It was the same old pantomime that went on between the men whenever the officers were out of earshot.

Albert looked out through a crack in the doors as the van crossed over the broad hump of the river bridge and the main town started disappearing from view. When they had entered the cooler leaf lined lanes he asked, 'Anyone know where we're going on this camping trip?'

Neville Cartwright a twenty one year old machinist was the next to join in from the shadows. 'Thought *you* were our bleeding Corporal Bert. Don't *you* know?'

Albert shot back, 'Sergeant Sanderson told me to mind my own beeswax when I asked.'

Doctor Jones butted in, 'Have you finished my car yet Bert?'

'Only outstanding thing is you putting some money in my pocket,' Albert shouted down the line.

'Unusual, to be kept in the dark,' Sidney said slowly. Sid was the youngest and often the most apprehensive of the bunch at seventeen.

'Always dark in here Sidney you twerp,' Doctor Jones pointed out.

Sid shook his head, but no one noticed, 'No, I mean he usually lets everyone in town know what we're doing, coz he puts it on the noticeboard.'

'If I'd seen her, I would have asked Fat Florence.' Albert took out the old newspaper he'd been reading and blinked through one word at a time in the available slither of sunshine.

'Yes bach, she'd 'ave known,' David Hughes laughed from the bench seat opposite Albert. He was a retired newsagent and the only Welsh man in the patrol. 'Is that archive material?' he enquired of the corporal.

'I think this paper's pre-Dunkirk Dave,' Albert turned back to the front page, lined up the crack of light and squinted at the date.

Mr Hughes sighed, 'Tidy. So, apart from the bloody Fuhrer, remind me what else *was* big news back then?'

Albert skimmed back through the headlines he'd read so far, 'Hitler, Hitler, Evil despot, Hitler again. It's pretty much just him and his mates in here Dave.' Albert read in silence for a minute then commented, 'The big story was the Netherlands. Those bloody paratroopers who dropped into the football stadium. They nicked all the locals vehicles and captured the town in buses and vans.'

'Bloody savages,' shouted Fred from the darkness. 'Invading a man's football is going too far.'

'Not sure they was playing an actual game at the time Fred,' Albert said reassuringly.

'Sounds a bit like us don't it? Dressed to kill in a knackered old van,' Neville suggested. 'Soldiers of fortune like, off to do who knows what and God knows where?'

'Well as long as Captain Cooke knows where and what,' one of the new lads added.

'Well none of us has jumped out of a plane and hijacked this old bucket, have we Nev?' Doctor Jones shouted across.

At that same moment the van caught a pothole and jerked the passengers several inches into the air before they slammed back down hard.

'Blooming Nora, I think I've put a dent in the roof,' Fred shouted, banging his fist on the back of the cab as he tried to keep the old chair upright. 'There you go lads, that's your training jump. They'll make real troopers of us yet.'

'It is different lads, see we're here to protect not attack,' Mr Hughes pointed out.

'And we're a bunch of virgins and old duffers.' Albert suddenly had to project his voice against the barrage of boos and cheers from the men as he corrected himself, 'Sorry, I meant old duffers and spotty virgins.'

William threw an apple core in Albert's general direction and shouted, 'I ain't no virgin.'

'Your mum told me your dad is though boyo,' David chipped in.

Albert continued sounding out his more sensible thoughts, above the banter, 'What I'm sayin' is, if we *was* invaded, how long would we last?'

The men stopped shoving each other and listened. Albert put the newspaper on his knees and addressed the crowd of eyes he presumed were staring back from the increasingly quiet interior.

'My service revolver was issued two decades back an' to be honest, it's as likely to blow me own head off as anyone else's.' The corporal had their full attention now. 'I bet your shot guns and hunting rifles belonged to your dads, or even your granddads before you. Right?'

The men with guns grumbled some agreement.

'Right,' Albert continued, 'so after that front line of decrepit defences, we're down to these young lads chucking rocks I suppose?'

'We do alright, don't we?' Neville asked impatiently.

'We make a good team Nev,' Fred agreed, but he sounded unsure.

'Yes we're great, but what I mean is,' Albert paused and took a deep lungful of the warm air. 'Well if thirty paratroopers dropped down right now and decided to stop this old bucket?'

'Against their own better judgement,' Fred quipped. 'Sorry Albert, go on.'

'Listen, if they took this vehicle and drove into town pillaging our women and eating our sausages. What *could* we do to stop 'em? We'd stop nowt, apart from a few German bullets.' Albert expected another protest, but no one spoke up.

'We do be a grand group of men, young and old,' David eventually said in an attempt to fill the void. 'With big hearts an' a fair bit of experience between us.'

'Some of us have experience, but that was a different kind of war. As for these young boys, well, experience of what exactly? We ain't fresh young German paratroops, with bags full of kit and bratwurst butties. It's nonsense that *we're* the only things on the ground. Now all those squaddies from the hill camps have buggered off to the front, we're the only thing between Gerry and the town.' Albert desperately wanted to say the right thing, but the truth kept spilling out instead.

'I bet we'll bloody well try though, eh lads?' Neville mumbled.

'My mum did me some nice pickle sandwiches,' Sid commented absently.

After a further ten minutes of conversational silence the van pulled up at what had been a local beauty spot before the war. The site was now a command post and camp area supporting a few out dated anti aircraft guns on the surrounding hills.

Albert peeped out at the car park and recognised the old moss covered tourist sign as soon as his eyes had adjusted to the light. 'Ding, ding. King's Hill, end of the line I'm guessing, all passengers please disembark and no spitting,' he joked, but no one laughed back.

Albert and David Hughes held back the doors as the men climbed down to line up and stand at something like attention, beside the van.

Captain Cooke saw less hope than usual in the eyes of his men as he walked down the bedraggled line. Even his two new recruits from the mill, whose eyes had shone bright with enthusiasm an hour ago, seemed weary now. The captain was not perturbed.

'Corporal Croft, put that newssheet away and your top pocket is undone. Jones there is something hanging from your first aid bag. Tidy your selves up.' Cooke removed his gloves and held them behind his back, then he nodded at Sanderson.

'Stand at ease men,' the sergeant said softly.

The men stamped their feet apart, shuffled about a little and settled down.

'We have some very interesting work to do,' Cooke shot them a smile, but all he got back was confused indifference. 'The majority of the forces previously stationed here are needed elsewhere. So *we* will now assist members of the Air Defence and Observer Corps to guard this post in shifts.'

This bought the squad back to life and aroused a glimmer of interest.

The captain quickly continued, 'I know many of you have performed similar duties in the town, but this is a gearing up of our activities and our equipment.'

The men looked around enthusiastically to see what they would be guarding. All they could see in the immediate vicinity were trees and vegetation.

Cooke could see he was losing them again. 'Right, I want half of you doing a quick plod up the slope,' he ordered with a big grin, 'to the observation post over to the erm...'

'To the East Captain,' Sergeant Sanderson interrupted with an apologetic grin.

'I was going to say East, South East actually Sergeant.' Cooke's smile had withered away for a moment, but his final instruction bought it bursting back, 'The other half will practise on the firing range with our shiny new weapons.'

All the men gasped at the news, some even muttered words of appreciation, but a wave of the sergeant's hand at neck level created an eventual silence.

'We will swap over later, so you will all get a few shots in,' Cooke beamed reassuringly.

It was hard to suppress the men's feelings as the dark cloud Albert had placed over them was instantly blown away. They whistled and cheered at the news.

'Now settle down men,' Sergeant Sanderson called out while stepping away to get a better view of the parade. He counted along and split the row in two with an outstretched arm.

The sergeant's group drove out to a firing range on the other side of the tree line. Once there the crates were opened to a round of whoops and cheers. The biggest box contained five rifles. Not the very latest design, but at least they could hold several rounds at once.

'Those are "Smelly" rifles,' Fred pointed out.

'I'll 'ave yours then,' Sid insisted as he reached past and grabbed one.

Albert held up part of the crate, 'No look here on the lid Sid, "SMLE" stands for Short Magazine Lee Enfield.'

'They do whiff a bit though,' Sid concluded as he shoved the greasy barrel up his nose.

'Point it away from your tiny brain Private, you might hit it with a lucky shot,' Sanderson said urgently. 'You two clever dicks can help me show the lads how to strip one down in a bit then can't you?' he added, pointing at Fred and Bert. The sergeant clearly wanted to get on. 'Now, let's have a look at what other goodies the MOD have sent.'

The second crate contained boxed ammunition, cleaning equipment, straps and even some bayonets.

Everyone looked up in anticipation as the sound of engines rapidly approached in the air. Then three Hurricanes appeared in a close formation, flying just above the trees.

'Wow!' was the general conclusion of the men.

'Come on,' Sanderson shouted over the noise as he walked off toward the range, 'screw those flash bastards, we've got some proper equipment of our own to play with now.'

Chapter Eight

Minnie stood in the middle of a wide and recently harvested field. Parched shapes illustrated the previous crops layout, but the farm workers and machinery were long gone. All that remained were the cropped hay bales and their twisted stalks sticking up between tramlines of earth.

The twins sat on top of a pyramid of stepped hay a few yards from the truck. Finn was still trying to show off his new police helmet, but Elijah was having none of it. He threw small pebbles in the air and every time one hit his brother's hat he sang out, 'PING!'

'If you don't stop that I'll 'ave to arrest you for public disorders,' Finn warned sternly.

'You ain't no real copper, just a part timer,' Elijah grinned, throwing up all the remaining gravel that came down like hard rain.

Patrick was standing on Minnie's flat back, surveying the skyline and brooding. He was even bigger than Elijah in height and girth and the complete opposite of his petite sister Mary. The twins had tried to make friends with him, but after introducing them selves to the giant Irishman, he'd merely grunted and moved away. Pat was clearly not in a good mood and the boys were getting tired of waiting for Harry and Edward to come back over and move things along.

'You sure no one's working round here today?' Harry asked. He was standing with Edward at the edge of the field, watching the hill road.

'All clear on the Eastern front,' Edward nodded as he latched the gate shut. 'Cook's van rattled past just after we arrived, but you said they were off out on an all nighter, right?' Harry nodded back to his friend who continued, 'The girls harvested this lot two days ago, an' it'll be a while afore they comes back for the bails.'

'Come on then,' Harry agreed after one more check. 'Might as well face the music.'

'Wait,' Edward insisted as they crossed back over to the others.

Before Harry could question why, the drone of the three fighter planes appeared in the distance and they sped overhead at the height of the near by hills.

'Just Hurricanes,' Edward shrugged indifferently as the aircraft fanned out and flew on over the town.

'So I got fined ten shillings,' Patrick sparked up with a strong Irish bark. 'Ten whole feckin shillings just for being a bit drunk and disorganised,' he boomed the words angrily then looked over at the twins rather than make eye contact with Harry. 'How can one man rob another of ten bloody shillings over nothing more than a disagreement?'

'We could all put a bit in to help out,' Edward proposed.

Pat roared, 'I ain't no God forsaken charity case.'

Edward glanced at Harry then added very quietly, 'Or maybe not?'

'You were there Harry,' Pat griped on as he jumped down heavily and threw up a cloud of dust. 'How come only I got fined?' he asked before scratching his head and flicking an insect into the scrub.

Harry thought carefully about the answer, not wanting to antagonise the huge man any further. 'When the police arrived you were, well you were a bit cross Pat. Don't you remember?'

Patrick pretended not to be listening.

'You were sitting on a pile of broken chairs and squaddies, smacking one poor lad on the bare arse with a shoe?'

'I remember finding the shoe, the rest is a bit of a blur,' Patrick admitted. 'You should have stuck around, instead of disappearing.'

'We couldn't,' Harry began.

Edward quickly stepped in with, 'We couldn't have both our best men locked up for the night could we? Who would've looked after everything?'

'True enough those soldiers were being offensive to the Irish, but you started the fight kiddo,' Harry risked saying. 'I only helped out once you'd got stuck in and your fine's not that bad really, considering all the damage you did.'

Edward stepped back in again, 'Good that Malcolm didn't add costs for wrecking his pub.'

'Harry said most of the witnesses got posted away to the front on the day of your hearing, and well, that's pretty lucky, isn't it?' Finn contributed softly.

Pat gave him a look, he still wasn't happy. 'Landlord wants me to fix up all the chairs and tables. He told my mam I'm barred from sitting down until I do.'

'Well at least he's still letting you in, we can all help with the woodwork,' Harry smiled, 'and don't forget the solicitor we sorted for you, he wasn't cheap either.'

'Pay you back for the law man, soon as,' Patrick insisted more humbly.

'Call it expenses,' Harry suggested.

'I do Harry, ten shillings is very feckin expenses,' Pat shrugged.

'He means the company will cover the costs of legal representation for you,' Finn explained.

Pat slowly nodded and turned away. He reached onto the flat back of the truck and hoisted off all three of the gun bags in one huge hand. 'Can we go and shoot things now, I think that would help me calm down?' Big blue puppy eyes hovered above a sad mouth.

'Course we can Pat,' Harry laughed.

Edward's eyes roamed along the edge of the field, seeking the sweet spot where they could get down into the riverbed and out of sight.

'You know it's gonna rain like feck later,' Pat informed everyone before moving off. 'Might not be a good idea to go down there for too long.'

'What do you mean, *it's going to rain*?' Edward asked, suspecting Patrick was just trying to get home early.

'That splat of clouds will likely come up the valley sooner than you think and give us a right old soaking,' Pat insisted, 'Seen it a hundred times back home.'

'But this is a very sunny day in England, the weather is fine,' Elijah argued as he jumped down from the bales.

'And they made us pour the cider away and bring water because it's so blooming hot,' Finn said with indignation.

'You won't need it Sunny Jim. I'm telling you it's gonna be a corker, one from the Devil's own arse hole, you mark my very words,' Pat decreed. 'Massive summer storm in the valley by tea time, want to make a bet?'

'How much?' Finn asked bravely.

Patrick smiled, 'Ten shillings.'

'Right then,' Harry raised his voice to address everyone. 'Lets get going. Well done Finn, but lose that tin hat; lock it in the tool chest with the jacket and the bag. Grab the ammunition box from under the front seats while you're at it.'

Though it was the first time some of them had met properly, the men had all been to the field previously, in one formation or another. When they reached the hedgerow, Elijah held back a springy wreath of greenery to reveal a man-sized hole in the foliage. Edward led the way, crouching down occasionally to check and move the tell-tales they'd left in place last time. These would show if anyone else had been along the track. Things like sticks and hoops of wire that animals would pass by, but intruders would find hard to avoid disturbing. Harry took up the rear and repositioned any disturbed markers once they'd all passed through.

At the bottom of the slope the men got onto a dirt path that ran down behind the overgrown stream edge. A few minutes later they emerged into an open area near a pool in the woods.

Pat and Edward leaned the weapon bags carefully against a large fallen tree then had a quick look around the clearing. The twins dumped the ammunition box next to the guns and stretched their backs near the waterside. After a quick splash of cold stream the men came back together. Four of them sat along the old tree trunk while Harry held court.

'Right, I have a few new gadgets for you to play with Pat. Have a look in that ammunition box and see what you can come up with.' Harry pointed at the metal case. 'Don't just spend the day poaching fish with them like last time.' He paused thinking back to home and normality and then said in a softer voice, 'Mum did say to tell you "thanks", for the trout.'

'She's a lovely little lady your mam. I can get her some more Harry no bother, just seen a beauty right there.' Pat pointed playfully back at the stream and pool.

'No, have fun over there instead,' Harry indicated a direction directly away from the water. 'See if you can clear a few more trees for us.'

While Pat opened up the box to see what was inside, the twins said in unison, 'What about us?'

Harry found a pointing stick. 'Ted an' me are gonna show you two what to do if you're being chased.'

The brothers raised their eyebrows.

Harry nodded, 'I know, but you can still learn new tricks.' He sketched out the pool, stream and trees in the dirt, as if being viewed from above. 'You have to cover each other see? One of you runs, the other defends him.' Little curved lines showed how to move and protect each other. 'Then you swap places moving out one runner at a time.'

'Is it not better to just, go for it and scarper?' Finn asked as he got up to walk around the plan.

'Or just stop and fight?' Elijah suggested.

'No,' Harry and Edward snapped together.

'All right, think of it like this,' Edward shook his head. 'I will be running down that bank, trying to catch you. Imagine I'm someone you know, someone who would do their very best to nab you. Like, well let's say PC Grogan or one of the other bobbies. Imagine someone that chased you down when you were nicking stuff as kids, right? And your job is to get away quick, without falling over or running face first into a tree.'

'Which tree?' Elijah asked.

Edward ignored the lad and carried on, 'While your doing your run Finn and gaining distance, Elijah will try and distract me and keep me pinned down into dealing with him. Then you swap over. You'll get it once we start,' he assured them.

'So *you're* PC Grogan?' Elijah mused thoughtfully. 'But he's a crafty old bugger. Wouldn't he just wait for us at mum's and cop us when we got home for our dinner?'

'Sergeant Roberts used to chase me a lot, but he's too fat now,' Finn commented while looking Edwards physique up and down.

Edward grabbed the biggest of the leather gun bags and thrust out the contents to the boys. Anyone else would have been surprised that the bag did not contain a big old fashioned double barrel shot gun, but the twins had seen it all before.

'You can do it the quiet way to start with,' Harry said before the boys could ask. 'No ammo.'

'Can we make the gun noises ourselves?' Finn asked.

His brother missed the joke and yelled, 'Rat, a tat a tat,', with real enthusiasm.

'NO!' Harry stated firmly, holding up two impatient palms. 'Now bugger off and leave me and Pat alone.'

The twins were the freshest members of the group, but if they'd made it this far into the woods then they were ready to handle everything that was thrown at them. The whole group had been schooled to a level where they should not be capable of doing anything too stupid.

'Bit young aren't they?' Pat said with a frown.

Harry nodded and shrugged simultaneously. After a short pause for thought he admitted quietly, 'You know I often worry that for the twins, this is all still too much like fun.'

Chapter Nine

Captain Cooke's half of the men had been taking turns to look around a seemingly small red brick observation post and its perimeter. The little building was wedged perfectly into a sandstone cliff, overlooking the river valley on the far side of the hill.

On arrival, the huts initial Royal Observer Corps occupants and an RAF flight lieutenant had made Cooke and his group feel very welcome. Then the observers had surprisingly abandoned the hut as quickly as possible, leaving only the flight lieutenant as host and guide.

'You may want to duck down a bit more here,' Flight Lieutenant Caspar pointed out as Captain Cooke completed his own personal tour.

The captain was looking at everything in great detail while also failing to see where he was going.

Lieutenant Caspar was generally a friendly fellow, but did not suffer fools and he'd already decided that the captain was definitely a baffoon.

The observation post's bomb proofed exit required some crouching and twisting from the officers to navigate its right-angled corners and sandbags. Behind them was a simple square room with a stove and a bench big enough for a man to sleep on. Aircraft recognition lists covered every wall with the dark outlines of friend and foe alike.

The next room beyond that was more of a short passage, which plunged straight into the embankment behind. It formed a connecting space between the hut and its rear bomb shelter, which was basically an old cave with new brick walls. To the right of the passage there was a wardrobe-sized alcove with a chrome and plywood chair. The recess housed a transmitter, a notice board, an illuminated wall map and a telephone receiver.

In the rearmost shelter section there were two more wooden benches and a couple of chained canvas bunk beds hanging limp and grey along the moist walls. The low wattage, caged bulb lighting was poor throughout the whole complex and sometimes grew much dimmer when the external generator coughed and faltered.

Back at the entrance Captain Cooke stooped a little further down and struggled through into the daylight outside. Once there he discovered that overexcitement had clearly got the better of the lower ranks. Several men that had completed their tour earlier were currently jostling for positions on the buildings side ladder and flat roof. They were making playful pirate noises and threatening to make Neville walk the plank. Several more of Cooke's men were sat around in the dry dirt, smoking and laughing at the amusing chaos.

Captain Cooke stood there beneath the dappled shadows of some camouflage netting and contentedly soaked it all in.

Lieutenant Caspar ticked off something on a small clipboard in his left hand. 'You look very pleased with yourself Mr Cooke,' he nodded with a smile as he stepped in front of the captain and blocked the view.

'Yes I am rather...' Cooke began to say wistfully.

Caspar's smile melted rapidly. 'Well get your shabby crew back in gear and snap to it man.' He went red with anger as he cried out, 'This is a military facility, not a sodding playground!'

Cooke stammered at first then momentarily regained his composure and batted back, 'Now look here young man, as a captain I expect...'

'You expect what, *old man*?' Lieutenant Caspar said abruptly. Then he completely lost his temper, 'You are not an officer in the RAF or the real army for that matter, so don't go kidding yourself. At best you are a platoon commander and to be honest, you are piss poor at doing even that.'

The men had long stopped laughing and playing. Those on the roof started to come down, those inside popped their heads out and everyone was paying full attention now.

Cooke looked the officer up and down, taking an age to simply ask, 'I'm sorry?'

The lieutenant took this as an apology rather than a question, but dismissed it all the same by continuing, 'Have you been listening to anything I have said on your tour, so far?'

'There is an awful lot to take in,' the captain admitted. 'We are more accustomed to guarding coal heaps and gasometers.'

Caspar was calming down a little. He nodded with a slither of sympathy, 'There is nothing to worry about. Professionals will still man the other lookout posts and the big guns. This one needs a refit, temporary decommission as of seventeen hundred hours today, engineers should arrive early tomorrow.'

'Decommission? But no, I thought, I mean we were supposed to be...' Cooke looked pale.

'Just don't loose this before the morning and you won't go far wrong,' The lieutenant poked him disrespectfully in the shoulder with a large key and tried to reassure, 'Look, the boffins say there's a storm coming in soon, a real pea-soupier. Nothing will be up in the sky tonight.'

'Oh?' Cooke replied uncertainly.

'Just guard the place until the engineers arrive tomorrow. Keep your men dry and that's it. Small groups can fit in here, but don't use the barracks.' Caspar pointed off right into the trees. 'They are due to be flat packed and moved on, first thing in the morning.'

'But I have bought my full squad with me tonight Lieutenant. I, that is we, my men and I, we thought we would be manning this post and guarding the entire facility. They won't all fit inside here.'

Caspar looked serious for a moment and then cracked up, laughing uncontrollably and leaning a hand on Cooke's shoulder to steady his convulsions. He managed to repeat the Captains phrase about "Manning the post", several times in a high pitch voice and then he stopped giggling just as suddenly. Finally he let out a deep sigh and wiped a tear from the corner of one eye. 'You can billet the additional "men" in the old education building near the barracks. It leaks a lot and smells funky too, but at least it'll still be there when they wake up. Use the woods or the old public toilet in the car park for anything else. Now get these men under control. I have some documents to pack away and then I'm pulling the plug. You have fifteen minutes to find me if you have any further questions.'

Cooke called his men over and ignored their sideways looks as the lieutenant briskly walked away, still chuckling to himself. The captain organised them into simple guard units and set them about patrolling the woods. Neville and Tim were given special duties to gather kindling then ordered to get a brew on inside the hut.

While Neville stoked the little stove, Tim was happy to get the chance to sit down in the chrome control chair and swivelled with delight. The little cockney thought he knew everything and was sure he could tune the radio into the BBC if he tried. With a pop he flicked the set on.

'You shouldn't mess with that equipment Tim,' Neville cautioned nervously from the main room.

'I bet you I can find something if I sweep through what's here and,' he stopped for a moment, 'Hang on, that's funny,' Tim turned up the volume.

'...EIVING OVER, TEST ONE, TEST ONE, THIS IS SD 9 CALLING ZERO 9, ARE YOU RECEIVING OVER. TEST ONE...' Then the broken voice trailed off and with a whine it was gone, leaving the receiver to just *whistle*.

Neville slammed down the tin of condensed milk he'd been wrestling with and crammed into the passageway behind Tim. 'What was that?'

'I tell you what that was Nev my old son, that was odd,' Tim rotated the dials in an attempt to get the voice back, but just as he found it again the power to the set died.

'That lieutenant said he was pulling the plug didn't he?' Neville suggested while his friend flicked at the switches seeking life in the transmitter.

'Dead,' Tim said as he got up to help with the tea.

Neville stared at the transmitter as Tim pushed by. 'She sounded nice,' he mused.

'Yep, a proper bit of posh crumpet and no mistake.' Tim agreed.

'What are you two up to?' It was Albert poking his head around the exit.

'Just brewin' up,' Neville said innocently.

'Blimey, you've landed on your feet with this Nev,' Albert whistled as he looked in from the doorway at what lay beyond. 'Get a mug on for me and Fred then, we've been sent over with all the bedding, kit and blankets on the van.'

Tim tapped a spoon on the side of a tin mug. 'No time Corporal,' he said before licking the spoon clean. 'Captain Cooke said, soon as it arrives, the kit needs to go down the track by the car park. Pronto!'

'And he is more than a little bit cross,' Neville pointed out as he began telling Albert what had been going on in their neck of the woods.

Albert and Fred eventually trundled the van back over toward the car park just in time to see the lieutenant leaving.

82

The officer stopped for a moment to let the shabby van pass by. He stood astonished as Albert let out a huge raspberry, then wound up the window and drove on. Caspar straightened his collar, made a final note on his clipboard then crossed over to a blue staff car waiting by the gates.

The driver got out to open the rear door as he approached. She was a very pretty young lady in uniform with neat blond hair; RAF sunglasses, a hat tilted to one side and perfectly straight seams stretching up under her blue skirt. She closed the officer's door and winked at Albert who had stopped abruptly to stare open mouthed from the cab.

'I wouldn't mind going to war in that,' Fred whistled from the passenger seat.

Albert nodded his enthusiastic agreement.

'Yes those Hillmans make a lovely staff car, don't you think?' Fred asked.

Albert looked back curiously at Fred and hoped the lad would discover women soon. Before the Germans came over and shot him at least.

When they arrived at the makeshift sleeping quarters Fred tripped backwards through the education hut's double doors carrying far too much and dropped half of it outside.

'I used to come up 'ere with my Edward when he was a boy,' Albert said as he stepped over Fred. 'Hardly see him nowadays, saw more of him when he was at sea.'

'We could 'ave a fag,' Fred said with a shrug as he sat up, 'and pick out a couple of good sleeping spots away from any draughts?'

'I reckon as it's all draughts,' Albert frowned as he poked around the room, which looked like it had been used mainly for storage since being requisitioned.

Mounds of damp and unusable toilet paper rotted in one corner. Dusty light bulbs spilled from mouldy cardboard boxes in another. Large windows on three sides of the room were covered in the familiar criss-cross white tape that framed triangular views of the real rows of barracks outside.

Early evening light cast zigzag shadows across the old hut's wavy floor and undulated as the two men walked around. The fourth wall with the doors in was papered with weathered example sheets of the kinds of butterflies, birds and flowers you might have previously seen in the woods outside. The posters were old now and curled up at the edges, brittle and yellowed by time.

'Stone me I remember those, let's have a look,' Albert turned and wobbled across the rickety floor which bowed considerably near the middle. Reaching the wall he pressed his fingers against a poster to flatten it out.

Frederick joined him and reached out to help uncurl the edge. 'My old man bought me up here a few times too,' he said softly.

'He was a great bloke your dad. A good soldier and an even better copper.'

Fred nodded. 'So, were you all mates together like, in the last war?'

'Some of the time yes,' Albert seemed to physically shrink a little as he remembered. 'We were in the same regiment, the same mud, same grub, just different bloody luck. I'm sorry they all got so sick.'

Fred shook away the sudden childhood flashback of his father curled up in a foetal position, coughing up blood on a bed in the front room. He turned to Albert and confessed, 'Even at the end, he'd still scream out in his sleep, "Oh the poor buggers, they're only kids", then he'd cry for hours. It sounded awful.'

'I know, he used to scream it even back then, in the trenches.' Albert wondered if the lad had ever fully understood what his dad was on about. He decided to explain it very simply, 'He was talking about the German lads mind you, not our lot.'

Fred looked puzzled for a moment then nodded and said softly 'I didn't realise.'

'He was the best machine gunner we had, your dad.' Albert paused, 'But I reckon as he paid for every bullet he fired, one way or another. I really am sorry lad. He saved my bacon a few times I can tell you. I just wish we'd been able to have saved more of the company. We lost two thirds out there and a dozen more since we got back.' Albert didn't really know what to say next.

'No Bert, don't worry it's fine.' Fred wiped a tear from each of his eyes and laughed as he looked around the room. 'I can remember sitting here too, with dad, before he got really sick. We had to sit in some really little chairs and he looked so ridiculous. Both of us trying to draw these bloody butterflies.' The young lad smoothed-down several of the buckled images at once with his palms. 'The real wildlife never stayed still for long enough.' He took one hand away and pinched his nose with a sniff.

Albert leaned on the wall and thought back to Fred's dad, just after the first war, talking optimistically about the future, a future that never was. 'Trust me, as someone who knew your old man. An' I'd like to say, as I knew him pretty well. He would have been proud of you these last few years and you should be proud of him too.'

Fred didn't reply.

Albert carried on, trying to change the subject, 'Seems like another life, back then. Up 'ere with our boys studying these beautiful butterflies on the wall. Now look at them daft buggers,' he pointed back in the direction of the lookout post. 'They're pissing about over there studying posters of the markings on enemy aircraft instead.'

As Albert moved away his palm stuck to the tacky poster for a brief moment and forced the backing paste to give up the last of its stickiness. The pastel coloured sheet fell away, swooping through dust motes as it looped the loop and glided along the floor.

Fred's head followed it down. 'Can you, can you be like,' he gulped, 'like my dad, just sometimes?'

Albert turned to him, void of words as he reached out and hugged the young man solidly. Seconds later he patted Fred firmly on the back and released his grip. Then he coughed a lot and moved about in the opposite direction. He wasn't sure what he was looking for, just something to change the focus for a moment. 'Fag break then?' he choked, rummaging in his uniform for some tobacco.

'Have one of mine.' Fred had the same awkward feelings. 'Let's sit on the steps in the sunshine eh?'

'Might not be much left of that,' Albert suggested as they opened the doors onto the fading daylight and dark clouds began to roll over the valley.

While they sat there surrounded by everyone's baggage and bedding, Albert said, 'You know I can't pretend to be your dad you daft sod, but I can be here to listen or compare memories. If you like?'

'Cheers,' Fred smiled through cigarette smoke. He said nothing more for a minute or two then got up and flicked the dog end into a bush. 'Better

85

get this lot stowed away then eh?' he sniffed, pulling up his collar and looking up at the rustling trees.

'Might as well take our time,' Albert grinned.

'Here what about that stuff then?' Fred pointed back inside. 'I reckon the toilet papers have had it, but if we can fill a box with a few of the *less* rusty light bulbs, well there could be a few bob in it?'

As they disappeared back indoors the sky above cracked and rumbled into the distant landscape becoming noticeably darker still. Cloudy grey fingers gripped the clouds tightly and caused dark blue bruises to appear across the heavens. A daytime moon came out for a trice before being swallowed and trapped with the sun, deep inside the growing torment.

This was the kind of storm that only ever appears at the end of a very dry and hot week. At first it was just the sound of something coming, like an orchestra tuning up. Then the wind came in for a dramatic solo, growing in intensity as it squeezed in and slotted itself between the trees. The sky became a solid mass, which fell as a myriad of molecules almost fused together. They landed with a thump on dusty leaves and dry earth, churning the condensed smell of summer into the air.

The wall of rain hit like hammer blows as it reached the last few men still training around the firing range. The fragile construction offered no real cover or drainage. It was just a narrow, rusting corrugated sheet above the shooting platforms that was lifting up like a comb-over in the wind.

Sanderson watched as one by one the men around him disappeared into the muddy spray. After a moments thought he pulled down his cap, picked up an abandoned rifle and ran after them through the woods.

Following his men and after an age of slipping and sliding through brush and ferns, Sanderson tripped over some netting, fell into a nest of sandbags and rolled over landing bum first in a giant puddle. He looked up and wiped the rain from his face with a claggy hand. It took a moment to ascertain that he'd made it back because he was distracted by the view, which was breath taking.

He had never seen it so dim in the day; it was magical, purple and dark blue shadow, rather than the absence of light. Ahead of him the dark valley floor stretched out for miles. Tiny factories, mills, farms, houses, cars and even boats were randomly being illuminated from thousands of little windows. The lights that in a normal blackout would be cut and masked off were all dot-by-dot, being switched on.

'Who goes there?' an indistinct voice called out from another new and nearer portal of light just below the ridge.

'Your bloody Sergeant *goes there,*' Sanderson spluttered out. Then fully realised that he was on the bank above the lookout post and moved onto the roof to climb down.

With his back to the town there was a different view consisting of dancing dark trees, a thick rag-rug of sky and semolina rain. Then for the briefest of moments he glimpsed something blip into the heavens. Several something's came and went through a slither of light as one cloud folded into another.

The entrance door was opened fully to allow his angry and wet body to squeeze into the cramped interior. Inside were just over two thirds of the full patrol, crammed into the main room and the shelter beyond. In turn, each man standing was encouraging Neville to get the fire going properly again and add more cups of tea to his current order.

'You can put me at the front of that list Cartwright,' Sanderson ordered as he pushed through their wet bodies, clocking every face.

The captain was sat alone and aloof at the little map desk in the middle of the complex. The flickering lamplight hardly glowed as the generator outside started to have real trouble sucking enough air through the watery wash.

'Sir,' Sanderson saluted, semi crouched by the alcove.

'Ah Sergeant, I was wondering when you would get here. Bloody weather. You know, I remember it being like this in India one Summer when...'

Sanderson interrupted before the captain could get going, 'Sir I believe there are aircraft approaching and the town, the lights are all coming on and the...'

'Calm down man,' Cooke snorted without looking up.

'We should call it in,' Sanderson insisted as he reached for the telephone and tapped vigorously on its little rocker to get a line.

'Put it down man,' the captain took the receiver away and replaced it, 'to the best of my knowledge we are no longer connected.'

His sergeant quickly nosed through to the shelter area and did another head count. 'There are a few men missing too sir.'

Cooke was annoyed at being shoved forward in his chair and for not getting to tell his tale of the Indian monsoon. 'I am sure they have all found somewhere to hide Sergeant,' he looked around vaguely. 'There is nothing to do now, nothing to even bloody well guard, don't you see? Just find a bench and dry off a little,' he snapped.

The sergeant did not sit down, instead he insisted, 'We have to round up all the men and at least try to report those planes.'

'Gerry won't bother flying in this,' the captain snarled.

Sanderson shook his wet head, 'They might if they're lost or if they took off an hour ago sir?'

'Now look here Sergeant,' Cooke took a deep breath.

Quite abruptly the telephone rang, making both men jump.

Captain Cooke cleared his throat and snatched up the receiver. In his very best telephone voice he said, 'Hello over there, Captain Cooke in here speaking to you over there.'

In response a tiny and tinny female voice could be heard screeching back at him through the speaker, 'Who the hell? This is control HQ, is that Sector Seven...'

'Yes I think it is, hello, hello,' Cooke tapped the phone on the desk then listened again. 'I say Sanderson, they seem to have connected, and then they have gone off?' he frowned.

'Probably the bad weather sir', Sanderson leaned in and took the receiver to listen for himself. It was dead, so he put it back on the hook. '*Ring, ring,*' the phone kicked off again the instant he replaced it.

'Oh just get on with it man.' Cooke sighed.

Sanderson ran a finger down the step-by-step procedure sheet pinned to the notice board in front of them. 'Hello, Sector Seven Charlie, Kings Hill East,' he said perfectly. 'We have aircraft approaching our sector post from the South East.'

'Well if there are, they are not ours. Everything is grounded over there,' a friendlier female voice pointed out.

'It was just a snap shot and a long way off, but I'm pretty sure there were several aircraft,' Sanderson recalled. 'Sky has gone as black as pitch and the town is all lit up, please they need to be warned.'

Sanderson could hear the operator shuffling paper and talking to someone else. After a few seconds she confirmed, 'No other reports yet, keep an eye out and update us on type, direction and numbers if they enter your grid.'

'Roger, will do. Over and out?' Sanderson was clearly unsure if that was exactly correct. He felt it was an improvement on his commander's attempt anyway, and put the phone down before any one could complain.

'So?' the captain enquired.

'We need to confirm direction and numbers sir.'

'Right men,' Cooke shot up reinvigorated and held centre court in the passageway. 'We might,' he looked at the sergeant for a moment then recommitted, 'we might have enemy planes to report in. So damn the weather and get back out there the lot of you.' With that he sat back down and picked up a book.

'Listen up,' Sanderson bellowed, pushing through to face the damp figures huddled nearest to the exit. 'Doctor Jones and I will head off and round up any missing men and equipment between here and the range.' He pointed at William and David, you two get on the roof and keep an eye out. As soon as you hear or see anything, you stick your heads back down here and let the Captain know. The rest of you stay put for now.'

As Duffy hauled Hughes up the ladder onto the roof there was a gigantic white flash. The men froze and counted together in the dark until ten seconds later the flash was followed by a colossal clap of thunder.

Chapter Ten

Two Heinkel bombers with escorts *were* approaching the hills. Their mission to destroy a new airfield had been going reasonably well up to a point. It had been a smooth flight at high altitude with little resistance met. The problems began ten minutes ago when they'd descended and found there was nothing here to blast. In their briefing the navigators had been shown aerial photographs of fuel bowsers, holding pens and planes. In reality they found only the empty patchwork of a farming landscape below them.

The crews had blamed their flight leader and navigator Stephan for getting them lost. In truth, a minute error on the vector intelligence he'd been given had taken the bombers many miles off course. With an oncoming storm swallowing the light and bouncing rain diffusing the entire scene, Stephan had decided that their mission was most likely now, all but failed. An order to gain altitude and go above the storm was the reason that Sergeant Sanderson had first seen them.

Ahead of the aircrafts current position, Private Hughes cupped his hands behind his ears and froze in place. 'I swear I can bloody hear something boyo,' he insisted.

'Well I can't see naff all,' Private Duffy complained.

'Listen then, down by there. Iesu mawr, aircraft it is.'

'Jessy mower?' Duffy turned around puzzled. 'Is that German or British?'

'Welsh it is boy,' Hughes said proudly. 'Iesu mawr, means big Jesus, it's a sort of swear word see?'

Duffy shook his head, 'Right well I'll keep looking, you shout down and tell 'em summat's coming over. In English mind, you daft old sod.'

David leaned out from the parapet and shouted down, 'Aircraft approaching from the East, tell the Captain.'

Neville's head popped out below, 'He says what type of aircraft you ninnies?'

Inside the captain was frantically tapping the telephone hook, trying to raise HQ again. 'Well Private, what type?' he called out impatiently.

'Small bombers and fighters sir,' Neville confirmed.

'Six, four, no six, erm? Tell him four medium bombers and four fighters, we think? Bloody rain.' Duffy's distant and exasperated voice grew a little louder as he leaned over the railings with Mr Hughes.

The captain got a line, 'Hello, hello, this is Sector Seven, erm Seven C, C for Charlie. We have incoming from the East...'

'Type and formation?' HQ insisted.

'I er, oh, well four bombers, medium sized and four escorts at least we think...' Cooke could hear the voice trail off repeating his inaccurate information questionably to someone at the other end.

Eventually the operator said, 'Who the hell is manning Seven C tonight, sounds like the bloody boy scouts?' This was followed by a click as the line went dead again.

Having wasted several minutes searching the countryside with the bombers, the two fighter escorts were out of time. At the limit of their fuel reserve the pilots gave a quick wave and swung away. The escort leader transmitted, 'Gehen müssen. Goodbye und good luck.' Then they were gone. The bombers had just enough fuel to go on, but it seemed pointless with no target, no support and extreme weather.

The navigators in both aircraft discussed all the variables, but neither of them could agree on exactly where they were.

'Rees du dumm Kadett, sind sie falsch!' came the crackling and angry voice of Stephan from the leading Heinkel.

Strapped inside the second bomber Rees couldn't argue with his superior, but he disagreed whole-heartedly with where Stephan thought they were. Rees was beginning to suspect they were actually approaching a small industrial town in the top corner of his map. All he needed was something man made on the other side of that horseshoe of hills ahead, to confirm it.

Below the bombers Private Duffy was forcing his way further inside the hut and pushing through to the captain's little telephone booth.

'Sir, sir there are more now. We can see two big ones higher up and something further out and quieter. Could be more fighters sir or, a transport?'

The rest of the men huddled around him calling out whatever outlandish suggestion popped into their heads. One man suggested it might be gliders, which led another to add the word paratroopers into the mix.

The captain got up and glared until the nervous laugher stopped and the men looked away.

Cooke addressed all of them from the archway. 'I need facts to relay to HQ, not fiction. Now settle down all of you,' he ordered sternly. 'Private Duffy, "Could be?" is simply not good enough. Get back out there and try again.'

On board the second bomber its out-dated equipment needles jumped and span then stopped briefly before fluttering on. Rees was distressed. Someone was trying to shout something at him, but the noise of the climbing plane was incredibly loud and there was a wavering whistle in his headphones caused by the storm. Rain crashed into the windows surrounding him and dragged back in rippled windswept fingers that obscured any distant detail from view. Occasionally something crackled behind the control panels as if a violent insect was trapped there. It startled the cadet when he reached out to tap a dial and neon blue sparks connected the gap between his fingers and the display.

The flights Technical Sergeant Peter Albrecht was crouched in the gangway trying to give advice to Rees over the noise. He calmly took off his steamy spectacles and used them to tap Rees on the side of his face. When he had the cadet's full attention he pointed outside to where electrical charges were trying to earth them selves along the other aircraft's antenna. The crew knew the fully loaded ship was old and difficult to control, even in the best of weather conditions.

Peter had a very worried face and that was all that Rees needed to know. Both crews were becoming more than aware that they needed to get away from here as quickly as possible. That meant either gaining much more altitude or going beneath the storm where obstacles and air defences would add to their problems.

'Klettern über dem sturm,' Stephan ordered over the intercom and both bombers roared higher up into the heavens at full power.

Moments before they reached the safety of a brighter clearer sky, a searching arc of lightening leapt over the lead bomber's tail. It whipped down lunging at the second aircraft before finding its way back to earth via the clouds.

On Rees's aircraft the environment exploded brightly, but not with burning fuel and shrapnel. Instead the little pockets of static stowaways suddenly pulled together and amplified as the lightning passed through them. A bright haze covered every line of the aircraft, inside and out. The Heinkel lit up like a backlit blueprint-schematic of itself then faded away to absolute black.

It happened in the blink of an eye, but the crew saw it all in slow motion. For them the electrical charge left a retinal imprint on the darkness and the taste of ozone on their teeth.

Everything was still and silent for a second, creating an empty stage which the valves, fuses and bulbs quickly erupted onto. Molten filaments and fractured glass burst out of the cockpit panels as atmosphere rushed back in to fill the void. Plastic coatings on wires, oil and grease, even patches of the men's uniforms and body hair were suddenly on fire.

Peter Albrecht was fast and knew his job well. He stumbled forward and dowsed the pilot with a plume of carbon dioxide from an extinguisher on the wall. Then he tore the whole device from its clamp and started putting out the electrical fires around them.

The big bird was dropping away now. Her big Daimler-Benz engines had not spluttered, they'd just stopped. Rees had watched the last silent rotation and seen the white spirals on the propellers red nosecones motionless and vivid against the darkening sky. At several thousand feet above the ground, the image made him feel sick.

At the lookout post several of the men were huddled by the door giving their own versions of what was happening in the sky above. 'Sid saw a glider and another plane towing it through the cloud Sir,' one man shouted in.

'Are you sure man?' Cooke's face demanded a clear answer.

Sid pushed his way inside. 'Positive sir,' he stated categorically. 'There was a whoosh of lightening on top of the clouds and it lit 'em all up. The first plane released the second and it started to glide down. It was going in fast sir. It must be bursting with troops?'

'Well get back out there and look for any more.' The captain waited then glared at all the men still skulking around. 'You lot get out there too,

NOW! Find some view points facing town and challenge anyone who can't speak the King's English.'

As the men filed out, Cooke picked up the receiver again and took a deep breath. 'Help, HQ this is sector Seven C, we have sighted transporter aircraft and gliders.'

'Are you sure Seven C? In this weather?'

The captain remembered his Sergeants words, 'This weather has only just started. My men saw clearly, bombers, fighters and at least one transport plane releasing a glider over the town and there are more coming. I think this is CROMWELL. Repeat CROMWELL! For heavens sake; send up some planes, get us some troops. We're bloody outnumbered!'

'Calm down will you. We can't send up planes in this. I will pass on your CROMWELL alert. Are you sure about this Seven C? Hello? Seven C, are you there?'

Pulling on the yolk as if he were trying to uproot a tree, Rees's pilot Second Lieutenant Rudolf Furch shook off his mask and shouted, 'Was funktioniert?'

The answer that came back from Peter was grim, 'Nichts funktioniert alles ist kaputt.'

Rudolf struggled to feather the propeller blades, but the mechanism was very heavy and stiff.

Around the hill tops the anti aircraft squads had been warned that something was coming. They tore back the rain covers they'd just put on their big guns and scanned the horizon. Searchlights swept across followed by flak bursting in lines as the only two visible aircraft were singled out.

The lifeless Heinkel dropped through the menacing beams and their accompanying pompoms, falling quicker than the gun crews could react to.

Rudolf began breathing again as he gradually pulled out of the dive and into a heavy glide. He tried futilely to restart any of the flight systems; it was time for a decision. Turning his head the pilot urgently shouted back, 'Jetzt springen, jetzt springen!'

Two fresh recruits manning the rear gun nervously followed his orders and left by the nearest exit hatch. Cold wind blasted in, removing any modicum of comfort or streamlining that had previously remained.

The cold air was what Rees the navigator needed to snap him out of his dream state. There was nothing he could do other than go. The cadet unstrapped himself to leave and Peter stood aside with a smile. Rees rushed past him and squatted at the edge of the open hatch, looked back briefly then crossed his arms and dropped.

The plane swooped away from Rees to the west. In the same direction, far below, he could make out a few speckled lights poking up in the dark grey blur. He snapped back to his own predicament and looked up, his canopy was buffeting, but mostly open. It swam away with him towards the town like a jellyfish caught in a current. Looking around for his companions he saw two other chutes spin apart further down behind him. Drifting around he thought he could hear a shrill sound travelling on the wind, then there was more flak very close by and he passed out.

The town's air raid sirens had started in unison with the flak guns, slow at first then winding up to a heart wrenching whine. It was designed to make you drop everything unimportant; grab what *was* important and run for your life. Most of the town headed for cellars, entries and little outside shelters or under their kitchen tables. Some people ran to the new public shelters, but the gates were all locked.

Wardens tried to usher these stray people into the towns old-fashioned shelter trenches, but these were already becoming overwhelmed with water and flooding fast.

Above the town Peter saw the flickering lights and had a terrible idea. He shouted out through the flak, 'Ich werde die nutzlast frei.' Letting Rudolf know he was going to try and crank open the bomb bay.

The pilot looked back at him in surprise and anger. He shook his head and shouted 'Nein, nein!'

Peter was a gifted flight engineer, but since having a training accident, he'd been much more afraid of jumping than of death itself. He was also a true Nazi and felt that if he was going, then he was going to take a bit of England with him. Dropping the huge bombs would mean more chance of him getting out in one piece. If they crashed with them still on board, there would be nothing left other than a very big hole.

Ahead of them the barrage balloons that had been pulled down out of the storm were now quickly rising again. Fortunately these defences buffeted in the wind and drifted sideways out of the bomber's path.

Rudolf had to agree that he desperately needed the aircraft to loose weight. As she juddered around him he held up the thumb and forefinger of his right hand and called to Peter, 'Zwei minuten!'

Peter confirmed he understood and replied,'Ja, zwei minuten, nicht in panik.' He had less than two minutes to dump the eight capsules that filled the bombers belly with more than a thousand explosive kilos.

At Sector HQ, reports were coming in thick and fast from many sources now. They had been told that everyone for miles around this one little town had seen gliders, bombers, fighters and worst of all parachutes. Sector control did not know what to believe. The hapless Home Guard at Kings Hill had started the frenzy, but the police, gun crews and ARP had also confirmed lesser, similar activity. It was a blind panic.

In their last communication Captain Cooke had simply screamed down the line, 'Paratroopers, OLIVER, OLIVER! They are here!' Since then the telephone had been dead.

His earlier cry of "Cromwell" had set unavoidable and official wheels in motion anyway. The confirmation message of "Oliver" meant there was no going back now. Troops would have to be found from somewhere nearby and dispatched to assist. There was a system for everything, even if the man, who had first confirmed the invasion force, appeared to be a blundering fool.

The stricken Heinkel's main gunner Harald, had been stunned when the lightning struck. He'd come around now and managed to unstrap himself before dropping down to assist Peter. With the air pulling at the double bomb doors, the men managed to wind out the planes clockwork caesarean in half the allocated time.

Peter knew if he could just push in the hydraulic rods a few millimetres, the fluid inside would release the bigger components holding the bombs in place. He searched around frantically for anything he could shove into the mechanisms little gaps.

Harald saw what was required and asked, 'Wird das helfen?' Quickly unzipping his jacket the gunner began to pull out a chain of dog tags.

'Nein, sie sind zu schwach!' Peter refused, needing something stronger than the brittle tags.

When Harald pulled out the remaining chain, it held something else. 'Es ist mein, erm, lucky schpoon.' he smiled.

Peter snatched the spoon, which snapped the chain and sent Harald's tags flying to the floor.

In Mrs Hill's dark office, upstairs at the town hall, Justine had been snoozing, slumped face down at her desk. It was quite jarring, as the sirens had woken her with a start then coupled with the sound of the rain beating wildly against the windows. Seconds later she was running in stocking feet down the carpeted stairs before skidding to an ungraceful stop at reception. She stopped to think for the first time since being stirred. People jostled past, as she stood there motionless, carrying her shoes in one hand and her bag in the other.

Instead of joining the long throng of bodies attempting to push their way through the exits, Justine decided to head out via the chambers corridor. There was another exit there and a staff shelter in the gardens just beyond that. That way she could also grab her umbrella and save her hair from attack by the rain, even if it didn't save her head from the bombs.

She bounded through flip-flop double doorways, pushing out as the wind forced its way further in. Conversely, this same force helped her to easily push open the door to chambers and then blew her inside as well.

Feeling around in the darkness for her brolly, Justine noticed someone else was there. Who ever it was had not noticed her, yet. The flapping doors, the din of the storm and the sirens had almost completely concealed the young girls entrance. Justine took a long shallow breath and waited for her body to catch up. She could hear the persons voice clearly now. It was Susan Hill.

A lightening bolt lit up the room creating a shadow outline of Susan standing at the biggest window. She was on the telephone with her back to the room. Her attention focussed on scanning the skyline and street intensely.

Thunder rolled through the room as Justine went over to encourage her supervisor to hang up the call and come to the shelter outside.

When the thunder had died away she was close enough to hear, 'What, now? It can't be, don't be absurd girl. Who told you that? The ARP said what? Well you can't be sure, no. No! What about the others?'

Justine shuffled inches closer, her feet leaving damp marks on the cool tiled floor.

'Well yes,' Mrs Hill continued quietly, 'I am always ready. You'd better not have this wrong,' she turned and slammed down the phone.

Mrs Hill seemed to hardly notice Justine. She glanced at her for a moment, said nothing then ran past the girl and elbowed her way out of the chamber doors. Justine wondered if she was invisible, then as the bombs started to land she realised she might possibly have just been insignificant.

Above the town the broken bombers evil eggs continued spewing forth, landing first on the outskirts and then marking a line of chaos across the whole metropolis. Gigantic and expanding dots of destruction erupted behind the aircraft, gliding heavily down, but still reasonably high above it all.

Rudolf reassessed if they could make it to the open land in the distance. As the last bomb clanged away he gave the escape order again with renewed urgency, 'Springen, sich schnell!' Looking back into the eyes of the men he'd served with for several months he added, 'Bitte Peter, Harald. Please!'

The men finally did as they were ordered. While Harald ran to escape, Peter saluted Rudolf then nervously closed his eyes and dived after the gunner.

The aircraft felt like a lurching brick, much lower now, but almost at the safety of the flatter fields. Some of the flak had struck the rudder and tail, tearing useless holes that dragged and pulled the ship off course.

Rudolf was tired of wrestling with the controls and this close to the ground the aircraft was no longer controllable anyway. With the last of his strength he let go the yolk and thrust out, releasing the canopy hatch. The panel blew away, spinning into the rudder and the bomber rolled nose down. Rudolf heaved and pushed out, his face skimming past a micrometre from the remains of the planes swastika tail.

Automatically pulling open his chute and checking its stability, the pilot looked around for his crew. Not far above were two white umbrella canopies fighting the wind and drifting away from him. As a gust blew Rudolf around he saw the line of carnage the bombs had created. Along that line he saw three more chutes far away and nearer the ground. He looked down just in time to see the last moments of his aircraft as it dropped onto a little church, alone in the lanes.

Hitting just between the tower and the chapel's sloped roof, the planes wings folded in and showered the remaining kerosene over everything. After one almighty whoosh of flame the chapel's tower leaned out at a horrendous angle causing the wooden beamed frame of bells to spew out through its brickwork. The carillon dangled, swaying in the wind. The heaviest bells twisted free of their mounts and swung around on the ropes, absorbing the energy and turning it into sound.

Jumping so near the ground meant that Rudolf was coming in way too fast. Smashing through trees, his cords and silk caught on branches that fortunately slowed the descent for the last few feet. Battered and cut the pilot finally stopped an inch from the ground. Pointing his toes, there was a vague feeling of solid earth beneath the tips of his boots.

The bells continued ringing around him as the harness crushed into his torso and groin. He could not breath and his ribs were on fire. Awkwardly thumping the release clasp he slumped down onto his knees and collapsed breathless in the mud.

A mile away from the crash site the verger of another church on the edge of town had heard the chapel bells ringing. Difficult to make out above the up and down of the air raid sirens, but it was definitely there. He had not heard them in a long while, not since Dunkirk. It was beautiful and frightening at the same time. He looked up and thought, *'It could mean only one thing, couldn't it?'*

As soon as the verger spotted Harald and Peter's parachutes he made a decision. He'd considered that it might not be an actual invasion, but some other silly beggar had started ringing the bells and he was only continuing what they'd begun. Someone had to do it and this was *his* moment.

The verger dashed out from the shelter of the gravediggers lean to, where he'd been crouching since the rain began. Explosions, sirens, fire engines and adrenaline surged around him as he pelted into the church entrance and ran up the bell tower. Flying over the steps two and three at a time he crashed into the heavy iron studded door of the bell room. Once inside he grabbed the biggest rope from its hook on the wall and pulled.

This was it, the invasion was on and he had a part to play. No one was going to stop him and he would do a better job than anyone else. The pumped up parishioner rang that bell with all his might. When soon after he heard more churches in the town centre joining in, he smiled like a mad man and bounced on his toes, pulling harder every time.

Leading Navigator Stephan's bomber had also lost some power and equipment when the lightening erupted over them, but only for a spluttering moment. At that time no one had noticed the other plane falling away behind.

Stephan had been trying to correct his corrupted equipment when he'd first spotted the flame filled cockpit of the second bomber dropping away to port.

When no one had replied on the radio, Stephan ordered his pilot to turn back and follow her in. It came as no real surprise when he saw men bailing out of the lifeless fuselage shortly after that. It did surprise him when only three men had jumped and Rudolf's bomber seemed to level out a little. When the bombs started to drop there had been even more confusion on board Stephan's bomber. *Why and how was Rudolf doing a bomb run if he was going down with no power?* Unfortunately the explosive activity had bought the full attention of the big guns on the high ground and Stephan's plane had been forced to peel away to avoid being shot down as well.

Flying higher and faster than the other Heinkel they had passed over her just before Rudolf bailed out. The best escape route home for Stephan's aircraft was going to be back the way they had come. With no working compass and hardly any sun, the burning town would hopefully lead the way East. The ungraceful bird swooped upwards doing a slow barrel turn and eventually dropped back down along her own flight path.

Flying low over the stepping-stones of the fires, kept them away from the flak above, but eventually they would have to rise up again to allow for the hills. When they were back at the end of the line of burning craters, Stephan called out that he could see something. It was in the distance near the bottom of the slopes and it looked just like, an airfield.

The first of Rudolf's bombs had started an inferno in the woods and the torched trees were now illuminating the whole area. In this flickering orange light Stephan could make out a large military truck in a big field and a sort of pyramid building made up of big blocks. It seemed to be surrounded by mud tracks and long straight take-off lines in the earth.

It was hard to be sure, but this could be their original designated target. Stephan thought. *Whatever aircraft had been down there must be under camouflage or have already scrambled to defend the town.*

The navigator decided in a moment that Rudolf must have seen the strip too and gone for it. It explained some of the confusion at least. 'Flughafen!' he shouted and flicked the bomb bay switches to open. With no radio, Rudolf must have dropped the rest of his bombs to help guide Stephan back on to the airfield? In which case his comrades were heroes, not just potential prisoners of war and the mission was definitely back on.

As they flew nearer he saw a group of men rush from the undergrowth towards the truck. Some were firing automatic weapons up at the bomber. The biggest man was struggling to run through the wash, with a large ammunition box on his shoulder. Stephan took the tiny mud covered men for ground crew in brown overalls erupting from a bunker.

Lying on the floor and pulling himself over the bombsight, Stephan held up one hand and said, 'Stetig,' wanting his pilot to level off and maintain the same speed. He used both hands to adjust his weight and change the aiming position. 'Stetig, stetig.' his voice was calm but firm. Several bullets hit beneath the cockpit, punching through the thin floor to Stephan's left and right, he felt the thumps, but didn't flinch. 'Stetig,' he said again calmly. He squeezed the release and counted off, 'Eins, zwei, drei, vier.' From his position he could feel the shudder of the first four bombs dropping in succession.

The plane was far too low, which meant the bombs did not have time to fully flip over, arm and detonate. One smashed side-on through the cab of the truck, decapitating most of the windows and roof. Full of energy it skidded onward to sink with a slurp in a flooded tyre rut. It released no more than a few bubbles then rolled over and sank down.

The muddy men threw them selves into the sludge, expecting to be obliterated as the other three black shapes hit the soupy earth like torpedoes.

101

One by one they sprayed plumes of muddy water, swimming between the men's bodies and on into the bushes behind.

One of the bombs detonated on a rock somewhere in the gulley beyond, throwing shrapnel and shrubbery out over the stream. The other two bombs found places to sit and hide amongst the undergrowth, waiting.

The Heinkel's gunners tried to get an angle on the five shadows now up and running again in the field. White lines of tracer bullets tore up the ground on either side of the brown shapes as they clambered aboard the remains of their truck. From their birds eye view the aircrew watched amazed as the wreck began rapidly reversing away; its occupants still firing up at the bomber with skill and determination. The Heinkel's engines screamed out as she desperately climbed away. Before long they were skimming over the hill again where the waiting flak guns picked out their shape and began bursting shells ahead.

As the truck pulled back, huge lumps of her twisted bodywork tore away and ploughed wide furrows in the earth. These new channels released the water surrounding the first rutted bomb, which rolled over a little more. A final bubble plopped to the surface next to it and then it went BANG!

Having almost reached the gate entrance, the truck was shoved violently backwards through it. A few inches of surface mud and several feet of dry compacted soil, roots and manure shot up and out of the ground. It was big, dark and messy. A dome of detritus spreading out, hovering in the air for a moment then falling back to earth with a sloppy thwack.

As the Heinkel finally breached the hill, another round of distant gunfire burst from the wooded area underneath them. The aircrafts machine gunners fired back until the muzzle flashes below died away.

'Schnell fallen die Bomben!' demanded the pilot. He was desperate to release the remaining cargo and gain altitude to get them away from this disaster zone.

Stephen let them all go unguided, but this time the plane was at just the right height. The final four bombs span down before finding their mass and letting gravity line them up to land around the lookout post, the firing range, the car park and near a van parked close to a row of huts.

As the bomber rolled away avoiding the anti aircraft fire, Stephan felt weak and tired. He didn't know if it was the battle he had just fought or the relief that it was over.

There was nothing left to drop from his position, so he tried to get up and find his seat. His arms pushed against the metal floor, but it was impossible. It felt as if his chest were cast from solid iron.

Slowly sliding a hand between the floor and his ribs, Stephan felt warmth spread between his fingers and jacket. This heat was immediately followed by the coldness of realisation. He tried to speak, but there were no words left in him and within seconds he was dead.

Chapter Eleven

The councillors from the planning committee had suffered many losses during the previous nights bombing. Most of them had lost money playing cards in the bunker for a start; a few were also deprived of large chunks of their property and income.

When the "all clear" had finally sounded last night, they were unsurprised to emerge into a wall of agitated voters. The mob had thrown a hail of questions, which the councillors instinctively ducked and dived away from as they moved to their cars. Answers needed preparation and were not the kind of thing the committee wanted to *commit to* at such short notice.

So Mr Burdock had promised to convene an emergency meeting, as soon as was humanly possible. For most of the men, that had meant going home to bed and waking up late to a large breakfast. That was followed by urgent and seemingly more important business discussions, thus leading them into a late lunch. Eventually they had all re-emerged to see what could be done for everyone else in the town.

It was early evening when the last few members pulled up in their big automobiles. The growing body of protesters outside town hall were tired, but they rallied themselves to meet each new vehicle with amplified contempt. They still had grievances to express, wanting to know why they'd huddled in tiny shelters, flooded slit trenches and cellars, while the vast new public shelters had remained locked. It hadn't gone unnoticed that the town hall staff's plush bunker had been open and well equipped for some time.

The majority of people killed and injured last night had been working at Mr Moor's munitions and tin can factory. Amongst the crowd, stories were spreading of locked doors, blocked fire escapes and inadequate organisation at his works. There were dozens of people within the mob who had been left bereaved or homeless by last nights raid. They seemed the angriest of all, ranting abuse and hurling insults, as you do when you have nothing left to lose.

Mr Burdock was the last to arrive and stood gormless on the noisy fringe of the demonstration as his chauffeur hastily drove away. The councillor was lost without Mrs Hill to hold his hand and haul him through any trouble. PC Thompson saved him today. The constable jogged down quickly from the steps, grabbed the gawping Burdock's pinstriped arm and dragged him back towards the main doors before anything sharper than insults got thrown.

Inside the main foyer a gaggle of administrative staff and pressmen were waiting to continue the flood of questions. Burdock did not like being manhandled by Thompson and did not thank him for it. He considered that it *was* merely *the man's job to protect an official from hooligans like that.* So instead of issuing gratitude the councillor ordered PC Thompson to throw the press out then ignored the other council employees completely and stormed off to the reception area.

'Locate Mrs Hill,' the frustrated councillor screeched as he tapped his knuckles on the wooden counter impatiently.

The receptionist answered quickly, 'Mrs Hill booked today off.'

'What do you mean off?' Burdock shouted angrily in response to the receptionists opening statement. He slammed his fist on her counter. 'Get her on the bloody phone girl.' The councillor glared red faced at the frightened young girl before adding, 'And what about Miss Page, don't tell me she's having a day out too?'

'Miss Page was injured sir,' the girl frowned as she held up a shaking list of all the town's known casualties.

Burdock snatched it away and scanned the names while muttering, 'Stupid girl, we told her not to go back out there.' His eyes flicked back to the receptionist, 'Well what are you waiting for?'

'Already tried her home number sir, but Mrs Hill doesn't answer,' the receptionist explained. 'She booked it off yesterday afternoon.' The girl rotated a large diary so that Mr Burdock could read her note. 'Said it was a trip to visit her aunt sir.'

'Well call her again,' Burdock scowled. 'And send two girls from the typing pool down to chambers.'

He walked briskly away before any of the swarming staff could get close enough to bend his ear about their own departmental problems. Several did manage to anxiously thrust typed pages and thin dossiers into the councillor's hands as he pushed his way through the corridors.

Without Mrs Hill, Burdock had to think for himself. It came as no surprise *to him,* that when push came to shove, he was quite good at it. The defensive weapon being fashioned inside his head was going to point the blame at everyone else and then delegate anything left over to other sub committees. He felt confident that he could turn all this into a positive before the week was out. Somehow he would clear his plate of these new bitter pills and refill it with the buffet of selfish prospects the committee had been chewing over yesterday.

In chambers today there were no actual refreshments to be seen around the big table. Today there was just a circle of grumpy faces below a dark cloud of cigar smoke.

Burdock noticed that the Chief Constable and Auxiliary Fire Chief had joined the group. Both men had looked at their watches with agitated body language when the councillor finally materialised.

'First things first,' Burdock threw his documents onto the table, 'I should thank the men of our uniformed services who have done their best to...'

The ad hock speech was abruptly interrupted. After an initial thud, two very young soldiers with floppy hats rushed into the room followed by a significantly older officer who had a whisper of a limp in his right leg. Strands of slightly greying and auburn hair poked out beneath a peaked cap that framed the handsome new face. His kind brown eyes took in everyone around the table, as he pulled over a chair and sat down.

With him seated, the soldiers closed the exit and remained on guard outside. Mr Burdock tilted his head slightly trying to remember what it was he'd been saying.

'Don't mind me mate,' the officer chirped with a strong Australian accent. While everyone stared on, he stood up again, placed his baton and cap down and leaned in to shake Burdock's hand. 'Major Jackson,' he smiled with a row of bright teeth set in a golden tanned complexion.

Two young girls were escorted in by one of the private's at the door. The girls stuttered to a halt, mouths wide as the Major pulled out a second chair and offered for them to sit at the main table.

The Australian officer had most likely started his day off looking smarter, but even with traces of soot, blood and sweat on his uniform, he still sparkled. For his entire audience, who had only seen the wider world in grainy black and white images, it was all a bit of a colourful shock.

'We are typists,' one of the girls said shyly, 'we have to sit over there sir.'

Councillor Moor interrupted, 'What can we do for you Major? We are very busy and...'

The major shrugged. 'I command the Company of diggers your town hollered for last night Councillor, Burdock is it?' he asked while noticing that the room seemed to have frozen in time.

Burdock broke the spell and snapped his fingers at the girls, 'Miss Crawford, Miss Dandle, just sit down will you.'

The typists found a space each at Justine's workstation as Councillor Moor asked the room mockingly, 'Company of, diggers?'

'Soldiers,' the officer explained.

'Well I hear they are very efficient at digging,' Burdock nodded slowly. 'I was just thanking Chief Higgins and Chief Scorn for their manpower dui...'

'We were sent here to save you lot from hoards of Germanic warriors dropping from the sky,' Major Jackson pushed on.

Burdock missed the thrust, but there was the beginning of a murmur from some of the other men in the room.

Chief Higgins stood up, 'Our personnel acted on the evidence at hand. Calls came in from all sides and control confirmed something big was going on.'

'My crews haven't stopped sir,' the Fire Chief chipped in.

The major held up a calming hand, 'Hold on, hold on. I'm not blaming your mob. Your men *and women* are still doing a fantastic job. Chief Scorn knows I appreciate all his fire crews commendable efforts last night.' Jackson gave a friendly nod then turned his glare back to Mr Burdock, 'A case of bad leadership at the top; trunks rotten, but the roots are good.' All eyes were back on the major as he added, 'Last night your town collectively panicked. I've seen a fair few critters do that when the bush is ablaze and there's nowhere to run.' He looked around the room begging everyone's attention. 'Last night we found kids shoved in coalbunkers, families and factory workers trapped or huddled in corners. Most of 'em just a dozen yards from your so called public shelters and their locked steel doors.'

As Chief Higgins sat back down the room remained silent.

'As you are no doubt aware Mr Burdock; when we arrived the German invasion had vanished, so we dug you bludgers out of trouble instead.' The major sat back down and frowned. 'I have spent half my day in the dirt and the other half trying to work out who was in charge of this cock-up. Then I got word that your little meeting was finally about to start,' he tapped his watch, 'at a quarter to flaming six no less.'

'Well we have all been very busy with, well with official business.' Mr Burdock felt he needed to show who was in charge here, 'Everything is under control now and your "diggers" are no longer required Major.'

Chief Higgins interrupted again, raising a hand, 'We still need their assistance to finish setting up a temporary camp for the homeless and also to round up the missing Germans.'

Burdock lowered his voice a notch, but was still very firm when he said, 'Other than that, we apologise for the confusion Major and you are now *dismissed*.'

The officer ignored him, 'Seems there's still plenty for us to do blue; could be more rescue work, bomb disposal and as Chief Higgins said, helping to find that enemy aircrew.' He paused as shouts from the distant protests outside trickled in through the open windows. 'Then there's our latest priority of course, protecting you lot from your own residents.'

Burdock's brain swam against the current and felt like having a bit of a crisis. His hands shuffled through the typed pages and thin dossiers he'd been given. His heart hoped the pages would somehow explain last night's fiasco in bold, brief and blameless detail. When he looked up his expression told the room that he was still lost.

The other council members chose to remain silent. So long as the rude officer was zeroed in on their chairman, they would probably remain that way.

'I, I err,' Burdock tried again to find anything in the notes to ratify his position and show this impudent colonial idiot what was what. When his finger had finished searching, Burdock reluctantly agreed that the major had a small point. 'We are sorry for the confusion,' he said quietly. 'It seems there were many factors that condensed into last nights debacle. Factors might I remind you, which were the result of a genuine enemy attack on our town.' He finally lifted his head to face the major, 'Not that many people were killed and we had well organised preparations for our services to the citizens.' The councillor stood up tall and confidently added, 'I *should* point out that some members here today, have suffered personal catastrophe and loss themselves.'

Major Jackson took a deep breath, weighed up the situation and blinked slowly before exhaling. 'I didn't realise that, I'm genuinely sorry.' He raised his hands and said with compassion, 'Look, maybe we should start over gentlemen?'

'Yes indeed,' Burdock triumphed. 'You see Mr Moor here has lost half his factory and Mr Humble has had a whole row of rented terraces, devastated.'

The major slapped a hand down on the table and said one scornful word, 'Unbelievable!'

'No it's true,' Burdock continued feeling he was almost back on top. 'Several of us have lost a lot of rentable income of one sort or another.' He smiled at his colleagues for support, but the look they returned said implicitly, *'You are on your own sunshine.'*

One of the typists raised a hand and flipped her shorthand back a page.

'Yes dear?' Burdock lowered his spectacles.

'Sorry sir, but they told me it might be over thirteen sir.' The girl looked almost apologetic for mentioning this possible factoid.

'Thirteen of our buildings, my word that is a lot?' Burdock tut-tutted, his face contorting as he considered the insurance and rebuilding profits.

'No, I mean d*ead. At least* thirteen dead *sir* and my sister, she's a nurse, she said it could be twenty by nightfall.' The girl sounded angry now, not apologetic.

'I see,' Burdock coughed and pulled out the list again with Justine's name on it. 'Ah yes, I hadn't seen all these figures before,' he lied.

'The actual count is fifteen dead so far,' Jackson clenched his grubby and grazed fist, 'but your town *was* still lucky.' The noise from outside rose again as the protesters began to chant together with more unison. 'And there's the people still missing or injured. Your hospital's overwhelmed.

Your public shelters should have been open,' Major Jackson waited for the information to soak in.

'We could not have done more or worked faster,' Burdock lied again, as his fellow councillors contributed their mumbled agreement.

'No mate,' Major Jackson shook his head firmly. 'And I'll bet you fountain pen fusiliers have made a mountain of money out of a molehill of a problem here.'

The major's assumption bought a gasp from every guilty man in the room. There was another gasp as a clot of new faces appeared at the chambers door windows, held back only by the determination of Major Jackson's two men. Then more soldiers and policemen arrived to force the onlookers back outside.

The major got up and leaned on the table, 'Whitehall assures me you plan for the shelters to be ready very soon? Why not *today?*'

'*I assure you,* Major, that we have only the public's best interests at heart,' Mr Moor protested.

'Well said councillor,' Mr Humble shouted up.

'My numbers man Private Evans, he tried to get a look at your records today, but had to make do with some local news paper archives instead.' Jackson waited for their faces to melt, 'He estimates that all this could have been wrapped up months ago.'

'Nonsense,' Burdock claimed.

'Fear is a powerful thing. You should be out there talking to those people.' The officer pointed toward the noisy corridor, 'Or more importantly, listening.'

Councillor Burdock tidied his papers, 'Well thank you Mr, I mean Major Jackson. Can I assure you we *will* endeavour to find out what went wrong and fix it.'

Jackson shook his head, but before the major could respond any further, a podgy private with black rimmed spectacles entered, saluted and said, 'They found a Paratrooper, Major.'

The major was the only man in the room not excited by this news. 'You don't salute an officer indoors Evans, not if he ain't wearing a cap.' He paused to consider his own statement then substituted, 'Or, maybe you do, could be a Naval thing?'

'Yes sir,' the young man half saluted again then quickly put his hand down.

'And he's not a Paratrooper,' Major Jackson insisted, 'he is just a bloke that fell out of a plane, right?'

'Yes sir.' Evans almost managed to not salute at all this time. He was a nervous individual at the best of times. About twenty-five years of age, but his short cropped black hair was already thinning on top.

The major put on his cap, which only served to confuse the private even more. Jackson nodded and followed his man out without saying another word.

Huge sighs of relief came from most of the remaining bodies around the table. Then Private Evans shoved his sweaty face back around the door and said, 'Major Jackson suggests you come with us too please Chief Higgins. We have a prisoner for you.'

At the bottom of the town hall's steps Chief Higgins stood and stared at an odd and badly parked vehicle. The half car, half pick up truck was camouflaged with a sand coloured bottom and pale sky coloured top, divided by a wavy line. It made Higgins think of a dessert island scene in a children's play, but without the fake ferns and palm trees painted in.

'Bute ute, but she sticks out like a saw thumb around here,' Jackson smiled holding back the passenger door. 'Jump in the front with me Chief.'

Mr Higgins felt mentally uncomfortable sat in the middle, next to the major. Primarily because the vehicle's oversized gear knob stuck up between his knees like a shiny walnut capped erection. He winced as the driver grabbed it and yanked it back hard to find the reverse gear.

'Don't panic Chief, he's a good driver, or at least, he's never clonked my cobblers,' Jackson assured the policeman as the ute bounced away with Private Evans and two burly soldiers on the flat back.

'There is always a first time,' Chief Higgins responded then breathed out slowly.

Jackson laughed and slapped him on the thigh, gripping hard. 'So, you up for helping sort this mess out then mate?' He let go his grip and changed the angle to shake the man's hand.

'Yes,' the Chief shook back.

'I meant those dung flies at the town hall mate, are you looking into their scams?' the major concluded.

'We haven't the evidence or the man power, what with the call up,' Chief Higgins stated sadly. He considered his two remaining unfit and useless detectives who were probably skulking somewhere near a barmaid, 'but I'll ask my desk sergeant to liaise with Private Evans if that helps?'

The two men bumped together as the car swerved and mounted the pavement opposite Albert's garage to avoid a rubble filled crater on the other side of the road.

The driver circumnavigated the entire street where Mrs Clark lived in order to dodge more disruption. After bouncing over a level crossing they used the rail yards tracks as a bumpy highway towards the woods on the other side.

The car arrived a few yards from a parked army truck and skidded to a halt, its horn honking three times. Word of the prisoner had spread quickly through the warehouse buildings along the yards and spread out onto the bombed streets across from the tracks. The frightened public were angry. Starting with just one or two onlookers, little clusters had merged into a circle of about thirty men, women and children around the sandy coloured lorry. The more curious had closed in tightly around the rear tailgate, just before Jackson had arrived. The cars shrill horn had semi parted the crowd to reveal a handful of weary looking Australian soldiers on guard within the melee.

The ute had overtaken many more civilians heading here and its occupants knew they needed to act fast. As the car pulled in a little closer, Jackson swung back the door and climbed up to use the cab as a lectern.

'Looks like we've caught one of the little blokes then eh? Good show everyone.' Major Jackson addresses the crowd, using body language to beckon them all in like a true showman. 'Now listen folks, I need your assistance here. We all want to get to the bottom of this crap storm as quick as possible, don't we?'

'He killed my neighbour, Mrs Adams,' a solitary voice said quietly.

Then a tall man with a spade over one shoulder continued more confidently, 'She di'n't never 'urt no one an' they blew up her house and our communal privy too.'

'And my cousin and our brew house,' a woman further back added with contempt.

Jackson nodded. 'We need to question him, find his friends and determine if the Luftwaffe are coming back again,' he said calmly.

There was no response, instead the audience watched as Chief Higgins hooked a leg over the gear stick and squeezed past the major into the open.

Before he was fully upright, a small boy prodded the Chief with a wooden rifle and said, 'My mum says they should all be shot.'

The boy's mother pulled him into her skirts.

'The prisoner will be held in custody by Chief Higgins and his staff,' Jackson stated firmly.

'Who are you to tell us, you ain't even British,' the man with the spade sneered.

'My men came here to help,' Jackson replied, taking it on the chin. 'They have worked shoulder to shoulder with all of you to save many lives.'

'That Nazi is our prisoner, not yours,' someone suggested. 'Hand him over,' another voice joined in and was instantly accompanied by ten more shouting similar remarks.

'He will be a prisoner of your police, until they arrange for him to be moved on,' the major said firmly then looked down at the Chief for support.

'This man will be questioned, processed and imprisoned. That is the only option,' Mr Higgins shouted loud enough for them all to hear. The policeman was not an impressive sight. He was as short as a policeman could be at five foot ten. He was well past middle aged and had become short sighted, pale and gaunt after years of being office bound and living alone.

The silence the Chief had created was broken when a railway worker disrespectfully banged a hairy fist on the car's bonnet and grimaced, 'Then he'll spend the war scratching his arse in the countryside, along with all his pals. We should string him up.' Everyone who was not wearing a uniform cheered their full agreement with this.

'What you gonna do to stop us, *MATE*?' someone strutting out of the trucks shadow asked the major directly.

'We won't do anything to stop you,' Jackson put a hand on the Chiefs shoulder and gave it a little squeeze. 'Will we Mr Higgins?'

113

The Chief shook his head cautiously.

'If you want to tear this man apart in front of your wives and children, if you crave to end their day with yet another nightmare then go ahead.' Jackson got down from the car's doorframe and moved amongst the confused faces. 'Lieutenant,' he called to the officer in charge, 'go and get the prisoner and hand him over to these, these gentle folk.'

'Yes Major, but Major..?' the young officer protested.

Jackson clarified himself sternly, 'We are here to assist these civilians in any way we can Lieutenant.'

The officer followed his orders and directed two soldiers to unhook the tailgate then bring the prisoner forward.

It was Peter, the flight engineer who had indeed fought so hard to drop the bombs last night. He did not look like a warrior now. His face was drawn and tired as he shuffled forward limping into the light.

'Right, where do you want to hang him?' Jackson said, watching for the prisoner's reaction, or lack of reaction as it turned out. It confirmed the major's suspicion that the POW didn't speak much English.

Chief Higgins saw it too, the crumpled German and his dirty twisted spectacles trembled with dread, but his fear was for the unknown.

Hidden away inside the vehicle, the magic had worn off. Hyde had become Jekyll; a dangerous curiosity instead of a monster. There was silence apart from the shivered breathing of the captive and no one stepped forward to claim the prize.

Everyone jumped as a dozen armed soldiers appeared noisily along the tree line around them. The patrol had zeroed in on the major's three horn blasts, which normally signified trouble.

Jackson used the tailgate foot holes to climb up next to Peter and stood the nearest men at ease with a simple flick of the head. 'Right then, I'll get Chief Higgins and some of my men up here to take this chap away into custody.'

There was a slow parting of the waves allowing Chief Higgins to climb up with Private Evans and two more escorts.

'That is all then folks,' Major Jackson said jumping down and helping to strap back the tailgate.

Two thumps signalled the wagon to move off, leaving behind a large oblong void. It was the space the townspeople needed to walk away; back to what ever they had been doing before.

The little boy with the wooden gun was the only one to speak up. 'I like Germans really mum,' he remonstrated. 'They blew up half the school for a start.' He got a smart clip around the ear and cried all the way back to the road.

When they were gone, Jackson pulled a map out of the ute and went around to the front. His men autonomously gathered around the vehicle's bonnet in a neat semi circle.

'Good work, now continue to search this thick woodland,' he pointed out their location then did a quick head count. 'Split up and fan out North East, until you meet the rest of the patrols, they should be moving this way.' The major's finger drew several sweaty lines on the map. 'There are a few British soldiers from the anti aircraft crews manning road blocks here and here.' The commander turned to his men, 'Search every bit of bush boys, they're out there.'

Jackson called over to a soldier who was carrying a medium sized radio pack and asked, 'Has Sparks had any luck setting up the full rig yet?'

The man nodded and smiled as he held out a handset for his commander.

'Just tell me,' Jackson shook his head and waved the devise away as he got back into the car, 'do you know where the Professor is working, or Corporal Jarli?'

'Yes Major, Captain Dreyer is helping with the flooding over at the stone bridge and Corporal Jarli is up on the hill sir. His team are trying to find a missing head wound who wandered off from a Home Guard patrol.'

'Send a message up the hill and tell Jarli to get his scouts back to town as soon as the injured man is found. Radio Captain Dreyer too and tell him I'm on my way.' Major Jackson casually pointed a finger and the driver took off, flinging him back in his seat.

Chapter Twelve

Justine had missed most of the last twenty-four hours, but the rest had done her body good. The sandwich, the never ending sweet tea and the bath had made her feel like a new woman. Now that her senses had returned, it felt like she'd missed a whole lot of other things too; things that had been happening right in front of her for months. After quickly drying and dressing she found Margaret, back upstairs looking out of the window in Harry's room.

'Anything new going on?' the young girl asked as she gently towelled dry the back of her head without disturbing the stitches.

'There was a big ruckus over by the railway yard just now. It looked like the natives were gonna smash that German chaps face in. Then some la-di-da ponce in a flash car turned up with Chief Higgins and stopped all the fun.' Margaret sounded extremely disappointed. 'They've all buggered off now.'

Justine smiled and turned away, 'I need to bugger off too.'

Mrs Clark nodded her approval and followed Justine down as far as the back door. 'What's yer plan then?' she enquired as the girl stepped outside.

Justine flung open the shed doors. 'I think I'll take the bike, try to check out Harry's old haunts, then get up to Edward's farm and see who's there. Maybe his wife Victoria knows something?'

Margaret scowled, 'You don't think they'll be up there then?'

'Of course they will,' Justine answered quickly, did half a smile and crossed her fingers.

'I just wish someone would fix the blessed phones,' Margaret sighed as Justine disappeared into the shed. 'Here, you won't make it up the valley on my old bicycle sweetheart.'

Justine reversed out of the shed doors dragging Harry's motorcycle. She was tiny next to the big bike, but turned it with ease before instinctively pressing a toe into the stand hook. This forced gravity to help bring the whole thing to a solid upright halt in the middle of the little yard.

'You can't take that monster,' Mrs Clark flapped as she stepped down onto the slabs. 'I know you wants to get up there quick, but you need a lift see? Mr Hornblower might take you up there in his taxi. Hang on, I'll go and ask him.'

'Margaret,' Justine hissed sternly, 'don't worry, I've ridden around the farm and the lanes loads of times. This is sure to be the quickest way.'

'But it's just so big, an' fast, an' you're just so, well...' the old lady was agog.

Justine reassured her, 'Trust me. I just tell her where to go and she's so well balanced, the hardest bit is staying still.'

'Well I can't let you go, I just can't, not like this,' Margaret stormed back into the house.

While Justine checked the fuel level and wondered what Harry's mum could do to stop her, Mrs Clark banged around the kitchen then scurried off upstairs. When she returned she was armed with a red hot steel skewer and a long buckled belt. Justine looked up in surprise, not knowing whether to laugh or hide behind something.

'I can't let you do it, not in that outfit. Everyone will see your daft knickers an' you'll get a draft up your muff. Quick, pull this belt round and we'll make another 'ole.' Once satisfied with the fit Margaret popped back inside and returned with more gifts. 'Harry's trousers, and here are the rest of them cigarettes, a pocketknife and a few coins just in case.

Two minutes later Justine was rolling out of the yard donned in leather jacket and goggles. She looked over at what was left of the terraces and considered that for the first time in her life, she actually felt in control of her own destiny. There was nothing here, no worldly possessions left to worry about. She was totally focussed on one single thing, finding Harry.

The first problem encountered was that the Bull and Bladder was in darkness, its doors bolted shut. The pub had not been damaged in the bombing, but a sign on the window stated that it was closed until further notice.

Justine's second problem was the drive through the rest of the town, which was difficult at best. The worst damage was in the road where she worked. Its corner school and surrounding buildings had been reduced to tooth like monoliths surrounding a hollow crater. Further down Harry's garage was full of holes too. It sat slumped and smashed, one ruin along from a second crater filled with broken brickwork. The end of the street was completely blocked by a huge gathering of desperate looking people outside the town hall. Justine dismounted before reaching them and inspected the damage near the garage frontage with trepidation.

The main door was buckled and jammed shut, but there was a smell of him on the air so she called out his name in hope. When there was no reply she cautiously walked around to the side of the yard.

The building had given some protection to the petrol pumps, but behind the garage a carpet of slate and masonry had rained down onto the floor. Three large bricks joined by cement had dropped straight through the roof of the outhouse and found the cistern on Albert's throne. A beautiful waterfall twinkled over the red ingots and down into the toilet bowl as it continuously refilled.

To her left the garage's side doors were hanging off on one side. There was the car within, which Albert had been working on yesterday. It looked fairly undamaged, other than a thick layer of debris and dust. Beyond that the two big wagons had been forced backwards far enough to wedge everything together. The rest of the rear structure was surprisingly intact. Justine called out again for Albert and Harry, but there was still no answer.

The easiest way in was to climb through the Austin then walk sideways between the tightly packed trucks. Cables, spare exhausts and welding rods hung down from the creaking roof rafters, forcing Justine to duck and dive. As she nudged around them, the parts clanged together creating a wind chime effect. Coming from the smashed in frontage, Justine caught a strong waft of that aftershave again and called out desperately, 'Harry, Harry, oh please don't be dead.'

In the floor debris behind the front doors she found the shattered remains of an aftershave bottle. Next to this was the garage's note spike. It sat bent and broken amongst a pile of old receipts, the hidden compartment wrenched a little out of line to reveal the dark void inside. She picked it up out of curiosity then used the pocket knife Margaret had given her to force the latch further.

As the flap squeaked open a tightly creased piece of paper fell out into her hand and sat there unfolding; a delicate square butterfly amongst the dust and chaos. On closer inspection it read, "Still working. Parts helpful. Need more of same for reserve. Ta." The note also had yesterdays date scribbled in one corner. Justine sniffed it. The paper smelt of explosion and garage, but there was a hint of something feminine and fragrant too. After tucking the note away in a pocket, she picked up an old receipt and a pencil stub, moved back to the Austin and used it to leave a message of her own under the windscreen wiper. Her note read, "Albert have you seen Harry? Let Mrs Clark know. Justine".

Back on the bike she thought back to Harry's bedroom and the conversation overheard from Margaret, Florence and Nurse Jones. Not wanting to waste any more time, she pulled off in a huge semi-circle and chose a new route. It would take her out of town, straight to Croft Farm along the narrow forest road.

After going back the way she'd come, the third problem she came to was a simple, but effective roadblock. Twenty cars ahead the traffic queue ended where a red and white wooden barricade blocked the lane.

'These cars are queuing for a reason, so you can turn that bike around and get back in line sunshine,' a chubby British soldier twirled his finger in front of Justine's goggled eyes. 'Coz none of this lot is moving for a while.'

She recognised him from one of the local gunnery crews that frequented social events in town.

A second and much thinner soldier came over and joined him by adding; 'There's a load of Australians with big guns in the woods, looking for Germans with little ones.'

The twirler halted his plump index finger and wiggled the little one instead. Then he leaned in to whisper, 'Told *us* to close the road see, 'till further notice. No one goes through.'

Justine pulled down the goggles and scarf that were obscuring her face.

The first soldier blurted out, 'Oh it's you luv, that bloke's missus, the chap who fixes stuff right?'

'That sounds like me, just that bloke's missus,' Justine agreed while looking past the men and up the otherwise empty lane.

'Sorry sweetheart, you'll still have to turn around,' the soldier apologised. 'Seen you at the dances ain't I, but we was never introduced was we?'

Justine shook her head.

'They call me Nipper,' he said proudly thumbing his chest pockets. 'An he's called Blinky, on account of his twitch.'

Blinky stopped gawping and started to squint madly at the mention of his ocular impediment.

'I need to get up to Croft Farm and make sure that *bloke who fixes stuff* is still alive.' Justine informed them while restarting the bikes engine.

Nipper shrugged and raised his voice over the noise, 'Everyone has a story today darling. Chaos ain't it.'

'NO ONE GOES THROUGH!' Blinky repeated demonically.

Nipper leaned in close to Justine's ear. 'You might fall off an' hurt yourself, or even get hijacked,' he warned.

'Or worse,' Blinky mouthed with a sinister grin. 'I mean, you know what those Germans are like?'

'Enough Blinky,' Nipper squeaked.

'Even with their tiny guns?' Justine pointed out.

As the men began to bicker she took the opportunity to throttle up and spin the bike around again, then drove back towards town as fast as she dared.

Nipper called after her, 'The bridge is out of action too darling, so don't bother.'

'She can drive that bike though,' Blinky admitted with respect.

'Smelled like fresh meadows mixed with a shot of erm?' Nipper pondered.

'Carbolic,' Blinky decided for him.

With a smirk Nipper said, 'Would have preferred it in a dress mind you.'

'It was wearing a dress,' Blinky blinked.

'No it wasn't,' Nipper argued, adding a playful punch.

'Yes it was, I saw it poking out,' Blinky punched him back.

'You don't see nothing pal,' Nipper said harshly bringing the argument to a conclusion with a hard flick on his friend's forehead. 'Not when there's a woman nearby.'

She drove the bike back through the rubble strew streets, around the demonstrators, bumped down a shallow flight of steps then charged over a canal bridge. The street after that was lined with more static traffic. Even from this far away Justine could see the fourth problem barring her path stemmed from the main river crossing. In the distance workmen and soldiers were leaning over its parapets facing upstream. At the junction a workman with a sign was trying fruitlessly to divert some vehicles away. From there to the river, all military and civilian transport was at a standstill.

As the bike weaved nearer Justine could see that a whole section of factory wall had collapsed on the opposite bank. Giant chunks of brick and concrete had smashed into the decorative parts of the bridge and badly blocked some of the flow beneath. Up close you could see that the angry storm water now washed around the structure as well as under it and most of the approach was cordoned off. At the top of the arch, the bridge's right hand lane contained a crane, its jib reaching down to haul out masonry from between the footings.

After a minute of study, a beeping car approaching from behind interrupted Justine's thoughts. She adjusted the bikes mirror and observed an oddly painted pick-up with flashing headlamps, honking along the pavement. As the flat back vehicle veered out in front of the traffic, Justine decided that enough was enough. *There would be no more problems and that was that.* She pulled out and kept pace with the car until it swerved away again to park up in the flooded road. Her bike pushed on past, it semi-aquaplaned through the water and hit the tarmac beyond with some throttle to spare. The spray she sent up landed on the major's car covering it in mud. Several workmen dashed out of her way and one dived over the bridge side to land in the shallow bank waters.

At the summit there was little room beneath the crane arm, but Justine ducked underneath with only a slight wobble.

Major Jackson jumped out of his car landing angrily, ankle deep in cold water and shouted, 'I want that man bought to me the next time he enters town. Now where the hell is the...'

His driver tapped the dirty window and pointed up hill, calling out, 'Captain Dreyer's over there sir, talking to the crane men.'

Jackson shouted and waved at the group, 'Hey Professor, when you're ready.'

A slender captain ran down the slope, jumped the flooded drains and saluted, 'Major, sorry not sure what all that was about?'

'Looked like someone in a hurry,' Jackson remarked as he surveyed the whole works.

'Cosmetic damage here really Major, nothing the men can't handle,' the captain stated with pride. 'Divisional Engineers think we'll be able to clear the other lane and relieve the flooding before the morning.'

'Are you still needed here Prof?' the major asked.

Dreyer didn't hesitate, 'No sir, these men can smooth things over without me.'

The major nodded, 'Remind me, you speak several languages, right?'

'I brushed up my Italian on the ship and my gramps were Dutch,' Captain Dreyer explained.

'Thought so. Come on, I need you to talk to a bloke we found in the woods,' Major Jackson said as he held back the passenger door.

Dreyer climbed in, 'Sir, I'm going to need a gander at my books from the hotel. I understand some German written down, but it's all a bit different as regional spoken word.'

Major Jackson tapped the dash with his baton. The driver nodded then pulled away.

'It is a German bloke, right?' the captain asked excitedly.

'I often wonder why we call you the Professor,' Major Jackson winked.

Justine had been busy negotiating her path out through the pedestrians and honking vehicles waiting impatiently on the other side of the bridge. Now that the motorbike was finally heading out of town, she relaxed and laughed, feeling a sense of release and relief. This direction would take her the long way around the valley peaks. It would mean following the river up to the place where it branched off near Kings Hill. After that junction she could follow the high road, before dropping back down into the lanes near Edwards land.

The Brough Superior's speedometer had never been accurate, but whatever the speed it took some time to reach the river's fork. The sun was still shining above the hilltops as she leaned into a long bend paralleling the water. Coming out of the turn, Justine barely noticed a scruffy looking soldier waving his arms and slowed down just in time.

The road beyond him was covered in a thick layer of soil and nature, which had been blown out of a field to their right. A single lane had been scraped out to allow one narrow vehicle at a time to pass through the rocks and mud.

Justine pulled over and realised that the soldier was Harry's friend Neville, from the Home Guard.

'What happened here then Nev?' she asked, pulling down her goggles and scarf as soon as the bike was stable.

'Bombs,' Neville said in an exhausted, matter of fact way. 'Four at the top of the hill, more over there.' He pointed out the bombsite with a shaky finger. 'They think there's still live ones down by the river bed.'

Justine moved closer and rubbed his arm. 'You look knackered Nev, how long you been standing there?' she asked.

'Not sure,' Neville yawned. 'Supposed to be slowing traffic and stopping anyone going in that field.

'Can I go and have a look?'

'No civilians!' Neville said, snapping to attention with theatrical authority.

'You should be in bed,' Justine suggested softly.

Neville coughed, he was always a bit nervous around Justine. 'Australians said they'd come back when the proper bomb disposal boys arrive.' He looked at his watch and tapped it, then remembered for the umpteenth time that it had stopped working last night.

'You know you look awful, right?' Justine smiled, trying to make light of it.

Neville shot his answer back through a fluttering mental slide show of vivid images from the night before. 'We didn't know what we were doing see? One minute we were laughing and then, and then,' his head dropped slowly as he mumbled to his shoes, 'some lads got killed.'

'Who, not your lot?' Justine lifted Neville's face with delicate fingers and asked, 'Is Albert hurt?'

'Everyone got hurt, Albert, Fred. Them flipping Germans, they bloody blew us up!' Neville pulled away. He took a few seconds before mustering the words to continue, 'Did you know them new lads, Ben and Mark? I didn't know 'em that well. Mark drove wagons for the far mill, Ben was his driver's mate. They only joined up at the weekend and now...'

Justine gently used both hands to hold Neville's face and demanded firmly, 'Albert's not badly hurt, is he, what happened to Fred?'

Neville was not really listening, he blinked, 'They both died. Blown to smithereens.'

Justine visibly shuddered and was about to demand proper answers when Neville snapped back into the here and now. 'Ben and that Mark chap I meant, they're just gone, see?' he announced as his blood shot eyes bulged open.

She squeezed harder.

'Albert, yes he's alright,' Neville confirmed through fish lips and reddening squashed cheeks. When she let go, he gasped for a while taking in air then continued, 'Most of us were safe inside the lookout to begin with, but the captain sent us all out after Sergeant Sanderson. An' he, he made them fire at the bomber and...' Private Cartwright wiped his nose on a sleeve and sobbed, 'There's bugger all left up there now, even the shelter's half collapsed.'

Justine gave him a hug and whispered, 'What happened to the others?'

Neville shivered for a moment then moved his eyes toward the top of the hill. 'Something got stuck in Tim's noggin and he's wondered off. Last I heard, they ain't found him yet,' he gulped. 'Most of the others are alright now we've dug 'em out, just cuts and bruises, but Albert got proper trapped in the fire. Don't worry coz Fred saved him and then he got burned. Doc Jones sorted them out and he said they'll be fine and, and.'

Justine noticed Neville swaying and helped him crash down into a sitting position on the grass.

'I told them Aussies that I got some kip before I come back up, but I didn't really,' he admitted with another shivering yawn.

Justine let go his hands and patted down her jacket pockets. Sensually lighting two cigarettes simultaneously from one mouth was enough to draw half of Neville's attention back. She locked him in with her best sunlit starlet pose and handed one smoke over whilst purring sweetly, 'Please can I have a peek, at the field?'

Neville reluctantly nodded then said breathlessly, 'But don't go past the gate.'

'Sure,' Justine smiled. 'Have a proper lie down Nev, I'll call out if anything comes up the road.'

'Ta,' Neville managed a smile back then did as he was told.

Justine stumbled occasionally when Mrs Clark's boots found big stones in the loose dirt. From the twisted gatepost it was easier to see where the material had come from. The field was now a wide brown bowl with a dirty pond at the bottom. Past the crater amongst a bent bramble border, she could see a large white sign. It read, quite unnecessarily in bold black letters, **"BOMB SITE!"**.

Around her feet, growing shadows vaguely outlined a truck sized oblong form and two ruts which curved away nearer the road.

'Hey, did they bring a big wagon up here to clear that muck?' she called over to Neville, who was now horizontal on the verge.

The sleepy soldier lifted his head and said, 'Nah. It was just me and a few of the locals, on a cart with shovels. Why?'

Justine crouched down for a moment and saw something else glistening on the peppered surface. Several shiny cases and bullet tips were lying just under the dirt. On closer examination the tips were much bigger than the cases. The typist reflected that she knew next to nothing about ammunition and pocketed samples of them for someone else to inspect later. *Someone like Harry*, she thought, *he'd know all about things like that.* There was a sort of moment of realisation in her brain. It was not enough to form a proper thought or idea, but it did condense into a feeling of pure and sickening panic.

Justine ran into the field, pursued by shouts from Neville to stop. She ignored him and carried on running down towards the giant puddle at the scenes epicentre. Inside the crater there were fist and thigh sized pieces of metal protruding from the wet mud. After plucking one free and washing it in the water she could see it was red. A second piece was pale RAF blue, the third was red again and then the next two were dark blue.

125

'Minnie,' Justine cried out, dropping the clanking pieces and scrambling back up the slope to where Neville was having a fit. 'Sorry, I have to go,' she burst out and rushed past him back to the bike.

It wasn't easy to see the muddy tracks through her tears and goggles, but she was determined to try. As the tyre prints faded away, big sods of dislodged mud vaguely marked the haphazard route until a mile or so further on, the sobbing rider was waved down again. This time by an old couple standing outside a solitary cottage.

The woman opened a little gate in a dry-stone wall and walked right up to Justine. 'What's happening down there?' she demanded. She was small, but strong looking with sharp hazel eyes set behind brown tortoise shell spectacles and her grey hair held up in a neat bun.

'Are you German? Do you speak English?' the old man shouted, trying to get to the nub of it. He was a much taller figure, but slighter in build and bounced along, following his wife with an open shotgun hung over a forearm.

'Of course she speaks bloody English you old fool,' the lady snapped. 'I told you it was no invasion, someone would've let us know if it were.'

Justine just about managed to park, then walked a few feet and threw her goggles down. Following them into the long yellow grass she cried out with emotion. After trying to catch up with Harry all evening, everything had suddenly flipped over and caught up with her.

'We saw the bombs,' the old lady said calmly as she sat down awkwardly next to the distraught visitor. 'Did you loose someone darling, were they caught out in the raid?'

Justine wept on, trying to talk but not finding a gap between sobs.

'There there now,' the lady put her arm around the tearful mess and held it tight for a few moments.

The old man leaned on his wall and waited as long as he could before piping in, 'Is it very bad? Sam the goat said there were a pile of folks dead an' plenty smashed up who might still die if...'

'Geoff, will you shut your fat gob hole. Go and put that gun away and stick the kettle on, go on,' his wife snarled, looking back at him from the corner of one eye.

'Excuse me,' Justine said meekly, 'I need to find someone, some people, well actually a truck called Minnie.'

Geoff did a U-turn and jogged back over. 'Oh yes I know Minnie,' he said, bobbing up and down with genuine excitement. 'Edward's lorry, you know him Maureen, the lad who brings the wood an' eggs an' all that.'

'He ain't your fellah, is he?' Maureen asked, looking down her nose at the young girl. 'That lad's married you know?'

Justine shook her head vigorously and explained, 'They all share.'

The old woman looked disgusted, 'What?'

'They share my Harry's truck, him and Edward, they built her together.'

'Will they be finished one day dear? Coz it normally looks like scrap and my lord it looked scrappy last night. Looked like they'd started unbuilding it.'

Justine stopped sniffling and sat up straight and attentive while Maureen described the scene. 'There was bits hanging off, an' it was all lopsided with just one headlamp.'

'So where was this Mo?' Geoff asked.

'Told you last night you scatter-brained old bugger. It was still bucketing down, but I thought the bombing had stopped. I came out to pull a cover over the log pile.'

'What about Minnie?' Geoff and Justine pleaded as one voice.

'I was just catching up with myself when the flak and four more explosions kicked off up on the top. Made I jump they did, I dropped me blooming lamp. I was down on my knees a pickin' it up when they came round the corner in that knackered truck. They seen me stand up with me lamp an' their headlight went off sharpish. Then they bumped it down the hill, off the road.' Maureen waggled a finger in the direction of a distant verge.

'Thank you,' Justine picked up the goggles, but didn't pull them back on as she pushed the bike away.

She could see deep tyre treads again now, heading over churned grass at the point where the old lady had witnessed the truck dive off. There were more clumps of mud too; carried here from the bombed field and a smashed wing mirror had come away to mark the point where Minnie had bumped over a curbstone. Coasting sidesaddle on the motorbike she followed the tracks down through a field. Eventually the prints curved away into the shadows next to another stream. After a few dozen yards of smashed up willows and ferns she came out again near an old and roofless animal pen. Its walls and beams sat crumbling around the remains of Minnie, jutting up from inside.

Fern fronds weighed down with branches helped to camouflage the sludge covered broken wagon. Something was leaking from the old girl and making a smelly slick beneath. It was a tight fit in the pen and Justine had to climb over the back in order to reach the front.

Behind the cab she found the dislodged lid of a toolbox and managed to clear enough shrubbery to open it near the broken hinges. There were tools inside as you would expect, but there was also a dulled uniform button caught on a wire brush. It was blackened brass, embossed with a crown and laurel and said "BEST QUALITY" on the back. It went in her pocket along with her collection of other bits and bobs and then the lid was closed to use as a step up.

Justine knew she was acting like some idiot from an adventure series on the radio, but it felt good. Peering anxiously over into the cab she saw bent, twisted window frames and jagged glass painted brown with dirt. Worst of all there was blood all over one seat. Crawling up onto the wall of the pen she scurried around looking for more of it.

Who ever had been injured may not have been badly hurt, as there were very few red drops to lead the way forward. She jumped down, circled the pen and found the tracks quite confusing. It was as if everyone had gone off in different directions leaving huge heavy prints in the wet soil and grass, then doubled back and moved away again more stealthily. Determining one direction to follow was a near impossible task.

The light was dropping a little more now as she climbed back up and sat on the rocky wall facing Minnie's shattered hulk.

'Minnie the moocher, a diamond truck with platinum wheels,' Justine laughed, half remembering the Cab Calloway song. She sang the final words with a broken voice, 'Poor Min, poor Min, poor Min.' After kicking her heels against the dry stone, the lonely girl filled her lungs and screamed out, 'HARRY YOU ARSE!'

Birds erupted from every tree then after a period of circling they noisily re-rousted. Justine circled again too and considered that the stream was the most likely exit route. If someone in those adventure stories had been hiding their tracks, that's the way they'd have gone.

At the waters edge you could see that someone had indeed come this way and they were still bleeding little spots onto the rocks. She made it five yards before almost dropping the bike in the shallow water. It was time to decide, either dump it and walk on in the dark drive to the farm, find Victoria and get some help.

She chose the road. The dappled scenery looked beautiful as the bike roared through setting sliced sunbeams along the tree lined high road. Then it turned sour as the route fell away towards lower land and unveiled the damaged landscape of the town again. Justine pulled over to take it all in. The dotted line of death drew her eyes away, landing on each impact point with a jolt.

Closest to her were the remains of St Mary's Chapel. In the graveyard a large yellow lorry with a hoist platform stuck out above the foliage. Between the trees, little figures directed the heavy vehicle as the twisted remains of a bombers frame pulled away from the crumbling bell tower and dangled from its jib. Nose high with the wings folded in, the aircraft remains looked like the skeleton of a monstrous dead bird.

Watching it swing gave her time to think. *Maybe the men would all be there at the farm with Victoria. Would they laugh at her and have a simple explanation? Or would it be just Victoria and the children, lost and confused like her?*

When she finally arrived the welcome party was made up of several chickens attempting to fly out of the way. Then as Justine pulled the bike onto its stand she noticed more players waiting in the wings. Twin barrels of at least three shotguns were poking out from windows and doorways around the yard. Justine slowly put her hands up.

'Christ you look awful, for a change,' Victoria stepped out of the kitchen door and raised the shotgun back onto her shoulder. ' Harry is gonna go ape when he sees the state of that bike,'

Justine put down her hands and brushed some of the bigger bits of grime off the fuel tank. 'Are they here?' she asked impatiently while getting off.

The other gun barrels were in the possession of Cassia and Bert Junior. When they stepped into the yard Justine crumbled a little. It *was* only Victoria then, with the children and they did indeed look very lost and confused. Just like she did.

Chapter Thirteen

Desk Sergeant Roberts *loved* forms. His life long stationery fetish was one of the reasons he'd ended up in this position, behind the aforementioned desk.

The German prisoner had passed through the sergeant's reception area on his tour through procedures about an hour ago. After stonewalling at the custody desk, the airman had been abruptly relocated for a wash and a brew. His round trip excursion would eventually end in a cell one floor below Sergeant Robert's boots.

Roberts didn't mind the lack of information at this stage, he had *some* details to fill in on his new forms and that was a good start. Unhooking red string from a cardboard washer he released the flap on a large grey MOD envelope. Inside there were pale yellow forms with heavy black words.

When he briefly held one up to the lamp it dissolved into a fibrous patterned sheet with delicate and surprisingly expensive looking watermarks. On the surface it stated, "F PW 788 UK (REVISED 5/01/41) THREE PART PRISONER OF WAR CAPTURE FORM SHEET 1".

'A thing of beauty,' Roberts said to himself then started spreading out all the other paperwork in a neat and perfect line.

The guidebook stated these punchy facts on what to do when you captured the enemy:

1. SEARCH – For weapons documents & equipment
2. SILENCE – Prohibit talking amongst POWs
3. SEGREGATE – By rank, sex and nationality
4. SAFEGUARD – To prevent harm or escape
5. SPEED – Remove POW from combat zone ASAP
6. TAG – POW, documents or special equipment

The sergeant stood back and sighed with genuine dismay, upset that someone hadn't taken the time to come up with a point six beginning with "S". While tapping a pencil on his teeth he considered a replacement heading; *STAMP, STICK, STAPLE,* all no good. Roberts decided STUB would work best and made a note for his future letter of complaint to the Ministry of Information.

The tags mentioned in point six were perforated dockets with unique prisoner numbers printed in triplicate down each sheet. These were to be attached individually to a prisoner's body, weapon and documents, thus ensuring that one day they could be reunited, on paper at least.

There was a clatter of doors as a more mundane prisoner was bought in. PC Thompson and WPC Birch placed a pillowcase stuffed with stolen property on the desk and nodded hello to their Sergeant.

Roberts looked up at a familiar face grinning between his constables and sighed dismissively. He took his time picking up the special yellow forms and placed them carefully to one side. Then he opened a drawer and pulled out a large black and well-worn ledger.

'So Monkey, what have you been nicking this time?' the sergeant asked before licking the nib of his pen.

Monkey looked hurt as he answered in a strong Midlands accent, 'That's a very mondescending statement Frank.'

'You mean condescending Monkey,' Sergeant Roberts explained patiently.

Monkey mulled over the words as he stroked his Fagin like beard, then pointed out, 'Nah, I'm a mon Frank. Only yow lot who keeps callin' me a con ay it.'

'He's been looting,' WPC Birch confirmed. 'From the bombed out houses in Humble Lane.'

Monkey shrugged his innocence and said meekly, 'I were just 'avin a bit of a tidy up and trying to 'elp out like, yer know? I was gonna ask around and see if anyone knew who this stuff belongs to.'

Sergeant Roberts picked through a few of the valuables spilling out in front of him and shook his head.

A corridor away PC Grogan was guiding Flight Technical Officer Peter Albrecht towards an interview room. Following a supervised hot shower, the duty medic had strapped the prisoner's leg up. Peter still limped, but with less frailty. The uniform had been searched and returned to him still smelling of damp and bark. His pistol had been reluctantly handed over by a trophy keen Australian and placed in Sergeant Roberts safe.

PC Grogan stopped at a doorway and pointed to a table and several chairs in an otherwise empty room.

Peter went in, sat down and folded his arms. Before being captured he'd buried his dog tags and any other items from his pockets. With the town bombed and his documents hidden, as far as he was concerned, his duty for now was complete.

He hoped his recent sacrifice had at least helped Harald to get away. The duo had stuck together after landing, but with the rain and wind and with one man limping they had only managed to travel in a rough circle. The next day Peter had rested his leg while Harald scouted around for water and some higher ground from where he hoped to discover an escape route leading towards the crash site. With no change to Peter's injury after a day resting, Harald had agreed to find Rudolf on his own, but vowed to return for Peter later.

Peter had wished him luck then slid down the nearest tree to dig a hole. Once down it was hard to get back up, the thick fern covered forest floor was comfortable and soon warmed up beneath him.

Some time later the sleepy airman had been woken by rapidly approaching boots and witnessed Harold running back past him at full pelt. Peter had not tried to delay his friend or call out. He was injured, he had done his job and capture was not a problem to him now, just an inconvenience. He was confident the invasion would come very soon anyway and reunite his fellow Germans in glory.

So Peter rolled out of the bracken onto the track, sprawled out as if he had fallen while running away. Twenty seconds after that the Australian soldiers had arrived hot on Harald's trail and calmly captured Peter instead.

Two burly grey suited men squeezed into the interview room now. They slammed the door shut and snapped Peter back to the present with a jolt. Detectives Thomas and Forbes were famous locally, for their self-purported ability to always apprehend the right man. Neither of them was sure what they would make of this apparently difficult Nazi.

Thomas consulted the arrest sheet and decided the language barrier was all a big bluff. He'd seen it all before with migrants and gypsies between the wars.

133

Detective Forbes just hoped the translator would arrive before his superior had time to get out of hand.

'Right,' Detective Thomas said as he pulled up a seat. 'What's your bloody name and where's your pal from the woods? Come on, two parachutes, two flyers and only one prisoner?'

Forbes smirked, 'Something doesn't add up, does it?'

Peter looked away and ignored them completely.

'I don't think he's a player,' Forbes continued. 'Australians said he wasn't likely to talk 'till their officer speaks to him, in German.'

'Nonsense,' Thomas said with disdain. 'He understands every word.'

As if to confirm the matter Peter asked, 'Wann kann ich schlafen?'

'Slaffen?' Forbes repeated, making a note, 'Sounded like "When can I slaffen?", what's slaffen?'

'Ja, ja schlaf' Peter looked up bright eyed for a moment, thinking they understood him.

'Maybe he wants a slash?' Thomas tapped the table in front of Peter, stood up and made some strange hip movements with his hands down by his crotch. 'You want go pee-pee?' he asked.

'Pipi? Was Pipi?' Peter responded with trepidation.

'There you go, he needs a slash,' Detective Thomas sat down again in triumph.

'He went for one boss, just before Grogan bought him up here.'

'Right then,' Detective Thomas slid off his jacket and started to roll up his shirtsleeves.

'This man has rights sir,' Forbes protested.

'He can have 'em, I just think he deserves a couple of lefts too,' Thomas growled as he leant in to get Peter's full attention.

There was an abrupt knock and Chief Higgins entered the room with Major Jackson and Captain Dreyer in tow.

The Chief turned to his Detectives and scowled, 'I don't suppose you two have got anywhere with this prisoner?'

'No sir, he might need the toilet,' Thomas said with authority. The detective picked up his jacket and added absently, 'He asked for Wankey Sloshin?'

134

'Wan can ik slaffen,' Forbes quoted from his notes with a tad more accuracy.

'I think that means he wants to sleep.' Captain Dreyer placed a phrase book and clipboard on the table then sat down.

'I can't blame him for that,' Major Jackson concurred taking out a packet of slim cigars and placing one next to the prisoner.

Peter examined the brown tube for a moment and responded, 'Nein danke. Zigarette?'

Dreyer nodded, 'He wants a plain old durry sir.'

'Does no bugger speak the Kings sodding English no more?' Detective Thomas huffed while rearranging his guts and belt line.

'You want fags right?' Forbes took out a half crushed packet and placed them on the table for the prisoner.

'If there is nothing more?' Chief Higgins thumbed his men away.

When the dejected detectives had left the room, Major Jackson retrieved his cigar and lit it. 'Name and number to start with Professor,' he said through the first ball of smoke. Then he leaned in to get a closer look at the prisoner, 'And ask how many mates he's got out there.'

Captain Dreyer began questioning in his best broken-German, 'Wie ist ihr name und, nummer? Wie viele von euch gibt es?'

Peter picked up the crumpled packet and smiled directly at Dreyer. Slowly he extracted one cigarette, sniffed along its length then put it in his mouth. As the major held out his gold Ronson lighter, Peter caught the flame on the tip and inhaled hard.

The prisoner took his time to savour the moment then responded, 'Neun acht null fünf sechs ein, Oberfeldwebel Peter Albrecht.'

'98056a, Master Sergeant Peter Albrecht,' Dreyer said quietly as he scribbled it down.

After a brief pause the captain pressed for an answer to the amount of men who had bailed out. Despite several attempts at further questioning Peter just smiled back, repeating his rank, name and number.

'I get it Professor, just the basics right?' Jackson tilted his head at Captain Dreyer, 'You stay here then, sweat him out for a couple of hours before he sleeps. If he tells you anything send Private Evans over with the good news.'

'And sir, did you notice he's been busy in the woods,' Captain Dreyer nodded over at the black dirt still caught beneath Peter's scuffed fingernails. 'I bet you'll find more information out there than I'll get from him in person.'

'Try anyway.' Jackson crossed to the door and held it open for Mr Higgins. 'The Chief and I will coordinate the remainder of the search and get someone to dig around over where this feller was found.'

Private Evans knocked on the open door frame and coughed, 'Sorry Major, Corporal Jarli and his men have reported back in town sir. I've sent a runner over to them with the witness reports, which Sergeant Roberts compiled from the raid.'

'Good,' Major Jackson smiled. 'Jarli will get things moving.'

'We need to find these Germans before Joe Public organises a search party of his own' The Chief moved behind the prisoner. 'If your Jarli chap doesn't find 'em, the locals soon will.' He placed a hand on the prisoners shoulder. 'Perhaps you should discuss that point with Mr Albrecht here, while we're away Captain?'

When the commanders had departed, Captain Dreyer checked his notes and roughly translated the Chief's parting shot for the German to digest. While Peter mulled over the possibilities Private Evans was directed to pull up a chair and sit down. The prisoner gave no response at first as each man smiled uncomfortably in a triangle of teeth and silence.

Eventually Peter stubbed out his cigarette on the table top, focussed on Dreyer and shrugged, 'Was ist Jarli?'

Chapter Fourteen

Jarli's family had not been in favour of him working with the "White Man". Nor had the Indigenous Australian League, who had tried to forbid it across the entire land. For once the all white Australian Defence Committee agreed and stated that the presence of natives was "Neither necessary or desirable" in any of their forces. Jarli, along with thousands of other aboriginal men and women ignored them all and enlisted as soon as they could.

Eight uncomfortable days after signing up, Jarli had arrived at Holsworthy Barracks near Sydney, over five thousand miles from his birthplace in Maralinga. At the gate a cautious guard had checked Jarli's papers twice before pointing him in the general direction of Major Jackson's Company. For over a year the little native worked and studied hard, volunteering at every opportunity. On really good days he would help with the horses or get to go into the bush and track down lost men. Eventually his reputation had grown to the point where he'd accompanied every search team dispatched from the camp.

When the company was ordered to take passage on a ship bound for England, little Private Jarli had half-expected to be left behind. Then on the night before departing he'd been flabbergasted to find the dubious title of *"Lance Corporal Charlie Jarli"* stencilled on a pile of new kit at the end of his bunk. Half of the men had thought it was a joke at first, just a nickname for their lucky, frizzy haired mascot. It wasn't.

Quite simply, Jarli was the most skilled tracker the major had ever seen or heard of in despatches. After working alongside him, it was logical to Jackson that Jarli should be treated with respect and also paid accordingly for his hard work and natural talents. Captain Dreyer had helped by pulling in several favours and the skills of an old forger before they'd set sail. Three forms, four signatures and a little light-hearted blackmail had transformed Jarli into one of the highest paid *black males* in the Australian forces.

The far-flung company and equipment had only been disembarked and in transit in England for a few hours when they were diverted. The convoy receiving a brief signal with new coordinates and orders to assist a nearby town that had been bombed. Jarli had spent that first night and most of the following day doing what he was good at. He had tracked down missing and injured people from the town and up at Kings Hill, using his skills to read obscure marks on the ground.

What Jarli was being asked to do now was altogether different, but still exhilarating. He was currently reading several witness statements from last nights raid. These universally affirmed that in the middle of the attack, a lifeless figure had drifted down on to a busy part of the town and then, disappeared. The surrounding streets were searched as soon as they could be, but even with the assistance of the major's men, not a trace could be found. No man, no parachute, no uniform, nothing.

'Bugger all,' Jarli said quietly to himself as he raised his eyes from the documents and craned his neck to the sky. *'If the reports were correct,'* he considered, *'there had to be something hidden in this tightly packed corner of the suburban sprawl.'* It was a riddle and Corporal Jarli was determined that his squad would solve it.

The rest of the team consisted of Privates; Cooper, Butler and Crook. Better known to each other as Noah, Nigel and John. While the Corporal continued to read the statements and mumble to himself, the others kicked dirt and smoked. All four of them were standing in what Jarli had suggested was a sighting hotspot near the damaged bridge. Behind them, Mr Moor's bombed out canning plant leaned over the river, while chimney fog drifted in from his meat factory and mingled unpleasantly with the grubby air around the waterlogged street.

'We going in this one, or moving on?' Noah asked as he dropped his cigarette and watched it sizzle in the grime.

'I think it's worth a look,' Jarli turned around and nodded.

On Jarli's orders and with Noah's tactful negotiating, the team passed through the works reception area to enter a high ceilinged production hall. The river garbled noisily outside as a pigeon flapped in through the missing walls and barrelled upwards to join his mates, cooing along the rafters. As the bird flew overhead, a tail feather dislodged and Jarli paused to watch it spinning down to the grey tiled floor. It landed amongst blood stained sawdust that clung to the windswept tiles like giant roses, waiting to be picked. Dusty shoes and other personal items still sat beside the blots, miming sad tales of their own.

Last night the sirens had started wailing while the evening shift was still swapping machines with the day workers. There had been too little time or organisation for many of them to escape. In the confusion of blocked and overwhelmed exit points, eleven people had died and many more were badly hurt. Some of the surviving workers were still here, trying to carry on. On the far side of the workshop where solid cover still remained, they were gathering tools and rigging sections of intact machinery together.

'Where do we start?' Noah asked.

'Not here,' Jarli replied then turned to the other two, 'Nigel, John go over there and help them people fix up their workshop for a bit.'

Noah looked up at the roof then back at his Corporal, following his gaze. After a moments hesitation he asked, 'We ain't going up there, are we?'

'I am.' Jarli spotted a ladder leading to a higher gantry and strode off towards it. When he was half way up he called back, 'You can come too, if you want?'

Looking out from the remains of the damaged side of the roof Jarli could see most of the bombers path. The next bomb along had landed amongst houses near what looked like a storage yard. Beyond that two craters dotted a street of shops and a school or religious building on the corner. Then more houses had been hit and after that in the woods outside of town Jarli could see gaps. The scout put out his wet tongue and let the breeze blow across it.

Without warning, several birds erupted from the void beneath Jarli's feet. Instead of flinching away he smoothly twisted and followed their path skywards. When his neck locked out he clicked it to one side and closed his eyes. Now he was flying with them, circling around and looking down. In his mind the landscape had transformed into simple, colourful flowing shapes. The river was a blue line dividing the town and the factory was a group of red ochre squares. Kings Hill was a vast splodge of green behind it all. Then an enormous black shadow started to roll over the colourful shapes. Above this shadow the silent form of a black hawk plummeted down with fingered feathers falling away from the wings. Two of these quills span back to the hill, another got caught in the up draught of the town and twisted in the cool air above the river before spinning away from the factory building.

Jarli's own flying form twisted to follow the third feather, but the hawk's shadow engulfed him too, until there was nothing left but black. In the emptiness he could feel his body falling, like the end of a dream.

When Jarli opened his eyes the real world was coming up to meet him fast. It looked solid, made of real red bricks and jagged grey concrete. In that instant Noah grabbed out at his friends webbing and swung the little man around to scramble up what remained of the crumbling walls.

'Took your bloody time mate,' Jarli smiled gratefully through the dust.

Fifteen minutes later a grazed Jarli was sat cross-legged on top of a GPO box, two streets over on the other side of the river. He was reading a solitary witness statement from a woman called Mrs Geller. Last night she had stood at this very junction watching the raid with her dog. She had watched the bombs and parachutes come down, so scared that she could not move. Though paralysed at the time, her later account was vivid and took in everything going on in the sky.

As Jarli quietly read on, a small crowd began to gather near by. It seemed the locals had overcome their curiosity about funny hats and uniform anomalies, now that the fuzzy haired dark chap in shorts had arrived.

'Here Jarli,' Noah called out, swaggering over to force a gap in the audience. 'You got any ideas, or can we give up on finding this blowie for the night?'

Jarli looked up slowly then sprang to his feet on the GPO box to stare down the road. The crowd gasped and cheered as he span around full circle and held up his hands to catch the wind. When Jarli jumped down several children gathered around him, attempting to touch his scuffed bare legs as he walked amongst them.

'Told you it don't rub off,' one of the youngsters revealed. 'And look, his blood ain't bleedin' purple neither, your nan's a blooming' liar.'

Jarli tilted his view to an industrial area straight ahead and said, 'Noah, I reckon he's over there mate.' His voice had a perfect sort of twang to it, like someone with a tuning fork for larynx. 'Up on them big round things.' Jarli measured the distant cylinders against his thumb then pointed his index finger. The crowd were amazed at the sound and sight of it all as their eyes followed his finger in awe.

The witness statements had told him very little, but at the same time, taught him a lot. No one from any angle had seen exactly where this particular parachute had finally come down. The interesting thing was, that they all thought they had.

'Those are gas holders mate, bet you haven't seen many of them before?' Noah gazed over Jarli's audience towards the giant man made structures that loomed over the terraced streets. 'Gas works, you know, whoosh?' He waved his hands around trying to mime an explosion.

'Don't matter what they are, our man's up on top an I reckon him been sunbaking,' Jarli replied without any expression. 'We need to go.'

At the gas works it took a lot more polite and determined persuasion from Noah to get himself past the gate man and into the site managers office. The manager immediately made a call to Desk Sergeant Roberts and was told to let the Australians do what ever they needed to do, by order of Chief Higgins. When the phone rang again moments later, Sergeant Roberts calmly confirmed that the rule still applied, no matter what colour the Australian happened to be.

While Jarli and Noah worked their way up the steps of the gasholder nearest to the river, Nigel and John ran over to ascend the second structure, which overlooked the town. It was a long climb through layers of criss-cross metal framework and flaking ladders with latched trap doors on every other gantry.

Near the summit, with just a few more feet to go, Noah stopped Jarli and signalled over for John's team to crouch down too. 'So what made you choose this tower for me and you?' he whispered in his Corporals ear.

Jarli looked down at the panorama of the town with its buildings, river and fields. Then he gazed up at the clouds moving over them. 'Angles,' he said wide eyed in his twangy tone.

Noah scrunched up his face and thought about it, then responded very quietly, 'Oh I get it. You mean angels mate? He nodded, 'Like ghosts and the spirits and all that mystical stuff, right?'

'No,' Jarli took a quick look over the top ledge and popped back down. 'Angles mate, like geometry.'

Noah smiled at his own underestimation. 'So you think he might be on this one then?'

141

'I know he's on this one,' Jarli said nonchalantly as he checked the rounds in his pistol.

Noah rarely questioned the corporal, but he had to ask, 'How can you be *absolutely* sure?'

'I wasn't sure when we was at the bottom. I was fifty-fifty. Now I'm convinced mate,' the corporal nodded slowly before popping up for another quick peek.

'But how?' Noah asked again. 'How?'

'Coz he's done the dunny over there,' Jarli held his nose and pointed his pistol over to where a fist sized organic pile stood out from the wrought iron rivet studded surface.

'Reckon if he's heard us coming he'll be as far away from that spot as possible then.' Noah suggested before taking his own snapshot look over the rim. 'And he'll be waiting.'

Jarli was right. Navigator Cadet Rees had awoken mid-way to the edge of the dome many hours ago, before daybreak. It had taken some time to untangle himself from the wet escape chute that had wrapped around him in the night. Ringing it out had provided him with a little water to drink at least. He'd spent some time thinking then folded the chute away, moved to the centre of the roof and lay on top of it for comfort. After making a difficult decision to stay on the run, it was a simpler conclusion that the cover of nightfall would be his best bet. Sorting out the rest of his minimal amount of kit and checking his weapon had taken no time at all.

The rest of the day had been waited out watching clouds go by with the parachute as a pillow. He knew he needed to stay low, but from that vantage point he'd only been able to see things far away, like the smouldering woods behind him and the ruined ridgeline of the hill ahead.

At one point the cadet had crawled over to check for the best route down, hoping that movement would also relieve the stomach cramps he was starting to feel. He felt very exposed nearer the edge, watching tiny people digging at broken homes while soldiers swarmed around the streets with weapons drawn. Outside of his previous circle of safety everything felt much more overwhelming and frightening, to the point where he had felt nauseous and dizzy. Then he had dropped his trousers and shat himself.

Now almost at sunset, following an entire day of waiting, someone *was* definitely coming up to get him. Rees had considered this possibility and knew the pursuers would block his only sensible exit. The frightened cadet did not want to be captured and tortured in the ways Peter and Stephan had often warned he would be in their awful and relentless stories. So the young navigator had shakily retreated to the other side of the dome where he took out his weapon, cocked the trigger and held it near the side of his head. He'd had plenty of time to decide on the only other way out of this dire situation.

Jarli signalled to Noah to stay low and go with him towards the middle. *If they could get to the high point,* he thought, *they could control the entire roof.* Looking over to the second tower he could see that John and Nigel were mirroring the move. When John made eye contact, Jarli signalled a thumbs-up pointing at his own tower, followed by thumbs down while pointing at John. John signalled back that he understood then moved to a closer position where he and Nigel could offer covering fire from their rifles.

Jarli went in low, crawling over the warm metal on his belly for the last few feet. At the very summit he lifted his head and could just make out some stray hairs blowing in the wind above the downward slope. The little scout lifted his view another inch and saw a side parting, which swung around slowly. It revealed a pale blue eye. The tip of a gun barrel came into view next.

As Jarli called a warning back to Noah and they both dropped flat on the dome, a single shot rang out. The corporal jumped up in a flash and ran straight towards his target leaving Noah floundering behind.

Rees was up and running too, heading down hill, toward the towers perimeter. He sped away on pure adrenaline, hauling the chute's strings to drag the unravelling bundle of silk which was now bouncing along behind. As soon as he got his stride he fired more backward blind shots with his free hand.

Noah dived again to avoid the bullets, but Jarli kept going, curving his path to stay outside the arc of fire. Rees struggled to increase the distance as the parachute began to fill. After two more steps he threw the weapon backwards and hauled on the straps with both hands, allowing the harness to pull the remaining chute wide open on the breeze. In that instant the German's body was heaved sideways and launched.

At the very same moment that Rees passed over the edge he felt skinny bones colliding with him, gripping his waist and knees from the side. Both men went down very quickly after that, moving away from the gas tower towards the river.

John and Nigel had realised quickly that they wouldn't get a clear shot and had run back to the nearest ladder cage at full pelt. Noah with more gusto had caught up to the launch point, got his balance and instinctively took aim. All he could do was watch as the two intertwined figures struggled together in his sights, dropping away over the river at an alarming rate. Eventually, he picked up the abandoned German handgun and paused for a moment to catch his breath and take in the amber sky. Then he ran back to the ladder swearing at every step.

Corporal Jarli had screamed all the way down then bravely let go just before hitting the water. Both men splashed down almost simultaneously with Jarli only slightly caught up in the trailing canopy. As the strong flow drew them nearer the bridge, the corporal began reeling his catch in. When they were swept under the semi-blocked arches he jammed the wet chute into the debris and held on tight.

Workmen's hands and ropes appeared quickly. They yanked the little soldier up and out with ease. Then more workmen came over the broken brickwork, heaving together to lift Rees out of danger.

As the sun finally set behind the hills, four Australian soldiers entered the police station with a new prisoner. There seemed to be only a little struggle left in Rees now, but he was still clearly very afraid.

Sergeant Roberts put down his crossword and stood back as a soaked Jarli placed an empty Luger and its ammunition clip on the counter.

'His parachute's outside and we need a receipt for the job lot mate,' Noah smiled, pushing Rees forward.

Sergeant Roberts ignored Noah and the fact that two of these men were dripping onto his freshly polished floor. 'You must be the black chap I've been hearing stories about all day?' the sergeant inquired. 'Nice of you to, *drop in.*'

Jarli tilted his head on one side and studied the fat man's big, balding and blotchy appearance.

'Is there something wrong?' Roberts asked.

'No mate,' Jarli replied rolling his head the other way. 'Just that, you is the pinkest bloke I ever seen.'

They laughed together and shook hands as John fished out Rees's tags from his breast pocket. 'This is R Heikling, serial numb...' he began to say.

'Hold on, hold on,' Sergeant Roberts broke in. 'I need the right forms first.'

'We was told to report to Captain Dreyer, is he still here?' Jarli asked.

'Just missed him, not more than three minutes ago.' The sergeant leaned in to examine the gun. 'Gone back to HQ after he'd had enough of the other German, Mr Chattypants.'

While the sergeant locked the weapon away Jarli tilted his head again and thought about the strange names white folks have.

'I have already had three excited phone calls on the matter, but I'll need a quick description of what exactly occurred,' Sergeant Roberts said once he'd got out his envelope of POW forms.

Nigel shoved the prisoner another step closer to the desk and announced grumpily, 'This flaming hoon fired at Jarli and Noah then he shot through.'

'Sorry to hear that,' Roberts looked each private over in turn, checking for wounds. 'So which one of you is Theroux?'

'He means this bloke tried to escape mate.' Noah laughed, slapping Rees hard on his wet shirt back, which made the prisoner shudder. 'Definite flight risk and he's a bit jumpy.'

At the Sergeant's signal, Constable Grogan came over and handcuffed the prisoner then towed him away to get cleaned up. When Jarli looked back, Sergeant Roberts had lined up his yellow forms.

Without looking up Roberts said, 'Now if you could help with a few more questions about your unit details and event locations? I could probably find a brew and a sandwich, or two.'

Rees was treated to the same shower and medical check as Peter had had. It seemed his previously semi-dehydrated body had been rapidly re-saturated during the swim and he'd come off no worse for wear. Cadet Heikling had maps and notes in his leg pockets when searched and according

145

to the police medic, he was quite a talker. There was no alternative but to drag Thomas and Forbes back from the nearest pub at short notice.

After trading tales of secret interrogations for rounds of drinks in the Artful Dodger, the two of them were fairly drunk. If Roberts had seen them come in, he would have thrown them straight back out. Which is why they entered the police station the back way.

Rees sat uncomfortably in the interview room, cuffed hands out in front, guarded by two constables outside. When Thomas and Forbes tumbled in together, Rees sat back a little startled.

Detective Thomas leaned on the table in front of Rees like a big silver back gorilla. 'Right son, what's your name and rank?' he demanded with spittle filled contempt.

Rees was confused; he'd volunteered this information twice and witnessed the soldiers handing in his tags. He recollected Peter's stories of drunken British men beating their wives for no reason. The frightened prisoner said nothing and started to turn away from the stale smell of drink.

SMACK! Thomas whipped Rees's attention back with the back of his hand. 'I asked you a question, now answer it,' the detective urged in an unexpectedly calm tone. Then he sat down to stare at Rees eye to eye.

The door guards looked in.

'Gov,' Detective Forbes began to say.

His boss held up a finger to silence the intrusion and demanded, 'Constables, shut that door and stay outside.'

Rees sat up stiffly holding Thomas's gaze, 'My name, is Rees Heikling and my rank is Fahnenjunker,' the airman confirmed.

'Hello,' Detective Thomas knocked on the tabletop as if it was a door. 'We don't have time to translate your Fritz words. What does "Fireman flipping Yonker" mean?'

Rees tried harder, 'Sorry, please don't hurt me. I am ah, I am Flying Cadet Heikling, yes?'

Forbes placed his bottom on the corner of the table and asked quizzically, 'Did you say your name was Recycling?'

The prisoner looked up wide-eyed, red cheeked and nodding.

Thomas laughed out loud, 'What, you mean like; make do and mend, or scrap metal?'

'I do not understand this make do the mend?' Rees felt sure they were going to hit him again and desperately wanted to get the answers right first time.

Both Detectives laughed until they coughed. Rees was the only one who did not see the joke. When PC Grogan popped a curious head back in, they let him in on it too.

'Here, I bet his wife is called Eunice?' Grogan quipped.

'Unicycling!' both detectives stammered as they fell about laughing.

Rees was even more confused now. *Had he stupidly bought information with him, like details of his family or a photograph of his brother maybe? He was sure he hadn't. And why were they chocking with laughter?* In an attempt to clarify the situation he stood up and called out angrily, 'Nicht, meine frau ist not called Eunice!'

'Oh,' Forbes said, a little disappointed.

Rees remained standing and completed his statement, 'My erm, my wife is not Eunice Heikling, but meine bruder is.'

The policemen were instantly off again. Between breaths Detective Sergeant Forbes managed to say, 'So, so your wife, she is not unicycling?' He wiggled his fingers like speech marks, 'but your brother is?'

'Well it's a difficult skill to master in a skirt, I believe.' Forbes added.

'Ja,' Rees nodded vigorously, 'have you seen of him, meine bruder, he was shot down over Birmingham last year?'

'On a flying unicycle?' Thomas cried with his head on the table, 'Oh my God, I am going to wet myself.'

The door burst open and Chief Higgins demanded from the doorframe, 'What the hell is going on in here?'

It seemed like their chairs were invisibly connected, because as Rees stumbled back into his seat the detectives were launched to attention from theirs.

The Chief took control, 'PC Grogan take this man down to a cell.' Turning his eyes on the detectives he roared, 'What, exactly, are you two doing?'

Thomas tidied himself up and apologised, 'Sorry sir, the interview got a bit, side tracked.'

147

'Very informative,' Forbes confirmed. 'Could do with a little more time to question him in the morning mind you.'

'Why did the prisoner have a hand print on his face?' Higgins asked, looking directly to Detective Thomas for the answer.

Neither detective wanted to admit the truth right now. They stared at each other, then down at the table.

'Go and get some sleep, both of you,' Chief Higgins groaned.

Chapter Fifteen

Half the town must have said their prayers and gone to bed early. The other half, as far as Albert could tell, seemed to be here at the hospital and they were generally getting in the way. While thinking the matter over, Albert also came to realise that he was an obstruction too. He had been checked, tested and told to go home, twice. With a stitched lump on his singed, slightly balder head and despite the chesty cough, he still felt that the waiting had done the most damage to his mind and body. With too much time to think he'd overdosed on worry, hard chairs and weak tea. Now they had said to go, but he wanted to stay, because he needed to see Fred.

Last night Albert had thought it was a great skive at first, to shelter from the storm in that smelly old hut. *There were enough men around with nothing to do, so why bother assisting them in doing it? Better to sit it out and do something useful, preparing somewhere warm and dry for them all to sleep later.*

As the storm had raged outside, Albert had pointed out to Fred that they had everything required and even managed to procure a night light candle and cribbage set from someone else's kit.

When the bombs started dropping it had sounded like no more than a second round of thunder, moving away over the town. When it returned again much louder, Fred had decided to go outside and investigate. That was almost all that Albert could remember.

Along the hospital corridor, flapping footsteps preceded an unfamiliar dark haired and flat-footed Matron. She looked scornfully at Albert sat outside Fred's door, as if his very presence was making a mess. With a snort she brushed past him for now and re-emerged moments later with Doctor Graves and a very pretty young nurse. The staff sped back toward reception in a neat line, leaving Albert's mouth and Fred's door ajar.

The pale coral coloured portal creaked further open and softly banged against a cupboard within. The rattle of bottles along the shelves caused the patient inside to stir. Fred struggled to focus on his surroundings as Albert jumped up and darted inside to help him.

Grabbing Fred's spectacles from the bedside, Albert noticed they were distorted and quickly bent them back into shape. 'Here Freddy,' he said and proffered them over.

Fred lifted his hands, but they were so bound in bandages that Albert redirected the frames over the lad's ears instead.

'Where did everyone go?' Albert asked while pouring a glass of water.

Frederick coughed and wriggled up the bed. 'I don't know,' he croaked out. 'That big woman came and said an Austrian soldier was knifed, then they dashed off?'

'Stabbed?' Albert glanced back toward the door then said softly to Fred, 'They ain't Austrian you deaf clot.' He pulled up a chair. 'Mrs Croft told me they were Austr...'

'I think I'm frightened Bert and I feel drunk in a bad way,' Fred interrupted before Albert could explain more.

Albert patted his friend's shoulder, 'Well that is probably just the medication, don't worry.'

Fred nodded unconvinced. 'We were happy yesterday Bert, now this,' he coughed and held up the bandaged forearms again.

Albert smiled, 'But if they've gone to fix that other chap, it must mean there's nowt too wrong with you. Apart from your hearing.'

'Pardon?' Fred said attempting to laugh.

Albert waited for the coughing to subside then helped Fred to some water and propped him up higher in the bed.

'You alright then Bert?' Fred spluttered once he'd regained composure. 'You were in a shit state before.'

'Thanks to you, I'm fine. Got a bit of a cough, but not as bad as yours.'

Fred put his head back and closed his eyes.

'Nurses said you saved me, pulled me out like.' Albert was close to tears. He took a sharp breath and rubbed his face before adding in a more confident tone, 'You still owe me three bob mind.'

'Prove it you old sod. Crib board went up in the fire, I made sure of it,' Fred tried not to laugh this time.

'I don't remember *what happened* after you went outside?' Albert confessed.

'My head's a tad foggy too.' Fred gestured for Albert to give him some more water. 'I remember opening the door just as the furniture van came through the side wall. Bloody thing was alight Bert, then the fuel blew up. Nev said there was a massive fire ball and that collapsed half the hut,'

Albert nodded with understanding and rubbed at the lumps on his burnt head.

'Nev said it went crash, flash, bang, whoosh,' Fred began to cough again. 'I was suddenly lying outside on the grass with a couple of blankets that we'd left out in the rain. I called you, but there was just crackling fire and pissing rain. So I sticks a blanket over my bonce and ducked back inside.'

'Cheers Freddy,' Albert went to thank him, but his friend was too excited now and cut him off again.

'You were down a bloody big trapdoor hole in the floor. And get this, you was surrounded by rusty tins of pork.'

'Pork?'

Fred nodded, 'I remember that bit clearly, coz I had to drop down next to you and avoid the heat.' Fred coughed again before he wheezed out, 'Then I dragged you through to the edge of the footings with them tins going off behind us like little meaty bombs.'

Albert poured more water and stated, 'I owe you a life then, or a new pair of hands at least?'

'They ain't that bad, just cuts and burns. Anyway Nev helped too. I couldn't kick out the weatherboards from the inside, not on me own. Then Neville came running past in a hurry.' Fred lowered his tone to a whisper and looked around as if someone might overhear, 'He told me after, that he'd been running away.'

Albert nodded and squeezed his bottom lip in contemplation, 'Sounds like the sensible thing to do.'

'That lad don't know how brave he is.' There was another bout of coughing from Fred before he continued, 'He heard me shouting and he came right back. Helped pull the first boards off, even though they were all on fire. Together we heaved you out.'

151

Albert shook his head and smiled, 'I saw the little bugger this morning and he told me it was all down to you.'

'Nah, it was all of us up there Bert, the Home Guard. You would've been proud, if you'd stayed awake to see how well they done,' Fred grinned.

'I think Nev's gone back out there to help today, in uniform,' Albert's brain was considering telling Fred the worst news on another day, but his mouth wasn't listening and burst out with, 'Ben and Mark died and Tim Walsh wandered off with shrapnel in his head.'

'I know,' Fred nodded with raised eyebrows. 'That was afore we left.'

'What about Sanderson and the other blokes, did they get away safe?' Albert enquired, trying to fill in the blanks.

'As far as I know, they're alright.'

'I only know what Neville and the Mrs told me,' Albert mumbled to the floor. 'Mostly gossip no doubt, but apparently Cooke spent the whole night hiding under a bench in the bunker. It took an age to dig the old sod out and he's gone a bit, doolally. Wants the remaining men to meet up later, in full battle dress.'

'But that's just barmy,' Fred looked around again as if someone else was eavesdropping in the room. 'What about Edward, your family and Harry, are they all safe?'

'Most of the telephones are out, but apparently Justine's gone up the farm in Harry's trousers and on his bike,' Albert said with a shake of the head.

A bell in the corridor signalled the end of visiting time.

'I should be off,' Albert looked at the clock. 'I just wanted to make sure you were alright.'

Fred held up his hands and turned them around. 'Better to be a bit burnt, than to lose you.' He looked cautiously towards the open doorway then advised, 'Be careful out there and stay out of uniform.'

'Alright?' Albert agreed with uncertainty. 'Did you get a bump on the head Fred, or did they give you something strong for the pain?'

'Well I couldn't feel a thing before, but it hurts a tad now?' Fred paused trying to recall what his friend had been saying.

Albert got up and pushed the chair back to the wall.

Then Fred suddenly remembered, 'Dressing up as a bloke, good idea. Coz they'd probably 'ave stopped a girl on a motorbike right?'

Albert nodded cautiously; still pretty sure that Fred was loaded up on something.

'Are there road blocks and lots of soldiers?' Fred burst out, suddenly animated again.

'Well I know the bridge is closed and one nurse told me there's about a hundred soldiers in town, searching houses and all sorts.'

Another nurse swept in carrying a small metal tray. 'Go home please Mr Croft, Mr Lloyd needs some rest,' she insisted.

Albert ignored her.

'You are due more morphine Mr Lloyd,' the nurse said ticking a box on Fred's notes.

Albert had to look away as she whipped back the covers and jabbed a huge needle into the lad's leg. 'What's this about a soldier being stabbed?' he asked over Fred's swearing.

'Mr Croft, go home, now,' the nurse repeated impatiently before turning to stare at him.

Albert absently went to shake Fred's hand, then removed the lad's glasses and patted him on the head instead. The boy's eyes looked more distant now, he was travelling somewhere else.

'He does understand that it wasn't a German invasion doesn't he?'

The nurse shrugged her shoulders then tailed Albert back to reception to make sure he didn't double back. Once there he saw Doctor Jones beyond the entrance canopy and stepped outside to say hello.

'Terry, you survived then,' Albert called out.

'Oh I'm fine, but I could do with another brew and a sleep. You seen the wife?' The Doc looked down patting at pockets for his pipe. He was still wearing boots and a dilapidated olive green uniform beneath a clean white medical coat.

'Seen mine, don't suppose you fancy a swap?' Albert smirked.

'No offence, but I'm happy with my lot.' Doctor Jones found his pipe and tapped it out.

'Thank you, for what you did for me and Fred,' Albert shuddered, trying to shake away a new memory.

153

The doctor put a steadying hand on his Corporals shoulder, 'You should rest up. Come on, I can give you a lift as far as the square.'

'But your car's still at the garage?' Albert half apologised.

'Doc Graves and I are, sort of sharing,' Doctor Jones said heading for a row of neatly parked cars.

'He never seemed the sharing type?' Albert puzzled.

'Well, he leant me this coat and,' Terry patted down his pockets again and pulled out a set of keys. 'Waste not, want not my dad always used to say.'

Albert frowned.

'Don't worry, you can help me replenish the petrol,' the doctor smiled. 'Don't suppose you know which one of these cars is his? Hey watch out!'

A fast paced policeman swerved past them and bumped into Albert with a grunt.

Albert shouted after the uniformed lout, 'Look where you're going son.'

'Who was that?' Doctor Jones asked.

Albert did a little shake of his head, 'Too quick for me, maybe they've drafted in some more men from the villages?'

The policeman zipped off down the first available corridor. It was a few minutes later before he found what he was looking for. The sign on the wall read, "Store Room". He went inside and closed the door, breathing heavily.

Fred stirred a little and spluttered, 'Who's that, is that you dad?'

The intruder was startled by the room's occupant and stepped back out to check the sign on the door plate again. On re-entering he calmly replied, 'Sorry wrong room, just after some supplies.'

Fred tried to focus and pointed limply, 'Try those cupboards dad. The nurses have been coming and going, grabbing kit out of 'em all day.'

The uniformed man guessed correctly that the patient was off his head and set about rifling through the shelves, filling his shoulder bag with anything useful.

'Someone stabbed a German. Dad is that you?' Fred yawned, closed his tired eyes and mumbled, 'I'm in here with a Gerry.'

The policeman momentarily lost interest in the medical packages and turned back to prod Fred, 'Where?'

'Hundreds of 'em all over town,' Fred giggled as he turned away. 'I love you dad,' he whispered, letting out a long sigh and then fell asleep.

It was a quick drive back to town for Albert and he was grateful for the doctor's insights into what had happened after the raid. 'So what was that about a man being stabbed then Doc?' he asked finally before getting out.

'A young rifleman,' Doctor Jones said, taking a moment to find the handbrake. 'He lost quite a lot of blood.'

Albert climbed out, but ducked his head back down to enquire, 'One of the Australians then?'

Doctor Jones nodded, 'Yes, he was on guard when someone attacked him from behind. Quite a professional job, clean and precise, give or take half an inch and it would have killed him.'

'Where was he stabbed?' Albert asked.

'Just here,' the doctor poked a finger under his own rib cage.

'No,' Albert shook his head, 'where in town?'

'He was guarding the junction near the railway yards, I think?'

Albert thanked Terry again and slammed the stiff door shut. In the semi-silence that followed the cars spluttering departure, he was sure he heard a thwack and a crack. Instinctively the old soldier ducked down behind a post-box and scanned the arena, but the entire square was empty.

Albert *had* hoped to return to his little end-terrace town house and discover that everyone he loved was well. After that he'd planned to put on some comfy slippers and sip at a dash of single malt. He shook his head and got up swearing under his breath, because all of that would have to wait now.

The police station was right there in front of him. At the top of the steps Albert huffed out loud, 'In for a penny.' Then the door opened before he could reach the handle.

'Hello Bert, we heard you were dead. It's not true is it?' Sergeant Roberts joked as he headed off duty.

Albert took it on the chin, 'Cheers Frank, I'm glad I found you and not just any old idiot with a truncheon.'

Frank mimed a touché then beckoned his old army friend inside the foyer.

'Look Frank, we've known each other a long time right?' Albert asked.

Frank looked at his friend examining several key areas in detail then nodded agreement.

'I know, I've got a bandage on my noggin and half me hair has been on fire, but...' Albert looked around the reception area to see who else was there. 'If I told you I just heard, well, what sounded like a silenced rifle shot going over my head, you'd believe me wouldn't you?'

'I would,' Frank replied, 'but is it something you're likely to say?' He needed no more than a nod in return. 'Right, well you make a statement to my colleague at the desk and I'll take a quick look.'

When the sergeant came back five minutes later, there was nothing to report.

'Look I know you think I'm crackers, but mark my words, something's going on.' Albert insisted.

'We believe you Bert,' Frank assured his friend. 'You've left a statement an' it'll all tie up in the morning, you'll see. Probably some cack handed Australian shooting at shadows in the woods?'

'No, it was right here,' Albert growled defiantly.

'Tell you what, I'm off duty now so why don't we walk and talk on our way home?' Frank smiled encouragingly and ushered Albert back to the exit.

As they got to the bottom of the steps, several drunken men hurried past shouting and jeering as they went.

'What now?' Albert said with disbelief before stepping back up out off the street.

Two women rushed across from the Artful Dodger pub and chased after their friends.

'Halt!' Frank shouted, but too late to stop the men.

The women didn't want to stop either, but they did, eventually.

'Oh come on,' said the first one, a dark haired young woman with ringlets. Her eyes followed the distant running men who were rounding a corner two streets down.

Her bottle blond friend was evidently a little tipsier. She was stooped near the steps spilling brown ale from a pint mug and mumbling about

Germans. 'Gonna miss all the action,' she suddenly slurred waving the beer around in a semi-circle.

Ringlets grabbed the pint glass from her friend and handed it to Albert in one smooth motion. 'Please mister,' she begged, looking back at Frank. 'They just cornered two more Nazi's on tuther side of the river.'

'Home Guards,' the other woman slurred. 'Chasing parrot troops towards the bridge.' She went to take a sip of ale then looked at her empty hand in disbelief, as if her drink had magically vanished.

Sergeant Roberts watched as more bodies left the pub and knocked on doors until small groups started to appear around the other street corners. They all scurried away under his gaze, heading for the river.

'You ladies go home, NOW,' Sergeant Roberts barked. He turned to Albert and asked more kindly, 'Make sure these two go the opposite way, I'll muster a few reinforcements.'

As soon as Frank had gone inside the women took one look at the dilapidated Albert and trotted off after their chums.

Albert shrugged, sat down on the steps and took a slug of the beer before sitting back to see what would happen next.

A couple of hundred yards away and out of Albert's sight, someone was shinning down a drainpipe onto a bevelled roof. They ran across it, dropped down again and leaned into the night to check the layout below, but there was little to see in the dark void. The figure wriggled to check its rifle was snug in the back and then carefully climbed onto an old pulley. From there it swung around until a foot found purchase on a ladder stave and there was an audible sigh of relief.

Half way down the shape froze, sensing that their movement had triggered a rustling from somewhere below. This sound was embellished by a growl, which became gradually more intense. Eventually a deep bark bounced around the walls of the enclosed space, behind the butchers shop.

Adolf couldn't climb the rungs, but made up for this by creating as much noise as possible. Occasionally the dog switched back to growling and pulled at the bottom of the ladder.

Lights were going on behind frosted glass, leaving the dark descender with only seconds before someone came to investigate. The figure quickly scampered back up and lunged for a decrepit winch just in time. As the dog pulled away the footings, the body on the pulley pushed out and swung back kicking hard. The rotting doorframe ahead of them burst apart while the antique ironwork dropped away behind, almost taking them with it. With a clanging it skipped down the inclined ladder and smashed heavily to the floor.

There was a yelp, a moment of silence and then a door opened at ground level. Before anyone below could look up, the runner scrambled inside the high doorway and was off and away. They crashed clumsily through boxes and down dark stairways towards an overpowering smell of pollen.

On the ground floor of the florists there was only one obvious exit and that was triple locked. Seconds later, an old milk churn filled with sand and fake flowers exploded through the windowed door. It left an equally sized and similarly shaped hole in the criss-cross tape covered glass, big enough for a way out.

Back up the hill at the police station the heavy gates next to Albert swung back and two black cars rolled through.

'Back on duty Bert sorry,' Frank called out over the din as the cars rattled their bells and headed for trouble.

'Don't worry, I'm off home to the wife,' Albert said to no one in particular, then he finished the pint, put down the glass and walked away.

Ahead of the police cars the darkly dressed figure was crouched in the open now. As shop windows lit up along the parade, the bulbs highlighted a uniform of sorts. The sound of motors and bells coming over the hill forced the shape to flee. As feet hit tarmac something else hit a rib and a bicycle clattered to the ground. Runner tumbled over rider, but when the police car lights rounded the corner there was only a swearing ARP man to be seen. The runner's heels dived away; caught for the briefest of moments in the two cars slit headlight beams and then who ever it was had gone.

'Are you alright?' Someone called out from the florists.

'TURN OFF THOSE BLOODY LIGHTS!' the ARP man shouted back angrily as he kicked the remains of his bike and swore at the sky.

The police didn't slow down again until nearer the bridge, where people had massed ahead to see tonight's show. Workers with dirty faces, families in dressing gowns and a mass of pie eyed bar flies blocked the route.

Bodies clambered all over the semi-repaired bridge, trying to get better views of the fields on the other side. At the pinnacle, the crane's engine was idling beneath the feet of two men and a woman. They were busy hooking up a massive makeshift work lamp slung from its jib. There was a burst of light as the cranes engine revved higher and the swaying beam came up to almost full power, picking out shapes in the scrub and trees far away. A nudge on the jib's controls meandered the light back along the road and verge while everyone's eyes followed. The audience all had an opinion to voice and their hubbub grew each time the circle of light swung back across.

'There they are,' the woman called down from the crane as the onlookers swooned towards a field.

'The Home Guard I mean,' her voice clarified.

At this, the crowd moaned as one, in pure disappointment.

The two police cars managed to beep their way through the throng as Major Jackson's car also appeared and joined their little convoy. Forced to stop completely on this side of the crossing, the uniformed men got out and tried to see what was happening.

'This is nothing to do with my Company,' the major shouted to the six policemen in front of him. 'Only just got word down the wire.'

Sergeant Roberts had a quiet discussion with some of the crowd then ordered all of them to move over and let his men through. As he turned back to Jackson he said quietly, 'Apparently this is a Home Guard thing Major, two flyers on the run, Captain Cooke's in charge. I suggest we get over there before he does something stupid.'

The crowd cheered as a tractor appeared and raced ahead of the Home Guard men, they in turn chased it down the hill. The farm vehicles spot lamp lit up some bushes surrounding a solitary tree as the crane's light honed in over the same spot. Caught in the bouncing and swaying stage lighting, two more figures grew from the scrub like magical beanstalks. They jostled around indecisive of whether to flee then stood motionless either side of the tree.

When the cranes lamp was cranked up another notch, the two matchstick men were drowned in a pool of sodium light. Even from the bridge you could clearly see them surrendering by holding up their empty hands.

A shot rang out, followed by three more in fast succession. Everything else stopped, as the two German's capitulating forms collapsed. Then the crane was swung back revealing a pistol drawn Captain Cooke on the tractor, surrounded by four of his men slowly lowering their rifles.

The silence lasted for another ten seconds then half the bridge mob began to cheer hesitantly while the others groaned. That moment summed up the confused feelings of the whole town.

Major Jackson and Sergeant Roberts had been trying to push forward. It became suddenly easier as many of the onlookers tried to move away from the guilt-ridden panorama.

Frank looked up at the crane and shouted, 'Put out that damned light!'

It took a few minutes to get from the bridge, through the crush and out into the pastureland on the slopes. The tractors little lamp still circled the scene where Captain Cooke now stood over the bodies. He was prodding one of them with his boot.

A couple of local journalists pushed ahead of the major, over to where the action had been. When they arrived Cooke directed the photographer who he knew as an old pupil. 'Here lad,' he said proudly, 'get a shot for the front page.' As he said it, Cooke put a foot on the chest of the nearest German and posed like the big white hunter.

Major Jackson stepped into the shot and punched Captain Cooke square on the chin at the very moment the flash went off.

Two of Cooke's men nervously reloaded and hoisted their rifles in the major's direction. He didn't even blink at the threat. Ignoring them Jackson pulled Cooke's fat leg off the airman and knelt down. The three big holes in the German's chest were enough to confirm his death.

Major Jackson quickly reached around to the other man and checked for a pulse. 'This boy's got a beat,' he yelled, carefully rolling the torso over to check for an exit wound. 'You drongos hand over those weapons to the police and grab a corner each.'

When no one moved, Jackson stood up to glare at them all. Neville and William stared back, looking very confused. Two more men lurked behind them staying out of the light. For a moment some of them had felt like heroes, now the Australian officer was treating them all like fools. They had no familiar leader, Cooke was out cold and Sergeant Sanderson had flatly refused to go on the unofficial and ill-considered search mission.

'Make safe and hand over those rifles immediately!' Jackson ordered again.

Three of the men did as they were told then heaved the body up between them, but Neville was still frozen to the spot.

'Constable, take that man's weapon,' Jackson ordered calmly.

As the nearest PC took Neville's rifle away he noticed something and checked the magazine. 'This gun's not been fired sir.' The constable held the gun out to show the major.

Neville was as still as a statue until Jackson stepped closer and gave the lad a slap. Consecutively another flash went off, blinding the young private as he jolted to attention then rubbed his cheek. Blinking back to reality, he took a look around and accepted his place on a corner of the damaged German. When blood oozed from the victims chest wound, Neville immediately dropped the leg and started to gag.

The PC shouldered Neville's rifle and took his place walking with the group down to the approaching ute. At the bottom of the slope they hauled the body on-board and Jackson jumped up to keep pressure on the wound. The police cleared the road as the car peeped its horn and slipped off into the night.

In the field Sergeant Roberts turned off the tractors engine and took control with a torch. Shining it around his own returning squad he said succinctly, 'I want Cooke in a cell.' Turning the light on the Home Guard men he growled, 'And I want the other body taken to the hospital, respectfully.' He was doing a lot of angry pointing, 'I want it put in that police car, by you and you can clean the seats after your done.'

Three Home Guard men fumbled back over to the prone body while Neville started to wretch again at the sight.

'Tomorrow morning I'll see you all down the station, no exceptions.' When Sergeant Roberts had finished shouting he stormed off.

161

PC Grogan called after him, 'Where are you going sir?'

Roberts stopped and looked around the scene. 'You are correct Grogan, the nearest pub is this way,' he huffed, then changed direction and strode off again, shaking his head.

Chapter Sixteen

Everything had slid back to some kind of normality after the incident at the bridge. Everyone eventually drifted home to their beds. When the major's exhausted body had been driven back to the Station Hotel after midnight, there had been only one thought on his mind, *sleep*.

Things started up again when several dull explosions had awoken some of the town in the middle of the night. Uncertain parents had assured their children that it was just a dream; some after effect of the previous nights raid or most likely the unexploded bombs being *sorted out*.

Major Jackson had not been offered the same uninformed option or a choice of sleeping on. Each thud had convulsed him back to the waking world as Private Evans rapped on his door and blew a whistle to officially sound the alarm. Jackson knew his limits and those of his company. He quickly gathered intelligence over the radio and discovered that the explosions had been small and only damaged the infrastructure of the town rather than any more of its inhabitants. So he issued orders to control the situation using whatever men were rested and then went back to bed.

He awoke again two hours later to yet more knocking and some refreshing information. Private Roach, the sentry who had been knifed near the railway yards and the young German airman were both still alive. Roach's stab wound would take time to heal and there were complications with the prisoner too, but it was still good news. Jackson was then informed by a runner that Captain Dreyer would do a full debrief over breakfast and he decided to get dressed.

When the major awoke for a third time, ten minutes later, face down and half decent, he decided strong coffee would be the best defence. It was unsurprising to confirm that there were no refreshments available downstairs in the hotel. The next best option was to see what the situation was in the hotel's car park and makeshift army camp. Following his nose to a catering wagon, Jackson poked around in what looked like fake scrambled eggs seeded with small, burnt, pink cubes. Still tired and unshaven he slumped down with a plate full at Captain Dreyer's table.

Private Evans immediately stood up like a rocket to salute; even Captain Dreyer made it half way to attention before the major waved their pleasantries away.

'Lets leave all that fluff for today shall we?' Jackson requested absently while examining the label on a bottle of sauce. 'We have business to discuss and I'm in a thinking mood this morning, not a soldiering one.'

Captain Dreyer poured out a coffee and slid it over, 'Looks like last nights explosive incident was caused by badgers Major.'

'Badgers? Is that some sort of Fifth Column group?' the major snapped, drinking the coffee in two long gulps and hammering the tin cup back down.

'They're like big stocky, black and white wombats sir.' Private Evans explained while topping up the major's mug. 'Corporal Jarli has found bits of 'em everywhere since sun up.'

'So the rail track damaged in the early hours of this morning, that was triggered by some mammoth, monochrome marsupials?' Jackson shook his head, stared at Evans and thought about the sleep they'd all missed.

Dreyer coughed and turned over a clipboard, 'They're not technically marsupials sir, but yes, they set off a chain of anti-personnel and demolition charges which would otherwise have gone off at...'

Private Evans' hand shot in and flipped a sheet on the captain's clipboard. He ran a finger down the roster, 'There would have been twelve small wagons of hogs coming in at 0500 this morning sir. The milk train was due in an hour after that, then at 0625 there was...'

'Shush,' the major held up his hand, he was thinking more than listening anyway. 'Private Roach was on guard near enough to that track when he got stabbed, right?'

Captain Dreyer agreed, 'Near enough sir, yes.'

Jackson pulled the clipboard across the table, 'So what else is in here?'

'I went back to take a gander with Jarli at dawn. Not much to see, just dislodged rails, scraps of detonators and a few pounds of badger barbecue.' Dreyer waited for the major to interrupt him; instead Jackson took a deep breath and casually waved his captain on. 'The men have completed a search North West of the woods and retrieved another parachute they found in a tree near the chapel.' The captain took out an envelope and poured the contents along the tabletop. 'These were buried at the first capture site,' he said, fanning out Peter Albrecht's dog tags with some damp documents and a dirt stained, folded map.

Jackson snatched up the map and sat back. 'So we either have stray Germans running around stabbing people and blowing things up, or a Fifth Column rescue team causing mayhem?'

Dreyer interrupted, 'But you wouldn't blow up a possible escape route, would you?'

The major smiled, 'Your right Prof, none of this makes any sense.' He opened the map on the table and prodded its landscape of empty fields, 'So what was their bomb run trying to blow up, and what do *these* words mean?'

'Piste', Captain Dreyer scrunched up his face. 'That could translate to track or runway and the second word means new, fresh. There were other group raids on airfields yesterday, but these grid references are well off. Comparing this with the more detailed map the navigator had, it looks like these boys got lost.'

'OK, so they were off course, but why bomb an empty field and half a town instead?' Major Jackson did not wait for any suggestions; 'We need to have another talk with the two men in custody Professor.'

Captain Dreyer nodded and drank up. 'How many men can fit into a Heinkel bomber?' he asked to Private Evans.

'Hard to say sir, they were used as transports in the Spanish conflict, but the bomber version is a tighter squeeze.' Evans thought about it for a second longer, 'Five for sure, maybe six at a push?'

Captain Dreyer jumped back in, 'Well we have four men accounted for so far and four canopies found. It's hard to get the full picture from those confused witness statements, but if you take them at face value.'

'Well then there were about fifty Germans, right?' Major Jackson sighed, then he was suddenly snapped wide-awake. 'The Professor and I will go and see what they've got from that chatty navigator.' He looked at his watch, 'The patrols might find one or two more silks over that side of the river, eh? Those Home Guard men can show us where they picked up the scent last night.'

Dreyer nodded, 'Yes sir the police passed word that they'd ordered the men to attend the station this morning.'

Evans got up to leave with them.

'Private, you need to get into the archives at the town hall. See what you can dig up on those bureaucratic horse thieves. Find out why the shelters aren't yet open *and* when they will be? Take your time Private, I need some facts to work with.'

'They told me it was all unobtainable sir?' Evans said nervously.

'Our standing orders in this *"Emergency"*, gives us certain rights and privileges Private,' Captain Dreyer winked.

Private Evans moved his lips as he ran over the words inside his head and committed them to memory.

'Tell 'em to come and see me if they've got any doubts.' The major managed a reassuring smile. 'And take my car. Reckon you'll need it to carry back all the bull dust you're about to find.'

The officers waited for Evans to leave. He didn't.

'Make like billy'o and go.' Captain Dreyer demanded.

Evans almost fell over himself in his sudden rush to leave.

Major Jackson tapped on Dreyer's clipboard, 'We are missing something here Prof.' He took a deep breath, stretched and looked around, 'I want to set some things in motion today, rather than just chasing my own arse.'

Dreyer felt this was becoming one of their common "talk freely" situations, 'I heard you spat your dummy and laid out a British officer?'

As Jackson raised an eyebrow, Captain Dreyer produced a copy of the local newssheet from beneath the table. The biggest image on the front page was a high contrast photograph of the major punching Cooke in the jaw. It had a bold caption stating "CAPTAIN COOKE DISOVERS AUSTRALIA!"

Jackson skimmed over the photograph to a small strip cartoon near the bottom of the page. In this he'd been caricatured as a kangaroo with giant boxing gloves and two pointy helmeted Germans poking out of its belly pouch. On page two there was a continuation of the shabby story and a moderately smaller photograph of Jackson slapping Neville.

The major pushed the paper away then lit a slim cigar, 'You know that Cooke fellah hunted down and murdered one of those Germans, mid surrender.' He left it at that and started to think about everything else. 'We need to look at the last few days as a whole. I want you to set up an incident room at the police station, like the ones you used back home.'

'But I've only taught and assisted detectives Major, I've never been one.' The captain got up to leave as ordered, but continued to protest, 'Half the blokes back home thought that my strategies were a waste of their time and these local boys will most likely agree.' Dreyer had learned the hard way that there was a certain etiquette to follow if you were sticking your nose into police business. That is, if you didn't want to get it broken.

'While we're here we'll do our bloody job, find the enemy and stop the locals from shooting our POWs.' Jackson turned back to the picture of Captain Cooke, 'Last night they were all jeering that hoon on, like bloody footy fans.'

The only thing the captain could squeeze into the conversation was, 'So our priority is to find the rest of that crew?'

The major ranted on, 'I suppose, but I also want those shelters open and those greedy vultures on the council *will* make it happen.'

Dreyer had to be forceful, 'With all due respect sir, we don't have time for a personal vendetta.'

After a moment of silence, the major laughed, 'Nah, it's not personal Prof, just necessary. And you're right; we need those Germans rounded up first. Sooner we do that, sooner we can see what's *really* going on around here.'

Dreyer was starting to buy into the bigger picture.

'Come on,' Jackson jeered as he got up. He flicked the end off the cigar, slurped a final mouth full of coffee and decreed, 'Lets go.' As they hit the main road he turned to Dreyer and asked, 'Can you smell dung?'

Miles away up the valley there was a very similar smell around Edwards Farm. In comparison to the army canteen, the scrambled eggs here were fresh and real, even if the conversation seemed like total fiction. Cassia and little Bert were outside mucking out, something their dad would normally have sorted before breakfast.

Another sleepless night without word from Edward had done Victoria no good. She had tried to keep things calm and normal by cooking everyone breakfast, but now she and Justine sat opposite each other arguing furiously.

'So you still think Edward an' his mates have driven away from a bomb site, in a truck half blown apart? Then hidden it in a field and run off into the undergrowth with one or more of them injured and bleeding?' Victoria waited for Justine to argue her side again.

Justine had had enough of arguing and chose to allow her friend time to adjust. Wearily she shrugged and carried on eating without a word.

'And all this, no more than a few miles from their own families front doors,' Victoria pointed out angrily.

'Well no,' Justine mumbled through a mouthful of toast. 'Look, *someone* must have driven Minnie, but I can't say I'm sure who. I've followed things as best I could, then when I ran out of time and tracks I came here to see what you knew. You have a lot more sense than I ever did.'

Victoria took the complement and softened a little. 'Why didn't you go and look for them around town, or the hospital? Someone must have stolen the truck and, and, well I don't know do I?' Victoria cleared away the plates noisily.

Justine had explained at least twice that the men were not at the hospital or simply having a pint in the pub. 'You really should eat something Victoria,' was another thing she'd said a lot.

Victoria was standing at the sink looking out of the window. She couldn't see the children in the courtyard, which was sort of normal, but not today. 'I spoke to our estate manager Mr Gibbs before you got up,' she said peering left and right. 'He told me Cooke shot two Germans a couple of miles from where you saw the big crater and Minnie.'

Justine shrugged again, 'I don't have any answers Victoria. Maybe you're right and it was those Germans who took Minnie. Still doesn't tell us where our boys are, does it?'

Victoria stopped washing up and spun around, glaring at her friend. 'I think we should all go down there and have a better look. Better than *you* managed anyway.'

168

Justine stood up to retaliate, but Victoria had turned away again to tend to the nagging thought in her head. The farmer's wife had one last peek past her curtains then went over to take down a gun from their dresser. Checking it was loaded she snapped the barrels shut and attempted to hand it across.

'What? I don't want that,' Justine protested.

Victoria pushed the weapon into her hands then grabbed another from the rack. 'Look, I'm sorry. I was tired before, an' I don't blame you for any of this really.' Victoria became instantly centred and calm as she creaked open the door and whispered, 'But the children, they should've come back in by now.'

When the women cautiously rounded the far corner of the yard they were relieved to see Cassia and Berty standing there unharmed. At the same time they were also surprised and confused to witness Cassia aiming a pistol towards the stream. Victoria moved closer and lowered her own weapon to meet Cassia's aim.

A leather-clad figure was lying face down in the soggy streambed, half hidden by the concrete culvert bridge.

Little Bert spoke first, 'Stupid Nazi's asleep. Cass took his gun right off of him and he didn't even budge.' He jumped down to prove his point by casually kicking the soggy man hard in the shoulder.

The German cursed in pain as his arm shot out and grabbed at Bert's foot. When the boy toppled away the hand let go and rested back into the mud.

'Stop that Berty, come back up here!' Cassia shrieked.

Other than two large snotty bubbles appearing near the German's nose, there was no further movement. Victoria waited for Berty to step back up, then un-cocked her shotgun, breathed out and propped the weapon against a gatepost.

'Cassia, give me that pistol and move Berty away from here,' Victoria instructed, holding out a pleading hand.

Cassia did as she was told, while her mother stepped down aiming the pistol at the German. She crouched to turn his face until the nose and mouth were clear of the wet ground.

'Is he the one who killed dad, tell me?' Berty demanded from the yard gate.

'No one has killed dad,' Cassia insisted, holding the boy back.

Victoria cautiously lifted one of the man's eyelids and gave her opinion, 'Well he's either out cold now, or dead.' She handed the pistol up to Justine and checked the rest of the body before shouting, 'Cassia, take Berty an' get a big plank from the tractor shed.'

Justine tucked away the pistol at the back of her belt then rested the shotgun over one arm just in case.

Soon after, as the children helped their mother slide the board and its limp load onto the kitchen table, Victoria began to fluster. She knew a few things like how to deliver lambs and de-louse chickens, but proper medicine was a job for someone else.

Justine could see her friend was out of her depth. She shook Victoria and begged, 'Someone needs to save him, he might know what happened to our men.'

Victoria shivered, unzipped the man's torn leather jacket and ripped open his shirt. 'It doesn't look too bad under the mess,' she lied. 'Justine help me to get this gunky blood off and clean up these big cuts. Berty, fetch some of the disinfectant and white powder from the chicken coops while Cassia fires up the kettle.'

After fifteen minutes work with hot soapy water and torn linen, things only seemed about half as bad. There was a lot of bruising around the ribs and several slash wounds.

'Right,' Victoria assessed what could be done rather than what couldn't. 'Well, we should be safe till you get back Justine.'

'Oh, I see, back from where?' Justine said with interest.

'Robert Gibbs has got the vet coming to look at his sweaty bullocks,' Victoria tried to explain.

That was all it needed, the tension was blown away, as if someone had opened all the doors and windows and let it out of the room. Everyone, apart from Victoria and the unconscious German, laughed uncontrollably.

'His show breeders 'ave got a fever,' Victoria was still deadly serious as she angled her view to look past them at the grandfather clock. 'You might just catch him, they'll be in the paddock, along Seagate Lane.'

'What if he wakes up?' Justine asked.

When Victoria poked the German in the eye, he didn't even flinch. 'I don't think we'll have that problem. Go quickly and we'll be fine.'

Justine did a shrug, 'Where is this lane?'

'Such a town girl,' Victoria sighed. 'Take the motorbike down the footpath, turn right at the pond and keep going on the gravel track through the fields till you see some really big cows with penises.'

In the smelly back streets of the town, on their own unfamiliar route, the major and Captain Dreyer were approaching a junction.

'Do we have to go the same way as, as this, shit?' Jackson stamped away some of the stickier manure that had built up in his boot treads.

An even broader track of animal matter extended along the next road. The streets residents were all busy with shovels and potato sacks, gathering up as much as they could scrape. The net result of their wet sweeping had created a slippery mess along the cobbles, punctuated here and there with mounds of crap.

Dreyer side stepped one of the muck molehills and asked politely to one of the nearby women, 'What's going on here then Madam?'

'Madam is it, and who's asking?' the middle-aged woman stood upright and arched her back. She took a moment to look the handsome men up and down before trying her luck, 'Well if you was a proper gentleman you'd be helping instead of asking daft questions.'

'Come come Captain, the nice lady has a point, get shovelling,' Major Jackson smirked slyly as he stood back and took out his unfinished cigar.

The captain glared for a moment then rolled up his sleeves. 'What happened here?' he tried again as the woman passed over the shovel.

'Train had to stop before the station didn't it? Took 'em an age to get all six hundred pigs off. An' they was so frightened as they flat refused to trot up the tunnel. Then they shat em'selves sideways as they squealed all the way along here.' The woman pointed out a few choice lumps which the captain had missed then turned to question the major, 'Why did you lot blow up the train track then?'

171

Jackson's cigar butt was flicked into Dreyer's manure laden shovel, landing with a hiss. He walked over to the lady, cupped a hand near her ear and whispered, 'It wasn't us. The badgers did it.'

'Get away,' the lady said with ample scepticism.

'What was that about a tunnel?' Captain Dreyer emptied the manure into her sack and leaned on the shovel.

'Pig tunnel,' she shrugged. 'They won't go in if they're frightened you see? Happens now and then, but we get all this shit for free,' she shook the half filled sack which had begun to drip at one corner. 'Everyone's a winner, 'cept the pigs.'

'Indeed,' the major mused. 'We need to go Captain, right now.'

As they took the last corner heading up towards the police and court buildings, both men voiced the same idea.

'What if there was something else, something that put those pigs off going into that tunnel?' the major began.

'Yes,' Dreyer agreed, 'I can get Jarli and Noah to take a look.'

Before they could say more the police station swung into view. Outside there were a lot of irritated men and women lining the pavements. The major recognised a few faces from the group that had forced their way inside the town hall yesterday. The mob parted to allow an ambulance to pull out of the side arch, then filled in behind as it drove away with its bell silent.

Sergeant Roberts jogged over to intercept the Australian officers and held out his hand to Jackson. 'We met before sir and last night sir at the bridge, but didn't get around to introductions.'

Jackson returned the handshake and introduced Captain Dreyer. 'And you must be Sergeant Roberts?' he smiled. 'Chief Higgins said you might be able to help our investigations.'

Robert's looked down at his boots, shook his head and explained the situation in five quiet words, 'Chief's been shot, he's dead.'

'How, where, when?' Jackson and Dreyer said.

'Germans shot him,' an earwigging woman separated herself from her friends and stepped around to push in front of Roberts. 'And they'll murder us all in our beds afore you lot do owt to stop em.'

As the rest of her friends gathered closer to voice their own opinions, someone by the police station steps whistled out and the whole scene went quiet again.

Everyone's attention moved to Captain Cooke emerging timidly through the police station's front doors. He held a bundle containing his tunic, hat, belt straps and an empty holster. The old school master's shirt was creased and ruffled, hanging out at the waist with the collar undone. His hair was a bed head mess and there was a large purple bruise on the left hand side of his stubbly chin.

When the dishevelled detainee stumbled on the top step and dropped some of his possessions, the crowd flicked instantly from wonder to mockery before the first item had hit the ground. Cooke snatched up what he could and pushed through the mob, down the steps. Those nearby roared with laughter now as he scuttled away, crossing the road to hide inside the nearest pub.

The major had no pity and saw no humour in him. 'Why is that man free?' he demanded of Roberts, before shaking his head and realising it wasn't important right now. 'Shall we move inside?' he suggested, then led the way himself.

Roberts followed them through the path, which Captain Cooke had cleared.

'How, when and where was the Chief shot?' Dreyer repeated as they entered the stations busy lobby.

Roberts directed the officers through to the privacy of a small rest room behind his desk. 'Rifle shot through his office window at about half past ten last night,' he replied running worried fingers through strands of remaining hair. 'There was a possible report of a gun shot outside at that time, but the cleaner only found him an hour ago.'

'So that was his body in the ambulance?' Major Jackson enquired.

As Roberts nodded, Captain Dreyer snapped, 'For Gods sake Sergeant, why did you move him?'

'Because he was dead?' Roberts responded blankly.

'Captain,' the major cautioned, 'Mr Higgins was a friend and colleague to the sergeant, not just a, well, shall we call it a body of evidence.'

'Sorry,' Dreyer apologised. 'Where is the Chief's office?'

'Three floors up Captain,' Roberts pointed skyward then moved to a small window and opened it, beckoning Dreyer to look outside. 'The shot must have come from over there.'

Captain Dreyer stuck his head through and scanned the surrounding rooftops.

'I sent word to the Chief's brother up in Carlisle, he didn't have no one else.' Sergeant Roberts stared into the distance.

'Has someone been over to search the roof of that department store opposite?' Dreyer enquired as he ducked back inside.

'Not yet, I need the men I have to control that lot,' Roberts glumly indicated the long queue in reception and the growing disarray outside. 'They all think they've seen something somewhere in the night. The ones in here want to report it and that lot out there,' Roberts allowed a moment to soak up some of their jeers, heckles and demands. 'Well they are *very* confused, but essentially I think they just want to string someone up.'

Dreyer was going to interrupt, but the major put up a hand and let Roberts finish.

'Then there's the old bombs, the new bombs, the Chiefs murder and your sentry being stabbed.' Roberts pulled out a chair and sat down with his head in his hands. 'Some of the phone lines are back on, but that just means more time being spent answering the bloody calls.'

'So what have you got in place so far?' Dreyer queried, as soon as the major allowed it.

'Nothing,' Sergeant Roberts admitted with a shrug then looked up with panic in his eyes.

Dreyer sat down next to the sergeant and said kindly, 'Best get organised then eh, make the best of what we have and work together, right?'

Roberts nodded and blew his nose on a spotty pink handkerchief.

'Well all right then, lets get stuck in,' the captain said slapping the table as he got up.

Roberts jolted then followed the captain out like a lost sheep. 'Where do we start?' he asked.

'We need an incident room,' Dreyer replied with enthusiasm. 'Major, if you could organise some men to check that roof out? Sergeant please lock up the Chiefs office pronto and I will take a gander at all the paper work you've got for the events of the past few days.'

The sergeant beamed with pride, 'Paperwork, yes sir.'

As Roberts and Dreyer moved away Major Jackson followed them as far as reception, there he noticed four Home Guard men looking very sheepish amongst the other faces. The man who hadn't fired his rifle last night was looking solemnly down at the booking desk. His friends tried other methods to avoid the Australian officers gaze.

Jackson stormed in and prodded the nearest man saying, 'Did you lot find those Germans dug into the bush or out on the main drag?'

Neville jumped and let out a little whimper while the other three clustered to attention behind him.

Jackson tried again, 'Were those Germans hiding in the woods with all their kit, or were they on the run when you found them?'

Neville fidgeted with his cap in silence. When no one else stepped forward he answered very quietly, 'Captain Cooke commandeered a big car on the other side of the bridge sir.'

'Speak up,' the major prompted.

Neville looked up, 'We headed out to search for the airmen sir, but after a mile or so they found us and flagged the car down.'

'Trying to take the vehicle?' Jackson butted in, attempting to clarify the events.

'Maybe, but they saw it was full of soldiers and they legged it. Captain Cooke fired his pistol out the side window and...'

William Duffy looked sideways at Neville and decided it was time to talk, 'Cooke said if we'd been civilians them Germans would have shot us right there, or slit our throats sir.'

'Where?' the major grunted impatiently.

When Duffy pointed a finger to his own throat then dragged it across to his ear, Jackson closed his eyes and shook his head.

Neville understood the question then, 'We came across the Germans just before the bombed out field, then dumped the car and pursued 'em back this way, towards the bridge, through the meadows and hedges.'

Private Duffy nodded, 'They were running pretty fast, but the captain found a tractor and headed them off.'

'You wait here,' Major Jackson ordered while pointing at Neville. 'The rest of you go back and see if there are parachutes or anything hidden near that road.'

'What's your name?' the major asked as soon as the others had gone.

'Neville Cartwright sir.'

'Why did you fail to fire your weapon last night?'

Neville shook his head in disbelief, 'Wasn't, right sir, not fair. Simple as that.'

'Have you slept recently son, you look clagged out?'

'Yes sir like a log,' Neville lied as usual, but this time he didn't feel tired.

'Come on,' Jackson smiled in an attempt to put the lad at ease. 'We both need to get some coffee down our necks, then we'll go and find the Professor.'

By the time they'd found Dreyer his makeshift incident room was already beginning to take shape. There was a wall-mounted blackboard on one side of the room surrounded by mismatched tables and chairs. Paperwork was accumulating quickly on every surface including the floor.

When Cartwright and the major entered, Captain Dreyer was on the phone.

'No worries, but if *any* of those names do show up you can get me on,' he glanced at the telephones dial, '152, yes that's right, thank you nurse.' Dreyer put down the receiver and waved a sheet of paper in the air. 'Seven locals still missing then,' he nodded over to Sergeant Roberts, 'and there's no one still trapped anywhere that we know of?'

Frank Roberts nodded back at him, 'Well they're fairly certain that everyone's out.'

The captain turned to pick up a red folder and saw his commander standing by the door. 'Major, take a gander at this interview with the man Jarli found,' Dreyer said holding out the file on Cadet Heikling.

Jackson turned to page one, but before he could read a word his captain excitedly filled him in.

'Says they were on a straightforward bombing mission, but with shoddy coordinates they got lost. Then a bolt from the blue took out their electrics and he bailed out behind two fresh recruits. He fainted soon as, and doesn't know what happened after that. Won't confirm or deny anything as far as total crew numbers go. Seems to be more afraid of his fellow flyers than he is of us.'

An office girl arrived with another pile of records from upstairs and coughed behind Neville. He cautiously entered the room to make way for her.

'Put them over here with the others, thank you,' the captain directed.

'Captain, this is Private Cartwright. He seems to have his head screwed on tighter than his mates.' Major Jackson pushed Neville towards Dreyer, 'I think he'll make a good runner for you, good local knowledge and all that.'

Dreyer shook the lad's hand, 'Can we arrange to borrow you for a day or so son?'

Neville eagerly replied, 'I work in the can factory sir, munitions really. To be honest there ain't that much left of it to work in right now.'

Dreyer nodded approvingly, 'Bonza, well we'll keep you busy in the mean time.'

'Yes sir,' Cartwright smiled, for the first time in days.

'Sergeant Roberts can you square things with his foreman?' Jackson asked.

A thumbs up sealed the deal.

The captain went back to leafing through incident notes on the nearest table, rearranging them in a rough reverse order. One by one he called out the events, 'One dead Chief Constable, a sabotaged rail road near our sentry's stabbing, some looting; in a flower shop?' Dreyer paused to read the brief details. 'And at least seven missing people with no known bodies trapped or unidentified. Germans sighted everywhere, some sneaking around last night, one spotted with a rifle. Before all that there's the bombing raid itself, oh and also, a missing dog answering to the name of, Adolf?'

'Don't forget the pigs and their tunnel this morning,' the major prompted.

Dreyer nodded, 'I sent word for Corporal Jarli's team to nose around at both ends then do a full sweep through.'

'He'll need a big brush,' Neville chuckled to himself.

Everyone's attention moved to the room's large window as the voices outside started surging.

'We need to sort that rabble out,' the major proposed as he crossed the room to gain a better view.

Scuffles were breaking out below as several women tried to drag their husbands and sons away. A few individuals were giving impromptu speeches, clearly stirring up the remaining crowd and every increase in noise drew more people in.

A sod of earth suddenly hit the window in front of Major Jackson's face and slid down a few inches before falling back to earth.

Sergeant Roberts reacted quickly, excused himself and headed back to reception to rally his staff.

Dreyer joined his commander at the bay. 'I ordered in two wagons and enough men to help out sir.' He checked his watch and turned to assure Private Cartwright, 'If that mob get angry we'll take control, don't worry.'

The damp soil had left a brown streak on the panes. The major peered past it and pointed out, 'They are already a tad past angry Captain.'

'I suppose that's what they call a dirty protest then sir?' Cartwright observed with nervous and caffeine fuelled enthusiasm.

Jackson tapped the glass to test its thickness, 'Bring the men and their wagons around the back when they arrive Captain, no point rattling the rattlers eh?'

Dreyer nodded, 'Yes sir and I'll have a proper snoop around the Chiefs office now while we're waiting. Did you send anyone over to check those rooftops?' He pointed up at the sign above the department store.

'We are a bit short handed for now,' Jackson scrunched up his face. 'But I know a bloke who's keen to get involved,' he said whilst handing the red folder back to Dreyer. Then leaving the conversation at that, he turned and left the room.

Chapter Seventeen

Near the pig tunnel Noah and Jarli followed their noses over a wall and saw an opening below the road. To their left there were steps leading down beside a red brick enclosure. A pair of six-foot high iron gates hung open twenty feet from the tunnels entrance. They were elegant and beautifully decorated in an Art Deco style that didn't fit with their purpose. One had the word "MOORS" intricately cast into it, the other said "MEAT".

Jarli ran down first to get a better view.

Noah held back. 'That would hold about a wagons worth of pigs at a time,' he suggested as he took in the scene. Then, leaning over the wall he described in some detail how they would probably be enticed into that smelly square with a single fat cabbage.

Jarli stepped into the pen, breathed in deeply and imagined the drove of beasts grunting around him. In his mind the ghostly pigs scurried past to squabble over a leafy ball, then ran off with it, following the cabbage smell into the tunnel. The corporal moved amongst the remaining apparitions towards the opening, then leaned on its rusty industrial shutter to duck his head beneath. He considered the sounds of the herdsmen, first closing the main gates behind him and then eventually releasing a rope or lever as the last hoof chased the other pigs inside. Then the shutter would have clattered down and cut off the hungry hogs decision making abilities, for the rest of their lives.

'Smells all kinds of wrong down there mate,' Noah choked out as he reluctantly descended the steps.

Jarli cautiously crept into the tunnel mouth, looked back at Noah and said, 'Captain Dreyer told *us* to check if some German blokes is hiding down there.' Crouching down he poked at the ground with a finger and examined the results. 'So that's what we do.'

'You're the bloke who finds people, then I shoot at 'em, right?' Noah did a similar ground inspection and added, 'So I think I'll just wait here to challenge any one that gets past yer.'

Jarli came back out and sucked his teeth at Noah. 'We both goin' in mate, with you thirty yards back. Like you say, just in case they is sneaky.' Jarli handed over his rifle to Noah and took out his trusty revolver. Before

179

going back in he added as an afterthought, 'No shooting mind, less you sure it's a white fellah.'

'Right-o, and should I check he's German too?' Noah asked sarcastically.

There was no reply.

Noah suddenly remembered the equipment he'd scavenged on the way over and shouted after his Corporal, 'Here, you need these.'

A second or two later a hand reached back out into the daylight. Noah placed a helmet containing a small metal box into Jarli's pale palm.

'What's this?' Jarli quizzed with a strange echoing voice.

Noah crouched down and pointed inside the helmet, 'That box of tricks is a torch, mate.'

Jarli switched it on hopefully, but the objects nameplate was about the only thing it illuminated. 'LAMP ELECTRIC NUMBER ONE,' Jarli read out slowly.

'And that's a helmet mate,' Noah tapped the upturned hard hat with his fingernail. 'Made of Duperite.'

'Sounds duper-wrong,' Jarli suggested with dissatisfaction.

Noah shrugged, 'There ain't enough tin hats to go around blue. Captain Dreyer won a crate of these beauts in a warehouse poker game before we boarded ship,' Noah explained. 'And *this,* is the only one left in town.'

The helmet was handed back. 'Them is for dispatch riders mate, I don't want it,' Jarli insisted as he moved further inside.

'Fair enough, you wouldn't fit yer fat frizzy head in there anyways,' Noah grunted.

As his corporal moved deeper inside, the private remained to sort out their remaining kit. It took him a while to get Jarli's rifle comfortable on his back and re-sling his own weapon up in front. Eventually he tugged the helmet on himself, counted to thirty and headed off into the hillside hole.

In another much cleaner world, back on the surface, the major was attempting to get past several dinner suited stewards in the foyer of the posh department store opposite the police station. Jackson had sneaked away out of the stations gated archway while Sergeant Roberts distracted the crowd. Reading his version of the riot act from the top step hadn't gone that well, but Roberts was safely back inside now and the major had at least got away relatively unnoticed.

'I am not asking your permission Jeeves, I just want to know the quickest way to the roof,' Jackson argued with a tall, eye patched bouncer.

The doorman signalled to several other stewards waiting near the food hall, then puffed out an ample chest and wheezed, 'New rules from management, no Australian soldiers permitted inside the store.'

As the huge penguin like reinforcements approached, Jackson saw that they were all damaged goods. *Probably medically discharged men with a natural hatred of uniformed authority,* he presumed. He also noticed that behind them two women were entering a caged lift set within an ironwork staircase on the far wall.

Suddenly the major darted left, narrowly avoiding the burly men's meaty hands. On the polished tile floor their leather soled shoes were no match for rubber bottomed army boots. The major swung out in a long right-handed arc and dived into the lift with not an inch to spare.

As the cage rose swiftly skyward the stewards slammed into each other, cursing at the officer through the fretted metalwork. A handful of them eventually untangled and made chase up the stairs. Jackson smiled back at them nonchalantly.

As the gap widened he tidied his uniform and addressed the lifts occupants. 'Sorry ladies,' he smiled, bowing slightly and touching the brim of his cap. Then he took out a shiny coin, flicked it toward the frightened liftboy and requested, 'Top floor please son.'

The boy looked once at the situation and twice at the money, then he decided the Australian was in charge.

By the third floor, there was only one bouncer left in the chase. As the lift climbed away the big dinner suit finally wheezed to a stop. The massive man leaned on his knees, huffing out spittle, slander and sweat, then sat down to consider how none of this was in his job description.

At the top the lift went "ting". Jackson got out and the cage slid rapidly back down its shaft. The major unclipped his revolver while his eyes took in the dimly lit surroundings. He had been deposited in a huge oak panelled dining room with upturned chairs on tables and no one else in sight.

Working his way over to a row of doors he soon discovered a grubby cement staircase that went up.

The top of the exit was bolted from this side, but Jackson cocked his revolver anyway, just in case. On the roof, although he moved slowly, the officer soon found what he was looking for. The parapet facing the police station had the best-unobstructed view. From the centre spot you could clearly make out across the skyline, the recessed balcony of the chief's office. In one of the shiny glass doors a silver spider web pattern surrounded an obvious black bullet hole.

Jackson stooped to look around for some time, but there were no handy cigarette butts or bullet cases to take back for Dreyer's investigation. 'A smart-arse, that'd be right,' he whispered, unsurprised.

When he stood up and stretched, the pint-sized shapes of Captain Dreyer and Private Cartwright appeared across the street. They were moving around the office looking for their own side of the evidence. Neville seemed to be trying hard not to touch anything, while Dreyer carefully opened the unbroken right hand door and stepped out onto the balcony.

The captain spotted Major Jackson and held up a pinched finger and thumb to ask if any evidence had been found. The major shook his head slowly and Dreyer confirmed his disappointment by nodding back.

There were enough disturbances in the hot gravel for Jackson to see where one or more people in heavy boots had recently trod and knelt on a board shaped indent. He followed the tarred boot marks through the dust of several descending rooftops and found a sticky plank that matched the indentation. It had been re-used as a shortcut between two stores. He found palm prints on the wood, but they were clearly from a gloved hand. Eventually he arrived at a cluster of chimneys and a gulley above a triangular courtyard. Leaning over a drain funnel he saw a ladder rested awkwardly half way down one wall. It was much too far away for him to reach.

Deciding he'd probably seen enough from this precarious angle, the major headed unhappily back to face the music from the department store's goons. At the highest point he stopped to look around the whole panorama properly. If he'd been gifted with x-ray vision he might have observed the strange slow motion dance his corporal was currently doing as he forged his way forward beneath the nearby junction.

Jarli carefully plodded through what he would one day describe in his memoirs as "Shitty brown stuff".

Thirty yards behind his corporal, Noah swore as the Duperite helmet thudded off yet another slimy slumped brick in the roof. He was still amazed at how well Jarli could find his way by day or by night.

Jarli stopped for a moment and listened as nearby drips and plops interspersed with the echo of swearing from Noah behind him. Rounds of "Rat shit!" and "Bloody far gone flop house!" drifted by and faded into the brickwork around him. The MOD torch had proved to be next to useless, so Jarli had turned the lamp around to lead Noah along, instead of damaging his own night vision. Since then, nature had slowly and softly illuminated the way.

On every wall surface a faintly phosphorous fungus grew in long psychedelic spirals. The strands were almost unperceivable, but the aboriginal scout was used to that. Since infancy he'd travelled the bush in pitch dark, rarely taking his eyes off the glowing leaves, which his father would attach to a short spear and lead the way ahead. He had to admit that despite the smell and the constant dripping water, down here it was still beautiful. He had to crouch down in places to prevent his hair from snagging on the roof. At one of these points he heard an almighty thud echo along from behind him, followed by a period of unusual silence from Noah.

'You right Noah?' Jarli shouted back down the passage with concern.

After a brief pause and another thump, the distant answer came quietly back, 'Happy as a boxing kangaroo in the fog mate.'

Jarli stopped to holster his revolver and covered one eye before crouching down and turning the lamp forward to examine the floor. Undulating drag marks showed where some cleaning device had recently raked pig dung smoothly over that from the week before. Close up, something also seemed to be moving. The corporal leaned in further and saw the ground was alive with beetles, worms and other tiny things. The torch glow followed a shiny beetle forward until it tumbled over the edge of a fresh boot imprint and squirmed on its back trying to right itself.

After finding that first impression, Jarli started to notice more partial footmarks in the thicker deposits. They were blurred by insect life and water flow, but you could still make out that each one pointed the same way.

Back above ground, no one had bothered to challenge the major on his way out of the department store. Instead of making a fuss and drawing more attention, he was politely escorted downstairs while the main door was opened wide. There had even been smiles given before the doormen slammed the exit shut behind him.

Jackson boxed around the buildings to avoid the crowds then took a short walk down the hill. At the florists shop PC Grogan was taking a more detailed statement while a glazier fitted a temporary cover to the door. Even though the place had been cleaned up, it was blatantly obvious that someone had broken out, rather than in.

Major Jackson nodded a quick hello to Grogan and entered a short alley that came out behind the shops. Down here at the more detailed business end, the ladder he had seen from the roof, revealed a worn metal plaque. Jackson stooped to read that it was the property of "Duncan Greene and Son Builders Merchants". At its feet were the remains of an aged pulley and some dark blood congealed between the cobbles.

'That be dog blood, afore you ask,' said a stocky man in an apron who'd appeared in a flurry of chainmail and door ribbons.

'And you'd be the bloke who'd know right?' Jackson said. He stood up straight, yet still didn't make it to the butchers eye level.

'Found the mongrel out here with that gear on top of him.' After wiping his hand on a once white tea towel the big man offered to shake. In that moment he made a connection and blurted out, 'My God it's you, the Australian who smashed Cooke's face in.'

'That man is not worth a pinch of billy-goat shit,' Jackson confessed, accepting the handshake with no sign of remorse.

The butcher looked sideways at the officer and tightened his grip, 'Young Nev's a good lad though, what'd you slap him for?'

'The lad was in shock,' Jackson assured the butcher. 'And you know you shouldn't believe what you read in news sheets, unless it's the date.'

The butcher nodded slowly and let the vice unwind.

Jackson looked up to the sky, 'This dog, big fellah was he?'

'Still is, I stitched him up. Alsatian, belongs to Drunk Dunc, but Duncan ain't no animal lover like me.' The blood spattered man put his hands on his hips, 'I might hang onto that doggy and we'll see how the old fart likes that.'

'You know what they say about the butchers dog mate?' the major smirked.

'What they been saying?' he growled back. 'That poof at the flower shop should mind his own flipping business.'

Jackson tried to get back to the real world, 'What time did you find the dingo Mr...?'

'Smith, call me Craig. What's a dingo?'

The major took a deep breath, 'When did you find the Alsatian, Craig?'

Craig scrunched up his face in thought, 'It was about five and ten to eleven, last night. We'd gone to bed, but the missus heard barking and woke me up to a crash.'

The officer attempted to translate, 'Five and ten to?'

'I always wanted a little doggy,' Craig mumbled, with a thousand yard stare. 'Dunc calls him Adolf, but I'm gonna change it to, Steve.'

'Sounds ripper Mr Smith, I hope you're very happy together. So about quarter to eleven, right?'

The butcher nodded.

'I need to take a gander up the ladder, can you hold the bottom?' Jackson enquired as he attempted to rattle the apparatus back into position.

Craig nodded, took over and slid the ladder fully upright with ease. 'If you see Duncan, tell him he can 'ave these steps back, but not the dog.'

As the major ascended he asked, 'How long have the ladders been here?'

Craig put a steadying boot on the bottom rung, 'They was dumped up that corner the day before yesterday.' He raised his voice as the major neared the top, 'We find all sorts round the back; bikes, tyres, prams, tramps.'

Jackson surveyed the broken upper storey doorway and carefully poked around in the fragments of rotted frame and board.

'You tell him mind, I'm keeping Steve,' Craig shouted up.

Major Jackson was oblivious; he took out a hanky and picked something shiny up. 'Do you have a phone number Walt?' he called down. The ladders shook violently as he rapidly descended and explained, 'Just in case my captain wants to ask you some more daft questions.'

In the darkness beneath the town, Jarli was shaking too, from his damp hair tips, to his soggy toes. The pig tunnel mechanically funnelled cool air over his wet clothing and drew away body heat as soon as it was generated. He knew that creatures could shake from cold or fear, but had never expected a personal capacity for convulsions like these. The skinny scouts lifetime above the red soil of home, had always been warm and life giving. Here underneath the dark earth of this new world, Jarli's little body felt weak and vulnerable.

The route sloped slightly upwards for drainage and seemed steeper now with each step. It felt overpoweringly colder upon reaching what Jarli presumed was the halfway point, and it was clear to see why. Several feet ahead of him in the roof of the passage, a ventilating shaft pointed straight up. Dim shadows and water cascaded continuously from around its orifice, where green stalactites of algae hung down. Jarli ducked under and stepped quickly to the centre to avoid the raining rim.

Clipping the torch away in the dull stroboscopic light of the spinning ventilator shaft, Jarli instinctively tuned out any sounds irrelevant to the hunt. His breathing slowed to almost nothing as his mouth opened wide to quieten any noises within. One by one Jarli's mind blocked out the dripping, the whoop-whoop of fan blades and the distant clunking of Noah closing in. Finally after considerable concentration everything was rendered silent. Everything, except for the slow in and out of someone else trying hard not to make a sound.

Over at the police station things were getting very noisy, both outside and within. The major had stealthily crept back inside the back way, and followed a steady stream of staff carrying paraphernalia towards Captain Dreyer's newly acquired room. At the doorway he watched a trestle table being set up away from the window where Sparks the signals officer was shouting out complicated technical orders to his men.

Neville was busy cleaning another chalkboard he'd wheeled in after the captain had almost saturated the wall mounted one. Dreyer was adding another arm to a huge spider diagram of names and events covering that boards cluttered surface. Behind all this Jackson sat down quietly.

'So,' the major said after a few more seconds of quiet observation, 'I found this.'

Dreyer and Cartwright turned together as Jackson unfurled his handkerchief and a brass shell casing rolled onto the nearest table.

'It was in the florists, so you can change that looting to an exit route for our shooter,' the major pointed to one of the spider diagrams feet. 'There was a big ladder out back, ready for an escape, but something happened and they ducked out through the florists instead.'

Dreyer approached and bent over the shiny stub of evidence, almost touching it with his nose. 'There's some details about a ladder in that lot,' he nodded toward a fan of reports on the floor.

'You can touch it Professor,' Jackson advised as Neville re-stacked and passed over the wad of papers. 'Who ever dropped it didn't leave any prints. Pretty sure they were gloved. It must have dropped out of their pocket as they jumped from the ladder.' The major thumbed through and found a page with the address of Duncan's yard at the top. His lips silently mouthed the words as he scanned down and waited for the captain to engage with the spent shell.

Dreyer picked up the casing by inserting a pencil into the open end. 'Could still be something there,' he said with anticipation. 'I wouldn't expect the Sergeant to have our man's prints on file, but...' The captain rotated the evidence, 'Have you seen what it says on the bottom?'

'Second thing I looked for,' the major smiled.

Private Cartwright loved his new roll. Compared to stamping out bits of metal or marching about being shouted at by Cooke, this was heaven. 'What does it say?' he blurted out excitedly.

'GB 1941 11A and it's a subsonic .22', Dreyer decreed before dropping the casing into an envelope.

Cartwright watched in awe as the captain scribbled on the package and placed it into a box tray. 'So that means it's army issue and relatively new,' the young private exclaimed breathlessly. 'And if it matches what they pull out of Mr Higgins...'

Dreyer tapped the pencil on his lips before confirming his own thoughts; 'It would mean the ammunition and possibly the gun, were British made at least.' He moved over to the wall and chalked the new details in before stating, 'On the enemy front we now have six parachutes in total Major. Those Home Guard boys sent word they'd found two chutes stowed in a feed trough half way up the hill.' Dreyer drew six sketchy parachutes with four stick men hanging from them and explained, 'Three canopies from the chapel and the woods in the West, one on Cadet Heikling's back and two from the slopes in the East.'

'But only four men captured or killed,' Jackson said as he got up and crossed over to the wall.

'Oh and sir, the workmen at the chapel found these,' Cartwright picked another envelope from the tray and poured two scorched semicircles into the major's awaiting palm. 'Loose tags, found in the crashed aircraft,' he smiled. 'They belonged to a H. Josten.'

Sergeant Roberts rushed in at that moment and cried, 'We have another German.'

'Where from?' Dreyer asked, chalking in another stick man.

The sergeant placed a pin on a wall map of the area, 'Found here, on Croft Farm, above the chapel.'

'Could be this Josten bloke, possibly the pilot?' Dreyer speculated.

Roberts nodded, 'I asked 'em to stop in on their way through, so a uniform can accompany him to the hospital.'

'Is he talking, do we have his name?' Jackson demanded impatiently.

Roberts shook his head, 'Still pretty beat up and no tags. Vet says they've had some fun just getting him fixed up and mobile enough to transport him here.'

Major Jackson muttered, 'Bloody vet thinks he's a doctor and Craig the butcher is stitching up dingos, doesn't anyone stick to their own job?' He picked up some chalk and took a turn at the wall to explain. 'I just met a feller who told me that ladder appeared *before* the German aircraft. So...' With a few quick strokes the major added the word "LADDER" then rubbed out Adolf's name and changed it to Steve.

Neville took a deep breath, coughed and nervously began his own little presentation. 'The captain has asked me to add some local perspective to these missing people.'

'Go on,' Jackson said, offering him the chalk.

'We have seven town people reported missing, no more bodies turned up at the bomb sites, nor in the morgue.' Neville squeakily copied out a list on the new board, calling out more details as he went.

'Harry Clark a mechanic and Edward Croft a farmer both best mates. Mary and Patrick Tremayne, siblings. Finn and Elijah Stewart, who are twins and also farmers. Finally Susan Hill, council secretary to Mr Burdock.'

'What do Mary and her brother do?' Jackson enquired.

'Family own the café sir. Irish and very nice people, mostly. Mary works there for her folks, quite near to Harry's garage actually and...'

The major gave him a look.

Neville gulped, 'Patrick, well he's a sort of odd job man, with the emphasis on odd. Can be a bit, erm?'

'Violent,' Sergeant Roberts interrupted, folding his arms.

'There is also some concern about a girl,' Dreyer picked up his own scribbled notes. 'A Mrs Clark telephoned earlier, Harry's mum?'

Cartwright and Roberts nodded.

Dreyer scanned his notated words then looked over to the major, 'She was worried about her son and also a Miss Page, Justine Page. She was last seen yesterday on a motorbike heading for Croft Farm.'

Jackson slapped the edge of the table, 'I bet she's the one who jumped the bridge.'

Dreyer nodded, added Justine's name to the board and chalked an arrow to Edward.

'Saw her yesterday, on her way up,' Neville confirmed.

Sergeant Roberts stepped forward. 'Justine is Harry's girlfriend and she's not missing any more,' he corrected. 'Farm manager just told me Miss Page is going to help bring the German in. I warned them about the situation here and explained we would keep the gates open for as long as possible.'

'Justine works in council chambers with Mrs Hill,' Neville said with ever growing excitement.

189

Dreyer drew another joining line then underlined her name. 'Can I assume that she's well acquainted with everyone else on the list? It will save on chalk.'

'Do all these people know each other well enough to be off on a jolly, together somewhere?' the major suggested.

Sergeant Roberts answered first, 'Mrs Hill is not a mixer, but some of 'em have connections sir, although you never sees 'em all together at the same time.' He pointed at Justine's highlighted name, 'She may have been attacked on the night of the storm too sir. Constable Grogan found the girl in a doorway by the town hall, unconscious after the raid.'

Major Jackson went back to the table and quickly re-read the missing ladder report. Holding out several paper clipped sheets he asked Neville, 'Do you and the Sergeant recognise any of the men on our list from the descriptions these children gave?'

'I saw that when it came in, big scuffle with the local kids and one lost two teeth.' Roberts tried to remember all the details, 'Something about a hand ball? PC Thomas talked to all the parents and all their kids told the same story.'

Neville read the children's words back aloud, 'Three men with a ladder started the fight.'

Roberts leaned over and looked at the given time and date, 'I think Pat Tremayne was in court that day, it would have been around then.' He glanced over the descriptions again then handed it back to Neville. 'The three men who had the ladder, the descriptions could be the twins and either Harry or Edward, I suppose. It's a bit vague though.'

Neville agreed, 'It is a bit vague like, but if a nipper described these men, then yes it could fit.'

'How does this tie in with the raid?' Dreyer stared at the names on the board. 'The sooner we speak to this girl Justine, the better.'

The noise level outside was rising again. Careful closer observation by Sergeant Roberts, confirmed that the numbers had risen too. Dreyer joined him crouching near the window until someone below spotted the movement and lobbed a half brick through.

The mobs more organised members had come up with a chant demanding, 'Send out the Huns, send out the Huns.'

The captain had ducked down as soon as the rock hit and dragged the sergeant with him. They both continued to look out of the window, but from a safer position.

Major Jackson took a quick scan over their shoulders and said quietly, 'Those two men back there outside the pub, they're the press from last night aren't they. Can you get word to them to come inside? I might have some *genuine* work for them.'

Sergeant Roberts scratched his head, 'I could telephone the pub and try to have a quiet word.'

'Thank you Mr Roberts,' the captain said, urging him to go. Then he turned back to the major with worried eyes and cautioned, 'I think we need a plan here sir.' He peered over the sill again as another less well aimed brick bounced off the frame. 'A bloody good plan.'

'Working on it,' the major insisted while keeping one eye on the mob's ringleaders.

Far away, below all this, at the bottom of the ventilation shaft, Corporal Jarli was static. He could have moved back towards Noah, or simply waited for him to catch up. He could have done a lot of things far more sensible than the thing he decided to do. Jarli looked up.

Two boots filled with a blonde German dropped down and made heavy contact with the little corporal's shoulder and ear. When Jarli buckled purposefully away the lamp's belt clip came free and it splashed down with him to dimly illuminate his muddy face.

The German gunner Harald, had landed with his feet on either side of his pursuer's hips, ready to take control. As soon as Jarli blinked away the light and pulled out his gun, the muscular German kicked the weapon away. Then he leaned in and picked up the torch with his own pistol pushed into Jarli's cheek.

'Schwarz?' Harald said with surprise.

'Me name's Jarli, not "Shorts", it means Owl.' Jarli pulled his arms back in, puffed out his cheeks wide eyed in the lamplight then did a loud and shrill 'TWITAWOO'.

In that brief moment of distraction, the agile scout twisted his head away from the gun and lunged backwards to grab onto Harald's testicles with his right hand.

As Harald shrieked, 'Owwwww!' and pulled himself away from the grip, it helped to roll Jarli over. When Jarli let go, Harald stumbled backwards, banging his head with a clunk.

'No mate, it's owl,' Jarli corrected. The feisty corporal attempted to get back up, but his struggle had served only to make the German very angry and untrusting.

Breathing heavily, Harald crashed forward and kicked out again then rested his boot on the little man's neck as he lay on his back in the torch light.

Noah was running as fast as he could now, crouched down and lumbering along. The rifle on his back sent out sparks whenever it made contact with the tunnel roof. Private Cooper was still swearing, but not the same phrases he'd issued when banging along at a snails pace. These condemnations were much worse and filled with pure venom, directed at who ever was giving Jarli grief.

When Harald swung his pistol around to fire two blind shots toward the oncoming noise, Jarli sat up a little to grab for the torch. Smashing it down hard on Harald's knee cut the light, but also jerked the German's foot. Although already deafened by the gunfire, Jarli clearly heard his teeth snap together as his head hit the floor.

Seconds later the scout came around to a burst of red and phosphor white as Noah lit a match.

'Jees Jarli you look like shit mate,' Private Cooper remarked as he knelt down to assist his friend. When he lit another match it highlighted his own injury. There was a neat semicircle where a bullet had parted the flesh next to Noah's thumb.

'You a noisy bloke Noah, man you deserve to get shot,' Jarli grunted. Then with more sincerity he added, 'Thanks.'

Noah shrugged and sucked at his wound while the corporal searched for his revolver.

'Shall we go, before he gets to the others?' Jarli suggested urgently as he stood up. 'Just one fellah, but him big mate.'

Noah and Jarli trotted along using the wall as a guide until someone called out and a crack of light appeared in the sidewall some way ahead. This light lit up the tunnel's dead end then spread out to touch the edge of

Harald's shape. The figure was crouched down; it raised a weapon and fired twice from the dark into the light.

As John and Nigel had swung open the door, Harald's well-aimed shots had hit Nigel's thigh and John's shoulder. Nigel fell headfirst into the tunnel while John staggered and slumped, using the huge doorframe to hold himself up as the German jumped out and yanked his machine gun away with ease.

Harald immediately shouldered the new possession, cocked the firing bolt and bellowed, 'Move back Tommy.'

'Trying to, you dopey dipstick,' John cursed in pain. As soon as he was upright he called down to Nigel, but there was no response.

'Schnell,' the agitated German rasped, grabbing John's webbing and dragging him back. Then he demanded, 'Shut this door or die.'

John reluctantly kicked the door and slowly threw the latches with his good arm.

In the renewed gloom behind the freshly sealed barricade, Jarli and Noah ran headlong toward the remaining hairline of light and the moaning sounds coming from Nigel.

'You right mate?' Noah called out just before tripping over the injured man.

'Christ sake!' The collision stirred Nigel back to life. 'Scumbag got me in the ginger meg,' he groaned in agony.

Jarli shouted and banged on the door, calling for help. It took an age, but eventually a few factory workers decided it was safe enough to stop hiding and let them out.

Noah and Jarli emerged into a large wooden pen, with gated channels leading off around a killing floor. While the workers helped Noah carry Nigel away, Jarli tried to calm his thoughts in the clangourous noise and visual horror of their new location.

As always, the smell was the worst thing. It was blood, bile and excrement condensed into a pure vapour of death. Vats of steaming offal and waste waited along narrow tracks that branched away between the tables and machines. From the ceiling, freshly gutted swinging carcasses slowly spun on hooks. The most surreal thing was the classical music being trumpeted out of speakers in every corner of the room.

Jarli vaulted over the nearest fence and looked down to where his feet had skidded through claret coloured goo. It made him flashback to the sawdust, shoes and belongings they'd seen at the cannery yesterday and he felt light headed.

Due to the delays, some animals were still squealing for their lives, death pending and penned in amongst the gore. High above them a row of half stripped corpses clattered along then one at a time disappeared upwards through a hole, with a percussive clunk.

The corporal shook himself and turned his attention back to the job at hand. There were footprints and blood everywhere, but the frantic marks left by John struggling backwards with Harald, stood out clearly from all the others. He went back over to the make shift first aid area, removed his webbing and dumped the belt packs down on the table.

'Use this lot on Nigel too,' Jarli said as the slaughter men looked up from their improvised doctoring.

'These blokes have stemmed his bleeding,' Noah advised, as he made ready to move out with the corporal.

Jarli shook his head, 'You stay here, sort your hand out and get a proper ambo down here for Nige. I reckon John was hit bad too.'

'But,' Noah turned away from Jarli's beady eyes then unhappily nodded agreement to the order.

The corporal pulled Noah forward, removed the rifle from his friend's shoulder and set off to follow the sporadic heel prints and drag marks.

Noah walked over to a small booth screwed to a brick pillar, grabbed the phone off a supervisor in mid conversation and thumbed him aside.

'Hello who's this?' he asked of the female voice at the other end of line.

'This is Anne, who's that, where's Stan gone? I was just saying to him that…'

'Look here Annie, I'm sure you're a lovely Sheila, but I need you to shut your fly hole and listen,' Noah said firmly.

'Well I never,' Anne crowed.

Noah talked over her, 'Get an ambulance here quick as you can and put me through to the Station Hotel, or the police station.'

The telephonist made the necessary changes to her switchboard in stunned silence. Then, the last thing Noah heard before the call transferred was, 'For your future reference *sir*, my name is ANNE, with an E. NOT FLIPPIN' SHEILA!' Click.

As far as Jarli could see, the trail ended beneath a set of pale green double doors with porthole windows on the far side of the pillared room. He cautiously moved over to one side and yearned to peek through, but knew the ruthless German would most likely put a bullet in his eye if he did.

'What's inside?' Jarli shouted to a bald dome sticking out above a stone topped butchers table.

'Re, re, refrigeration and sto, sto, stores,' the slaughter man stuttered, resting his fingers and nose on the table's edge.

'Any other way out?' Jarli asked patiently.

'What, n, n, n...' The man attempted to reply, but he'd run out of words.

A middle aged woman in a bloodied apron popped up next to the man and explained quietly, 'The river tunnel's down there, past the refrigeration area, but it's been padlocked for weeks.'

'Any people down there?' Jarli urged.

The woman shrugged at first, then remembered with fright, 'Lucy and little Wayne were in there, cleaning down the racks.'

Half a dozen panicking pigs were rattling their pen to one side of the butchering bench. A trolley vat, with its empty tub half tipped forward, awaited their innards nearby.

Jarli ran over and quickly examined the vehicle's working parts. There were two simple levers, one with "BRAKE" embossed into the handle, the other said, "TILT". Jarli pushed the latter and as the bucket sprang back up he said, 'Help me get them hogs in.'

Between the three of them they loaded four wriggling pigs over the top of the tall container. At which point the stuttering man had had enough of being helpful and scooted off through the aisles. With the container full, the woman also backed away to join her beckoning colleagues across the room.

Jarli checked his weapon, clicked his neck and crouched down. The pigs jumped, kicked out and squealed violently as he heaved the wagon along the floor runners. It wobbled down the gouged cobble track and bumped through a branch connection, accelerating all the time. With a final surge of effort it slammed through the doors and into the cold storage area with Jarli tucked in behind.

Rapid rounds rang out, pinging off the truck's bucket. As soon as the doors had batted shut behind him, Jarli pulled back the lever to tip the enraged swine out. They tore around the available space in frenzy while Jarli hunkered down and kept pushing.

Ahead of him Harald fired another burst and three fat bodies slapped down around John's feet, oozing air and blood. The fourth pig took a bullet and cannoned sideways into a storeroom, evicting the two workers who'd been hiding inside.

The net result was two fleeing humans and one wild pig crashing around Jarli, just as he tried to jump up.

'Surprise,' the little scout grinned as his rifle caught on the trucks lever and clattered away.

Harald reacted quickly, ramming a hot gun barrel under John's chin and vowing, 'I kill him.'

Jarli raised his arms slowly, allowing the civilians time to escape. In a much faster motion Harold braced himself against the wall and raised a boot.

The trolley jolted back, its corner knocking the wind out of Jarli who slumped over and moved away with it. The little scout watched helplessly while the abductor dragged John away and disappearing down the corridor, which curved off into distant darkness.

Harald rapidly reversed along the cold tiled wall for some time until his buttocks discovered a dead end. A wide singular exit, which felt like it was padlocked shut.

'What is way out?' Harald demanded angrily from his hostage.

John wanted to give an uncooperative shrug, but the bullet in his shoulder prevented that. 'Must be a fire escape somewhere, right?' he snorted through the pain. 'Let me go and I'll have a look for you, eh?'

Reverberations of the last injured pig floated down the curved passage. It was still squealing whilst clattering around in the cold-room. Harald shushed John and listened as the pig lived a second more of struggle and gave a grunt, accompanied by an echoing click that faded into grim silence.

'God's truth,' John whispered, 'the corporal's coming down here to kill *you* now.'

Harald swore in German and turned, holding John up by the throat as the passage lights began flickering on in the distance. The men struggled in the approaching strobes until John went limp and slid down like an unloved doll. Harold used his last bullets on the exit, stepping back to fire three single shots into the padlock.

Jarli stayed low, but kept moving. As John heard his corporal coming he stopped feigning death and wrapped his legs around the big German's feet. Harald grunted, yanked open the heavy cast doors and tried to drag John inside. Failing to move far, the German smashed the machine gun on John's bleeding shoulder and leaned in to free himself. John used the surge of pain to launch himself up and grabbed near Harald's belt with his good arm. A solid backwards punch knocked the skinny Australian back to the ground again with a thud.

Jarli was down on one knee, waiting for a line of sight that wouldn't hit John. When Harald lurched out of the man-tangle, the corporal shouted a clear and threatening, 'HALT!'

The bullets impact made Harald spin around. As his body slumped he nodded respectfully at John and fell backward through the open doorway. John dropped the smoking Luger he'd taken from his assailant's belt. As the adrenaline depleted and his energy level fell to zero he lay back down and panted heavily next to Harald's bloodied boots.

Jarli came forward, rifle trained in anticipation that this panther might yet pounce again. Close up he could see that there would be no more rounds in this fight. The entry wound was in Harald's groin, the exit through his left side. Dark blood pulsed out, flowed down the floor's trolley track and pooled inside the room ahead.

The corporal checked John over first then moved in to try and slow Harald's bleeding. After a few more seconds Noah cautiously appeared with a group of burly workers in tow and ran down to attend to Private Crook.

'Is Nige alright?' was the first thing John asked as they helped him up.

'Nige, he'll be right,' Noah assured his friend and dropped the remains of Jarli's belt kit next to Harald.

Jarli grabbed some bandage packs and tore them open. Two workers supported John between them while Noah and Jarli worked to slow down the German's demise.

Before John was taken away Noah had to ask him, 'Why did you two drongos let this toey bastard out? Me and the corporal had him cornered.'

John stopped and turned his head, 'We heard two shots and Nige shouted, "Is that you blokes?". Then that Nazi hoon answered, "This is Jarli mate, open up!". John shook his head, knowing it was a stupid move and that things could have ended better.

'You should have double checked, not just believed him,' Noah scalded.

'But I'm a believer,' John smiled as he was helped away.

'A believer in what John?' Noah called after him.

'Most things,' John's voice echoed back down the curved corridor.

Noah shoved some wadding into Harald's side and stated, 'Bloke's gotta believe in something I guess?'

'Could have been worse mate,' Jarli pointed out.

'I *believe* you're right mate, Noah laughed, shaking his head.

Harald started to come around, grabbed Noah's sleeve and spluttered, 'We all believe, in fear. I afraid of you, you of me,' he coughed bubbles of blood. 'We both should fear the black soldiers.'

'Now hold on mate,' Noah said sternly.

Jarli looked up, he didn't seem offended.

Harald laughed then screwed up his eyes in pain and explained, 'Not him, not your black owl.' He gasped for air then added, 'I was near, when they plant the traps and stab your friend.'

'Did someone get an ambo?' Jarli shouted over to the growing parade of factory workers gathering around them.

'On the way,' Noah nodded as he got up to throw all the light switches inside the newly opened doorway.

As bulbs buzzed and clicked on around them illuminating the scene inside, the crowd gasped as one, but not at the blood, nor at the curious little corporal with his fingers buried deep in Harald's groin. The slaughter men were looking at something beyond all that, something which was much more unusual to see.

Harald let his head roll sideways to follow their view. Inside the previously locked under river chamber, there was an Aladdin's cave of goodies. Pipework, tiles, toilets and sinks were stacked high along the centre passageway. Overflowing pallets, crates and sacks of food and medical supplies lined the curved walls. 'Toiletten und milchpulver,' the dying man laughed through pink froth.

'Who them black soldiers?' Jarli asked hastily.

Harold beckoned him closer and whispered, 'No one is their friend. They think you German, with your motorcycle helmets and machine guns.' Harald placed a hand on the empty black gun by his side. 'The silver fist he chased me, but did not follow into tunnel of shit.'

'Probably afraid of the dark?' Noah kidded as Harald slumped back exhausted.

Jarli took out a water bottle and poured some in, but the patient coughed it all back out as he suddenly lifted his head again and cried, 'Blacker than you my friend, black faced green shadows.' With that and a deep, rasping last breath, Harald died.

199

Chapter Eighteen

The mass of unhappy pedestrians around the police station clearly wanted someone to hit out at, someone to blame for all the losses and the chaos. It seemed odd though, that their riotous ringleaders, men known to the police for petty crimes, would rally a protest sparked by the killing of their adversary, Chief Higgins. The local racketeers and thieves *had* risen to the occasion and were for once, doing a really good job.

Sergeant Roberts studied them from a small stairway window and worried, but not about the troublemakers and villains. He was more concerned about the previously innocent town people who were being sucked in to the vacuum. The commotion was like a human vortex, drafting in anyone curious enough to be drawn near.

Gossip about an injured German pilot heading this way had spread quickly down the valley. Phones rang, children ran messages, people whispered and the chants outside became more threatening and more graphic. Sergeant Roberts wanted to do something, but with no real manpower or ideas of his own, *what could he do?* No matter how sceptical, he would have to wait it out and stick to Major Jackson's orders.

When the vet's car appeared along a cobbled street to the left of the station, everything went quiet. The crocodile crowd opened its jaw to let the vehicle in, then instantly snapped shut and swallowed it whole. The throng of bodies had had enough of all this mess, enough of seeing no justice and of getting no revenge.

As the crowd swarmed in, Mr Gibbs and the vet were roughly manhandled from the car and cast aside. The two men bobbed up and down in the sea of hysteria, fighting for buoyancy until an odd bespectacled woman took Mr Gibbs by the hand. She tugged him over into a tiny void and winked at him from beneath her headscarf as she kicked back twice against the Artful Dodgers locked doors.

As soon as the car's front seats had been emptied, half the mob had tried to dive in. A snarling pack of hands and faces fighting to pull the German out from beneath the horse blankets on the back seat. Unfortunately, other than the blankets, the wide seat contained only a hat and some straw covering a medical bag and a half dozen Croft Farm eggs. Confused brawling broke out as more people crushed forwards while the front row of car raiders attempted to bail back out.

Around the surrounding buildings, the uproar from outside had triggered a more official response. The major organised his vehicles and rallied the men in the parade area behind the station as Captain Dreyer sorted out the police constables and a handful of soldiers in reception. Behind the mob the Artful Dodger's doors had opened to haul in the vet, Mr Gibbs and the woman who had winked at him along with two dozen women and children reaching the safety of the pub just before the doors were slammed and bolted shut.

'Any news of the vet and the farm manager Mr Roberts?' Captain Dreyer asked as the sergeant burst back into reception.

'They're fine,' Frank panted, 'I watched WPC Birch do her bit.' More panting. 'She got them and a bunch of stragglers through, she's safe too.'

Neville had been left alone to man the phones in the briefing room. As he sat there nervously biting his nails, the radio started to crackle and then a faint female voice began repeating something too quiet to make out. He quickly turned the volume up while gingerly nudging the tuner back and forth.

When Neville had got it just right, the voice repeated clearly, 'SD 9 CALLING ZERO 9, SD 9 CALLING ZERO 9. OB TWO NOT REPORING. OB ONE HAVE BEGUN ACTION, SEALED ORDERS COMPLETED. OB ONE WORKING TO THEIR PREPLAN NOW OVER.'

Neville scribbled a note of the frequency and message content and dashed out to find someone more important than himself. When the room was empty the message repeated again. If Neville had still been there he would have also heard a clunk and an older female voice moving closer.

The new voice said crossly, 'I don't know what you think your silly trap sounds like on there? What have you done to this? I can't even switch it off. Click, pop, click, pop, pop, pop. Well you do it then, if you think you're so damn clever. You really are an annoying little, CLICK.'

It was too late to stop the momentum of the riot outside. The group that had squeezed inside the vet's car were trapped by the others clambering up behind. All of them were trying to occupy the same space and half of them were oblivious to the fact that there was a severe lack of anyone to lynch.

As they circled like wasps on jam, a motorbike rolled slowly to a halt on the tarmacked road to the right of the police station. It was forced to slow down behind a loose gathering of less decisive agitators who were blocking the junction.

Justine saw the commotion ahead at exactly the same moment that *it* spotted her. She turned around them, smoothly mounted a dip in the pavement and accelerated along behind the puzzled protesters. Several yards later she turned the bike through a semi-open gate at the side of the police station and disappeared.

As the motorcycle revved along the passage and into the parade ground, it narrowly avoided being sideswiped by a large military truck.

An Australian soldier clinging to the cab door shouted a welcoming g'day, then pulled himself in tight as the lorry rounded into the cramped archway. At the end he slid down and shoved the side gate fully shut, latching the bolt. After a thumb up from him the truck lurched forward another yard, forming a solid barricade against the gates. Almost simultaneously, the rest of the building went into lock down.

On the pavement the noise rapidly multiplied at the same speed as the rushing mob. They crashed towards the side gate and poured up the front entrance steps, trying to gain entry. The ground floor was locked up tight, heavy doors shut, steel bars and blackouts down.

Out of sight at the rear of the building, everything seemed a lot calmer.

'You would be Miss Page, I presume?' the major said sharply.

'Are you in charge? I need you to help me find some people, right now.' Justine was clearly in no mood to argue the toss. The tone of her voice meant, *If you're not the person I need, then get out of my bloody way!*

Two soldiers moved in to take the weight of her pillion passenger as she unbuckled him from an improvised harness.

Major Jackson helped steady the handlebars and did his best to reassure her, 'Everything is very much in hand Miss. We have been looking for your friends with all our resources.'

Justine eyed him suspiciously as the German's weight was removed, then she angrily pulled the bike out of Jackson's grip and onto its stand.

The major moved his attention partially over to the new prisoner; he helped to steady the man then saluted and introduced himself.

You could almost hear the ribs grinding as Rudolf's body moved to attention, without asking his brain for permission first. His arm made it half way up then stopped dead, so the major gingerly shook the German officers hand instead.

'Second Leutnant Rudolf Furch, Luftwaffe, number 924...'

The major cut him off, 'We don't have the time. Having a bit of a mufti-day you see? Non uniform, you know?'

Rudolf shook his head bemused and stared around at the major and his men, who were all in full uniform.

Jackson continued unabashed, 'It will be a while before you get to the hospital now Lieutenant, sorry. We considered diverting you on route, but there just wasn't the time.' He waved a hand around the parade ground and said with a smile, 'This is plan B. You alright to walk?' The commander strode off towards the police stations rear entrance, not bothering to await his reply.

'Yes, I am being a lot better now,' Rudolf admitted, hobbling along behind at half the major's pace. 'The horse doctor has given me the needle stitches and strapped up the ribs you see?'

The major stopped and turned to look, there was a large bandage wrapped around Rudolf beneath his torn leather jacket. 'Looks *smart-as*, but we must push on now Lieutenant so, this way please.'

'This is why I am to travel with the lady, I could not, into the car get.' Rudolf stayed where he was and patted his chest very softly.

Major Jackson nodded, 'Yes we heard about that.'

'The other English lady has gave me much water and a small food, also many Schnapps yes?' Rudolf smiled.

The major shook his head and scurried back to hold the lieutenant's arm. 'It sounds like you've landed on your feet. Sorry, no pun intended. Come on we have to hurry.'

Justine dismounted and took something out of a small leather tool bag that swung beneath her seat. She tucked it back into her rear waistband then swung around to confront the major again.

'Please hurry *Miss* and we'll help each other reach the same footy post,' Jackson called back, pausing just long enough for her to scowl at him and catch up.

The three figures moved off unsteadily toward the building, leaving the men outside to complete their work. The first truck had been abandoned in gear, to block the archway gates. You could hear the crowd banging the wrought iron against its heavy bumper, but to no avail. The second truck had been reversed up to a loading bay off to one side of the main building. Once in position, the driver bailed out, moved the motorbike into a shadowy corner out of harms way then hid himself too. The rest of the men grabbed weapons and equipment from the truck, cleared the courtyard and ran inside to do their part in plan B.

The major was already inside. 'Please take a seat Lieutenant,' he urged to the prisoner as he directed the way into Captain Dreyer's briefing room.

Justine waited in the corridor as four soldiers pushed through with a heavy looking filing cabinet, balanced sideways on a porter's trolley.

'Ah Captain Dreyer, this is Lieutenant Rudolf Furch and Miss Page.'

Neville nodded a hello as Justine entered the room suspiciously. She sat down in a huff, folded her arms and legs then proceeded to waggle her foot impatiently. Rudolf remained standing, leaning on the back of his chair for support. He was sobering up and worried that sitting down would start off that firecracker pain in his ribs again. Dreyer and Cartwright moved towards the major so that they could talk discreetly.

'The radio sir,' Neville whispered excitedly, 'a woman's voice came out of it.' He took a scrunched up note from his top pocket and handed it to the major.

There was a pause while the major deciphered Neville's scrawl. 'Interesting,' he eventually said. 'And did you recognise the voice Private?'

'No sir, very English she was mind, like the BBC. We heard a similar thing the other day, up at the lookout post on Kings Hill. Should I see if I can find the signal again?' Neville started to move off towards the radio.

'Not now son,' Dreyer called out.

'Professor what do you know?' The major ushered his captain further from the new prisoner and Justine.

Dreyer turned back to his commander and quietly said, 'I don't know what to think right now. I bet this young lady has a lot of the answers that'll open things up, but that will have to wait a tick or two. The press men have agreed to stick with us and help sort out the print works for you. So long as they ultimately get an exclusive?'

The major looked down at the note Neville had given him, 'Starting to wonder how much we'll be able to give them to be honest Prof,' he sighed. 'Or how much they'll be allowed to print?'

Justine had started drumming her fingers on the wooden chair base. 'I don't have time to sit here, I'm going to talk to Mr Roberts or one of them detectives.' She stood up and stormed past the whispering officers, insisting very loudly, 'Now!'

As Cartwright gave her a look of embarrassed pleading she turned to face him and hissed, 'No offence Nev, but I want to speak to a proper policeman and if...'

Justine trailed off, suddenly aware of her lovers name along with her friends and colleague's names laid out on the room's blackboards. It was alarming for her to see the women's names on what must be, she presumed, a missing persons list. Most worryingly, her name was there too and it had been underlined with vigour.

'What the?' she pointed at the list and glanced over all the other scribbled notes and sketches about Germans and people being stabbed, shot and potentially blown up.

'We will explain everything soon, but we've got a tiny bit of soldiering to do first,' the major insisted.

'Tell me what the hell is going on around here,' Justine scowled, 'because every time I wake up things have gone, madder.'

'There is real danger here. Trust the major and do what he says. They really are trying to help,' Neville pleaded with absolute confidence.

Everyone jumped as a succession of eggs and a medicine bottle broke against the crack-crazed window to confirm his point. They jumped again when the phone rang and Dreyer took the call.

Justine put her hands on her hips, threw back her head, huffed then said, 'So, what can *I* do to help?'

'Just be ready to go quickly. Neville will get you up to speed on the gist of things,' the major smiled and moved away to leave them to it.

Before reaching the door, Captain Dreyer passed the commander a hand written note and told him, 'This is the latest from the hotel, I mean HQ.'

Major Jackson read it and digested the contents. He sighed, turned back to Rudolf and said solemnly, 'We have news of your officer, Harold Josten. He was killed, attempting to escape.' Then in a much more direct tone he clarified, 'There were six of you, right?'

Rudolf nodded.

'We have Rees and Peter, here in the building. The two young boys,' the major looked to his captain for their names.

'Karl and Elias sir,' Dreyer contributed, 'Karl is at the hospital, recovering from a gun shot injury and I'm sorry Lieutenant, but Elias was killed last night.'

'This is most sad news, it was Elias first mission and Unteroffizier Josten, Harald, well he was a good friend, a good German.'

'He shot three of my men. Might have been him who stabbed my sentry last night and it's still possible that he shot a police man,' Captain Dreyer snorted.

Rudolf didn't seem to care, he cocked an ear to the ever growing noise outside on the street and asked, 'All this anger, this is because of the bombs and Harald? Or, or because *we* are prisoners in here? Ah, I see it, they wish to find some satisfaction in me and my men, yes? They wish us dead also?'

'Can't blame 'em really,' the major said with a shrug. He edged closer to the windows to gauge the current level of animosity below. 'I don't reckon they're big fans of us Aussies right now neither.'

Behind him the German officer stood to a semi-attention, as best he could and stated, 'This is war, no? I admit it was not our primary mission, all of this that I see on the journey here, but...'

'You were sent to bomb a bloody airfield, not an innocent town,' Captain Dreyer said angrily.

'Innocent?' Rudolf shook his head nonchalantly, 'One of my men, he thought bombing it would be good for to save me, to save our aircraft. I am not sure if he considers the consequence for everyone else, but is this town innocent? Is anyone innocent any more?'

Dreyer turned away.

'Never parachute into a town you've just bombed, eh?' the major mused out loud. 'First rule you fly boys get taught, I would have thought?' He straightened his hat and walked over to interrupt Neville's briefing, 'Miss Page, you said you wanted to help. Please assist the lieutenant on his way down to the cells.'

She looked confused, but nodded and offered Rudolf her arm.

'Lieutenant if you go with Miss Page one of my men will show you both the way,' Jackson said dismissively then gave a long blow on his whistle.

The soldier on guard outside the briefing room door leaned in, beckoning Justine and Rudolf to follow him.

The major took one last look around the room, addressing Dreyer and Neville, 'So you two Sheila's know the plan right?'

'Simple really, we bravely stay here and keep our heads down while you run away. The angry mob outside come in and, to quote your earlier statement, they "hopefully" won't bother to kill us.' Dreyer was trying not to sound too sarcastic, but it was difficult.

'You make it sound a lot worse than it is Prof. Keep the door locked. Barricade it if it makes you feel better, just pull your necks in till Mr Roberts gives the all clear. Besides, there's always the fire exit.' He pointed to the window where bric-a-brac was still occasional bouncing off the frames.

'Do we wait for them to set fire to this place first then sir?' Dreyer frowned.

Major Jackson left them with a smile, closing the door behind him. Someone inside turned the lock, furniture scraped and that, was that.

As the commander walked along the emptying corridors he blew his whistle three more times. That was all his men needed to know. They abandoned the main building, leaving only the major, a handful of constables and Sergeant Roberts stood to attention behind his desk.

207

'Is everything in place here Sergeant, and did you get me those pictures of all the missing people?' the major asked as the hammering on the locked outer door became more and more frenzied.

Mr Roberts gulped and nodded, handing over a fan of images. 'Best I could do, Patrick is the thug in the first mug shot, and this is a blow-up from the Harvest Festival. It's not perfect, but I've ringed all the faces and numbered them on the back left to right. I'm still waiting for pictures of the women.'

'Are you sure you're happy with this little stage show?' Jackson asked while tucking the images into a pocket.

Roberts answered firmly, 'Yes sir.'

'Bonzer, I'll pass the pictures on, soon-as.' The major took out his revolver and placed it on the desk. 'Please take this. I recommend you keep it out of sight and close at hand. Mind, you'd be best to shoot the ceiling, not the public, *if* everything goes wrong.'

'Thank you, but I have a small collection of handguns in the safe and the armoury. Plus the Home Guard rifles locked away upstairs,' Roberts insisted as he pushed the Australian's weapon back toward its rightful owner. 'I think we'll manage without.'

Jackson returned it to his holster with a nod. 'Now,' he said tapping his fingers on the desk, 'I think it's time to depart? Sorry to leave you in the lurch. Can you spare someone to come along and close the door behind us?'

On the street outside there was a disconcerting drop in the droning as some individuals started to think and act, instead of just stand and shout. Not many of them at first, but enough to form a few small ideas that rippled out from those growing pockets of activity.

Sitting at the epicentre of it all was the vet's car. Other than a couple of dents, a cracked window and bent mirrors, the stocky little vehicle had remained relatively undamaged. It was still upright and even ticking over quite nicely. A small man in overalls was the first to see that idea form. He and his flat cap climbed inside and revved the engine. While his cigarette drooped at the lip, his friends cleared a path toward the gates. There was real anticipation as the revving continued and the glowing tobacco burned away in time beneath the caps shadow. When the cigarette tipped swiftly up, the onlookers hushed and drew breath, awaiting the inevitable collision noises as the car sped forward and struck the gates.

That did not happen. Instead the man took it very slowly as he found a gear and rolled gently over the cobbled street. On reaching the entrance there was a dull and modest clang as metal kissed metal and the car began to apply pressure on and off. As more people cottoned on, they flocked behind the automobile and rhythmically pushed, rocking the gates and the truck beyond. It was quite exactly David and Goliath, because the man in the flat cap just happened to be called David and the truck had its biblical name stencilled in white above the grill. The pressure pulses were *just* enough. Half an inch at a time they began to slowly move Goliath back.

From the top steps, at the main door of the police station another group watched the activity below as another idea began to form around them. A long pew like bench to the side of the doors was quickly converted with a simple realignment in space, to use as a battering ram. It was just a case of coordinating enough people to move away and let five strong men pick it up. The windows went first and then everything stopped as someone delicately reached in and released the bolts and blocks. After that brief pause and a colossal cheer, the resulting cascade of shouting bodies piled over each other through the foyer, advancing in a surge of motion and noise that swept toward reception like lava. It burst through the inner doors with a crack and spilled out in front of Sergeant Robert's desk, ready for action. At which point, nothing really happened.

In the same way that a huge wave hits a sea wall and rolls back to wipe out the next crest, so the noise and rage was dying away amongst the foaming mass. The desk's high oak panels acting like a dam against the decelerating yet still vociferous flood of heaving chests and flailing arms.

Sergeant Roberts stood firm, when he moved it was unhurried, almost graceful. He was using skills learned long ago in battle, coupled with experience gained as a policeman in this town. Most of all he used perfect timing, which had been more recently developed in amateur dramatics. Looking up briefly from a newspaper on the desk, he turned a page then took a casual sip of tea.

It was not just the sergeant's nonchalant response, which had an effect on the mob. As they quietened, their interest had moved to a tune which was crackling out from an old and battered gramophone set up to the side of the sergeants desk. Its orchid trumpet towered above everyone's heads, feeding a sweet piano solo into their souls.

'Good morning gentlemen, ladies,' Roberts eventually said. He put down the mug of tea and looked slowly around into all of their eyes. 'How can I help you on this lovely sunny day?'

A tall man standing directly in front of the sergeant raised an accusatory finger and then forgot what he was going to say.

'Can I have that paper after you please?' the constable behind Sergeant Roberts asked informally.

Without taking his eyes off the front row of faces, Roberts folded the paper and passed it back. As the music tinkled on he asked again, 'How can I help you?'

John Stokes, a local car dealer and serial felon, pushed through to the front of the group. He was not as stuck for words. 'You know exactly what we want Frank,' he shouted, banging a fist down hard on the desk.

The gramophone needle jumped clumsily out of its groove, causing the arm to skid off towards the centre. There it remained, clicking and popping, popping and clicking as the turntable continued to spin.

With the music dead, the crowd came back to life. Their voices filling the void with slants that morphed rapidly into threats, threats aimed toward the policemen and anyone else helping to keep the Germans safe.

At the side of the building the gates had been opened enough for a teenage girl to squeeze through. There was a sudden lurching breach as she found and threw the brake then clunked the truck into neutral. She steered it well, rolling backwards with body after body joining the strident throng. The first mob roared around the lorry as it clipped a wall then curved away and settled in the courtyard, but there was no one there to meet them. Apart from the other army wagon and an old horsebox, the parade ground was empty. There was some confrontational shouting as the gang pulled up canvas curtains and searched the trucks for any signs of life. Again they were disappointed, first the vet's car, then the trucks and courtyard, each time there was nothing on board.

It took but a moment to unanimously decide what to do next. Seeing the buildings open back doors they migrated on mass up the steps to join the on-going melee in reception.

As the numbers surged, Sergeant Roberts casually removed the needle from the record and placed it safely on its rest. 'I would presume,' he began, but as he spoke the crowd took a while to stop and listen. He waited patiently then tried again, 'I would presume that you lot want me to hand over my prisoners, right?'

No one replied at first, some nodded excitedly then looked away embarrassed.

'We want justice,' shouted one of the few women at the front of the group. Several others patted her on the back and agreed loudly with the comment.

'JUSTICE, JUSTICE?' the sergeant boomed, doing his very best *Mr Bumble* impression. Then in order to remain calm he stole a second to compose himself.

'Up yours Frank,' a short someone remarked from the back.

Before anyone could add more, two constables clattered out of the main entrance to the cells. This drew everyone's attention sideways and the PC's did their very best to block the protesters as they swelled toward the opening. Inevitably, there was a scuffle as they tried in vain to push back the bodies nearest to them.

'Stand aside men,' Roberts ordered clearly. 'These citizens have a right to their "Justice", let them through.'

His men dutifully broke away and took up positions on either side of the welcoming entrance.

'Hang about, hang about, where's all the Aussies?' Stokes asked with suspicion in his eyes.

'You frightened them all away,' Roberts said folding his arms.

'I seen that Major skulking off to the department store ages ago,' a voice at the back recalled. 'I seen a few of 'em creeping off too,' another voice chimed in, but with apparent less certainty than the first.

'Last chance,' Sergeant Roberts persisted. 'Some of you know the way down without a guide, eh Monkey? Or Mr Stokes, perhaps you would prefer to lead the way?'

211

A cheer went up as the overexcited crowd pushed Stokes reluctantly towards the entrance. The double doorway opened onto a wide corridor, at the end of this two much stronger doors stood open and unguarded, allowing access to a wide stone staircase.

'I bet you've fallen down these a few times eh Monkey?' Mr Stokes said to the town's unluckiest criminal as the scrawny man pushed his way up to the font.

'Are, but never on paper John,' Monkey laughed.

The Witch Hunter duo forged their way down, rolled up sleeves and shepherded the flock of vengeful villagers down into the depths. At the bottom there was another long corridor looping back towards an area below reception. Monkey was the first to reach the main door of the cellblock itself. He grinned a gappy smile at John Stokes as they pushed down the handle together.

Once the door was open Mr Stokes flourished his hand saying, 'You first Monkey, my good man.'

Beyond the door was a little anti-room with a desk, a chair and a large filing cabinet standing against one wall. The opposite wall held the final door, which separated the gleeful group from their targets.

'You first this time Mr Stokes,' Monkey said while bowing to his friend.

John had no choice anyway. Both men were jostled inside, thrust along by the others surging behind them, pushing and shoving to see what lay beyond the cast iron entrances. The men and women tumbled into a long tiled corridor that ran off left and right. In front of them and stretching away into the distance, were the individual cell doors. Ten of them, all dark blue, solid and shut.

'They'm in them two down there,' Monkey pointed off to the left.

Mr Stokes raised a questioning eyebrow.

'Spent the night down 'ere yesterday I did,' Monkey shrugged. 'They diddled me for shopping out of hours like, down near the old post office.' He guided the men and women down to the end cells.

The names of Rees Heikling and Peter Albrecht were chalked on two matte black squares on the substantial doors. Rudolf's name had been added to a third cell, further along.

'New lad,' Monkey smirked, 'must be that pilot.'

'Hello in there,' John Stokes wrapped firmly on the riveted surface with his knuckles. 'We 'ave come to take you outside for a nice *little* walk.' There was no answer so he flipped open the spy hole and peered around. 'Aww bless him, he's hiding under the bed.'

Everyone laughed at this.

'Don't be afwaid little Nazi pigzy wigzy.' Stokes mocked as he slammed down the handle with one hand and released a bolt with the other.

The door swung open and he stepped inside, quickly checking both sides in case the German was waiting to surprise them. Monkey followed and together they flipped the bed upside down, but there was no one cowering beneath. It was the same in the other two cells.

Monkey had an epiphany. 'Of course,' he shrieked, slapping a hand to his forehead.

'What?' Stokes grabbed Monkey by his jacket collar. He was starting to realise they'd been had too and wanted to know how.

'That room we come through,' Monkey smiled before pulling away and pushing his way back to the antechamber. 'Oh I'm so stupid.'

Many of the people around him agreed loudly while they awaited a fuller explanation.

'This room, it's also the court's underground entrance, it takes you to the dock in the courts next door.' Monkey pushed his way through into the little office space. 'That big cabinet, it warn't there when I left this morning.'

Mr Stokes followed him in and together they heaved over the giant filing cabinet. It clattered down sideways, revealing a door in the wall behind. It was made of solid steel and heavily locked, from the other side.

Echoing thumps travelled along the passage as two more thick metal doors were closed off above them in reception. These cells were designed to hold back an angry bunch of prisoners. Which is exactly what they were doing now.

The only prize the mob could find in their dismal pit, was a storeroom with a load of salad sandwiches, four empty buckets and half a dozen urns filled with water.

The only natural light in the prison block came from a row of small slit windows, one in each cell. Monkey climbed on the bench in cell nine and looked through the thick glass and iron bars. Out on the parade ground at surface level, he saw a distorted set of soldier's boots drop down in front of his face.

The driver had been lying on top of his truck in a roll of tarpaulin, waiting for Mr Robert's "all clear". After jumping down he bent over and smiled at a correspondingly distorted face trapped inside.

Monkey shouted something extremely rude, but only his friends could hear him clearly. He continued to add phrases to this little string of expletives as the truck reversed away and out of sight.

Back in reception the two constables whom Mr Roberts had ordered to stand aside, returned to his desk and placed some large old-fashioned keys upon it. Mr Roberts was busy examining a new scratch on his record.

'Oh dear, did that get damaged Sergeant?' asked one of the men.

'Seems to be all right, I think I can polish it out,' Mr Roberts replied.

'What was it anyway?' the constable behind him asked.

'It's Johnny Mercers, Fools rush in,' Sergeant Roberts said smiling and sliding the thick record back into its paper sleeve. 'I never really liked it before, but now I think it's become one of my favourites.'

The sergeant pulled across his ledger and began to fill in the events of the last hour or so. When he realised the men were standing around waiting for further orders, he looked up and asked politely, 'Can you put the gramophone back in the evidence room for now please, oh and someone make us another pot of tea will you. Cheers lads.'

Chapter Nineteen

As Elijah opened one eye and struggled free from his clammy blanket cocoon, he wondered if his life would be lived entirely in the dark from now on? At first his mind had to conjure up its surroundings from memory, rather than actually being able to see them. It was uncomfortably cold and damp down here. The only light in the room came from a solitary snub of candle, which drooled flickered from a slot in the opposite wall.

The strongest sounds and fragrances were emanating from Patrick some distance away, thankfully. As far as Elijah could ascertain, the enormous Irishman was currently taking a dump and eating an apple simultaneously. Down here there was a faint yet constant flow of air that blew over them like bad breath. It generally repeated the same odours over and over in an endless loop. Never refreshing, but absorbing everything else into a mixture of gun oil, smoky sweat and stale farts. Elijah preferred to wake up to the waft of his mother's bacon butties or a fried egg roll, whenever possible.

Quiet gunmetal clunks, swearing and finger sucking sounds occasionally came from Edward in a small room at the opposite end of the dark cavity. It suggested he was assembling something very badly next door.

'Finn?' Was the first solid question that popped into Elijah's head and out through his mouth. It echoed back into his ears before he'd really realised the word had escaped.

'Sure we're all brothers now sonny boy,' Patrick shouted with a distant grunt. After a few seconds of quiet contemplation he drifted off into a quieter moan about the lack of dry quality toilet paper down here. 'Given us everything we need so they have, except decent feckin bog papers.'

'Finn is still up on lookout,' Edward said as he came in with a tin mug. 'We thought you should have a bit of extra kip, seen as you had such a restless night.'

A torch came on beyond an archway as Patrick read disembodied from the box in his hand, 'The greatest necessity of the age it says, "Gayety's medicated paper for the water-closet". My arse. Mam uses this rubbish downstairs at the café, but upstairs we have the good stuff.'

'Are you alright now?' Edward asked Elijah.

'I just keep seeing that man's eyes,' Elijah shuddered while accepting the mug. He sighed disappointed that the cup was so cold and most likely contained only spring water. He tried to sound more confident by adding, 'It was so dark last night, I'm amazed we saw anything at all.'

'Forget what you saw, it's the best way,' Edward suggested.

'Not just what I seen, there was a muffled shout too,' Elijah continued. 'It was the last word that Gerry made.' Elijah stood up to stretch and clattered the cup against something nearby. 'You know I've killed things; chickens, foxes, sick and injured animals on the farm, but I've never...'

Edward gave him a little one armed hug around the shoulder. 'He was the enemy and you likely saved Pat's life too, you know?' Edward reassured Elijah with another squeeze.

'Oh, saved my life did he? I can look after my flaming' self you know.' In the distance Patrick farted, dropped his apple core into the slop bucket and hauled on his trousers. 'My people have been watching their own backs for centuries, from all you bloody English, long before the Germans started,' he ranted on.

Re-entering the main chamber, Patrick picked at an ear then examined his fingertip in the candlelight. The movement made the little wisp of flame and carbon flicker more. Elijah studied what little he could make out of the darkly dressed figure. The big man looked different now, ever so slightly smarter. Especially in this very low light, as you couldn't quite make out the stubble or missing teeth. The simple uniform and a hand made woolly shepherds hat, gave the thug a look of belonging and purpose. Elijah determined that Pat had the appearance of a boiler man rather than a soldier. Either way, it was an improvement from his string vest and shorts.

'Seriously,' Pat stopped and thought about what had been said so far. 'Thanks a million for what you did kiddo.' He reached out and found the curly head in the gloom, then patted him on the cheek. 'To be honest, we don't think you killed him. Well not outright any ways.'

'Leave it,' Edward stepped forward and quickly explained the latest news to Elijah, before Pat could interrupt, 'Finn didn't want to say anything before, but when you were sleeping...'

'What?' Elijah insisted.

Edward was still hesitant. 'He, well he said there was talk of a stabbed German up at the hospital.'

Elijah was elated and instantly sad in the same moment. 'Dead or alive?'

'Makes no difference,' Edward said sharply. 'Just chalk it up to experience and move on.'

Patrick decided to help reconstruct the previous nights activity, 'After you stabbed that Gerry, when we moved off, I found him again, sort of tripped over him in the dark. He was still groaning a bit like, so I gave him a good kick and his little helmet came spinning off. I thought it was his whole head at first.'

Elijah sat back down, a little woozy and took a sip from his sloshing mug.

Patrick looked towards Edward who was slowly shaking his head and asked. 'What, seriously what?'

Edward rubbed his eyes, 'Just stick to the main facts Pat, please.'

Patrick rolled his eyes up remembering, 'So I went to finish him right, but well, it looked like he was done for. Sure the man was all blood, froth and bubbles you know? So I didn't waste any time on making more noise.'

'But he wasn't, was he?' Elijah said angrily.

'Like I said I thought he was a goner, but?' Pat scratched at his hat to relieve an itch.

'Well it seems he made it as far as the hospital and that's all we know. Now how about some biscuits and jam?' Edward asked in an attempt to move on.

'I need to speak to Finn ,' Elijah insisted.

Edward put a hand on the lads shoulder to hold him back. 'You can speak to Finn soon. You know the daytime rule, one man on watch and everyone else down here.

Patrick ducked down to look beyond the nearest doorway. 'Oh is that right, so where has Mr Marvellous disappeared himself off to then?'

Edward looked at his watch but couldn't make out the hands very well. He considered the timing in his head and added, 'He went to relieve Finn.'

217

'Lucky mare he is, getting to stretch his legs. Why do I have to stay all cramped up in this feckin tomb? I can do lookout?' Pat sat down grumpily on a crate.

'Because you have things to prepare down here,' Edward sighed. He was getting sick of answering the same questions all the time. 'You know we're lucky really? At least we *can* stretch our legs occasionally and we have plenty of options for escape in a crisis.'

'You realise this place also has the disadvantage, of there being a few too many ways *in* too?' he warned, still snorting. Patrick had done his crash courses in terrorism at a different location to the others. While they had been learning how to be more mole-like, Pat had spent his training days blowing things up on the surface.

'Most of the other operational bases are a lot less cosy than this one,' Edward went on.

'Haven't you seen 'em up at Coleshill House?' Elijah asked.

Pat shook his head, 'Nah, I was supposed to be going up to Coleshill with Harry this month.'

'Only one way in and one emergency way out. Can you imagine that?' Elijah sat up distracted from his other thoughts for a moment. 'They only have a dinky room and it's not much bigger than a gypsy caravan, made of elephant iron and covered in soil. Horrible they are, nothing quality, not like this.'

Patrick laughed at the fact that this boy wanted to celebrate the splendour of their overcrowded grotto.

Edward ignored the discussion; he was too busy toasting the Radium dial of his watch near the candle.

'Least we can store more than most and have it near to hand,' Elijah argued. 'Those Royal Engineers did us proud when you look at it in the light,' he insisted, patting some of the newly laid brickwork behind his head.

'We can't look at it can we, it's always too fecking dark to see anything.' Pat tried to find his cigarette papers in the multitude of pockets and pouches his uniform offered. When located, they were so moist that they had stuck together like a paper concertina. 'Why didn't you ask me to relieve Finn on watch?'

Edward had moved away and gone back to cleaning his gun next door. He paused for a moment and called back as calmly as possible, 'Because, you're so bloody big and noisy. You're a good explosives man I grant you, but you ain't no ballerina.' Something pinged away from Edward's grip, followed by the word, 'Bollocks.'

'I can be quiet,' Patrick assured them, then accidentally knocked something over with his size thirteen boot.

In frustration Edward slammed down the remaining weapon parts and switched to a much more official tone, 'When Harry left you were off taking a dump and as I keep saying, you need to prepare some more explosives for tonight.'

'Too bloody dark,' Pat said quietly while trying to separate a cigarette paper from the bunch.

Edward had had enough. He came back in, lit another candle and used it to find all the things required to get the storm lamp working.

As the mantle burst into life, they were all blinded and amazed by the difference in their surroundings. There were boxes, bags and bits of this and that stacked up everywhere. Almost every package had the same clearly stencilled purposes of death or destruction. There were one or two luxuries dotted around too; a tiny stove, some bunks, rations, water and even a gallon jar of rum.

On the whole it should have been alarming to be suddenly reminded that you were in an enclosed compartment filled with so much stuff that went bang. None of the men seemed too bothered. Instead their interest moved to a crate between two of the far bunks. Someone had placed a bowl of apples, a welcome to your new home card and a five-pronged candelabra on top.

'From my ma,' Pat smirked. 'House warming gift don't you know?'

'You didn't tell her we were down here did you?' Elijah gasped, astonished.

'Sure don't be daft,' Patrick dropped the smile. 'And I didn't tell her I was borrowing the family silver neither. I had to come by here the other day and I just thought, well you know? Seen as it was all nearly complete and that.'

'Very funny, here,' Edward handed the lamp to Pat. 'Now find what ever else you need and pack it away for later.'

Pat shrugged and got on with his job, disappointed that the others hadn't appreciated his joke. As he left for the main storeroom, the gloom swallowed the room again.

'I don't trust the dark,' Elijah said quietly. 'I think it's one of the worst things about all of this. That and the, well you know.'

'Is that why you didn't chase the other German guard into the pig tunnel last night?' Edward asked bluntly. 'Sorry, but I need to know?'

Elijah said nothing at first.

'Pat said you were great with the knife and then you just stopped and let the other man go?' Edward persisted.

'It was more a case of common sense, he was a very big bloke,' Elijah said eventually.

'So are you,' Edward pointed out. 'And Pat was coming to help.'

'But that second soldier would've had us in his sights, soon as we rounded the tunnel entrance. Plus the gunfire would've alerted every other German within a mile.' Elijah looked up and rubbed at his face. 'I pulled out soon as I heard that bloody Irish King Kong coming up behind me, then we both ran and found our way back here.'

'There you go then, so you did save Pat's life.' Edward sat down next to his friend.

Elijah was still feeling awful and would have bluffed it and puffed out his chest to any of the others, even Finn. 'Thing is, I thought I'd killed that man and it shook me up. There, I admit it.' It felt better to have said something out loud and it seemed safe to go on with Edward asking the questions. After checking to make sure Pat was still out of earshot he continued quietly, 'The strangest thing was the word the man said when I grabbed his face. It sounded like, "Cheeses".'

'Cheeses?' Edward gasped, trying to get comfortable on the damp blankets.

'All I can hear when I try and go to sleep now is CHEESES!' Elijah bit at a fingernail. 'What does that even mean?'

'Probably just a swear word. It's a very angry language. *I love you,* sounds like *get lost* in German.'

The conversation came to an abrupt end as Pat returned with some detonators and pencil timers in one hand, a paraffin lamp and lit cigarette in the other. The light came from below giving him an eerier appearance than usual. Some cable or fuse wire was coiled loosely around his neck and a wad of cotton was stuffed in his mouth. Edward thought it made Pat look like a big white-lipped minstrel or African idol with his up lit blackened face. When Pat spat the cotton out to talk, Elijah caught it.

'Did someone mention cheese?' the Irishman said, looking around for a snack.

The others couldn't be bothered to answer him with more than a sigh.

Pat waited for a few seconds then carried on regardless, 'What am I blowing up then?' He put down the lamp and took a drag on his damp roll up. 'I could really do with seeing what effect those bundles had on the tracks last night.' His eyes were bright, switched on and excited. 'Any chance we could swing by later and recce the damage?'

'NO!' Edward said firmly. 'Most likely it'll be harder this time, now they know we're here. Just do as much damage as you can. Stick to the plan. Take out the fuel and supply dumps before they get their mitts on it all.'

Patrick grumbled, 'I know what I'm doing, but I still need to see what I've done. Professionalism, you see? We could go that way round to the target, couldn't we?'

Edward shook his head, 'We are still on schedule, but it's tight. Should have been the munitions factory tonight, but they blew that up them selves. An' that's forced us to do tonight's raid close to yesterdays. It's gonna be tough enough, without you going off sightseeing on the way.' Edward started to cough as he ran out of breath and winced.

Elijah wanted to change the subject and let Edward calm down. He needed to confront one elephant in the room, before moving on to the other. 'You don't think that might be a bit dangerous do you?' he pointed out Patrick's burning cigarette, then nodded at the explosives and timers.

Pat looked from left to right and shrugged, 'In separate hands aren't they? That's safe enough, unless I decide to clap.'

Edward coughed again, he was clearly in a lot of pain. Elijah could see that Edward had a sweat on too, yet he looked pale and cold.

'This stuff is state of the art,' Patrick bluffed on, oblivious. 'They told me it's safe enough, until you stick all the bits together.'

'Just be careful. Things are chaotic down here already,' Edward spluttered.

'These are just toys, the good stuff is stuck over at the old quarry,' Patrick moaned.

'I needed more time,' Edward wiped some sweat from his brow with a shirtsleeve. 'Without Minnie, that'll be a long four man job now,' he said with some regret, leaning against a wall for support.

Elijah motioned towards Edward with his eyebrows and Patrick finally noticed Edward's discomfort.

'You still hurting?' Pat asked with rare concern.

Edward stood up straight, 'No, I'm fine. Just get out from under my bloody feet will you, so I can sort through all the sodding mess you've made.'

'My mess?' Patrick shrugged as he took another nonchalant drag on his soggy smoke.

Edward snatched away the roll-up, which sizzled out in his sweaty grip. 'New rule,' he snarled, 'no smoking in storage areas.'

Patrick would normally have punched something by now, but this time he shrugged it off and went away quietly to look for a kit bag.

Elijah broke the silence. 'Are you still bleeding?' he asked, knowing that Edward would probably lie.

'I think it's getting better?' Edward frowned and patted a hand on his abdomen. 'I get pains sometimes, when I move about too quick. Listen, can you store some of the more dangerous boxes in the other cavern?' Edward pointed at the supply crates around their feet.

'I will,' Elijah nodded, 'but I think we should have a good look at that wound first. Did Finn find anything better to dress it with at the hospital?'

Edward was more deflated now, his little burst of energy had taken an instant toll. 'Not really, more of the same, but it's a bit less damp.' He thumbed over his shoulder to the table in the other room where the medical kit was stacked. 'I was going to have a look later.'

'I think *now* would be best,' Elijah insisted.

Eventually, Edward gave in, pulled up his shirt and revealed a bandaged field dressing around his waist. It was not soaked, but there was still fresh blood coming through near his side. 'I got as far as this myself last night, not bad eh?'

Elijah carefully pushed past him, grabbing the ornate candleholder on the way. He lit all five wicks and placed it down on the table in the end room. 'Come in here,' the lad requested as he opened a cardboard first aid box. While rummaging through the contents he also noticed Edward's Sten gun, still half dismantled on the table top. 'You should put that back together first, just in case you need it.'

'I have tried to get that sodding spring in three times, then I decided to argue with Pat instead.' Edward admitted with a shamed face.

He moved around the table and lowered his aching body down onto a chair. It was a sorry sight.

'OK, forget the gun for now. I'll do it for you. Thing is, I think you might have bits of Minnie or maybe the bombs, still stuck inside you. That's what's slowing you up.'

Edward nodded without really thinking through what that meant.

'So I'll get them out,' Elijah said quickly as he examined a pair of curved scissors in the candlelight.

'What?' Edward got up with a sharp intake of breath and tried to move away.

There was a brief stand off and some muttered curses. Eventually Edward huffed, undid his shirt fully and leant against the nearest wall as if being frisked. This allowed Elijah to at least remove his friends dressing and have a proper look at the damage.

The official medical kit's contents included alcohol to clean the wound and a sterilisation pack for everything else. As Elijah rummaged deeper in the neatly packed box he pulled out a full morphine pack with syrettes of brown liquid, small dark blocks of soft resin and some shiny syringes. Most of the other paper parcels at the bottom of the bag had drawn in the damp from sitting around below ground for too long.

Elijah laid everything out then picked up Finn's yellow shoulder bag and tipped its contents on top.

'I think we should stick with the dry dressings Finn nicked,' Elijah said as he picked up some wadding.

'That morphine looks dry,' Edward joked. 'Give me some of that.'

'Alright then,' Elijah continued the joke to keep his friend's mind off the inevitable. He picked up one of the packets and began quoting the instructions out loud, "To administer segmented resin blocks. If the patient is in severe pain, but will recover, give a quarter block. If the patient is in severe pain, but may not recover, give a half block. *This will not inhibit recovery should it occur.* If the patient is surely to die, give one whole block. *This will cause them to pass more rapidly.*" Elijah found a bit of wooden packing for Edward to bite down on and set about his work.

'Better make it a whole piece then,' Edward hissed through gritted teeth.

After sterilising, Elijah prodded around as carefully as he could in the dim light and found several metallic fragments beneath Edward's skin. The puncture wounds were small, which made the tweezers difficult to use without causing a lot more pain.

Edward bit down hard on the wood in his mouth as tears rolled from the corners of his eyes.

The most difficult and hopefully final piece to remove was a half-inch rod of old barbed wire. It seemed to be just a tiny section, like a bent carpet tack, but it was deep in muscle. Elijah dragged the candelabra closer to the edge of the table, knowing he would have to relax the patient and get the barb out in one swift go.

Edward reached up and removed the wooden block to take a deep breath. 'Get on with it,' he urged before replacing the wedge in his mouth and tensing up in preparation.

'You know what Patrick said, about these being his mom's best silver?' Elijah asked.

'Mawf?' came the patients muffled reply.

'Well it made me think about my parents. Do you think they're alright, up there on the hill I mean?' Elijah dipped the tweezers into a mug of alcohol and sloshed them around in preparation.

'Meff!'

Slowly Elijah pushed deep and got a good hold on this end of the wire spike as Edward simpered. 'Only, I was thinking, would it be alright if I just popped over to see them and let them know we're alright?' he said, expecting a big reaction.

'Mo, moo oopern marnt,' Edward replied with amazing calm and control between his breaths.

'So I take it I can't pop along to the hospital and see how that injured German is doing either?' Elijah asked, softly bracing one hand against Edwards ribs.

That was it. Edward had heard it all now. He dropped his shoulders, relaxed his tight frame and began to turn his head just as Elijah yanked out the shrapnel in one quick plucking movement.

As the chunk of chewed wood flew forth from Edward's mouth, so did one of the longest barrages of curses Elijah had ever heard.

'You bloody, shitty, son of a bitch, useless, stupid scabby-cocked...' Edwards's words finally trailed off into a high pitched, simultaneous cry of relief and agony.

Elijah dropped the bloodied object into his metal cup along with the other bits of metal and sloshed them around.

Hearing the commotion, Patrick came back in to have a gander at the gory scene playing out ahead. His lantern illuminated all the random bits of metal, which mostly twinkled. All except for the fragment of barbed wire that was quite rusty and black.

'Feeling better?' Patrick asked.

Edward did not answer. Instead he stretched to look at the bloodied holes for himself. He did at least seem to be in a lot less pain and discomfort now. Then Elijah washed away the blood with a slosh of the surgical spirit and the swearing kicked off again.

'I think that was all of it. I can poke around a bit more if you want?' Elijah offered patiently beneath the noise.

'No thank you,' Edward eventually whispered sharply. 'Just patch me up and we'll leave it at that.'

'I think it would be best if you just lie down on the bunk and do nothing now,' Elijah suggested as he applied more alcohol, a dry field dressing and fresh bandage from Finn's haul. 'At least until the others get back.'

'Did you do all this at the training camp?' Patrick asked, examining the mug closely.

'No, just that mostly, our farm just can't afford to pay a vet,' Elijah said. 'We learned a bit in the scouts too, an' there's a lot in that handbook they gave us in that old calendar.' Elijah drifted away on a thought. 'Do you get the impression when you read that thing, that we're only gonna be here for a short time? Afore they finds us like.'

Patrick shrugged, 'Well we have enough weapons to take on the devil him self, but there's only enough grub to feed us for two weeks.'

Edward buttoned up his shirt and tried to think of a more positive slant on the information they had all been given. 'I hope it's more a case of us being reinforced by then and we can easily replenish the supplies.'

The conversation ended there as the lads let Edward settle down on a bedroll and curl up, almost comfortable at last. He'd only pretended to sleep before, lying there listening with his eyes closed. Lying to his self about the pain and the possible trouble he was in. This time it was completely different and after two tots of rum he was able to sleep, deep and comfortable.

When Finn returned and checked him over later, Edward didn't even stir.

'How long has he been out?' Finn asked, stowing his weapon on the rack.

'An hour or so I think. He still goes a bit hot and cold, but he's stopped mumbling now. We pulled all this out,' Elijah said as he held out the cup.

'Ewe, I was just about to drink that.' Finn smirked. 'He looks a tad better, well done.'

'Yes, I guess so,' Elijah agreed, 'at least, he does in this light anyway. I thought you was coming back ages ago?'

Finn had returned to the chamber via a long brick lined passageway. At the far end of it there was a ladder made up of iron rungs sticking out of the wall. If you climbed to the top of that you would find a trapdoor that opened out into an old abandoned access tunnel. The space in there was tiny and just big enough for a man to climb out and walk along while crouching.

Harry and Finn had both been through that trapdoor today, but you would not know it, or even that an entrance was there, unless you knew exactly where to look. From the outside the closed door looked like all the other square slabs of rock making up the floor.

In the outer access tunnel there was no light at all which meant you had to feel your way along until you escaped its claustrophobic shaft and entered the train tunnel proper. A seemingly locked iron gate covered in rotting planks separated the in from the out. What little light there was along the track came from the railway tunnels entrances, some way off in either direction. The dimmer end took you towards the countryside through embanked and tree-lined slopes. The brightest circle of light framed a Victorian viaduct which flew out over this side of the wide valley and on into high town.

Harry had been sat statue still, hiding behind the low wall of the viaduct for some time. Forty minutes earlier he had lain here next to Finn and debriefed all the things the lad had seen throughout the night. In the blackout Finn had seen very little, but you still had to ask.

In the daylight Harry could see for miles. He was extremely tired and had fallen asleep in the sunshine twice since Finn's recent departure. During each sleep he had drifted into the same dream of Justine and his mother being grabbed and tied to the tracks by bald, fat Germans with handlebar moustaches and pointy hats.

The nightmares played out in black and white, soundless movie style, with a dramatic organ accompanying the flickering frames. His beloved Justine wearing heavy makeup and a skimpy outfit like some dessert maiden. His mother was always dressed as a dark wintry widow, thrown to the earth by Germans as her weighty shopping bags spill out over the floor. Both women raising frail hands, palms out as they silently mouthed his name and a mute steaming engine approached them at speed.

When the dream train hit, he would always wake up and for one confused moment, expect to be splatted by the ghostly locomotive as it screamed past him and evaporated into the tunnel.

Harry knew he needed to stay alert and tried to make himself as uncomfortable as possible. He shook off thoughts of saving loved ones and concentrated instead on doing his job. It amounted to the same thing, sort of.

Harry knew that if a real train did come, he would hear it, feel it and eventually see it a long way off. A workman's cubbyhole was set back into the wall at the tunnel entrance and once inside he could remain invisible to any passing eyes. He had also organised access to the monthly maintenance rotas and each week's timetables, just in case.

During the debriefing, Finn had confirmed that Patrick's devices had gone off consecutively in the early morning. He also reported that after the pig train had come and gone, no more traffic had been sent this way. So at least the disruptive mission had worked, one way or another. Although the trains had not stopped arriving from other directions, the damage had prevented them from getting to the loading yards.

Harry peered into the heart of the town below and wondered if Patrick could muster enough materials to take one of the other lines out tomorrow. In Harry's head there were ambitious plans to blow up a section of the viaduct, but that would require more supplies from the quarry.

The most worrying thing was the amount of soldiers that kept appearing. Harry couldn't see any detail from this distance, even through binoculars, but the titchy military wagons were moving around near the railway yards and the police station regularly. Their shapes were not like his beloved British Bedford's. These trucks were ugly, long nosed things. Even their camouflage was different, a fuzzy sand and khaki green pattern.

It worried him. If the Germans were here in such numbers and so quickly, then the whole country must be overrun, or a large proportion of it at least. Harry had convinced himself that the beaches and harbours must be in enemy hands already, somewhere near by.

Soon after this thought, Harry woke up again slumped over the wall. It was no use being up here if he couldn't stay awake, so he decided to go and find a *volunteer* who could do the job properly.

When he got up his ankles went rubbery, his feet felt like clogs. It took a minute or two for the blood to recirculate and he made a mental note to be more careful. He swept gorse behind to hide any boot marks and hobbled back into the dark train tunnel.

The locked gate simply lifted on the hinge side and allowed enough room to squeeze by. In the darkness he ran his fingers along the wall at waist height until they passed over an indentation. Poking a finger up inside, he pressed a release. A square of floor clicked out an inch and he lifted it up and over before feeling for the edges of the hole. A moment later and the hatchway had gone again, becoming just another innocent rock slab.

When he returned to the main chamber everyone seemed to be asleep. Three of the bunks were full and something big was snoring from a neatly stacked row of crates at the far end.

Harry carefully woke Patrick up and whispered, 'Your turn up top Pat, I need a few hours kip.'

There were a few Gaelic curses for good measure, but the big man was generally happy to be vacating the uncomfortable crates to spend a few hours on watch outside while the others slept on.

Harry was surprised and pleased to find the candelabra. Once lit, it gave him enough light to look at the small map they had all helped draw up of every known track and route into and out of the town.

With so many Germans turning up it was going to be a lot harder to achieve their goals from now on. So far he and his men were ticking boxes and as long as they continued to do so, everything was worth the effort. He tried to consider every possible event that could occur later. Taking into account all the things that could go right, or wrong and how to move on from there.

In his mind an imaginary flow chart of possible outcomes formed in little bubbles, all joined together by dotted lines of footprints. After half an hour of this mind mapping, he blew out all but one of the candles, found his cot and fell into a deep sleep.

One of the other men silently counted off five minutes inside his head then very quietly got up. It was not a completely silent exit, but had obviously been planned to avoid making too much noise. The stealthy non-sleeper slid a bag out from under a bunk and crept off toward the nearest exit.

Outside this particular escape route a raft of ferns covered a hole in a sandstone bank. Some weeds had even been nurtured inside the opening, which made it all but disappear from external view.

Who ever it was crawled carefully past the foliage and dropped down onto a ledge of harder rock. Once there he swapped his olive uniform for the contents of his kit bag. The outfit was tight, but it would have to do. Newly dressed, the escapee crammed everything left over into the bag then threw it back up into the hole and out of sight.

Chapter Twenty

Around the Court House and square it had taken some time to tidy up. Following that the antipodean soldiers had been regrouped and reorganised. A good strength of them were posted to rest up and help out Sergeant Roberts. Anyone still fresh and awake had been sent to relieve Jarli and Noah, guarding the supplies they'd discovered beneath the pig factory.

The last truck to depart contained nine Australians and three Germans, squinting in the sunlight as they headed for the hospital. The prisoners sat near the tailgate, Rees and Harold handcuffed together with their lieutenant propped up uncomfortably opposite. Sergeant Roberts had arranged for them to be handed over to the proper authorities later this evening.

Dreyer watched from the briefing room window until they had gone and the street outside was left quiet and still. He was on the telephone to Private Evans.

'I see, got it. That's ripper. So bring all that back here then, quick smart. Oh and well done.' Dreyer slammed the receiver down with enthusiasm. 'Right, that's the lot for now,' he said, handing a final scribbled note to a young runner who was clutching a folder near the door.

Soon after the messenger burst into the Court Room over the road, saluted and said, 'Sit-rep from Captain Dreyer sir.'

Major Jackson started to go through the fresh paperwork as his runner coughed, 'Sir, the captain asked when you'll be back?'

'Tell him I need some space to think,' the major waved him away without looking up from the new notes. 'Soon as I've fully debriefed Miss Page, I'll come.'

Justine raised an eyebrow and blushed.

Desperately trying not to break a smile, the young messenger saluted again and left them to it.

No matter how rude it sounded, Justine was pleased, because she'd tried to talk many times, but the major was always too busy. Her mind yearned to spill out its observations and get back out there, clear headed.

Jackson slumped into a chair at what was normally the prosecutor's desk, temporarily unaware of her existence. So much so that it made him jump when Justine decided to get stuck in.

'What is that?' she asked politely, sitting down at the next chair.

Jackson briefly read on again until he'd finished the page. 'This top one is the report from your bomb disposal boys,' he finally replied, leafing through the last few pages and sliding it across.

Justine appreciated that he wanted to concentrate and not talk, despite the fact that she was bursting with questions. She smiled, accepted the documents and flicked through them quietly, for now.

If Jackson had been honest he would have admitted that he was holding back because she unnerved him. Justine was frighteningly confident, stunningly beautiful and smelt so nice it made him giddy. Instead he'd convinced himself that he needed to know all the facts, not just the ones she was waiting to flush into him. He leant forward to digest several chunks of datum, but it wasn't very long before that girl derailed his long-lonely thoughts again.

Justine had taken out a cigarette and when it was finished she tried again. 'Is this important?' she asked, snatching up a curl of paper as it was rolling away. She unravelled what looked like a lengthy hand written receipt and read it out in astonishment. 'Ten crates of tinned ham, *eight crates* of processed pork, *four palettes* of plumbing fixtures, light bulbs, paint, cement, medical supplies, copper piping, condensed milk, tea, coffee, sugar, tools...'

Major Jackson tapped the summary he was reading, 'Sounds like a catalogue of the haul they've found under the river, between Mr Moor's factories.'

Justine whistled at some of the rare luxuries further down the inventory and passed it back. 'I was up there yesterday,' she added trying to bring the conversation back to Harry and his friends.

'At the pig factory, why?' The major put an elbow on the desk and looked at her directly.

'No silly,' Justine pointed back to a diagram from the bomb disposal documents, 'Up there, in this bombed out field.'

'Wait, I need to take this one step at a time,' Jackson insisted as he shuffled all the papers back into a neat pile. 'Sticking with the shopping list;

you don't seem surprised that Mr Moor has hidden all these materials beneath the river? You worked with him, did you know about all of this?'

Justine answered frankly, 'Everyone around here is on the rob one way or another. Them who's got it sells it on to those who don't, you see?'

Jackson sat back and listened.

She looked down, 'The thing is, those men in chambers, those lucky few, they've got more than all of us put together. So, it makes sense that they're at the top of the pile.'

Jackson disagreed, but waited for her to continue.

'They own the land, the factories, houses, banks, the lot. They *are* the council, the magistrates, the landlords and the bosses of the jury, don't you see?'

'But it's wrong, they're terrible people,' Jackson argued back.

'Old Mr Burdocks not that bad, he's not really. He's just upper class that's all. At the end of the day, he's an alright bloke, to work for anyway.'

Jackson let rip, 'An alright bloke? You don't think he's a shallow horse thief then? A flaming leech, sucking the energy out of this place to fill up his overburdened lifestyle?'

Justine didn't hesitate, 'Well he ain't never touched me up, not like the other old farts do.'

'One saving grace,' Major Jackson conceded while pinching the brow of his nose. There was an awkward silence and then he took a deep breath, picked up the papers and got up to go. 'Can we amble while we ramble on?' he asked.

Justine furrowed her brow, 'You mean walk and talk, right?'

As they left the building he tried to clarify her remarks, 'So, you all know it's going on, but no one does anything to stop it?'

Justine turned away momentarily then swung back and glared at the major enraged, 'No, actually, I didn't *know* about *all* of this.' Rolling her eyes she stated, 'Well it isn't the kind of thing they'd discuss in chambers, is it?' When he didn't answer, she added sarcastically, 'Because they pay me to write down every word they say.'

Jackson grabbed her arm and for a second she struggled against his grip, thinking of Harry. When a bicycle clattered past her on the cobbled street, she understood the major's intentions. The rider was a chubby looking policeman; his tin hatted head so far down that he wouldn't have seen her.

The couple were face to face briefly, until Jackson turned and shouted, 'Go dip your eyes in hot cocky cack you flaming blind gink.'

'Bloody hell!' Justine exclaimed, 'I hope he's on his way to something important.'

The bicycle wobbled around the corner, stopped rattling and accelerated as it hit the smoother tarmacked section beyond.

Major Jackson ran over to see which way the bike had gone, but a bus coming the other way had obscured the view. Justine caught up with him in front of a big public notice board outside the police station.

'Sorry,' he said trying to remember where the conversation had got up to. 'You were saying something about me being a great gala for not understanding the situation at town hall, right?'

'I did overhear things, but it's not just a Planning Committee, it's a War Time Planning Committee. They made me sign the Official Secrets Act on day one.'

Jackson looked confused, 'Official Secrets Act, are you sure?'

Justine nodded, 'Well that's what Mrs Hill said it was.'

'But what about Sergeant Roberts or Chief Higgins?' he tilted his head to one side, 'You could have said something to them.'

'Look,' she pointed to a row of posters pasted below the notice board. 'The walls have ears see? And there, 'loose lips sink ships'. All their conversations are protected by His Majesties propaganda. So I knew things weren't right, but who am I to say it was wrong? Dammed if you do...'

'And dammed if you don't,' the major agreed with an apologetic nod. 'Sorry.' He tried to keep the facts flowing, 'So, moving on, what about that bombed field?'

The question knocked the steam out of the previously empowered girl. 'I found stuff there, bits of my boyfriends Bedford truck and,' she fished out a bullet case and tip, 'these were all over the place.'

Jackson looked at them and muttered, 'The bullet is from the bombers guns, but the smaller case,' He examined it more closely, 'Different calibre to the one that killed Mr Higgins.'

233

'Sorry, did you say Mr Higgins was killed?' Justine glared into the major's expressionless face.

The major frowned, 'Yes, I thought you'd read the blackboards?'

'I only glanced at them, didn't realise it meant someone had bumped him off.' She took a moment to remember Chief Higgins then said softly, 'Harry introduced me to him once, he was, well, he seemed very nice.' It took a few more seconds for her brain to register what she had seen. 'Hold on, why were Susan and Mary on those black boards? Was that a list of missing people, dead people or, or suspects?'

'Honestly?' the major tilted his head again and scrunched up his face, 'All of the above.'

'And what does that mean?' Justine started swaying and moved to a nearby bench, wanting to sit down before she fell over.

The officer sat next to her with the documents on his lap. 'We both agree your Harry and his mates were up there then?' He pulled out the Bomb Disposal Report, 'But doing what?'

Justine looked up, 'Maybe they weren't there, but Minnie was?'

Jackson turned the top sheet, 'Minnie?'

'My bloke's Bedford,' Justine explained as she leaned in to read the main points again, 'This says five bombs dropped on an empty field, on dead stalks and dirt? That's not a standard military target is it?' she pointed out.

Jackson found a copy of the statement Rees had given, 'The bombers were looking for an airstrip that wasn't there. A ploughed field could have looked like a runway I guess. Especially if someone was shooting back from what looked like a military vehicle.'

Justine considered the problem, 'So something about my friends and their transport made the aircrews think *that* field *was* their target? It doesn't mean they were firing back though.'

The major shrugged, 'Disposal boys found a lot of this spent ammunition too, like I said, it's German *and* British.' He jingled the pieces she'd given him. 'If there's vehicle debris, but no vehicle and no skin or bone...'

'Oh they got away, I'm sure of it, but someone got hurt. I found the rest of Minnie, she's up on the lower bank below Rose Cottage, hidden in an animal enclosure. I found this too, in the toolbox.' Justine dug deep and pulled out the dulled black tunic uniform button.

Jackson studied it and stood up to look back down the street in the direction the fat policeman had gone. 'Rose cottage?' he asked, rubbing the button thoughtfully with his thumb.

'It is about a mile or so to the West of this road,' she pointed out the turning on the field map, 'but how, why would they shoot back *or* hide, instead of running or seeking help? He's a mechanic not a soldier?'

'That report says there were lots of footprints in the mud, leading up from the stream where the unexploded bomb was found.' Jackson sat back down and pulled out a sheet from the pile. 'Here, third paragraph, they found a clearing down stream with a makeshift firing range, shelter, brewing up kit and three empty shot gun bags?' He pursed his lips, 'Do you have anything else in that magic pocket of yours?'

Justine reluctantly dipped in a hand and pulled out the note. 'I found this at Harry's garage.'

Jackson said nothing as he read the note.

'There was something else. I noticed a calendar in Harry's bedroom too, which was four years out of date. I didn't really think anything about it, but then I remembered there was one exactly the same in Edwards office up at the farm.'

'Did you open them, did you have a look at the contents?' Jackson begged enthusiastically.

Justine shook her head, 'Not really, there's been so much going on and then what with that German pilot and,' She bit her lip then announced, 'I could get the one from Harry's room, if you think it can help?'

The major had read the note from the garage again and absently repeated one word out loud, 'Valves?' He thought through all the bits and pieces of information. Before he could think of how to frame his next question.

Justine interrupted, 'Hang on, you said the bullet that killed Mr Higgins was a different calibre? Now look here, shooting at Germans is one thing, but you don't think my Harry was involved with killing Mr Higgins? He couldn't, I mean he knew him, I told you that.'

The major sat back, took off his cap to wipe away the sweat and tried to think of an answer based on facts. He drew breath to speak, but was too slow.

'My Harry uses spanners not guns, he's not a killer?' Justine insisted tempestuously. 'Edward's practically a vegetarian. Patrick, well yes he could probably kill a man, but those two boys from the next farm, they're just babies.'

'In my lifetime I've seen quite a few boys, killing and being killed, both in and out of uniform.' Jackson breathed a heavy sigh, 'No doubt with Nazi's at the helm we'll all see a damn sight more.'

'But, but,' Justine had no more questions that made sense.

Jackson went on, 'As for Mr Hitler, he's a flaming Christian you know and a vegetarian. It doesn't seem to hold him back. Face it Miss Page, there's more going on here than a few farm boys taking a picnic in the woods.'

It was like someone had let the air out, Justine slumped, wounded by it all.

Jackson knew this was hard, but carried on in the hope that the detail would push her through. 'Who ever killed Chief Higgins escaped down a route set up before the Germans had even arrived. If we question a few locals properly, well I'm sorry, but I think they'll confirm someone matching your mates descriptions set it all up. Mr Higgins was killed with a British bullet, most likely a Brit gun. Stolen, purchased or issued I don't know, yet, but your Harry's involved.'

Justine remained silent at first then as if slapped by an invisible hand, she bolted sideways into a tiny garden behind the notices. Jackson followed in time to see her being sick and knelt down to comfort her. Captain Dreyer started tapping on the window above, but the major ignored him and placed his jacket gently around the sobbing girl's shoulders.

The sudden contact made Justine jump, it was everything she wanted right now, but from the wrong man. 'That keeps happening to me, I'm sorry' she confessed and sat down to get her breath back.

The major watched as she pretended to fix something on her shoes.

'I made a promise that I would find him.' She looked up with her chin on her knees, 'Please, help me get Harry away from all this and promise you won't shoot him?'

While the major was considering an honest answer, two rabbits appeared from beneath a bush and began to jump around them on the lawn.

Justine wiped her eyes and asked, 'Where did they come from?'

'I imagine they belonged to one of the smashed up gardens down the road, unless there's a magician near by?' he suggested. Then after a pause he asked directly, 'Would you say Harry had a secret life, as well as the one you knew?'

Justine twisted her face up and tugged at the grass, 'I don't know.'

Major Jackson plucked out some daisies and offered them to the rabbits. 'Let me put it this way then; did you always know where he was and what he was doing?'

'Of course not,' Justine began, then as the bigger rabbit hopped over she cried, 'Stop, daisies are poisonous to them.'

Jackson slowly withdrew his hand. He looked around at the minefield of bunny toxic weeds peppering the lawn and the rabbits hopping amongst them. Thinking back to the rabbit fence he'd helped maintain in a previous life back home, he had a flashing thought and exclaimed, 'Bloody hell!' As the bunnies frolicked around them, Jacksons mind had cleared. He could see now what was happening. 'We need to go inside, quickly.' The officer jumped up and put out a hand to assist her.

'What, tell me?' she begged, allowing him to haul her up. 'Tell me, I want to know.'

Before he could reply Dreyer threw open the window and shouted down, 'Major, we need you on the balcony upstairs.'

'Right behind you Prof,' Jackson called back with thumbs up. He squeezed Justine's hand and assured her, 'Come on, we really have to go.' After taking several steps up toward the doors of the police station he stopped. For a second he pondered whether anyone could honestly know *what* their family and friends were up to, at *all times*. Turning to face Justine he asked softly, 'There were times when you couldn't really account for him, right?'

'Sundays,' Justine replied, as if she'd been holding her breath. 'Harry and one or two of the lads would go off. They'd say they were working on Minnie, or fishing or, well all sorts of things.'

'But they didn't always come back with any fish and Minnie never looked any different on a Monday morning, right?' He held open the doors and flourished a response to the men who saluted him in reception.

A young soldier pointed over to the inner staircase, 'Captain said to follow him, that way sir.'

Justine trotted along behind and continued to think aloud, 'It was subtle, we didn't live our lives in each others pockets.' She took a moment to collect and accept her own thoughts before admitting, 'But yes, you're right.'

'Anything else?' Jackson urged as they headed for the stairs.

Justine reached out and grabbed him by the arm, 'You mean apart from the guns, the death, the bombs and all the other bonkers stuff?' She looked at him like all this was his fault.

He got it. If the war hadn't come it would've been all right and not all wrong, but men like him in suits and uniforms were planning everyone's future now. For the first time in his entire professional life, it felt unscrupulous.

'Victoria, Edward's wife, said I was being selfish when I suggested the boys were making excuses, even when they went away for the whole weekend.' Justine pushed past the major. 'But Edward used to be away for months at a time in the Merchant Navy, so a few days away was no price for her to pay.'

'And did either of you ask your men what they were *really* doing?' The major challenged as he followed her to the first floor.

Justine held open the door to let him pass.

'The enemy's just over the horizon and people are being asked to do all sorts of strange things. No one really asks questions any more, that's the deal, remember.' Justine huffed. 'Your lot don't understand, you're all too far away from this, this England.'

'I think in this case, I do bloody understand,' Jackson said as Justine passed back his jacket. 'Australia *has* had a few invasions too, one way and another.'

'I haven't seen anything about it in the news,' Justine said bluntly. 'Who would invade Australia?'

'A handshake from a foreigner can invade a long established society in more ways than you would care to imagine. In Melbourne our forefathers took ships up river, clearing a channel which allowed the salty sea to invade a fresh water food chain.' He thought back to his revelation on the lawn outside, 'Or something as innocent as a couple of flaming rabbits.'

'I read about that one at school, but what *people* have ever threatened to invade you? Admit it, you're all safe down there, Hitler won't bother your lot will he?'

Jackson answered swiftly. 'Oh we know an awful lot about invasion Miss Page,' he sighed. 'Australia's in the middle of one right now.' Jackson took a very deep breath, allowing time for his words to sink in. 'Didn't you know, *we* invaded her.'

'You mean you took it off the savages that were there before you? Australia was colonised, we did that at school too.' Justine went over the history she'd been taught, 'Let me see, there were a few hundred naked natives running round and killing each other. The British Empire did them all a favour, educating them and making them into proper Christian people.'

Jackson was not that shocked, he'd heard it all before, even from men and women who'd seen the truth with their own eyes. 'The Aborigines *were* a real and capable people.' He was not berating her, just redressing what had been put into her mind. 'They had democracy, trade routes and sustainable civilisation long before we showed up.'

'Oh sorry, but we were told,' Justine apologised uncertainly. 'What about us, here and now, I don't see the connection?'

Jackson started moving along the upper corridor, 'The things they did to resist our expansion, it gives me an insight into what might be happening here.'

'How?'

The officer checked a few empty rooms then found more stairs. As they climbed he explained, 'There is some strong resistance at times, even now. Once, we woke up in the bush to find our vehicles were all dead, with dirt in the engines and fuel tanks. We stayed on mission, using horses to trek the saboteurs further into the bush.'

'Go on,' Justine urged him, 'what happened then?'

'Soon-as we made the next camp the mules became spooked, restless and agitated. These were army trained and reliable horses, but that day they got randy for the smell of fillies up wind, some wouldn't eat. Those that did eat, got crook.'

'So what was the mission?' Justine asked.

'Tracking some blokes who'd been re-wiring the local telegraph lines.' Jackson looked deep into her eyes to see if she understood yet. 'Before that they'd contaminated generators too and water towers were being drained on homesteads for hundreds of miles around that spot.'

'So you think Harry's some sort of native resistance fighter, but who is he resisting?'

Jackson had a think and concluded, 'Well on the night of the bombing, looks like they resisted the aircraft. Thereafter, I think they started resisting us, us rabbits.'

Justine stopped him, 'You have lost me completely now.'

'Old Australia didn't think ahead, they had to learn the hard way, that it makes sense to be prepared. A third of the country was overrun with little bunnies before anyone had formed a decent plan.'

Justine nodded, 'I get it. Our German proof fence; the Navy, Coastal Defence and the RAF, they are the outer barrier, but if the enemy break through, well, we have soldiers in reserve don't we?'

'But if your troops are pushed back and overwhelmed, you need some diggers dug in, hidden away, ready to slow things down and disrupt the invader,' the major suggested.

'But why would Harry decide to take on the entire German army with a few of his pals?' She shook her head starting to loose faith in the whole idea.

'Imagine there are lots and lots of little cells waiting to go. Maybe there are one or more, in every town in the country? So it's like your Home Guard, but the pick of the crop. Men, and probably women too, with excellent local knowledge and skills that make them better than the rest. They are told to carry on as normal, don't give up the day job, tell no one else. Then one sunny day there's a panic, church bells ring, the proverbial balloon goes up and bingo, they're off out the starting gate, without looking back.'

Justine got it now, 'They know the land, they can be resourceful and they're fit and strong. That's just the boys, it still doesn't explain Mrs Hill, how is she involved, or little Mary? You realise she cleans tables for a living? Can't see how that would be a deadly skill, can you?'

'Around the world men *and* women are fighting battles of resistance right now,' the major insisted. 'What if the top brass here in Britain used that insight and had the clout to get things going in advance? Ordinary working class heroes stowed away in reserve, well trained and well equipped ready to take the enemy on after they have invaded. There's always a way around a fence, no matter how high or how deep you make it.'

Justine felt empty, 'So they are all hiding somewhere, waiting to pounce? On the farm or in the town, but that doesn't explain why you think they killed Mr Higgins does it?'

Jackson leaned on the stairwell windowsill and waved his hand across the limited panorama of the town. 'You tell me where they might be and we can ask 'em that very question.'

Outside the major's car was returning with Private Evans who all but fell out of the passenger seat. He adjusted his spectacles and waved up at them like an excited school boy, but they did not see him.

'Honestly, I don't yet understand *why* Mr Higgins was shot,' Jackson admitted.

He tried to visualise the injured Private Roach on guard in the dark. He thought about the company supplies being limited since disembarking and that his men had only been reunited with half the equipment they'd sent ahead. His platoon had an assortment of different tin hats, helmets, mismatched uniforms and equipment. Some of it their own and some on loan. The major considered the Australian made Austen machine guns they used, copied from British Sten and German MP40 designs.

'One thing's for sure,' he eventually said while scratching an ear. 'They think we're the invaders. We turned up on their patch, just when they were expecting the enemy.' He looked down at a group of squaddies having a smoke in the shadow of a tree further down the street. 'We even look the part, kitted out in hand me downs and fancy dress.'

'So what are *you* going to do to find them?' Justine insisted, grabbing his arm so hard it left a mark. 'How will we talk them down?'

The officer was too distracted, suddenly more aware that his men and the town were in as much danger as Harry and the others. He said nothing for about twenty seconds and then in a very matter of fact way he stated, 'Well, I think we should start by throwing a bloody big party.'

Before Justine could think of a good response, Private Evans burst up into the lower section of the stairwell, breathless.

'Catch your air Private,' Jackson ordered.

Evans took a giant lung full of dust and oxygen, stood to attention and smacked himself in the forehead with a leather bound notebook.

'Sir this is Mr Burdocks private ledger, I think it has everything you were looking for.' Evans handed over the notebook.

'How did you manage to find this Private?' The major asked, leafing through the pages.

'I, I had a bit of a row with him sir. About what we were doing there.' Evans huffed away for a second or two then continued, 'It got a bit heated to say the least Major. Thought someone might reprimand me for speaking out so I went back into his office to apologise and...' Evans was totally out of breath.

'And...?' Justine demanded grabbing Evans by his collar.

Eyes bulged behind steamy spectacles as Evans spat out the words, 'He was ripping out pages from that book Miss, trying to burn them in a metal bin.' The private pulled away from her and pointed out several specific pages to his commander, 'Catalogues every penny they've stolen since before war broke out. Staff and vehicles hired, fake vouchers printed, even their plans for the future.' Evans put a hand inside his tunic and pulled out a handkerchief containing the singed pages he'd salvaged from the bin. 'We have a tonne of other files on the back of the ute outside.'

'Well done Private,' Major Jackson said very pleased with the result. 'Did he just hand it over to you then?'

'Not really Major, he came at me with a big letter opener, had a handle shaped like a parrot.' Evans looked at his feet guiltily, 'Sorry sir, but I pulled a swifty and laid him out.'

'Tut tut Private, striking a civilian, consider yourself on double ration,' Jackson winked as he accepted the burnt sheets of paper.

Justine interrupted, 'On the day of the bombing we had a guest at our meeting. Odd fellow from the MOD, I think? He called himself Mr Stevenson.'

Evans and the major looked at her expecting more.

'Well he wanted the councillors to stop expanding their plans and to stick at what they'd done so far and leave some areas alone. Asked me to keep an eye on them all, in case they hadn't listened.'

'Which areas?' Jackson said adding the leather book to his pile of documents.

'I don't know, there were so many plans and maps and he pointed here and there then took some with him.' She struggled to remember the reference numbers from the list Mr Stevenson had prepared, but it was no use.

'Do you have the minutes for the planning meetings Private Evans?' the major asked hopefully.

'Yes sir, I think so?' Evans turned to head back down to the car.

'Wait, you're wasting your time, I'm sorry.' Justine apologised. We did what Mr Stevenson asked. 'He wouldn't let us keep notes of anything he said or did, you see?'

Major Jackson slapped the wall.

'But,' Justine went on, 'all those plans and maps were checked out from old Mr Stibbins in records. I could ask him which ones didn't get checked *back* in?'

'That might just do it,' Jackson beamed, guiding her back down the stairs. 'Can you get someone to track down those calendars from the farm and Harry's house too?'

'I can try,' Justine stopped at the door, 'but what did you mean when you said you were having a party? It doesn't sound very appropriate in the circumstances?'

Jackson took a moment to answer, breathing through his nose, 'I want to try and get the whole town together in a safe place. Let's just say I have something to share with everyone. Well almost everyone.'

'Alright then, I'll be right back,' Justine said, still confused.

The major pulled some photographs and documents from his pocket and used the reverse of the largest one to write out a note. 'Private, take these over to the Express and Herald, their office is round the corner. Ask for Mr Pulfrey, I have a deal with the local press so they will be expecting you. Tell Pulfrey we need a few hundred leaflets printed up with this message and get him to put it in the afternoon issue too.'

'Yes sir,' Evans accepted the photographs and the notes.

'Use your own initiative and get the leaflets delivered into as many hands as possible before tea time.'

'Take one and pass it on, yes sir,' Evans nodded.

'Rope in some locals to help and give Mr Pulfrey those mug shots. Tell him I need a dozen copies as discussed, but to keep them out of the news right?'

'Yes sir.'

Jackson left him to it and ran off upstairs to look for the captain. At the top he found several rope like extension cables, which curved away into the chief's office.

More cables snaked out to the balcony where Dreyer, Cartwright and Corporal Tony Chambers the signals man, were engrossed in something on the floor.

Tony was the best signaller in the world; at least that's what he told everyone else. Most people called him "Sparks". All three of the men outside were wearing headphones.

'What you up to Prof?' Jackson asked, patting his captain on the back.

The men bobbed in a Mexican wave as their entangled headphones snagged on each other and Neville's were pulled off his head.

Captain Dreyer held back his own ear speaker, 'Cartwright was playing with the set in the briefing room, listening out for those ladies. When he found them again, Sparks suggested we set up something a bit more directional.' Dreyer picked up Neville's headset and handed it to the major, 'Listen.'

'...ALLING ZERO 9. ARE YOU RECEIVING? OVER. (Crackle) EXCURSION YESTERDAY. TROOPS ALL OVER (Whistle)AIN YARD AND WOODS. (Pop, pop, pop.) FURTHER TODAY. OVERHEARD

TALK IN TOWN MANY CIVILIANS LOCKED UP (Pop, crackle.) STATION (Fizz) GERMAN PROTESTS. TURNED BACK (Pop, long whistle) HIGH NUMBER OF TROOP VEHICLES (More whistles and pops) TRUCK FULL OF (Whoop) OFFICERS. THIS IS SD...'

The major waited, but there was no more to the message, just more crackle and pop mixed with extra fizz. He raised an eyebrow and said, 'Very English, but there's a hint of Irish in the way she says "nine, excursion" and "over".'

Dreyer agreed then pointed out, 'If she saw the truck with the German officers on-board? Well, I mean, they didn't leave that long ago sir.'

Major Jackson looked over the balcony at what he could see of the town, 'She could be sat within a few minutes walk from the main road up to the hospital then?'

Dreyer nodded and tried to give a technical explanation of what they knew, 'Sparks thinks it's a fluke that we can hear her at all Major. Might be why they're not using cypher, because they think *only* ZERO 9 can hear.' He turned to Corporal Chambers, 'What did you say it was Sparks?'

The signaller lifted his headset, 'Right now it's sending out overlapping waves sir, some sort of double modulation. That's why it's all crackle and whistles. Occasionally, we can pick it up on a frequency range of 48-65mcs. That's when the double modulation gadget on her set shorts out, I think?' Sparks smiled triumphantly at the blank faces.

'What the devil is he on about Captain?' The major asked as politely as he could.

'Well it's all very clever really sir. If he's correct then she's got some pretty amazing radio equipment. The signal hides, it kinda rubs itself out. If you've got the same technology you can decode it, but anyone with normal equipment gets whistles and dead air. We're only hearing it because her kit's broken. Which could be the same reason Zero Nine doesn't answer?'

'Or Zero Nine isn't there? Maybe Zero Nine is doing her hair or at the post office queuing for stamps?' the major grinned. 'So, Corporal, can we get a fix on it?'

'Sorry sir, too far away and intermittent to get a lock from here,' Sparks explained. 'If I could get some proper equipment out there,' he pondered. 'We would need to be very close to the source, but it's possible.'

Jackson was happy with that, 'Get this lot on a wagon with a generator and zone in. Cartwright will show you the main drag, but don't go walkabout 'till I get there.'

'Yes sir,' Sparks said as he began directing Neville to help take down the antenna.

'And what did you mean about Zero Nine being at the post office?' Captain Dreyer asked with interest.

The major put an arm around his captain. 'Oh Professor we have much to discuss,' he smiled. 'Before we do, we need to speak to Corporal Jarli about all that angry bacon he was caught up with. Can you get hold of him?'

'Yes Major.'

Major Jackson gave his captain a friendly punch in the arm, 'You know I'm surprised you haven't worked all this out for yourself Prof.'

'Could it be that you've been privy to some information that I've not yet seen?' Captain Dreyer queried.

'Sort of,' Major Jackson admitted. 'Oh where to begin, let me see, do you know anything about rabbits Professor?'

Chapter Twenty-One

'You sure you alright back there Noah?' Jarli asked as they rounded a corner aboard a horse drawn meat wagon.

'Just a scratch digger, no worries.' Noah flexed his bandaged hand and gave Jarli a thumbs-up to prove the point.

The two-wheeled butchers cart had only one proper drivers seat behind the horse. Noah had used the beast's oat sack as a cushion, but it kept sliding down the polished wooden roof of the vented cooler.

Jarli made a clicking noise and flicked the reins to try and accelerate the cart's powerhouse. When it didn't work, he sat back impatiently and resigned himself to clip clop along. 'This is nice, right mate? Fresh air and sunbaking out here in the open.'

Noah ignored the question. 'How do you know where to go Jarli?' he asked after looking around the next street junction.

'Bloke at the factory said this fellah knows where we going mate,' Jarli shrugged and flicked the reins a little harder.

This time the horse stopped dead in its tracks. It turned to stare at Jarli in disgust then snorted a cloud of rank that stank of rotting grass.

When Jarli gingerly attempted to turn the beast's head back to the road, it yanked the straps half out of his grip. The corporal held up his hands in surrender and once it was happy, the horse trotted on at its own pace.

'Don't think he likes you Noah,' Jarli suggested to his friend in a whisper. 'Him knows you is sitting your smelly arse on his grub mate.'

Noah shook his head and changed the subject, 'So what was all that gear down there in the tunnel then Jarli?'

'You blind mate?' Jarli turned to face him. 'It was tins of grub and stuff for houses and that.'

'No mate, I mean why was it down there, locked away in that tunnel? Surely they need all that kit up here? I mean, is it some sort of *back up for Britain* thing?'

There was silence while they both considered the mountains of supplies.

'Noah, you think we all get to share some of it?' Jarli asked eventually.

'Nah mate. We're just lucky we got away before they asked us to carry the flaming lot of it back upstairs. Best we keep our necks in Jarli. Get as far away from all that trouble, quick as possible.'

Jarli covered his mouth with the back of his hand so that the horse wouldn't hear, 'Not gonna be quick on this old fellah mate.'

After a long few minutes the cart stopped outside a row of shops. The sign above the nearest one read "Craig and Irene Smith, Butchers". Craig came out to greet them, rubbing his hands together and beaming from one cauliflower ear to the other.

'You must be Mr Jackson's men?' the jolly butcher replied, 'Noah and Charlie right?'

'You Mr Smith?' Jarli asked as they got down.

The big man nodded, holding out a hand. Jarli didn't enjoy shaking hands, but he'd learned to cope after years in the army. In this case he felt physically lifted off the ground.

'Captain Dreyer says we going to leave these pigs with you, for safe keeping or something?' Jarli moved around to open up the back of the cart.

'IRENE!' Craig shouted, beckoning his tiny wife from the shop. He heaved two bloodied carcases onto his good lady's narrow shoulders and took two him self, one under each ample arm.

'My captain said you gonna show us where to go next?' Jarli asked as Craig turned to walk away.

'Flower shop, just around the corner there,' Craig nodded towards the other shops. 'Stuck up old poof he is, but my Irene's told him your coming.' He lowered his voice and added, 'Don't be afraid to pop back 'ere for some scratchins or baked faggots for your way back.'

Jarli and Noah looked at each other, shrugged and moved on. 'What about this horse?' Noah asked as the butcher twisted his porky luggage through the doorway of the shop.

'Don't worry about old Brian, my boy will trot him back. Cheers lads.' With that he winked and followed his wife inside.

As the two soldiers stood there in the sunshine, Noah had to ask, 'Scratchings, faggots? Brian?' He shook his head and thought of a better question, 'So why did we just deliver four pigs to that bloke instead of our canteen?'

Jarli shrugged, 'Orders mate. Then as they walked away he pointed, 'Could be something to do with all that mate.'

At the corner of the street was one of those newspaper boards with the latest headline. At the top it had Express and Herald in red and gold. Beneath that and behind diamonds of wire, was a bold message saying, "Celebration of good will in the Clock Square and Park, Today 7.00pm. Food and drink supplied. All welcome"

'Better crack on with finding the trail from that shop then,' Noah waved towards the only shop entrance not yet criss-crossed in sticky brown tape.

Jarli nodded, 'Major thinks some fellah came through here after them was shooting a copper in town last night.'

Noah was hot and tired. After a quick scan of the area he walked over to a nearby bench and slumped down. 'Go on then,' he said sulkily. 'You know I'm no good at all that. I just tread my big boots in it all an' make things worse.'

Turning his back on Noah, Jarli moved back to the florist's door and took in the whole arena. A lot had happened since last night; people and vehicles had come and gone all morning and in every direction. When Jarli eventually stepped inside, a bell above the opening jangled. An aroma hit him in the face like some sort of tropical oasis, although the flowers smelt nothing like the ones Jarli had known at home. It was nice, a welcome difference to the smells in all the other locations he'd been sent to in the last two days.

'Morning Miss,' the bloodied corporal said to an immediately frightened looking girl standing behind a long glass counter.

She tried to smile but ended up looking like she was having a stroke. The manager came in, responding to the bell and froze. He took in the dirty pig stained soldier and dismissively waved it through to the rear of the shop.

'Sorry boss,' Jarli apologised, suddenly seeing himself in the mirrored decor.

The shop manager took out a hanky and waved the dirty little man through.

Jarli took the welcoming for what it was and got on about his business. He moved cautiously up the stairs, taking in every bit of detail while trying not to disturb anything. At the very top the smell of flowers faded away and the dank odour from outside broke through.

Inside the smashed doorway, where Jackson had leaned in earlier to retrieve the bullet case, there was mess everywhere. It looked like someone had started a clean up, re-stacking boxes and re-rolling ribbons. In the old carpet a small amount of gravel and tar were mixed in with splinters of rotting wood near the broken doorframe. Tubs of glitter and gold paint had spilled out over the top flight of stairs and dripped down to the landing below where grave pots and posies covered the carpet.

The hurried escapee had thrown up a few marks, here and there where little blobs had been trampled in or brushed off, but it was not like there was an actual trail of footprints to follow. The runner had been stealthy or maybe just lucky enough to avoid treading in most of the incriminating paint and powder, but there was still a little to go on. While following these few thinning globs back down to the shop, Jarli approximated the runner's height, weight and shoe size.

Downstairs beyond the glass counters the shop girl was set up ready to hold the new door open wide. The manager stood beside her holding his nose and flapping his handkerchief as Jarli nodded politely, took one last look around and departed. The ting of the little bell sounded sweeter as the door slammed shut behind him.

Once in the street Jarli got down to scan the pavement for any more fragments of debris. The clues were even fewer and farther between out here. The ground had been disturbed by the police and local footfall this morning, plus the glazier had obviously swept up after fitting the door. A faint trail did remain, caught between the pavement cracks on one side of Noah's bench. At that spot there was a slightly larger amount of glass fragments and glitter than elsewhere.

'Murrmarti,' Corporal Jarli whispered in his native tongue. Then when Noah screwed up his face for an explanation Jarli tried to translate, 'Like rain can add a time frame to a footprint instead of washing it away. If you brush up, it don't mean you spotless.'

'It didn't rain much last night though mate?'

Jarli smiled down at Noah then closed his eyes and conjured up an image of a wild thing that was trapped. A shadowy creature spawned in a corner of his mind. It crouched there quivering, ready to spring forth if the hunt closed in.

When the scout turned around and opened his eyes the animal image emerged again, hiding inside the florists. It had the appearance of a creature somewhere between a wallaby and a wild boar, all blood eyed, spiky haired and snorting red dust. Its inky breath steamed a misty ochre circle half way down the glass door. Then all at once, from the centre of that shape it burst-forth trailing wisps of crimson.

Jarli turned quickly, allowing the spirit creature to pass. Ignorant of them, it crouched down near the bench where Noah was calmly smoking his cigarette. The private raised an inquisitive eyebrow and followed Jarli's gaze down to a seemingly empty space on the floor.

Beyond Jarli's eyes the mutant reared on hind legs, trailing misty fingers of colour around Noah like fog. Noah blew smoke rings, which mingled for a moment before the creature dropped back on all fours and turned to run. It shot a look back up the hill and bolted away in the opposite direction. The shadow ran between Brian and the cart then disappeared into the nearest alleyway on the other side of the road.

This was not the first time Noah had watched his friend reacting to something he could not see himself. Experience had taught him to ask specific questions rather than hear the whole story.

'How many, how fast, how far?' Noah asked while thoughtlessly dropping his cigarette amongst the tiny fragments of evidence. He got up, put on his wide brimmed hat and rubbed out the burning butt with the toe of a boot.

Jarli stood stock still, contemplating his vision and the trail signs he'd found so far. 'Big feet like you, big feller, new boots and he be tired.' He pointed towards the alleyway and added, 'Him go over there mate.'

'Anything else?'

'Yeh mate,' Jarli sighed, slowly nodding his head, 'I need to spend some time away from flaming pigs.'

Now that they both knew what they were looking for it was easier. As soon as they entered the passage Jarli pointed out an area where someone had squatted down to catch a breath. He allowed Noah to think he'd found the first boot prints in the sludge that lined the edges of the passage, then moved on.

The shooter had moved along close to the wall last night. This had kept him out of sight then, but now in the light of day it was like a dot to dot of his journey. There was also enough dog mess and other material along the ground to keep the trail going.

Lying flat out at times, Jarli found little beads of tar covered grit with specks of the powder and paint on board. Most of all, to him there was always a very faint waft of that scent made up of flowers, stale aftershave and body odour.

The long track they followed did not ultimately lead to a secret hideaway or a room stacked high with guns and ammo. At the end of this trail there was only an old lady, hanging out a rug to dry in the sun.

'Oh,' she said when Jarli peered around the corner of her yard. 'So they sent the clever little darky then?'

'Good day missus,' Noah said as he stepped out and unconsciously swept around the scene with the barrel of his machine gun.

Mrs Clark ignored Noah and his weapon, 'Florence was right then, you are good at finding people.'

The corporal bowed and introduced himself. 'Names Jarli,' he said, scanning every window and door with beady eyes.

'There ain't no one here as'll hurt you,' Margaret assured them. Then she carefully sat down on her back step and took out a half finished roll up from a paisley pinafore pocket.

Noah offered a light as Jarli took another glance through the window of the shed, just in case. He shook his head subtly so that Noah knew there were no instant surprises to be had.

Mrs Clark continued her tale, 'I think he came here last night, our Harry.' She was clearly upset at the full realisation of this fact in her own head. 'But you see, I'd had that sleeping draught that Heather left for me.' She took a long drag then blew out a smoky sigh, 'That was a long time before he came mind you, but I was still out for the count, you know?'

Noah offered the old lady a real cigarette and she lit it from the tip of her roll up.

'Thanks,' she nodded, 'So, like I was saying, I heard someone having a good old rummage around the house, they came upstairs. He probably wanted to ask where his bike had gone? And, well I wanted to talk to him, but I couldn't. It were like someone was sitting on me, stopping me from moving. It was hard to even open my eyes. When I did, I thought it was all a dream, what with him having the gun and the black face, he looked like you son.' She pointed to Jarli stood in a shadow with his rifle on his back. 'It was him though wasn't it? Silly sod.'

'This Harry, is he your boy then misses?' Jarli asked.

'He was my boy, our boy,' she sobbed for a few moments. 'Now he's just a silly man, who should be here helping out, not...'

'It's alright honest, it'll be alright,' Noah cooed.

'Balls will it, I've seen it all before. You stick a gun in a man's hands and he thinks he's in control of everything. He, he,' she struggled to see the words through her tears. 'They was going to have a baby.'

'There there,' Noah tried again, patting Mrs Clark on the shoulder while making an odd face at Jarli.

Jarli ignored him and asked, 'Can I have a look around the house please Mrs?'

Margaret waved him in, getting up out of the way then stubbing out her cigarette in a cement birdbath.

Noah continued to try and get some answers as he opened the shed door and had a quick look around. 'And what did you say?' he asked without really understanding exactly what it was they were talking about.

'Well I was drowning in fresh air wasn't I, an' I couldn't speak. Can you imagine?'

Noah came back out, shook his head and let her continue.

'It was no dream was it. Cos when I woke up, hours later mind, I looked around and some of his stuff had gone. The bible has gone and he were never a religious boy before, that old calendar that Justine was going on about, that's vanished too.'

Noah nodded back without really understanding.

'He took a bit of food too, nothing as would leave me short, but I know what I has in that pantry and it's missing a few bit an bobs.'

Noah interrupted, 'When we arrived here, you were expecting us.'

'I was, yes. Our Florence had not long left see? I didn't say nowt to her, not yet. She told me, about Mr Higgins being shot. Word spreads faster than warm butter with Florence holding the knife.'

'Florence?' Private Cooper asked, passing a cup of tea that Jarli had poured and handed out from the pot inside.

'Flo is a big old bird with a massive gob on her. She came and told me all this for our entertainment see? She doesn't know the truth, she just gossips. After the first few sentences came out I couldn't hear her. Like the silent films my husband used to project in the parlour it was, her big gob flapping around with no sound.' Margaret took a long slurp of tea, made an "ahhhh" sound and then carried on revitalised. 'My mind was just going over last night and trying to work out the timing with what Florence had said so far. Then when she left, I thought, well I thought that's it then. So I've done all me chores and I'm ready to go.' The old lady balanced her cup on the birdbath and held out both wrists to be cuffed.

Noah gently pushed them back down and smiled.

'Nothing here mate,' Jarli stepped back into the yard. 'This place is as clean as my whistle. Apart from these.' He held up a pair of army boots with some traces of glittered paint on the top. 'Reckon them too uncomfortable. You know what new boots is like?'

Noah took the boots, handed them to Mrs Clark and walked away to consult with his friend. 'Fair dinkum mate, I feel uneasy about all this,' he whispered. 'I reckon we go and see Captain Dreyer and take the old girl with us? If her son killed that copper, that's pretty flaming serious.'

'I know,' Mrs Clark said from beneath Noah's armpit making him pirouette away.

Jarli smirked as he tapped Mrs Clark on the shoulder from behind, 'Mrs, we need to go back now. You mind coming with us?'

'Nah, I've been ready for over an hour,' she replied, grabbing her coat from a fence nail and handing the boots back for Noah to carry.

As they were leaving the curtain twitched next door and Florence watched the two soldiers politely point Mrs Clark back the way they'd come. When someone suddenly stepped out and tapped on her window she jumped back in fright.

'Sodding Norah,' Florence cried out with a shiver.

'All right Flo,' the little postman's words vibrated through the glass. He was waving a pile of leaflets and pointing toward the front door.

Florence went around and opened it, 'You scared the life out of me Charlie, you little twerp. What do you want?' She snatched up one of the leaflets and started to read it.

'Post Master said to help the Aussies spread the word with these, quick as we can.' He waved the rest of the papers in front of Florence's fringe. 'And I thought, who better than you to give my first flyer to?'

'Have you been drinking Charles?' Florence asked the postman.

By the time Jarli, Noah and Mrs Clark got back to the police station, an overburdened Justine was also arriving outside.

'I was on my way back to yours next.' Justine slumped a little as she weighed the words, 'We need to talk.'

The two women grabbed and hugged each other tightly, letting go of everything. Words and emotions poured out onto the pavement along with all the rolls of paper Justine had been carrying.

Noah grabbed Jarli and they hung back while the women cried and talked. It was near impossible for them to understand the blurted words the women were sobbing out anyway.

Eventually Noah concluded that this must be Margaret's daughter in law and decided to calm the situation down. 'Mrs,' he said tapping Justine on the shoulder, 'Mrs, you should have a sit down really. There's a lot to take in, about your husband you see?'

There was a very brief pause before the women started to talk again. The result was more hugs and blurted half sentences stating what each thought they knew about Harry.

'Please if you could both stop crying and shouting we can all go inside and work this out,' Noah asked lamely.

'MISSES!' Jarli shouted above the noise, 'If you is having a baby you should calm it and have a sit down.'

The two ladies stepped back leaving a gap between them, saying nothing more at first. Justine looked at Jarli open mouthed then slowly moved her gaze down to her own tummy. She had stopped crying all together, but Mrs Clark was still sobbing a little.

'You said it was, concussion,' Justine managed to say before she looked up and turned her full glare on Margaret.

'No, you did,' Margaret smiled. 'Anyway, you might have had that too?' She held out both hands, seeking forgiveness and comfort, 'Nurse Jones said to wait and I wanted to tell you both, together.'

Justine nodded and moved closer to embrace. 'We should go inside then and do whatever we can to find him,' she said quietly with her chin on Margaret's shoulder.

'Rather that than stand out 'ere like blooming bollards, chin up,' Margaret agreed.

They looped arms and walked in together, heads held high.

Noah looked at Jarli and rolled his eyes, then followed them inside.

'What?' Jarli asked before grabbing the rolls of paper and chasing after them all.

In reception, Justine directed Jarli to deliver the rolls of maps to the briefing room while Noah introduced Mrs Clark to Captain Dreyer and helped her to explain what was going on. Justine earwigged on their conversation at first then followed Jarli to keep an eye on what everyone else was up to.

Corporal Jarli found the major and told him briefly what they had discovered on the journey from the flower shop. Jackson listened intently at first, but then the story and his eyes drifted toward the maps.

'She said these was for you Major. Said to say they was not exactly the same maps as the other feller took away, but they shows the same ground.'

Suddenly filled with curious excitement the major stood back saying, 'Stick 'em down on the table Corporal.' He pushed all the other papers aside, forming one messy pile that spilled over onto the floor.

With a little help, Jarli stretched out the biggest map over the remaining surface. The colossal chart was a very basic plan of several farms, a dairy and a wide area of scrub sitting way out on the estuary side of town.

'Don't think so?' Jackson said, allowing his end to roll up.

Jarli let go too and the waxy parchment neatly dropped off the edge of the table. The second map he put down looked more hopeful. It detailed a little coppice and timber track on the edge of a wood. According to the hand written notes it had been owned by one of the sawmills until 1939. A big government stamp signed in triplicate said it was now rented to the Government, namely the Ministry of Supply.

'Could be?' the major mused, rubbing his chin and directing Jarli to slide some weighty objects onto the corners.

'Boss, what we looking for?' Jarli asked as he unfurled another map and placed it over the top.

'I don't know son, I'll tell you if I see it.' The major pulled the third map to one side and tried another.

Jarli picked up an old flat folded map from near his feet. As he unfurled it he noted, 'This one's the same place.'

The corporal laid it out over the big forest plan. It was indeed a good match, but on a different scale and showing much more detail.

The major scanned the map with interest. 'There,' he said eventually, pointing to a faint horseshoe shape. 'The hospital, right here at the edge.'

Jarli slid and aligned the two diagrams so that they sat next to each other.

'That could be it Jarli my man,' Jackson slapped the corporal so hard on the back, it could have been considered an assault, but Jarli just smiled.

'Bring both of them, I'll explain on the way,' Major Jackson urged as he left the room in haste. 'We have a possible winner Professor,' he called out across reception. 'Let's go.'

Dreyer politely handed Mrs Clark over to Sergeant Robert's care and ran after his commander.

Justine had left the shadows and followed the major over to the entrance porch. 'Where are we going?' seemed the most logical question for her to ask.

'We can't take you with us,' Captain Dreyer insisted. He took out a service revolver and checked down the barrel. 'It could be dangerous.'

The major nodded his agreement and smiled as he said, 'If they are there, we'll do everything we can to talk them down first.'

Justine stopped staring at the gun in Captain Dreyer's hand and shifted her gaze up to the major's eyes. He looked keen to get away, but waited patiently while she assessed his words worth. When she closed her eyes and nodded a reluctant acceptance, he broke free and ran down the steps towards his ute. Dreyer followed and swung into the vacant passenger seat as Noah and Jarli jumped on the flat back.

Justine waited to see which way they were heading out of town. When she ducked back inside Sergeant Roberts was leading Mrs Clark away, towards the interview rooms. At reception WPC Birch was busy womaning the phones, while PC Thompson brewed up in the little rest room behind her.

Ultimately, no one was paying any attention as Justine stepped back into the foyer's shadows. With slow movements she checked that Rudolf's pistol was still tucked safely out of sight then entered the reception area wearing a huge grin.

WPC Birch finished her call and smiled back, raising an eyebrow of disdain at who ever had been on the other end of the telephone. As soon as the pretty constable dropped the heavy handset back down, it rang again. Justine walked by confidently, heading for the rear of the building and trying hard not to seem in a rush.

One step away from entering the exit, Birch shouted after her, 'Wait, Miss Page STOP!'

Justine hovered and wondered if Captain Dreyer had arranged for the young WPC to be her personal minder? When she turned around Birch was holding out the receiver.

'A call for you Miss, rerouted from town hall,' Birch said matter of factly and wafted the phone in the air.

'This had better be important,' Justine muttered as she stomped back across the tiled hall.

'Something about a caretaker that needs to speak to you?' WPC Birch noted as she passed over the earpiece.

'What?' Justine said with alarm.

'Work, they always find you don't they,' Birch whispered with a wink, then walked away to join PC Thompson in the rest room. 'I will leave you to it,' she smiled and closed the door behind her.

'Miss Page?' a tiny, crackling voice was calling far away.

Justine lifted the phone and gulped, 'Yes, is that you Mr Ste...'

Stephenson sighed, 'I need to ask a few questions, time is short so please try and answer them briefly.'

'Where is Harry, do you know where they are? Why are you making them do this?' Justine demanded.

'Me first,' Mr Stevenson sounded agitated. 'My office has received a request from a Captain Dreyer, for rather specific information. You wouldn't know anything about that would you?'

'Someone shot the police Chief,' Justine whispered franticly. 'I don't know what's happening here; it might have been my Harry? The Germans came down, then the Australians arrived and the men all disappeared and...'

'Miss Page, calm down,' Stevenson said more patiently.

'You don't seem surprised?' she asked.

There was silence at first, then he replied, 'I am surprised that things can go so wrong so quickly, but that is war.'

Justine pleaded into the receiver as quietly as possible, 'Tell me where they're hiding?'

It sounded like he was tapping his fingers on a desk and thinking. Eventually Stevenson said, 'I can help to find them, but it will require your assistance.'

Justine shook her head, 'But you must know where they've dug in, you are part of all this aren't you?'

Stevenson considered her words carefully before replying, 'Do you really imagine we have a big map here on the wall with pins in it? No one knows, apart from the men assigned to be at each location and the handful of engineers who fitted them out.'

'No you're lying to me, tell me,' Justine tried to pull herself together.

Stevenson calmed himself, 'I have some idea of the zones they should be in, but I need your help to pin point them. Honestly.'

'Get them here, those engineers. Get them here and we will see what they remember?' Justine urged.

'It is all about local knowledge. They would have travelled blind, taken into the actual spot by someone stationed there,' Stevenson tried to explain.

Justine thought he was just being difficult, 'Ask them anyway, speak to them, do something.'

'Please understand, if the war ended today, the exact chosen location for most of these hides would remain secret, to all but the men and women who use them.' He waited patiently for this to sink in then added, 'Please, tell me everything you know?'

Chapter Twenty-Two

Now that things were slowing down, Rudolf had time to reflect on whether his remaining men would become prisoners or get added to the list of corpses. It felt as if his aircraft and crew had been removed from the battlefield by some almighty hand. They'd been swatted from the sky and abandoned into a box, a box filled with broken tin men.

Several minutes ago, two noisy porters had unknowingly informed Rudolf of the latest news. Through thin blue curtains he'd overheard that Karl, his injured rear gunner was still alive elsewhere in the hospital. The lad was apparently getting slowly better, but would not be well enough to travel on with the rest of "them Nazi's" later today.

After being wheeled back from treatment Rudolf was relieved to be reunited with his engineer. The room they were being kept in was bright and clean, but very minimal now. There remained a bed, a table and chairs, but everything else had been removed during his absence. He was happy to see that although Peter was still pretending to hobble, his sprain no longer seemed to really need the crutches for support.

Peter stopped at the other side of the room and rested his forehead on the cool glass brick wall, which separated them from the outside world. As the sun came out from cloud his eyes were drawn to a deformed reflection of the yellow paper tag that Sergeant Roberts had tied around his neck. He slumped down on the crutches, straightened his spectacles and turned the tag over twice. The only bits he really understood were his name in the top corner and his prisoner number, neatly written in blood red ink at the bottom.

As Rudolf came over to stand at his side, Peter turned his head on the glass wall and looked hard at his friends tag. It was numbered five digits higher than his own. He speculated that Rees most likely had the next higher numeral, Karl, Elias and Harold would have got the ones in between.

Peter visibly shuddered as an awful thought hit him. The thought that Harald and Elias would probably be wearing their tag's on smaller strings tied around their big toes.

Rudolf walked away and eased himself slowly onto the edge of the bed. It was an uncomfortable mistake to make without a nurse to help you up again.

'Drei kleinen schweinchen,' Peter muttered.

Rudolf tried to stand up then grunted out, 'We are three wolves Peter, not pigs.' Peter swore at the ceiling while Rudolf shook his head and repeated in German, 'Wölfe Peter, nicht schweine.'

Peter nodded and wedged a crutch on the bed so that his friend could lever himself up with it. Once the pilot was back on his feet, Peter crossed over to check the view of the corridor outside. The room's inner windows were frosted up to eye level, but he could see at least two Australian soldiers through the clear section. They had their backs to him, chatting up a pretty nurse some way off to the right.

Peter span around quickly, opened his jacket and pulled up a military knife. Its blade glinted in the light as Peter grinned and whispered, 'Ich packte es, wenn der wagen hielt plötzlich.'

Rudolf tried to gather his thoughts. It felt as if the big hand was rummaging in the box again. Trying to find a handful of twisted toy soldiers that could be bent back into shape and made ready for action.

The door opened and Rees stood there holding a tray of food and drink. Peter instinctively let go his jacket, rearranging himself to look as innocent as possible.

The soldier accompanying Rees stepped inside and let him put down the supplies before handing over some towels and wash kit. He looked from Peter to Rudolf suspiciously, then grunted and left to take up his official post outside the room.

Peter elbowed the door shut and continued to glare down the corridor for a while.

'What is matter with him?' the navigator asked in a whisper.

'He has a knife,' Rudolf whispered back. 'Stole it from one of the major's men. Remember when the wagon stopped suddenly and we were jolted on way here.'

'Yes, when that young girl stepped out and all the men were whistling at her.' He did a quiet wolf whistle and Rudolf nodded back. 'He will get all of us killed,' Rees concluded as he forgot about the girl and thought about the knife.

Peter groaned, and urged, 'Wir sollten die türsteher zu töten und entkommen sie jetzt!'

'No. I will not be killing anyone, I want stay here,' Rees implored nervously.

'Sprechen Deutsch jungen,' Peter demanded, grabbing a cowering Rees by the ear and spitting the words into his face.

Rudolf stepped in and ordered them quietly but firmly to break it up.

When Peter turned away in disgust, Rudolf reassured Rees, 'Don't worry Cadet, I am not to be running anywhere soon either.'

'Kommen,' Peter begged as he peered out over the back of the guards scalp.

'Peter nicht, nein!' Rudolf ordered.

The angry engineer swung around so fast that his crutch caught the table edge and almost knocked the contents over.

Hearing the commotion the guard opened the door and looked inside. 'You dags sit down, drink yer chokkie and eat that fruit or we'll take it off you,' he scowled.

Peter looked at his commander, waiting for the nod. Instead he was directed to sit down at the table and shut up. Satisfied, the guard huffed and slammed the door back into place.

Behind the hospital a fat policeman had arrived and stowed a bicycle out of sight in the shadow of a side entrance. The big bobby tidied himself up quickly, dropped two cycle clips on the ground and loosened his helmet's chinstrap before charging in.

Doctor Jones stepped aside and held open the inner door to let the rushing officer pass. 'Still as rude,' he grumbled as the policeman's shoulder number brushed past his chin and trotted away. 'Chap looks bigger in the day light?' Jones said to himself as he stepped into the light. Tapping out his pipe caused the doctor to notice the big boot prints and subsequently the bike hidden against the far end of the porch wall. 'Tut, tut,' he said quietly, shaking his head.

Elijah had no clear idea where he was going. His plan had been to come in the back way and then to stay out of sight. The plan was pretty vague from there on in. The building was unfamiliar, the signs were confusing and he was getting nowhere other than lost. His eyes flicked sideways over medical words and notices, seeking clues as he bolted up to the next level. What they should have been doing was looking straight ahead.

His nose felt very happy and warm as it swung back to face forward and gently met with a soft bottom.

'What the?' the nurse startled before stepping to one side of the boxes she'd just dropped.

'Sorry,' Elijah squeaked with embarrassment.

The nurse weighed up the situation and forgave him with a little headshake. Then she asked, 'Now you've introduced yer self, can you help me with this lot then Mr Policeman?'

Elijah automatically panicked and tried to show more hat than cheeks. 'Not seen you around before?' he said while nervously stacking up the boxes and using them to shield the rest of his face.

'Well you wouldn't have.' The nurse climbed onto the next step up to get on eye level with him. 'We got bought in to help, from the convent hospital,' she smiled and moved the top box aside.

Elijah managed to smile back without looking odd and then launched himself on up the stairs.

'Careful now,' the nurse chirped from behind him. 'You don't want to split that lovely outfit of yours.'

'You might be able to help me with my enquiry actually,' Elijah said in an impressive impression of a policeman tone. 'I need to check on the man who came in last night.'

'Oh we had a few in last night. Not as many as the night before I'll grant you, but.' The young nurse skipped past Elijah in a race to the top and cooed, 'You'll need to be a tad more specific, Constable.'

'The one who was stabbed,' Elijah clarified as he stumbled along behind her.

'Oh yes I heard about that, not my thing I'm afraid. I'm a bit more the laundry and bed baths kind of girl, don't you know?' She stopped outside some double doors and allowed Elijah to push them open before following him in. 'If you plonk that lot down near those other boxes,' she suggested a spot with her foot, 'then I can put this one on top.'

Elijah did as instructed then softened out some of the bulges between the remaining buttons on his jacket.

'You know, I'm thinking to myself, you're not the smartest policeman in town, are you?' she smiled. When Elijah looked instantly sad and bashful the nurse quickly added, 'I meant your outfit, not yer mind.' After brushing some dust and green marks off his shoulder she put a hand on his cheek. 'You really could do with a shave as well.'

The girl was so bright eyed and beautiful Elijah had a sudden and strong youthful urge to kiss her. He caught himself just in time and thought better of it, based on several past experiences.

'Can you tell me where he is at least? The chap who were hurt? Is he still alive?' Elijah asked the questions rapidly then grimaced at the memory of the sound of stabbing him with the shiny steel blade of his knuckleduster knife.

'As far as I know, no one has passed away in here since yesterday, which is nice. He *was* on the recovery ward with the other man, the German flyer. I think they've moved the soldier to a separate room now.' She stepped back out into the corridor beckoning Elijah to follow. 'Down there, turn left and go down to the row of doors at the end. Last but one should be him.' She pointed into the distance then checked the watch on her chest. 'I have to go now, but maybe I'll see you later at the blow out in town?'

'Alright,' Elijah said absently as he started to walk away. Then he came back with, 'Blow out?'

'The gathering, you know?' She paused while he covered the remaining few steps towards her and then added, 'Sure everyone's talking about it. The major and his men are throwing a great big bash in the centre of town at seven tonight. To introduce them selves properly, no doubt.'

'The Major, at seven you say?' Elijah looked hard into her eyes then had to look away. 'And *all* the soldiers will be there?'

'Oh well, I imagine they'll leave a few at your place.'

'My place?'

'To guard all them folks they've locked up so far.' She checked the time again. 'You do know they've promised a gigantic feast and there's a rumour they're going to give away all sorts of other stuff.'

Elijah shook his head in confusion, 'What? I mean who is locked up and why are they giving out gifts?'

'Ah your kidding me, you must know?' It was her turn to look bemused.

Elijah thought on his feet, 'You see, I've been drafted in to help, just like you. No one tells us anything.'

The nurse nodded, 'Well I just keep my ears open and my mouth shut, like my good mother always told me to.' She still felt he should know more than he did, or at least more than she did. 'I suppose the Major wants to cheer everyone up and get them on side. So have you not been back to the station today or something? I heard they have half the town in the clink. Is it not true?'

'Oh yes, sure they do,' Elijah pursed his lips in thought. 'And you're alright with that, the Major giving out free food and gifts to make everyone behave?' He had anger in his voice.

'There is only one man that makes me behave and he does not wear a uniform,' she tutted. 'You are an odd bobby you know? Look, I have to go, your man's down there.'

The nurse turned to leave, but Elijah grabbed an arm to spin her back and kissed her hard on the lips. *Time was short and what the hell,* his mind kept saying. Something had reignited the hero in him like a spark to petrol. He suddenly felt like a movie star and wanted to save the town, his town from the wicked foe. Eventually he stood back and asked, 'What's your name?'

After slapping him hard across the cheek, the nurse looked up through her long eyelashes and fluttered out a breathless, 'Teresa.' Then she coughed and recaptured her senses, 'Sister Teresa Ahern actually and yes, I do mean the bloody holy kind.'

'Sorry,' Elijah went purple and ran off around the nearest corner, as fast as he could.

Teresa touched her lips with a fingertip and sighed, 'Don't be.'

In a room directly below Teresa's feet Peter's breath steamed up the glass behind their one remaining guard. Even now with the odds much more in his favour, Peter waited for a minute more, just in case anyone returned.

'I think he is going to do it,' Rees whispered anxiously. He was slightly surprised by Rudolf's abrupt answer.

'Fähnrich Heikling, you know it is technically your duty to escape? I am in no fit state yet, but Peter thinks he is recovered enough and you are fit, yes? You should both go together, I think. To watch the backs of each other.'

'I can't,' Rees pleaded.

'You can help Peter get to the railway or take from someone a boat? Go home and serve your country again. I will follow when I can.'

Rees shook his head, 'But that is not my wish.'

Rudolf weighed up the possibilities and also the liabilities each of them would bring to an escape attempt. He stood beside Peter and watched the corridor with him for a short time, then went back over to Rees. 'Then I have another thought,' Rudolf said, lifting the cadet's chin. 'You will not like it, but this will make better for the chance to get Peter from here away.'

'Yes Hauptmann Furch,' Rees nodded lamely, knowing he would ultimately do whatever he was ordered to do.

'Rees bleiben, werden wir zeit geben,' Rudolf began to direct Peter.

Peter turned away from the window and replied, 'Rees ist ein feigling. Was ist ihr plan?'

Upstairs Elijah moved cautiously along and stopped outside the door Teresa had indicated to him. When he knocked lightly, there was no reply. After taking time to check around the hallway he slowly turned the handle and crept inside. The only occupant was in bed, wearing striped pyjamas beneath crisp linen sheets. One arm was outstretched, connected to a long rubber tubed drip. Most importantly the rest of his body was asleep and snoring loudly.

Elijah walked over and looked down on the man with curiosity. He had come to find out if this person was alive, or dead. No thought had been put into what would happen after that question had been resolved.

Just to make sure this was the right man, Elijah pulled back the sheets and checked for a bandage in the area he had stabbed last night. Then he carefully pushed the man's head to one side and found the boot mark and bruising Pat had given him in the dark.

Teresa's words had rattled Elijah. She had been so complacent to the concept of these Germans taking over the town. Like it was the best thing for everyone to just get on with it? Beneath the police helmet an angry thought rose to the surface and spread out. It polluted Elijah's mind like oil on water until there was no more guilt on the surface.

Part of him just wanted to finish the job he'd started, the job he was trained to do. He visualised the hateful Sergeant Major who had screamed at him for three days, telling him to be a man. "Shake away the guilt boy and fight", the snarly little bulldozer had shouted at every training session before knocking Elijah back down into the dirt.

The Sergeant Major had trained them to use lethal weapons with lethal force, but not pillows, never pillows. Elijah didn't know where it had come from. It was in his hands and yet that was the first time he had noticed it. He rotated it several times then folded it over to make a thicker pad.

Removing the pillow had changed the angle of the patient's head and as a result he was now beginning to stir from sleep.

The solitary sentry on guard downstairs was not aware of the handle behind him slowly turning. When he did hear the door scrape open and began to spin around, it was too late.

Peter and Rees yanked him into their room. Rees was no fighter and quickly got pushed aside as the guard lashed out and tried to call for help. Peter squashed the air out of the soldier with a knee. The weaker looking and deceptively bespectacled German then let rip several hard blows to the man's face with the palm of his hand.

As soon as the guard was face down and subdued, Rudolf stepped forward and thrust something into the back of his neck. It seemed to the confused soldier that his prisoner suddenly had a weapon. The way Rudolf held it, the shape and proximity were real and frightening. The Australian gave in and put up his hands.

Rudolf stepped back, allowing Peter to reach around and yank the guards rifle strap from beneath him. When the guard bravely tried to call out again Rees was ready to shove an apple in his mouth.

'Get his uniform off and tie him up Cadet,' Rudolf urged to Rees as he put down the crutch he'd been pointing at the guard and tied a pillowcase around the man's face.

Rees passed over the guard's garments and Peter helped Rudolf as he struggled to put them on. Once dressed the commander turned to Peter and ordered, 'Gib mir die gewehr.' Then in a more friendly and joking way he added, 'Die Australier müssen es uns mit zu schießen.'

Peter passed him the rifle then turned on his heels, took a sideways look down the corridor and jogged away still limping a little.

'*Walk, don't run you fool,*' Rudolf hissed as he closed the door and took up the sentries position in the hallway.

It was all a waste of time.

As Peter bolted away head down, he smashed into something coming around the corner. Where there had been one fleeing German, there was now also a wheelchair and two very angry Australian patients. One was in full uniform with a sling; the other was in an army shirt and pyjama bottom combo. All three men and the chair ended up wrapped over and around each other as they tumbled to the floor.

The German kicked and punched at anything soft as he tried to push himself free. The two rattled men fought back as best they could until Peter produced a long knife.

As the tip moved closer to Nigel's eye, he reversed his arm, letting go of Peter's trousers and belt. 'All right mate, calm down,' Nigel raised his hands.

'Yeh, no worries, off yer go then,' John spat out some blood and tried to use the overturned chair to get up on his feet.

Peter pushed free and palmed the wall to help to climb upright, then after one last sharp kick he circled around John and reversed away towards the exit. He could see Rudolf in the distance, aiming the rifle to cover him. Peter nodded his thanks, turned away and was gone.

'That was one of our dovers he had in his mits,' Nigel scowled.

John righted the chair and held it steady for his friend. 'I saw you had your eye on it mate,' he joked.

'Bloody deadhead thieving Germans,' Nigel cursed, ignoring his friend and climbing back on board. 'Well are you going to get after that garlic muncher or do I have to drive us?'

John frowned, then patted Nigel on the head and chased off after Peter. Nigel span the chair to see whom his attacker had nodded to, but the corridor was empty.

As Rees closed the door behind his commander he asked, 'Change of plan Herr Hauptmann?'

'Ja, Peter is on his own now,' Rudolf nodded. He slid the gun's bolt forward expelling the bullet then placed the weapon safely against the wall.

Rees looked at the rifle, 'Did you mean it? The last thing you said to Peter, when you said they would need the gun to shoot us with?'

'We have captured our own doorman, also helped a prisoner escape, and I am now technically dressed as a spy.' The pilot looked deep into Rees's worried face, 'Major Jackson is how do they say, an understanding fellow, but all this will be pushing his boat out too far I think.'

Rees started to panic, unable to think.

'We will be alright Rees, as long as the men here remain calm,' Rudolf consoled him. 'Now quickly, help me get out of this enemy uniform.'

Outside the hospital, through the frosted glass brick wall you could just make out the small and distorted figure of Peter. He popped out through the side doors then slowed down a little about ten yards out and caught his breath.

John was soon smashing through the same exit, but he didn't stop for air and easily caught up with the limping escapee. A flying Australian rules tackle bought Peter down ten more yards from the doors. As the men climbed over each other in a wrestle, John got in a punch with his good arm. Peter flipped back over and slashed out angrily with the stolen blade. The steel drew a deep crimson line across the Australian's beige shirt just above the breast pocket.

As John defensively fell back, Peter sat up and raised the blade high above his head ready for a kill. It was time for John to die.

As a single shot rang out behind them, Peter dropped the blade and collapsed backwards clutching his throat.

High above all this Elijah was startled by the noise of gunfire and paused in his task. Private Roach had woken up very drowsily just as the pillow was fully applied. The injured man had been confused and dazed, but revived enough to struggle for life each time Elijah shoved down. The drip pole had swished past the men's heads in the tussle, smashing its glass bottle noisily across the tiled floor.

'Damn you,' Elijah shouted, knowing he had to go now and go fast. He dropped the pillow and hooked the man square on the jaw with his right, knocking him unconscious. Stealing a few seconds to look out of the window, he saw the backs of several soldiers. They were moving away with machine guns aimed down towards two more men lying on the ground. One was a German officer for sure, the others were just backs and braces.

John slowly lifted his head to look past his fellow soldiers and saw Doctor Jones standing off to one side of the hospital doorway. The doctor was holding a smoking service revolver in one hand with a similarly smoking pipe grasped between his teeth.

'Are you alright young man?' Jones called out as he casually tapped his tobacco out on the wall. He then checked to see if anyone else was about to burst through the exit archway before walking over to the fight scene.

'Shoulder might need another patch up Doc and I think I've got some new work for you,' John called back. He looked down at the dead German and asked, 'That was one hell of a shot. How the hell did you manage to be right there and right then?'

'Actually I was aiming for his hand.' Doctor Jones shrugged off the uncomfortable applause that the other Australians were now giving him. 'And I was expecting to have a chat with a big dodgy looking policeman,' he added, looking back over at the bike, 'not to shoot this swine.'

'Well fair dinkum Doc, I'm mighty pleased you were expecting anyone to be honest.' John ran his fingers over the warm wet gash in his shirt and asked, 'But why did you want to shoot a copper?'

'Oh I didn't want to shoot anyone,' the doctor replied as he inspected John's wound. 'I just wanted to ask the bobby why he had my wife's bike?'

As far away as you could be in the same building, Elijah had left quickly by the front doors. He walked over to a row of vehicles, seemingly without a care. Once there he assisted a middle-aged man to haul a pregnant lady out of a small car. Squishing himself in along side, Elijah manoeuvred around the man until all of them were free.

'Thank you officer,' the man said, moving a hand towards his rain coat pocket to give the lad a tip.

'No need sir,' Elijah smiled out from beneath the helmet. When the couple had moved off, he added, 'All in a days work sir, all in a days work.' Then he threw the car keys he'd just stolen off them, tossing them high up in the air and catching them again with a broad grin.

It was more than time to flee now, but Elijah was in no immediate rush to get back to base. He was obviously not happy about how any of this had turned out and felt like a grade one bungler.

For starters he had failed again and knew that Harry would rake him over severely on his return. Edward, Patrick and even Finn would probably have a few words to say too. He did at least have some solid intelligence to give them.

While driving Elijah removed the helmet and tunic and changed his disguise to a simple pair of sunglasses from the car's glove box. A mile away from the hospital he saw a big camouflaged vehicle moving towards him. Even from this far away he could make out an aerial with a broad loop at the top sticking out of the trucks roof. He decided not to risk getting any closer and turned off down a side road heading for home.

Behind him, on the main road, someone banged on the cab of the radio wagon. The engine revved as it dropped gears and pulled over on the kerb.

'I got something then,' Cartwright shouted over the noise. Sparks let go the antenna wheel and listened as the lad added, 'Sorry, it's gone now.'

'May as well stay put for a bit then, see what we get and wait for the others to catch up?' Sparks suggested. 'I figure the radio we're homing in on is a bit far-gone mate. A fizzer that's fizzled out, right?'

'Right?' Neville agreed without really understanding what he had agreed to.

Sparks ushered Neville away, 'You blokes go and have a smoke in the sun, I'll take a punt on the headset. Trust the expert eh.'

'Yeh, right then,' Neville complied, but also wondered *how much of an expert you needed to be in order to turn a knob?*

'And tell the driver to shut down the engine for now, but keep the genny going,' Sparks called after him.

With a crunch of gravel the ute pulled up behind the wagon and Major Jackson leapt out. He climbed up the tailgate while Captain Dreyer ushered everyone else to assemble at the rear.

'Right folks,' Jackson said while unfurling a map. 'I think we have something here, take a gander.'

Captain Dreyer, Noah and Corporal Jarli joined the flock for an eye level view, but Sparks stayed at his post within.

'The other end of this service track is up the road a ways,' Jackson thumbed the general direction. 'This old sawmill, yard and bush area is about half way in. You're looking for a signals hut, could be an old building or an outhouse with an antennae of some sort?' He prodded the map, 'This place is as likely a candidate as any for now.'

Captain Dreyer called up to Sparks, 'Corporal Chambers have you got anything to help seal the deal?'

'Definitely coming from the right direction. We caught a few bursts driving back and forth, then,' Sparks flicked a switch and held up his hand as something else came in on the main set. The signaller held his neck microphone in place and replied, 'Unit Two receiving, go ahead.' He tilted his head towards the others, 'Sir it's a message from the hospital.'

It took seconds, but it seemed like an age. All the men could hear was the generator and the wireless whistling as they waited impatiently for the news.

'Relaying message, over.' Sparks looked up again, 'One of the prisoners attempted to escape Major. He tried to kill Private Crook.'

'Not again, is he hurt?' Noah asked abruptly.

'Crook, is OK. Some bloke, a doctor shot the prisoner, Peter something?' Sparks held one of the headphones against his ear as more details came through, 'OK, there's a lot of confusion, but I think they're saying a copper tried to bump off Roach then stole a car?' He pressed the transmit button again, 'We got that, anything more? Over.'

The men leaned in so much that the trucks suspension dropped an inch.

Sparks took the microphone away, 'The hospital surgeons have confirmed that a .22 bullet killed Chief Higgins sir. Got that. Over and out.' The signaller looked across the row of expectant faces and held out his hands, 'Sorry guys, but that's all she wrote.'

'Right men, let's go, the major ordered.

Minutes later the service track melted from grey bitumen to potholed brown rubble beneath their vehicles. It was all the men could do to hold down bits of radio and other equipment as it skipped around on the shuddering floor.

Not far behind them, a motorbike and rider were idling against a gatepost. As soon as the little convoy disappeared from view, Justine slowly pulled away and followed the little convoy along a parallel track, mirroring their moves.

When the truck had crossed a broad flat stream, the ute pulled over behind it and an outstretched hand signalled them to stop. According to the map they were almost there and the major sought to complete the journey more stealthily, on foot. He climbed out and drew a finger across his throat. The truck driver immediately cut the engine and generator, leaving bird song and the sound of trickling water to drift by in the gap.

'Have you got something more portable?' Captain Dreyer asked as Sparks stuck his head around the wagons tarpaulin to blink in the sunlight.

'Yes sir,' he nodded enthusiastically, 'If Neville carries the back pack I can work him from behind, so to speak.'

The men strapped Neville into a heavy harness and handed him something shiny to hold out front. 'What the heck is this?' he asked, twirling it around in Corporal Chamber's face.

'TDA,' Sparks explained.

Neville furrowed his brow in response.

'Transportable Directional Antenna.' A pat on Neville's shoulder seemed to signify the end of Corporal Spark's explanation.

'Looks like a couple of coat hangers held together with window putty and tape?' one of the men probed.

'Had to improvise mate,' Sparks sounded hurt. 'Not as powerful as the big rig, but I reckon if we're nearly on it, we should be good enough.'

'And what do I do with it?' Neville had begun to wave the receiver above his head.

'Just hold it like this out in front then walk in a straight line mate.'

Dreyer signalled and the rest of the men spread out forming a wide concave crescent with Neville, Sparks and the radio pack taking rear centre stage. It took a few minutes to clear through the remaining trees, at which point it was easy to see there was very little cover ahead of that.

All of the trees surrounding this side of the old lumberyard had been mown down as far as the next hill. There were no buildings left standing, no huts or storage areas and barely even any foundations. Just lines of rubble here and there and an old cinder track with several weedy paths leading to more patches of nothing. It was stark, just a spotty landscape of mossy stumps and skinny mutated coppiced fingers sticking up here and there.

Major Jackson cautioned everyone to stay alert as they moved out. When they'd crossed over the flattest part of clearing Sparks called out crossly, 'Nev, don't just swing it around like that.'

Neville argued, 'I ain't moved nowt but me feet pal.'

Sparks turned the dial all the way around then back again just to be sure. 'Thing is mate,' he whispered, 'the signal is coming from behind us now.' There was a pause before he smirked and said excitedly, 'Major.'

The major flapped a hand and everyone crouched down in the thicket between the stumps.

Chapter Twenty-Three

Still squatting down, Jarli scanned his eyes around the seemingly empty landscape again. 'Maybe them is under the earth sir, like a mud frog?' he suggested.

The major nodded, 'They must be, but did you see any tracks back there that don't belong?'

Jarli shook his head, 'But if they comes up near that shale path, they could easy walkabout in someone else's old feet.'

Captain Dreyer motioned to Sparks and pointed along the track. The signaller took Neville and ranged along it, stopping twice at one particular point. At that spot there was a narrow oasis in the sea of roots and bare earth where ferns and wild flowers had flourished around a big old Hazel stump and a tall, spindly sapling.

'Can we talk to them?' the major shouted across to Sparks as they moved in closer, 'I know you said it was all double module thingamajigs, but right here on top of them, can we talk back?'

'If their ends still shorting out, well I can try,' Sparks agreed and reversed some of the transceiver's settings.

Captain Dreyer had a thought, 'If they still think we're Germans they won't answer, I know I wouldn't.' He turned and walked backwards toward his commander swathing huge arcs with his eyes and weapon, checking the perimeter for any movement.

Neville stepped up, 'The lads know me sir and Mary, I asked her out once. She said no, obviously.'

Jackson approved, 'They might think you're being coerced son, but let's give it a go.'

Neville scratched a bristled chin. 'What should I say?'

'Something short mate, and make it sound very Pommy?' Sparks winked, passing the throat microphone over Neville's shoulder. The signaller threw a final switch and tuned the dial carefully. 'Your on the air Nev, just push it against your neck and talk.'

'Hello this is Nev, is there anybody out there?' was Neville's feeble first attempt.

The other men glared at him.

276

'Say something British mate, something you all know?' Sparks insisted.

After thinking hard about this Neville blurted out, 'Can you hear me mother?'

'Is one of 'em his mum?' Jarli whispered to Noah.

Sparks played with the dial, 'I can hear something, like an open channel, but no one's talking?'

'Shall I try again sir?' Neville asked nervously touching the microphone. The officers nodded. 'Honest it's Neville Cartwright here. We've come to help, because you've got it wrong see?' Neville gave it a moment or two. 'The men in town are British soldiers, well Australian ones anyway, some of them are really nice.'

Captain Dreyer interrupted, 'Can you ask if they'd like to come out now please?'

'The Australian captain is wondering if you'd like to come up? We don't want anyone to get hurt, we...'

Something came crackling back.

'We got 'em,' Sparks said and switched the voice onto a speaker.

"...LLO, HELLO, NEV IS THAT YOU? CAN YOU..." The sound was cut by a sharp slap and the tone changed to say, "PUT THAT DOWN YOU STUPID GIRL!" Followed by another slap then a scuffle and finally a click. After that there was nothing more than static.

'Keep trying son,' the major insisted. 'Get ready men, Jarli you lead the way. Captain, Noah, follow us. The rest of you fan out in the tree line facing this clump of green.'

Before anyone could really move, Jarli put up a hand and cried, 'Snake,' but he sounded uncertain.

Several feet from the old hazel stump a tall spindly tree started swaying as what looked like a thin brown reptile helter-skeltered down. It juddered around the base then disappeared into the ground with a tail whip.

As the officers crouched for cover around the stump, several gunshots thudded under their feet. All but one man dived away with them, falling instinctively into the dirt, but no bullets broke the surface. Jarli was still standing, he counted off the seconds and got to nine. Before anything more could be done there was an audible click and a scrape. Directly in front of Dreyer's eyes a square of weeds and earth surrounding the Hazel stump rose up several inches. Its hidden mechanism engaged and revolved the cover aside revealing a dark square that dropped away into a brick built hole. Peering over the edge with great caution, Jarli could see a woman's hand; it was waving a white handkerchief.

'Coming up,' a big Irish voice shouted. 'I surrender.'

With guns aimed at her from all over the site, Mary emerged squinting into the afternoon.

'Keep going,' Jackson ordered, getting to his feet and waving his pistol. 'Has anyone else decided to leave?'

'What? I can't hear you properly, speak up?' Mary cupped her raised hands around her ears. Noah raised his gun toward her and panned across as she stepped clear of the opening. She abruptly understood what the major was asking her and explained quite simply, 'Oh, she died.'

As her vision and hearing returned, Mary smiled with the relief that these men *were* Australian after all. Then she slowly nurtured the realisation of what that meant. Of the damage the others must have caused by now. The soldiers watched her crumble as huge waves of confusion and guilt hit home. 'Oh Patrick,' she sobbed.

It seemed madness now, but getting Pat to join up over here, had been her way of keeping him out of trouble. Political fighting had earned Pat a place on several hit lists back home. That had been the reason they'd all emigrated here.

Convincing him to fight for King and country was difficult, but not as bad as getting past the local Police Chief's checks and interviews. Finally they'd both been called to London and a few days later on Mary's oath, Patrick was approved. Eventually, he became happy to be back amongst brothers in arms, protecting all their families from a far worse enemy than before.

Mary imagined him out there now, armed to the teeth with everything but the truth. Her final mental image was of what had just happened to Mrs Hill. She began to chant out loud, 'Hail Mary full of Grace, the Lord is with thee. Blessed are thou among women and blessed is the fruit of thy womb Jesus. Holy Mary Mother of God, pray for us sinners now and at the hour of our death.' She stopped suddenly and sobbed.

Captain Dreyer tried to ascertain what had happened, but every question made her cry more deeply. When she had eventually calmed herself, he tried to verify if it was safe to go down the ladder. Mary nodded.

Noah volunteered Jarli and himself for the job, but the corporal was far from keen. Seeing the wooden stump rise out of the ground had unnerved him.

'Me old fellah told stories of them people in the earth!' Jarli fretted, backing away.

'Come on mate, just like the pig tunnel right?' Noah smiled.

Jarli started to move forward again, then noticed a black, downy feather caught on the bark of the tree stump. 'This ain't no factory,' he said with genuine fear. 'This is Kurdaitcha.'

Noah swapped his weapon for the corporal's pistol with a grunt of understanding and descended into the darkness alone. Thirty seconds later his voice was back, 'One dead Sheila and an exit tube at the rear.' Noah's head came out beneath the major's feet and looked up. 'Someone could have escaped that way? Must come up over there somewhere.'

Jackson followed the private back down. When he'd gone the captain escorted Mary over to a small pile of corner stones on the other side of the path.

'The cow didn't believe you. I had my doubts all along, about everything, but...'

'Captain Dreyer crouched down to the girls eye level. 'You need to fill in the gaps as quick as you can, there's still a lot to do.'

Mary nodded, 'Susan outranked me and well, well she's a bloody fanatic. When she thought we were done for she said we had to get rid of everything, smash the equipment and then I reckon it would have been me.'

Dreyer hesitated, 'A suicide pact?'

'Not one that I had agreed to, it's a sin. God forbid and all that. She got her husbands crappy old gun out, then she told me to pull in the aerial and I thought, here we go.' Mary paused and fiddled with her hair. 'Well I didn't think to be honest and that's the truth. Soon as she turned away I looped the cable around her fat neck, stuck my boot on her arse and pulled.'

'So she tried to shoot you while you were,' Dreyer chose his words carefully and pointed to her ear. 'While you were resisting.'

Mary felt around her hairline and said with genuine surprise, 'That old bitch shot me.'

The major emerged behind them and shouted excitedly from the opening, 'Amazing signals bunker down here Captain, come and take a look.' He climbed out and crossed over to them. 'There's a sleeping section, transmitter room, stores and well, if you could run your *professional* eye over the *scene* please.'

Dreyer understood and left Mary in the major's care. While descending the ladder he caught a glimpse of Noah popping up behind some bushes, twenty yards away. Noah waved, looked around quickly then shot back down and disappeared.

'So where are the others, the men?' the major asked as he passed over a packet of cigarettes and a handbag he'd found in the bunker.

'Not here, we don't know where they are. It's supposed to be safer that way you see?' Mary rummaged in the bag for a light.

Jackson signalled for his men to stand down then noticed the lighter. 'Where did you get that?' he demanded as he snatched it from her and turned it over. It was made from a bullet casing, exactly the same as the one that had killed Chief Higgins.

'The bitch stole it from *me,*' Justine called out angrily as she ran out across the clearing. On arrival she slapped Mary hard across the face and the cigarette went flying. 'She must have snatched it after whacking me over the head.'

Jackson pulled Justine back and called out to his men to lower their weapons again. 'Had a feeling you wouldn't be far behind,' he admitted.

Justine tried to pull away and kick out. 'You said you hadn't seen him. Where is he? Mary, tell me,' she screamed.

The major hoisted Justine around behind him, but as soon as he let go she ducked down and darted back under his arm. Mary put up her hands and Justine snatched the bag, getting several good swats in with it before the major could restrain her again.

'I seen him,' Mary croaked through a curtain of hair and tears, 'He fetched me some parts for the radio.' She calmed herself a little, snatched the smouldering cigarette up from the dirt and took a long drag.

'What exactly happened to your radio?' the major probed calmly.

Mary laughed and shook her head. 'I bloody dropped it. Simple as that.' She let out a huge cloud of smoke. 'That cow said I had to stow it all away after every scheduled transmission. It was days ago. I was rushing so I was, it's a long ride out here on a bike, see? First I dropped the secret panel down, it's hidden in the wall behind the map bench and, well then it hit my other hand on the radio and I dropped it. Sounds daft, but there it is and it feels grand to tell someone the truth.'

Jackson nodded, 'Tried to fix it yourself, right?'

'I was so frightened and when Susan asked about the damage, I just lied and said it had burnt out. Did my best to fix it and I got it working again with some components from the Bakelite radio down there and the parts Harry got us.'

'Yes I spotted that domestic radio under the bench,' Jackson confirmed. 'But it didn't work right, none of it worked? No one replied and you couldn't be sure if it was the broken transmitter or because you'd got *everything* else wrong too.'

Mary laughed again, but not because she thought this was funny. 'I bluffed old Susan, I logged that they'd responded yesterday and ordered us to keep up the good work. She didn't need much convincing.'

'And Mrs Hill couldn't get the news on the old crystal set because you'd gutted it for spares.' Justine folded her arms and shook her head. 'You really are a piece of work Mary, you know people have died because of you?'

'Miss Page,' the major snapped. 'It is not all her fault and don't forget that her broken radio is the reason we've got this far. Now pull your neck in and give her a chance.'

Justine turned away in disgust and started going through the contents of her reclaimed bag as a distraction.

'Susan must have thieved it, your bag I mean,' Mary suggested.

Justine swung back around, but did not lash out at her this time.

'I bet it was her who whacked you out too, she loved a scrap.' Mary lifted her fringe to display a newly forming black eye and bright red cheek.'

Justine felt a tang of compassion as her fading anger crept away and made room for it. 'Where are they Mary?' she begged, 'Where are our boys?'

'I don't know where they are,' Mary insisted. 'Do you think I wouldn't want to save my own brother?'

The major stepped back in between the two women, 'Earlier I saw a message you sent.' He struggled to remember the notes Cartwright had shown him, 'It mentioned something, a report; OB One had completed their orders?'

'Yes that's right, Operational Base One. SD Nine, that's us and Zero Nine is a weather station somewhere in the middle of the county. I swear, when they didn't answer I just convinced myself it was the set not receiving.' Mary put her hands up to her face and cried out through her fingers, 'God I wish I knew where they were.'

'So how can the men talk to you from Operational Base One, if you don't know where they are? Do they transmit too, do they come here?' Jackson scanned quickly around the clearing and signalled to his men to go back to full readiness.

Mary considered the answer, 'They have been here, sort of, but we don't see them.' She tried to explain, 'They drop a note inside a tennis ball, it comes down a fat tube hidden somewhere way out there. You hear it coming for ages and then it rolls out under the radio desk.'

'When?' Major Jackson demanded.

'Could be any time, or not at all,' Mary sighed.

Justine had a go, 'So your job is to come up here and send any messages you get from them?'

'I am supposed to go into town and help observe what the enemy are doing too.'

'What if Zero Nine have a message to pass along for OB One?' Jackson asked, hoping he was onto a winner.

'I report troop movements and messages back to the boys while I'm in town. There's a few dead letter boxes where I can leave notes. We've been using them for months, even before the, before we thought there had been an invasion.' Mary brightened a little, 'Yes, we can tell them that way. Tell them that it's safe to come out and...'

'If you mean the one at Harry's garage, it got blown up. Where are the others?' Justine tried to force shut the bag, but its contents had grown to include a dozen sovereigns, a wad of bank notes and several items she'd lost weeks ago.

The major passed back her lighter for safekeeping.

Justine looked at it thinking back to better times and said, 'Harry made it, does that mean he's the killer?'

Major Jackson gave no reply other than exhaling and looking away.

Justine slumped down next to Mary and they held hands.

'What, what killer?' Mary stopped at that, realising she knew what it could be.

Justine had tears forming in the corners of her eyes as she burst out, 'Help us please Mary, help them.'

'I will, if I can,' Mary said dizzily, 'I feel sick.'

'Not you as well?' Justine groaned.

The major passed his canteen to Mary. He waited while she slurped down half the flask then asked, 'Where are those other dead letter boxes?'

'There is one outside the vicarage in a line of stones around the drive. Susan put hers inside a fake brick near the old school house.' Mary bit her nails and remembered another, 'If the town got overrun we were supposed to only use the big old key at the far chapel, it unscrews clockwise at the handle.'

'The vicarage it is then,' Justine tried a smile, 'Everything else has gone.'

Mary was not ready to smile back yet, 'I am so sorry, this is all my fault. PC Grogan told everyone to shelter, then the sirens came on and someone said there were paratroopers everywhere. I went to check and be sure, but then the bells kicked off and that should mean only one thing, shouldn't it.'

'What ever you've done Mary, this is honestly only partly your fault,' Jackson stated again soothingly.

Mary nodded between sniffs, 'They trained us to drop everything. Everything, if we heard those bells, even our families and friends. I called Susan at the town hall, but I didn't have time to find the boys.'

Justine put an arm around her, 'Well if they've gone to ground, then they made their own assumptions just like you.'

'I went back to town the morning after, but I was so afraid. I, I just couldn't go all the way in. I didn't have the balls.'

'If you had...' Justine stopped.

'I listened and watched from a distance, but I should have been braver.' Mary suddenly remembered something important, 'But today I made it as far as Derry Street and a whole lorry load of Germans nearly ran me down. I saw them with my own eyes, all sat in the back.'

Jackson gave her a sorry expression, 'Captured aircrew I'm afraid and more of my men.'

Five minutes later when everyone had resurfaced and gathered in the clearing for debriefing, the major set out his plans. Contact was the priority.

Noah used the lengthy antenna cable to probe deep into the tennis ball message chute beneath Mary's communication desk. He'd attached a red ribbon from Susan's collection and Jarli was dispatched to scout around for any sign of it breaking the surface. He hadn't found it yet. Once discovered, Jarli and two riflemen planned to hide up to monitor the drop point from a distance and the first trap would be set.

Sparks joined Noah to study the radio bunkers, documenting the equipment and gathering up any intelligence while they waited for movement from above.

Dreyer, Jackson and the girls returned to town in the ute, where they would drop a dead letter inside a rock. As their car departed, Mrs Hill's body was being hauled out along the escape duct with as much respect as possible. Her corpse was loaded onto the truck with the last of the men and driven away on route to the hospital.

The ute's journey to town passed in relative silence, other than a brief discussion about what to put in the note. The final version read, "OB One surrender. Not Germans. Not an invasion. Stop fighting." The car pulled over a couple of streets away from the vicarage and Mary got out nervously to walk on alone. Justine followed her at a short distance while Captain Dreyer climbed down from the tailgate and got into the passenger seat next to his commander.

'So,' Jackson asked him immediately. 'Where do we go from here?'

When Mary reached the vicars house she pretended to have a pebble in her shoe and Justine held back. The little Irish girl crouched down and removed a pale boulder from the paths border.

Justine stood next to a bus sign and watched as her friend picked something else up, it glinted. Mary took a last look around, hid her note inside a void in the boulder and replaced it in the line of rocks. Once this was done she continued along the road and around the corner with Justine closing in at her heals. The moment she was within striking distance Mary swivelled around and flew at her blindly, sending both of them sprawling into the bushes.

'Wait,' Justine shrieked as Mary straddled her and raised a shiny fist. 'Please, I'm pregnant.' Justine had promised herself she would tell Harry first, but even in this awful scenario, it felt good to confide in her friend.

'Well if it's a girl, call her after me,' Mary scowled, raising her fist another inch. It took a moment to find the hope in Justine's fear filled face. After that she rolled away beside her and said calmly, 'No, you're right, bad idea. Sure call her something else.'

Justine sat up angrily, 'What the hell Mary, we were trying to help you.'

'You just don't get it do you, I killed Susan and those bastards will string me up for her murder.'

'Who, the Australians, how can they?' Justine tried to calm herself. 'You were acting in self defence.'

Mary sat up, pulled off the newly acquired knuckle-duster and prodded a finger at the empty air between them, 'I mean the men in Whitehall. They'll either hang me in a corner to rot or lock me away till the end of the war. The best I can hope for is being sent on a suicide mission somewhere real bad.'

Justine thought about everything long and hard then looked around for her bag. 'Here,' she said, urging Mary to take it. 'Please, it's full of money and none of it is mine. There's lipstick, sunglasses, your fags, the lot.'

Mary took it and the two hugged briefly. While they embraced she said, 'I won't forget you.'

As they helped each other up Justine brushed away some leaves and advised Mary to clean herself up, 'There's blood on your shoulder, we should swap.'

When they exchanged tops Mary noticed the gun down the back of Justine's waist line and asked, 'Where did you get hold of such a thing?'

Justine shyly admitted, 'It was the German pilot's, I just kept it. I don't know why.'

'Well be careful you don't shoot off yer own arsehole with that temperamental German crap,' Mary winked. 'Will you give a tale to my mar and pa and tell Pat I'll be with friends?' She rummaged in the bag then donned the sunglasses to hide her eye. 'Look if I'm going, then I have to go now.'

Justine nodded, lost for words and held out a hand for Mary to shake.

Mary stood on tiptoe and kissed Justine on the cheek. Before her lips pulled away, a salty tear rolled through the same spot. She turned before her friend could see that she was also crying and strolled briskly away.

Justine wiped her face and headed back around the corner towards the major's car, as slowly as she could.

'You let her go didn't you?' Dreyer scalded through the open car window when Justine arrived.

She nodded.

The major smiled, 'I win then, which means you're filling out all the paperwork Professor.'

'I had to,' Justine admitted guiltily as she got in.

The major felt he needed to explain his own thoughts to be fair. 'Relax, it's fine,' he said reassuringly. 'We were pretty sure you'd help her if she chose to make a run for it.' He pointed at the captain, 'This ding-a-ling didn't think you were up for it. You realise I sent him down that bunker to check out the murder scene, not to look at shelves and brickwork?'

'Mary acted purely in self defence,' Dreyer confirmed. 'From the pattern of shots, it was a close thing either way.'

'That woman would have killed her,' Major Jackson sat back and mused on the scene in his head. 'Then possibly some of us, I reckon she'd only have saved the last bullet for herself anyway.'

'We can still cut Mary off if you think letting her go is the wrong thing?' Dreyer urged as he got comfy around the gearshift. They both chose not to answer him.

'Time to move on then, where next?' Justine asked.

The major brushed the stubble on his chin thoughtfully, 'Better get ready for the party I guess. I feel a bit daggy, need to get rid of this face fungus and grab a fairy bower.'

'A shave and a shower?' Justine guessed. 'Are you serious?' Justine couldn't believe the man's depth of impudence. 'What about Harry?'

'Not a fat lot else we *can* do for now,' Jackson began as they drove away. 'If those fellers are coming out, I reckon it'll be after dark and I want everyone else tucked up safe by then.'

'Then when we track your bloke and his mob down...' Dreyer noticed Justine was glaring at him in the mirror. He coughed a little and continued with less enthusiasm, 'Well, empty streets means safer streets, right?'

'But where is safe?' Justine demanded impatiently.

'Trust me,' the major tapped the side of his nose. 'To the pub then, it's been a flaming long day.'

The ute drove to the Station Hotel, going the long way round so that they wouldn't catch up with Mary along the route. After dropping them off, Captain Dryer climbed over and drove on toward the police station.

Justine remained outside at first fumbling with the pockets on Mary's jacket, not knowing what she was supposed to do or think next.

Jackson popped his head back out of the reception doorway and asked, 'You mind having a sit in the bar with a cold drink while I change?'

Justine looked at him trying to decide if he meant he would be changing in the bar while she drank. After a period of uncomfortable indecision she decided to go around and wait in the beer garden instead.

Sat in the sun she began to relax, more out of tiredness than anything else. Two floors above her someone who sounded suspiciously like the major had just started singing, "Hang Out the Stars in Indiana". If it was him, he was clearly caught in the moment and unaware that she and several of his men were listening to every note.

When the fresh faced major eventually returned to the fold, his men stood to acknowledge him with embarrassed greetings.

Justine burst the bubble by slurping up some dregs of lemon squash through a paper straw. Before Major Jackson could order more refreshment, the army cook bought over some curled up sandwiches and two cold looking bottles. As the catering Sergeant departed he made agitated sideways head gestures to the other men. *They* got the message and cleared them selves away with haste.

Jackson adjusted his top button and sat down. When they were alone he asked, 'Was it something I said?'

'No,' Justine giggled, 'It was something you sang.' She considered how much more dashing he looked with his face, hair and uniform all polished up and tidy.

'You could hear that?' he said quietly and looked around, deeply ashamed.

She wondered if he had someone at home to sing to, then felt guilty for even considering that he might have been serenading her.

'Those diggers haven't been bothering you have they?' He checked again, just to make sure everyone was still on the move.

'They have all been perfect gentlemen thank you,' she smiled.

'The captain tells me you're in the pudding club?' the major said casually without a hint of judgement.

She took a moment to catch his drift and then shot him an offended look.

'No worries, good luck to you, both of you obviously. Thing is, it's going to get a bit dangerous around here, tonight, tomorrow, who knows? From now on I think you should follow your friends lead and get out of town.'

'He needs me and so do you. No matter what, I'm staying till the end.' Justine leaned forward, 'Look, I am going to your bloody party, you did say we would *all* be safe there.'

The major took a swig from one of the bottles and shrugged, 'Well that was the idea.'

'That man from the government called me earlier. He said not to tell you.'

'Mr Stevenson, what did he want?' Jackson put down the bottle and rested his chin over its neck.

'He asked me about everything that was going on, but, well he seemed to know most of it without my help. Apart from the last bit, about the radio bunker.'

The major showed little reaction as he said, 'Go on.'

'Well, he implied that any information I could give him would help to coordinate his limited resources.' Justine blushed, 'He promised me, if I kept quiet, he'd find out where Harry was and get back to me as soon as he could.'

'So why aren't you keeping quiet?'

'I trust you now, more than him, more than Harry, more than anyone.'

'Well like you say, the bloke knew most of it anyway.' He smiled back and reached out to put a reassuring hand on hers, 'Don't worry.'

Justine gently pulled her arm away, 'You will try *not* to shoot Harry, or any of them? Only I keep asking and you never give me a straight answer.'

'If they shoot first we won't have a choice.'

Justine shuddered.

'Look, Captain Dreyer is getting the word around as we speak. So my men will know what's going on around here, before they start shooting. I'm giving everyone a fair crack of the whip that way.'

'But,' Justine struggled.

Major Jackson slid the other bottle of beer across the table and reasoned, 'Some say my nations creed is, "If it moves shoot it, if it doesn't, chop it down". I've asked the captain to suggest a more lenient approach to the men.' He gave her his most serious of expressions.

'Thank you,' Justine picked up the beer and used the cold bottle to cool her neck.

'But if push comes to shove,' he shrugged, not wanting to finish his train of thought. Instead he grabbed a handful of sandwiches and got up saying, 'Why don't we go and find everyone else then?'

They walked towards the centre of town where the streets were swarming with pre-revellers. They were all waving the leaflets that the

Australians had been distributing. Men cheered as the major and Justine passed. The women gave accusing looks and whispered to each other instead.

'Word seems to have got around then?' Jackson smiled.

'Yep, and in more ways than you'd think,' Justine added. 'How exactly are you going to get this rabble organised and into one place?'

'Haven't you heard? I'm like the Pied Piper of Sydney Harbour,' Major Jackson bowed down and swirled his cap, playing to the growing crowd. 'Besides,' he whispered to Justine, 'Who said there was only *one* place?'

They continued along with the spawning congregation heading towards the grand park at the centre of town. By the time they'd climbed the hill to the bandstand and turned around, the numbers behind them had tripled. It looked like the whole town were gathered on the grass and in the streets and pubs that surrounded them.

Jackson knew that not *everyone* would come, but at least he could guarantee a fair percentage of the inhabitants would gather to be safe under his wings tonight.

'Hello sweetheart,' Mrs Clark shouted from behind them as she pushed herself in between Justine and the major. 'Any news of Harry?' she cooed.

'Not really sorry, but there is a plan,' Justine apologised, then added awkwardly, 'Major Jackson this is Harry's mother Mrs Clark.'

Jackson nodded hello, 'My captain tells me you've seen more of Harry than anyone else, since he disappeared.'

'And our Flo tells me you've seen more of Miss Page than anyone else since, my Harry buggered off.'

Jackson mulled over the remark then asked, 'And do you have any useful gossip?'

'Now don't be a smart arse. I was out half cold when I seen him, nowt I could do, but you've got an 'ole army ain't ya?' Margaret poked a finger in his chest as she spoke. 'What you gonna do to find him?'

'Patience Mrs Clark, we don't know where to look so it's safer for them to find us,' Jackson said absently, ignoring her pokes and tallying the crowd to judge rough numbers. 'We need them out in the open where we can talk, not sneaking around like Robin Hood in the bush.'

'So you're the bait and we're the sandbags,' Margaret Clark scowled.

The major finished counting and looked directly at her, 'I reckon almost everyone has come out and soon they'll be safely under my guard. We'll have loudspeakers in key locations and when the men come we'll be ready, you'll see.'

'Loud speakers? What you gonna do, tell 'em off an' give 'em a good scalding is it? You better be as good as everyone says,' Mrs Clark's eyes drilled deep into the major for quite some time. When she was satisfied he'd understood, her mouth turned to Justine and said softly, 'I was just telling Nurse Jones, oh where has she gone?' Margaret twitched and looked around the crowd like a bird. 'Anyway, I told her what's been happening since you woke up. Here, did you know her Terrance saved a man's life today? Not in a doctory way mind. No, he shot a German lad in the neck. Right mess it was apparently.'

Justine shook her head and turned a little green.

'I heard it was the face,' Florence suggested as she squeezed her bosoms into the group.

'Florence, where have you been?' Margaret huffed impatiently.

'I been 'ere abouts, saw you ten minutes back I did, when you was chatting with Mrs Jones. I had summat to discus with our Enid,' Florence waved at someone nearby then turned back to Margaret. 'Woman's troubles,' she said with her lips, while hardly making a sound. Then the big lass hoicked up one of her breasts with the back of a hand and smiled at them all, 'Anyway, I'm here now and, who's this handsome bugger?'

Before Florence could be properly introduced, the four-faced clock in the square below chimed seven.

'Well if you will excuse me ladies, I have to go and get things started,' Major Jackson bowed and walked away.

Half way down the sloping path he took out a shiny whistle on a lanyard and blew it hard three times. This had two immediate effects; firstly a wave of expectant silence spread throughout his surrounding audience. Then as the silence enveloped everything, several big muffled engines began to start up sporadically and rev away somewhere out of sight.

The noise grew as lock up doors beneath the viaduct swung open to reveal exhaust smoke and a row of colourful military trucks. These rolled out of the nearby railway arches and began to beep and honk their way through to the square at the base of the park. Bunting, flowers and coloured whitewash had been applied to all of the vehicles in wild organic aboriginal patterns. From roof mounted smoke canisters, waves of different colours were released and towed into the air. The roads cleared smoothly as the jaw dropped residents backed onto pavements to allow the rainbow convoy through.

From his desk at the police station many streets away, Sergeant Roberts tapped on a microphone three times and said, 'Testing, one, two, one and a two.' His massive audience roared with laughter as the words boomed out from speakers mounted on the trucks cabs and echoed around the streets.

Then with a clunk he transmitted the first gramophone record of the evening. From the wagon's funnel speakers the piano and saxophone combo from "Sunny Side of the Street" began to trumpet out.

The vehicles rolled noisily around the roundabout, circling a memorial to the first war while everyone applauded the smoky, colourful musical vision. After several more rotations the vehicles sounded their horns to clear a path and departed with each truck peeling off via a different junction.

As soon as the trucks hit straight road their rear tarpaulins were hoisted away and the tailgates dropped down. This released another cloud of dramatic and aromatic smoke into the air as the crowd cried out from shear hunger. From within the rolling vapours soldiers emerged, removed their gas masks and began to hand out steaming pork and sausages in bread rolls. Before anyone could take a bite the side covers rolled up to distribute goodie bags as the wagons passed. A separate ongoing cheer had gone up for each of the previous revelations, but now they all combined, intertwining into one tremendous roar.

Watching the spectacle from the hill in the park was like seeing the movements of a colossal machine. As each painted wagon cleared a bow wave in front, the pedestrians would fall in and follow on behind like clockwork. In no time at all the square was nearly empty and the park all but abandoned.

'Pied Piper you are,' Justine applauded, a little sarcastically, 'but where are you taking them all?'

'Aha, well that would be phase two. Would you like to take a look?' Jackson continued down the path to follow the last of the stragglers. 'Come on, you deserve to see this more than anyone.' He held out his hand and they ran down the hill like children.

When they stepped out of the park a voice behind them bitched, 'Oh dear, how romantic.'

Mr Burdock was standing out of sight to the side of the park gates. Mr Moor, Mr Humble and Mr Smith were with him.

'You don't have permission for any of this, this,' Burdock wafted a hand through the remaining smoke, stuck for a word to describe it.

'Fracas?' Mr Humble suggested while swatting at the smoke with his hat.

'Débâcles?' prompted Mr Smith, looking up from the notes he was taking.

'Too bloody French,' Burdock winced, turning on his friends. 'Abomination, that's the word,' he said proudly as he and the other councillors stepped forward.

'I was ordered to take control of this town and ensure it's safe return to normality,' Jackson replied stepping between the men and Justine.

'Normality?' Burdock and his cohorts snorted their disapproval. 'Safe return?'

'What you *have* ensured Major is a bloody carnival of chaos with people being killed daily as a result of your bollocking blunders. I mean, for instance, today you shot my bloody secretary.' Burdock left the protection of his group and challenged the major head on, 'Now hand what is left of my town back to me, along with all the papers and emergency supplies you *STOLE*.' He forced the final word out looking up into the officer's face with contempt.

'Reckon I've got a fair few bodies to count before I catch up with you blokes and your disorganised death rate,' Jackson protested angrily.

The councillors shrugged, snorted and folded their arms in a simultaneous show of disregard.

'This town belongs to the people and I'm here to help *them* look after it.' Jackson leaned forwards yearning to thump the fat face in front of him, 'Your note book will stay safely locked away until someone high up orders me to hand it back.'

'That has been arranged,' Humble smirked.

'Shut it Humble,' Burdock snapped.

Jackson shook his head, 'You got the updates and bulletins we sent through right? You know there's a group of armed men out there who think we're under German control? And yet, you boys want to stand around and argue about an account book?' He looked up at the setting sun. 'I need to go and make sure *your* citizens are safe from Harry and his mob. Good day.' With that Jackson walked away.

'We read your briefing; it's nothing more than fantasy and coincidence. All these events were the doing of the Germans,' Burdock called after the major and Justine. When they didn't stop he added, 'I added my own reservations and explanations to your report before forwarding it to my, friend.'

Still there was no reaction from the departing couple.

'He sent it to his friend at Whitehall,' Mr Smith huffed.

'And they're going to send your soldier boys back to the front where they belong, pretty damned quick,' Mr Humble shouted, but there was nothing humble about the way he said it.

That did it. The major twisted around so quickly it made Justine wobble. He strode past her and back towards the pudgy agitators with one thing on his mind.

'You are just covering up your failures,' Mr Burdock insisted, but with panic and fear showing in his voice.

As the major closed the distance and rolled up his sleeves, Burdock put up a shaky hand and clicked his fingers rapidly. On cue Mr Humble stepped forward and placed an envelope in his associates sweaty palm.

'This is from *very* high up,' Burdock smirked, confident again with the telegram in his hand. 'It orders you to leave immediately.'

Face to face, Jackson breathed like a raging bull, trying to decide between taking the envelope or punching out this smug and contemptuous man. Justine stepped in just in time. She took the note, opened it and handed over the contents.

The telegram was short and to the point.

MAJOR PHILLIP JACKSON 9TH DIVISION STOP TAKE COMPANY DIRECTLY PORTLAND HARBOUR DORSET STOP TRANSPORT TO PORT MASSAWA AFRICA STOP SORRY PHIL HANDS TIED STOP LIEUTENANT GENERAL JOHN GERALD MOORSHED STOP GOOD LUCK STOP

With apparent calm the major returned Burdocks smirk and said, 'This does not order me to hand anything over, and as far as leaving...' He took a second look at the wording. 'The General would expect us to prepare properly for such a journey. I bet you that boat doesn't sail for a few days yet.'

'Oh no, *Philip*. I have it on good authority that it departs tomorrow night,' Burdock grinned.

The major was shaken now. Burdock could see he had scored a hit. 'I know some powerful people Phil,' he taunted, twisting the knife. Then just for good measure he supplemented, 'Don't make me call them again.'

'Fine, well that still gives me a few hours to open the shelters and spread the word.' With nothing more to say the major turned his back on them and moved on.

'Spread the word?' Burdock taunted. 'The only good decision you've made was to keep all this under your silly floppy hats. The towns people can't cope with the, with your perspective of what's going on. Those inbred idiots will panic like sheep.'

When there was no reaction Mr Moor added his two penneth, 'You can't open the shelters, the gates are locked, your festivities are cancelled Major. You have nowhere to go and *we* will open *our* shelters when *we* are ready.'

'Probably tomorrow,' Humble blurted out.

Burdock, Smith and Moor glared at Humble then back at each other, then over at the disappearing shapes of the major and Justine.

Moor scalded Burdock, 'Don't let him go, stand up to him. You said your Mr Stevenson would sort this out for us. Give me his number, I want to talk to him myself.'

'Shut up Bernard,' Burdock shoved the other men out of his way. He was heading for the solace of a brandy bottle, hidden away in his leather bound and oak panelled council office.

Smith grabbed Mr Moor before he could make chase and continue the argument. 'He doesn't even know that Stevenson chap, not like he says,' Mr Smith explained. 'I heard him on the phone. He spoke to a Great Uncle something or other over at the War Office.'

Mr Moor spoke firmly, 'I think we should start packing my old friend. Just in case.'

Chapter Twenty-Four

'You could've been killed,' Edward scalded.

'Or worse, been captured and told 'em where we were.' Patrick joined in as Harry kicked a bunk.

'But I wouldn't,' Elijah protested.

'He just needed to know one way or the other, right?' Finn stressed.

'Right. I had to check and I used the disguise so,' Elijah tried to turn the tide of blame, 'I found out about that radio wagon near the girls and the police station stuff. Oh, and the gathering tonight. I did didn't I?'

Harry put his head in his hands then pulled them down over his chin while letting out a long sigh. 'So you've killed this bloke now?' he asked bluntly.

'I told you he's a goner, no problem,' Elijah insisted again. They'd had this same argument several times since his return.

'Better have this back then,' Patrick slammed down a dagger next to the candles for everyone to see. 'Found it shoved in with my kit,' he said with a tone of suspicion.

The dagger was long and thin with a shiny knuckle-duster handle. Even in the dim candlelight you could make out patches where globs of blood had settled on the grip and in the blades gulley.

'Cheers,' Elijah said as he nonchalantly picked it up. 'Must 'ave dropped it when I was moving all your junk.'

Patrick shot a look back at him, but everyone else was losing interest.

'SD Nine should have been invisible?' Harry turned to Edward for an answer.

Edward didn't have a ready made solution and surmised, 'Obviously it didn't work very well. You said she was asking for spare parts, right?'

'Do you think we've lost our Special Duties post then?' Harry asked, half worried for the crew down there and half for the impact it would have on the men down here.

Edward scratched his chin. 'Well, I suggest we should stay away from SD Nine, for now.'

'What about Mary?' Patrick muscled in, 'Bugger that, I'm going up there quick sharp. You can't stop me.'

Harry tried anyway, 'Stand down Pat, if they stay hidden they'll be fine.'

Edward tried some logic on the thick-skinned giant, 'If we all blunder around we might take the Germans straight to them. When Elijah saw that lorry with the antenna it was only nearby, not on top of them.'

'If the Germans have dogs like the ones the Brits use back in Ireland, they'll find 'em in no time. The same goes for us.' Pat looked accusingly at Elijah's muddy boots then up at his commander. 'You said an Alsatian stopped you escaping Harry?'

'I think that was just Duncan's guard dog sniffing out lost property,' Harry protested. 'Elijah, did you see any search dogs?'

Elijah shook his head and said softly, 'Not a sniff.'

'Right then, we do the cells tonight,' Harry frowned. Then to get Pat back on side he flicked Elijah in the forehead and pointed out, 'PC Stupid here, says they've locked a load of people away, remember? So if they did find Mary and Susan, that's where they'll be.'

'And we let everyone out and bring the girls back here?' Patrick mulled over the idea.

Harry stretched an arm around Pat and continued to hash out the plan, 'That gathering or what ever it is, will make good cover to get the girls out, you'll see?'

'So you want me to blow a hole in the police station and forget about the stuff we were going to do?' Patrick picked up some of the kit he'd prepared earlier.

Harry thought quickly about all the new variables, 'No, you and Elijah stick to the original plan, but make me up four more of those small cutting charges.'

Patrick nodded enthusiastically and moved off to get on with the new preparations.

'I need to talk to Edward,' Harry said dismissively to the twins. 'You two go and check our exit points just in case someone followed Elijah back.'

There were plenty of soldiers all around the town, but none of them had been specifically pursuing Elijah. They were all too busy.

Chapter Twenty-Five

Justine and the major were just catching up with the nearest group of squaddies and their colourful parade. The lorry ahead of them slowly swam in a sea of revellers then pulled over outside the town's brewery and honked its horn. The soldiers inside poured out to clear enough space to set up a serving area while the driver jumped down with a large set of bolt cutters and a big grin.

As if following a timed script (which he was), Sergeant Roberts changed disks and more tunes came tinkling from the big speakers. This time it was Louis Armstrong singing "When The Saints Go Marching In", everyone did as Louis instructed and sang along.

During this furore, two soldiers accompanied each driver over to their designated shelter gates and took up guard positions on either side. Cheers and applause grew as locks were cut and the barriers were flung wide with an echoing clatter. At the old brewery, along a deep stairwell beyond the blast doors, lights flickered on and the crowd whooped as they pushed forward to see inside.

'Not full of building supplies and tinned tongue is it?' Justine commented after catching up with the major.

'Hope not or it'll be a tight squeeze,' Jackson smiled and pulled his cap back on. 'Evans thinks we've already found everything to match the ledger. Everything that Burdock's mates haven't recently sold off, but you never know?'

Justine offered him her arm, 'Shall we have a quick look then?'

The tune playing from the speakers changed to Will Osborne's "Needle In A Haystack". It wasn't on the script, but it had been on Sergeant Robert's mind for several days.

Justine noticed the entrance guards had blow-up pictures of Harry and the others on clipboards. She felt odd seeing them portrayed like wanted men.

'You know they're the good guys really?' she lectured to the nearest soldier.

The guard looked to his commander for advice. Jackson gritted his teeth, 'Just follow your orders Private and you'll be right.'

Justine looked around them as she queued to get further in. 'Is this going on at every shelter?'

'All the big public ones yes,' Major Jackson nodded approvingly at how things were shaping up.

Justine had to ask, 'How on earth did you organise all this?'

'Delegation and trust,' he winked. 'Oh and Mr Moor supplied the pork, fresh and tinned. I probably should have thanked him earlier?' Jackson grinned cheekily.

Within a few claustrophobic minutes they reached the bottom of the queue at the base of the steps. To their left a metal shutter and doorway opened into a brightly lit first aid centre equipped with sinks, beds and overflowing supply cupboards.

'These places are very well set up, so why couldn't the councillors open them?' Justine noted.

The major pulled her into the first aid area and closed the door. A row of inquisitive faces still slowly conveyed past the open shutter. He ignored them and whispered, 'The ledger shows that until recently these places were all overstocked. They've been shipping stuff out and flogging a whole load of crap around here for the past few weeks. The police found a warehouse full up at one of the mills, following a tip off the other day.'

Justine spoke quietly, 'And they dumped what was left in the river tunnel while the inspectors were here?'

Jackson nodded.

'But how did a few overweight old men manage all that?'

'They paid local men with vans and labourers to organise the heavy work and other rogues to sell stock on the black market for miles around,' Jackson informed her.

A man at the shutters called out, 'Two teas please luv.'

Jackson pulled a lever and the man clattered away. 'They started small somewhere, before the shelters existed. Earliest records were for toilet paper, ham in a can and light bulbs. Whatever they could knock off. I think demand caused supply to just mutate into something big, too big.'

Justine flicked her eyes, 'So as it snowballed, the shelters gave them room to expand *and* over-order on equipment and supplies from the ministry.'

'That and a few other dodgy deals they had going. Evans reckons it got out of hand and half the haul was bought and sold in bulk from some very dubious sources in the big cities.' Jackson opened the door and looked out into the wide tunnel packed with people. He imagined the wagonloads of goods that could have passed through here, disguised as building works in progress.

'What about the rest of the things your men found?' Justine asked as they moved along another packed corridor.

The major stuck his head into the next open doorway. A hastily painted sign above it said "FREE STUFF". He pulled Justine through and said with pride, 'Well if you need a dunny, but you ain't got the money. Look over there, some of my quartermasters. They're offering new facilities to anyone who needs 'em.'

Several uniformed young men were busy setting up an extra trestle table to deal with the growing demand for building and plumbing equipment vouchers.

'All we ask is that they pledge some labour time and we will kit them out with all the bits and bobs to rebuild. Your town will be up and running again in no time, I hope.'

Justine stepped out of the way as more eager people pushed into the room. 'But that telegram, it means you have to leave much sooner. You don't have time to do all this now do you? And what about finding Harry?'

'Gears in motion and all that, not all my men are working on this evenings bunker activities, these blokes are mostly cooks and admin folk.' Jackson looked up, he suddenly seemed sad and worn out.

'What is it?' Justine asked.

The major took her arm as the doorway was becoming swamped. When they reached a quieter alcove he said, 'All this has been good for us, for them, mostly. A lot of my men are fresh-faced recruits, so these events have honed their skills and bought 'em closer together. Do you see?'

'You just wanted more time to get them ready for fighting in the real war?' Justine hugged his arm.

'Half of them could do with training for another few months, at least. That's why we're here in England. At least, that was the deal when we left home. Burdock's action has cut some of my men's lives shorter today and no mistake. If we sail tomorrow, they'll be pretty unprepared. He's as mad as a gumtree full of galahs.'

Burdock was indeed quite mad if not livid, mostly because he needed a calming drink. He'd started at the town hall, but found it locked up tight and the Bull and Bladder shuttered up for the evening too. As he stomped along the emptying streets, his mind conceded the battle and raced to conceive a method of destroying any accumulated evidence that pointed the blame his way.

When he'd crossed the almost deserted town and discovered the Artful Dodger was also shut, he'd been very upset. Unable to think clearly, Burdock had screamed blue fire and kicked the door in frustration, only stopping when he'd heard it being unlatched.

'Oh it's you,' the barman said, unimpressed. He looked up and down the empty street, tugged thoughtfully on his grey whiskers and beckoned sullenly, 'Come in.'

Inside the smoky lounge Captain Cooke was occasionally shouting nonsense at anyone who passed his table. There had been signs of remorse when he'd arrived hours before, following his night in the cells. Now the drink had forced any sense out of the man via the urinals in the yard.

Burdock went to approach him and then realised the area was being looked after by a few of the Captain's men. Young William Duffy, David Hughes and two more men whom he didn't recognise were at the next table.

Albert was there too, getting his coat from a rack near the snug. He'd come along out of a previous respect for his captain, then quickly determined that he no longer *had any* esteem for the incoherent oaf.

At the far end of the bar, Dunk the drunk had come in to find refuge. Since the yard had been bombed it seemed there was no safer place than inside a pub at the bottom of a glass.

Burdock sat down at the other end of the slop-covered counter, tapped two fingers between the puddles and a double scotch quickly appeared.

'Howd'you do that?' Duncan slurred rapidly to attention.

Burdock ignored him.

'You would be amazed what you can get when you own the pub,' Albert said as he stepped in between them. 'He's the landlords landlord.'

'Ah Mr Croft, sorry to hear about your little business being bombed,' Burdock smirked. 'You should have let me buy it when I offered.'

'Damage ain't too bad,' Albert said without thinking, then wished he had disregarded him. 'Sam, can I get a strong coffee for the captain?' he asked the barman while putting on his jacket.

The landlord nodded agreeably from behind the bar as Burdock took the opportunity to muscle in. 'We can look after the old fool if you're leaving, don't worry,' he assured and slid down to meander over to the captain's table. 'Mind if I join you?' the councillor asked on arrival. Then he shouted, 'Mr Cooke,' trying to wake the captain from his semi-stupor.

'He comes and goes see?' David Hughes noted as he moved over to prod Cooke in the ear.

Burdock sat down and leaned forward, 'I hear the major is probably going to have him court marshalled for murdering that German. Going to sort it out before he leaves I'll bet.' It got the right response.

'Snot murder,' the captain woke up and blurted out. There was a brief moment of contemplation before he half closed one eye again, slumped to the left and mumbled, 'Twas a soldier defending the ranks.'

Hughes pushed the captain upright. 'Please don't start him off again,' the old newsagent begged as he struggled to retrieve his pint from the other table.

William Duffy helped him out and bought over the rest of the drinks, he was keen to join in the prohibited conversation. 'That can't be right,' he sparked in as he sat down with a wobble. 'Bloody Aussies.'

'I agree, they shouldn't even be here should they?' Burdock signalled casually to the barman to bring over a round of shorts. 'I mean you boys can look after the shop without their help, can't you?'

'Did you say they're going?' Duffy asked as he finished off his old pint.

'Good riddance,' the captain slurred, opening both eyes with a slow flutter.

'Indeed they are William, but not before taking care of business I fear.' Burdock tried to agitate the men further, 'I see your holster is empty Captain, did they take away your side-arm?' He swept a look across the younger men's faces and asked them directly, 'Didn't I hear the rest of you had some nice new rifles too?'

'Sergeant Roberts took 'em away,' William needlessly explained.

Cooke shook himself awake and yelled, 'Took everything they did, an' said I'm not the captain no more.' He mulled over the words, 'I am though, I still got the hat.'

Mr Burdock tried to draw the younger men further in as a tray of sloshing drinks arrived. 'Here have one on me,' he smiled. 'You should be the heroes, not them.'

'What a load of old codswallop,' Albert stormed back over and slammed a coffee down. 'Sorry lads, but Frank Roberts and half the town swear those Germans were surrendering when you lot, when you all...'

'Your pal Frank flipping form filler Roberts can eat my rubber stamp,' the captain stipulated as he tried to stand up.

Mr Hughes steadied Cooke who tottered vertically to face Albert. The men grabbed the tilting table and their drinks as some of the empty glasses rolled away and smashed with the coffee cup on the floor.

'Cosy he is, hopping about in the pouch of that wallablobby from down under, sodding sell-out.' The captain let out a huge burp and collapsed back onto the bench. 'Snot been same since they arrived, has it?' he asked to the whole out of focus room.

Half the men nodded and raised their remaining glasses in support.

Albert felt it was almost time to leave. Instead of arguing he shook his head, bit his lip and headed for the toilets.

Mr Hughes felt the same way and followed his friend out. He hadn't been on the mission to hunt down the Germans and didn't want to join the party now. He also needed a pee.

The Councillor took a tiny swig of whisky and raised his glass to their departure. He grinned, happy in the knowledge that men like Albert and David would never have seen things his way. On the other hand, the four men who remained looked like they had just enough intelligence, inebriation and stubborn loyalty between them, to get the job done.

As soon as Mr Hughes was out of earshot the councillor continued his assault, 'Major Jackson has tried to make you look like a bunch of fools.

What you need is some way of disgracing that awful man and his Company of cowards. Show them up for what they really are.'

As the men leaned in to hear more, Private Duffy suggested, 'We should take our town back from them.'

'Exactly, let's drink to that,' Burdock insisted, while avoiding his own glass. 'You could lock the major away and make the town safe again, if you believe his nonsense?'

'What d'you mean?' Cooke snapped.

'Haven't you heard?' Burdock asked very seriously. 'The Major insists that Harry and his pals are running around killing people and blowing things up.'

'Nah,' William said as he sat back to finish his drink.

Burdock nodded and pointed along the row of drunken faces in turn, 'You need to get your weapons back and guard our homes tonight.' His words pulled the men back in like fish on a line. 'I can sort out Sergeant Roberts and arrange everything, but I'll need some help from you lads.'

Private Duffy and the captain nodded their approval of the concept. The other two men were also keen to get back on the winning team.

'What d'you need?' Cooke asked.

'Shall we start with another round of drinks?' Burdock proposed, as if there was a choice.

Around the various shelters, the entertainment was now in full swing. Live fiddles, tin whistles and ukuleles resonating different versions of the same songs through the various vaults had added to the broadcast of gramophone music. The catering had moved inside to avoid the impending daily blackout. As the Sun set, several performances and even a small football match began playing out deep below the ground. In the past half hour the major had refused more dance partners, drinks and food than he could remember. It was as if the King and Queen were leaving the ball, whenever he and Justine tried to get away. They moved in stops and starts, shaking hands and nodding away conversations as they forged through the engorged passages. Both of them with but one thought in mind. It was time to find Harry.

Harry was unaware of any plans other than his own. He was currently moving his men out from their hide, plodding down the long shadows of the furthest sections of viaduct, leading them into the cover of the river bank below. From there on in, on the approach to town, they scrambled along the gullies, culverts and hedge-lines in absolute silence.

When they reached the main road Patrick extracted a roll of leather from his shoulder bag and handed it to Harry along with a large green backpack. After a handshake the patrol separated into two groups with Patrick and Elijah climbing a slope to the crossroads above. Harry checked the packages contents, shouldered the lot and moved on to skirt around this side of town with Edward and Finn close on his heels.

Inside the Artful Dodger, Cooke slapped a crisp pound note down on the moist bar surface.

'Take the lot,' Duncan said, handing Cooke the keys to his yard's office.

'One box of padlocks should be more than enough. They're under the desk you say?' Cooke waited briefly for a reply, but Duncan was too busy unpeeling the sodden money and reviewing the mirrored optic shelf behind the counter.

Once the Home Guard had departed Burdock moved through to the snug, making sure a few faces witnessed him being there. After a couple more circuits he found a dark corner alcove to sit in, right next to the back door.

The roads in town looked almost dead when Harry, Edward and Finn occasionally emerged onto them to lay charges. Yet it was easy to hear where the metropolises heartbeat still pulsed and even easier to avoid it.

'Sounds like everyone else is having fun down the shelters while we risk our lives,' Finn said quietly, but with genuine indignation.

Edward couldn't help himself either. 'Do you think Victoria and the children are down there somewhere?' he pondered as a cheer went up from the bottom of the next street.

'Right, shut up,' Harry ordered. 'They're just getting the town drunk on lies. It's better than shooting at them. Now come on.'

'Sounds like they're having a bloody good time despite the occupation,' Finn pointed out again.

Harry turned on Finn, pushing him back into the shadow of a wall, 'Think like them. Smell the food; imagine having a safe place to hide if counter attacks start up? I'd jump at that wouldn't you? And it's more than our councillors and officials ever gave them.'

'Two of our farm girls are from Jersey,' Edward quietly interrupted. 'They were glad to get news that their families hadn't fought back.' After a moments thought he added, 'Coz they'd 'ave been slaughtered like swine if they had.'

There was a sudden clatter from around the next corner. Harry slapped a hand over Finn's mouth and signalled a quick change of direction across some low fenced gardens as drunken voices broke out in the next street.

'Do, do we, have enough bicycles now?' Cooke asked, squinting in the dark.

'Check,' his men replied as another bike fell over.

'Padlocks?' Cooke called out.

'Same to you,' Duffy joked to the lads.

'Got them,' the other two men grumbled whilst trying to untangle their cycles.

'Well if your washes are as sickronised as your hansers, we might jus time this in do,' Cooke slurred and looked at his watch, but found it hard to focus on.

'Some of us haven't got watches sir,' one of the men grumbled.

'I will cowt to two hubdred and soon as you hear me doing my thing, you can do yours,' Cooke garbled and wobbled until the men's sniggering snapped him back. 'Now bugger off and get round 'em.'

The men mounted up badly and meandered down the street in different directions. When they'd gone Cooke remembered his own task and began counting loudly as he staggered along towards his goal.

Minutes later he reached a car park, 'Hubdred n'eighty one, hubdred n'eighty two, hubdred n'eighty four.'

'Who goes there?' a voice called from above.

'Who blooming goes there?' Cooke shouted back. In the moonlight he could make out an industrial spiral staircase and began throwing himself up it. 'I go there you imbecile.'

'What do you want?' the distant voice shouted down with more urgency.

Cooke rounded the penultimate corner with drunken confidence, straightened his cap and saluted. He only tripped on three out of the five remaining steps. 'Hello, Simon?' he grinned at the ARP warden.

'Your pissed as a fart, go back down,' Simon declared as Cooke arrived on deck. 'You can't be up here Mr Cooke, there's new procedures since the other night.'

Simon tried to stop the captain getting any closer, but Cooke crashed drunkenly into him. The ARP man landed flat on his back, ten feet below on the works roof.

'That went better than expected,' Cooke surmised, sticking his head out through the handrails. He could hear Simon's spread-eagle body beginning to groan and the man's left arm was at a very peculiar angle. 'Oh well, one hubdred and ninny nine, two hubdred!' he declared. Standing upright he focussed on an arrow cast into the mechanism before him. After several attempts to grab the handle he cranked away at it like mad.

At first the siren's rise and fall mingled with the song and dance leaking out from below the earth. As the warning grew steadier it cancelled out the power of the music, which died away to leave only alarm.

The guards on the street side of the shelter doors immediately began ushering any strays back inside. All of them were asking if it *could* be for real? Justine and the major had only just fought through to the bottom steps when the stragglers from outside formed a new oncoming blockage ahead.

'It can't be, not now,' Justine insisted. 'We need to be out there finding them.'

'The party was no secret, maybe Harry's men have done this to keep us all down here?' Jackson suggested as they reached the top step and ordered the guards aside. 'We had better take a quick decko.'

There was a scrape, quickly followed by a clunk and a click as the doors slammed shut before their eyes. The major tried the handle twice, but it wouldn't budge.

Justine pushed him aside; yanked at the handgrip herself and then demanded, 'Shoot it!' The major's scornful face answered for him as Justine turned back and banged on the barricade shouting, 'Harry it's me, Harry, Harry.'

The siren continued long enough for several drunken cyclists to lock up every public shelter in town. Anyone who'd stayed at home dove for cover, without the "all clear" they'd probably remain there all night.

About half of the Artful Dodger's customers had relocated to the air raid bar in the cellar. The rest had gone home. Burdock took the opportunity to creep out of the Dodger's back passage avoiding them all. The streets had seemed dead to him before, but now they'd gone that extra mile. They had passed over, been laid out under the blanket of night and come back as a ghost town.

Then out of nowhere the silence was polluted by the distant sound of a small racing engine. As if someone or something were returning from the dead, on a motorbike. It grew louder, then almost disappeared. Burdock stopped to listen. Loud and then quiet again as the noise bounced across the empty road junctions surrounding him. He decided not to care, shook his head and hurried over to the police station. When the engine noise finally faded away, something else made him pause again. He could have sworn there was another note on the wind now, like a horse clip-clopping far away and in the opposite direction.

He made himself ignore all of these interruptions and ducked down behind a vehicle, seeking cover. While crouched there surveying the building, he rested a hand on the car ahead and gasped. Unlatching a heavy fuel can from the back of the major's ute he whispered, 'That is a bonus.'

At the top of the stations dark deserted steps he peeked through a side window and discovered that even here the siren had done its job. There were no lights on anywhere in the building and not a soul in sight.

In reception he was unsurprised to discover the desk safe was locked. He tipped out drawers and searched desks, but to no avail. Then Mr Burdock thought back to Frank Roberts as the diligent junior office clerk he'd been long ago in the past. Frank the clerk, working for Burdock's father. Frank the man with a reputation for tidy detail, who had then become a soldier in the first war, along with half the shop floor. He considered that Frank the army clerk had notoriously got the local men home quicker than most, after the campaign. Those men who all had the right documents, papers and tickets in neatly labelled packages.

Finally Frank Roberts had become the formidable policeman, with his bloody annoying forms for everything. One last rummage with a lit match found a folder in the filing cabinet, stored under "S", containing an envelope marked "Safe Key – Spare 001". The safe contained Burdock's leather bound ledger lying beneath Cooke's revolver, two Lugers and a box stuffed full of ammunition and clips.

Burdock took the ledger, swung the door shut and went back to the heavy petrol can. He placed it on the desk and then he took out his matches again.

In a dark corner just outside the same building, three figures huddled against a wall drawing breath.

'Do you think that siren meant something?' Finn whispered, peeking around the nearest wall.

Harry stepped out to look for aircraft and hissed, 'It usually means there's going to be an air raid you nit.'

'You did say you went to school?' Edward asked quietly while tapping Finn on the head.

'Yes, but our lot wouldn't bomb civilians and Gerry won't bomb himself,' Finn reasoned.

Edward thought about it. 'Maybe it's Gerry's way of signalling something's up?' he suggested as quietly as he could. 'Go and check if we've been rumbled.'

'Where's he going?' Harry asked.

Edward nodded back down the street, 'Checking back the way we came.'

Finn reappeared minutes later carrying a massive helmet shaped coal bucket sloshing with water. He sat it down quietly and began removing his shirt as if all this behaviour was the most normal thing in the world.

'What the hell are you doing?' Harry asked and then quickly moved men and bucket out of sight.

'We need it to bend the bars,' Finn insisted, 'I read it in a book about cotton at the library.' He dunked the shirt and began twisting it up.

Harry and Edward looked at each other in disbelief.

'We have some equipment to do the bars with,' Harry pointed out, waving the leather roll in front of Finn's face.

'Ah, yes, but reception just lit up like Blackpool Illuminations, so I borrowed some water from that bombed out back yard.' He pointed along the street opposite. 'It will be more stealthy on the iron bars than your explosives. Trust me.'

'Utter bollocks,' Harry unravelled the roll of leather Patrick had given him and shook his head. 'These will do the job stealthy enough, they're smaller and neater than the post-choppers we left along the road.'

The men jogged down the passage and scurried along the back of the police station until they reached some steps leading down.

'Wait up here and stay switched on,' Harry ordered as he crept down toward the basement of cells.

At the bottom of the outer stairwell there was a locked cast iron door and a heavily barred window. Harry attached several shaped copper tubes to the bars, looped a yard of safety fuse between them all and set a delay. Moving quickly he returned to the others and got his head down.

At first nothing happened, then with a whoosh the room above them erupted into bright light that twinkled on the men's eyes as they looked up in confusion.

'Did we do that,' Finn asked, standing up to get a better view.

Edward and Harry reached for Finn's belt, pulling him back down onto the ground. They hit the dirt together just before the detonators went off. The shaped explosives cut through the bars and glass of the basement window with an impressive whooping suck.

'No I didn't,' Harry admitted as they got up. He crept forwards then turned to Finn and said, 'Go and see who's burning down the police station, we'll go down and look for the girls.'

At the top of the shelter steps, the fuse of Justine's patience had also burnt out. It set off an emotional outburst inside her head, which was far more dramatic than Pat's devices. 'Get out of my sodding way,' she screamed at everyone in earshot as she shoved her way back down the steps.

'We need to stay up here while my men break through the doors,' the major insisted.

'No we don't, follow me,' Justine called back.

As she disappeared amongst a sea of blank faces, it occurred to the major that they were more interested in her than the situation at hand. Then as one their attentions turned on him, awaiting his response.

Jackson did his best to keep up, but as she moved along more bodies spawned in her wake. Emerging from doorways they pointed and whispered then stepped aside and gave him the same treatment. The joy and laughter had been replaced by words whispered on the wind; missing, murdered, married, mother and major. He paused and lost ground, only just able to make out Justine's red hair trapped in a crowded canteen area ahead. Fighting to catch up he clasped her hand and they pushed on together, elbowing their way into the next zone.

It was quieter there; the people in these back rooms were older and wiser. Some of them had bagged bunks or benches and were busy setting up camp for the night. The rest of them were sitting around chatting as they swapped the contents of their goodie bags with each other.

One old lady moved her legs for them to pass and said, 'You won't find Mrs Clark's boy down there sweetheart.'

Justine was still oblivious. 'Come on Mr Slow,' she said, letting go of the major's hand and racing ahead.

The major waited and asked, 'Where *will* we find him?'

With a huff the lady replied, 'I don't bleedin' know, that's your job ain't it?'

A younger woman beside her joined in, 'If what my Gilbert said is true you should be out there finding those murdering bastards, not running around down 'ere chasing skirt.'

Jackson didn't have time for any of this and made off after the sound of Justine's heeled shoes.

'Off they trots, into the dark,' the old lady purred.

'And with her pregnant at that,' her friend threw in as the major ran away.

The old lady nodded, 'Well if they ain't out in two ticks we'll know they're up to a bit of *how's your father* and no mistake.'

The unlit and seemingly dead end that Justine had entered became narrower the further she went in. At the bottom she crouched for a moment and was gone.

The major was impressed. 'Good girl,' he called after her.

'Don't say good girl, I really hate that,' came the dulled echo of her reply.

Jackson apologised then waited gallantly below. He could hear her releasing what sounded like handles, then with one more grunt she must have shouldered up a hatch, which clanked open. The major felt a sudden chill as air rushed in.

'They all have these emergency exits, in case the street gets blown up,' she called down, climbing out into the fresh breeze.

'Coming up,' the major called out excitedly.

When his head cleared the top Justine recalled, 'I had to get the blue prints signed off for these, weeks ago.' She sat down on the grass to catch her breath.

'Your committee thought of everything, eventually,' Jackson sighed, crumpling down next to her.

'They may have been on the take, but what they built was solid and fit for purpose.' Justine smiled and rapped her knuckles on the hatch. 'To be honest, they were never fussed about the finer details, all this was down to Susan, the engineers and the men from the ministry.'

The major wasn't really listening any more. He stood up again and stared out into the distance.

'What is?' Justine asked as he helped her up.

Jackson pointed across the town and asked, 'If this is a blackout, then why are the lights on at the police station?'

Finn had been too late to stop the fire taking hold of the dry old building's reception area. He had dashed back to the archway for the scuttle of water and emptied a further two fire buckets of sand over the nearest flames with no lasting effect. Glass cracked and floors creaked in the rooms above by the time he'd got through to the foyer. The big reception table had been dragged in front of the doors to the cells. It was covered in burning information leaflets and magazines. An empty petrol can lay on the blue flaming carpet near the front doors.

'Is someone there?' Finn coughed out seeing a shadow move through the smoke.

It was Burdock returning with a second can of fuel from the major's ute. Seeing Finn he flung it through the doorway and ran away down the front steps. Finn tried to follow, but the spilling petrol erupted with a fireball that knocked him off his feet.

By the time he poked his head back up the councillor had gone and the entrance was engulfed. The only temporary safe place left to hide behind was the booking desk. Finn picked up the empty coalscuttle and wore it like a huge helmet as he dived for cover over the counter top.

As he squatted there it was hard not to notice an olive coloured radio transmitter lying amongst the scattered drawers and papers. It looked like a military set, but not German. The box, battery and dials were all labelled in English.

Outside, when no one came rushing into the courtyard from any direction, Harry had helped Edward climb through the hole where the prison window had been.

Monkey appeared in their torchlight on the other side and greeted them with, 'Bloody hell, yow two make a good entrance don't yer.'

Harry and Edward ignored him and moved on.

'Thanks anyway our kid, but they're letting us out in the morning,' Monkey winked as they passed. 'Yow joined up have yow, good pay is it?' he nodded at their uniforms and black faces.

Edward stopped and asked bluntly, 'Where are the women? How many uniforms are there upstairs?'

Harry moved off further down the corridor to check for guards as more faces appeared at the end of the passage.

'There ain't no uniforms up there Harry, they went out with the lights.' Mr Stokes stepped out of the end door and pointed up at the ceiling, 'When that siren sounded they turned off the awful music and shut up shop.'

'Who am yow looking for?' Monkey asked as he and several of the prisoners took a peek out of the new exit hole.

'Mary from the café and Mrs Hill from the town hall,' Edward replied.

'Not here pal,' Stokes answered with confidence.

'They ain't in the gang see, which is a shame coz I quite fancy that Mary,' Monkey sneered.

'Shut it Monkey,' Stokes growled.

'Harry, they're not here, we need to go. Harry,' Edward urged from behind.

'You lot need to get away, quick as you can,' Harry said to the curious faces around him.

Mr Stokes looked beyond him at the hole in the wall, 'Well I'm tempted to exit via that new aperture, but as Monkey said, we're all being set free tomorrow.'

'Most of them got let out earlier; Mr Moor's Lawyers sorted it. Sergeant Roberts said we was more *exciting,*' Monkey shrugged.

Mr Stoked shook his head in dismay, 'No Monkey, they said we was *inciting*, you moron.'

'How can lawyers…?' Harry looked to Edward for some answers.

Edward looked blankly back in dismay. He decided to keep things simple, 'Upstairs is on fire, sooner we all leave the better.'

The mob of faces looked around the corner to where smoke was now collecting at the top of the curved stair well. Then unanimously, they voted with their feet.

Finn's feet had also made it outside. He'd climbed through the tearoom window and headed back around to the parade ground coughing all the way. 'I don't think, there's any one, inside,' he choked out, dropping his bucket down in front of the escapees.

'You dow think yow lot might 'ave gone a bit far?' Monkey asked from the top of the basement steps. He stepped back, fag in mouth and took a moment to admire their work. 'Anyone gorra light?' The scrawny man checked his own pockets then realised what he'd said and chuckled before asking, 'Yow gorra problem with authority then gents?'

'Why are you all dressed up like soldiers?' Stokes asked as more people made their way out of the basement. 'And where did you get those guns?'

'We want to hurt them, slow them down, just like you,' Harry said cautiously.

'Oh, so Burdock sent you over to finish the job,' Stokes nodded, then suddenly looked concerned. 'You're mob aren't taking over from my crew, are you?'

Monkey came back over and prodded Harry with a bony finger, 'We still get paid dow we?'

Harry pushed the little man away dismissively.

'But he promised, Burdock said to cause them Aussies as much hassle as we could and we'd get a bonus like,' Monkey argued.

'What did you say?' Edward grabbed Monkey's jacket collar and pressed him for more.

Monkey dipped and twisted out of Edward's grip with ease then explained crossly, 'We was told to start something. He said try and get to them Germans in the cells, but just our men and no guns.'

'Your men?' Finn asked.

'And women,' Mr stokes wife shouted over.

'What are you talking about?' Harry demanded, 'What Germans were in the cells?'

'Them airmen what got shot down of course. They've gone now,' Mr Stokes replied. 'Probably got their feet up somewhere in a nice camp eh?'

'But the Germans are everywhere, they're all over the town right now?' Harry said, looking from face to face for confirmation.

'Are they? Nah, that's the Aussies that is and a right bunch of trouble causers they am too.' Monkey spat some tobacco strands onto the floor.

Mr Stokes stepped in and explained, 'We had to shut down most of the black market business this week. All because of that Major Jackson and his men. I mean, we wouldn't have been part of all this, not if we'd had any proper work on.'

'Been living the high life last few weeks we have,' Monkey thumbed his collar. 'Then those bleedin' foreigners drove into town and put pay to our pay checks, you see?'

'No we don't,' Harry confessed.

Harry and Edward stared back at each other in a sort of mystified shock. Harry's face melted and contorted into relief followed by self-loathing and finally disgust. It was horrible being zapped by these lightening bolts of realisation.

'Yow lads am a bit out of touch ain't ya?' Monkey mocked their confusion. 'You been hiding down a hole somewhere or what?'

Finn was only half listening as he crouched down fiddling with something that had started glowing in his bucket. When he got up again, he did have a question, 'If your mate Mr Burdock knew you'd been locked up, then why did he just try and burn you all to death?'

Every face turned toward Finn.

'What are you still doing with that bloody bucket?' Edward asked through gritted teeth.

'This thing has saved my life at least once tonight and besides, I wanted to show you something I found inside the station.'

From the slope behind the brewery Justine and the major heard fire bells heading towards the distant police station, realised what was happening and ran down to follow.

'Tell me Captain Dreyer wasn't in there?' Justine gasped.

'You want me to lie then?' the major replied. 'Told me he was going to finish the reports, then find somewhere to have forty winks.' At the first junction Jackson looked left then right and asked, 'Which way's quickest?'

'This way,' Justine nodded towards a narrow lane. 'But what about the people back there?'

'I reckon they're safer where they are, now come on.' Jackson took her hand and headed off along the cobbles.

Behind them at the shelter, another head popped out of the exit hole and shouted, 'Yep, they've buggered off and left us to it.'

There were muffled responses from below.

The head looked down and continued, 'Well I don't know, they're probably heading towards that fire.'

More excited voices this time, growing louder as they pushed the man off his perch and out into the open.

'Bloody terrorists again,' said the next head out of the hole.

'Looks like they're seeing the police station off this time,' someone confirmed as they helped two more bodies climb out onto the grassy knoll.

'Well if the army ain't capable of stopping 'em, we bloody well will,' the next man out shouted while waving an angry fist.

'You will all have to get past me first,' Albert said as his horse scampered up the slope behind the emerging towns people.

A large local woman stepped forward, 'You know it's your lad who's doing all this Bert. They're lookin' for him and his mate Harry. They've been terrorising us all since the bombing.'

'You know my boy, and the other lads, they're not trouble makers are they?' Albert asked openly with a stern face.

'Pat is,' the next head shouted up from the hole.

'Granted,' Albert agreed. 'Look, just tell the rest of 'em down there, I'm opening up the front doors. Then we all need to have a little chat.' With that Albert lit a roll up and trotted his horse off towards the main street.

Chapter Twenty-Six

Approaching the centre of town, Noah was roaring along on Harry's Brough motorbike. Jarli held on tight behind, with Mary's transmitter squeezed between them. Every time they hit a bump the scouts light body would float away for a moment then thump back down onto the saddle.

'Is he still with us?' Noah shouted above the noise.

Jarli stole a quick glimpse behind and saw the black sedan swinging around the last corner right on their tail.

'Yes mate,' Jarli shouted into the wind.

'Fire,' Noah called back.

'Not got my gun mate,' Jarli called out helplessly.

As a ball of flames erupted over the rooftops ahead it lit up several thin wires stretched across the road.

'Duck mate,' Noah screamed at his pillion.

'Where mate?' Jarli asked, turning back and craning his neck over Noah's left shoulder.

Noah leaned forward, grabbing Jarli's hair with his left hand, taking him down and preventing him from sitting back up.

They struggled along together with a slight wobble until something went ping behind them and Jarli understood. He looked back just in time to see a lamp post flare at the base and crash down behind them, narrowly missing the pursuing car as it swerved out of its way. There was another ping as the sedan accelerated, trying to close the gap.

Bike and car shot along just beyond a falling telegraph pole as two more streetlights flared and fell together directly ahead. Noah hit full throttle and popped through the shrinking triangle as lampposts and ground scissored together. The car's long bonnet was caught in the criss-cross crash.

Jarli craned his neck further to observe an upside down view of glass and debris exploding from the car as the clanging poles ripped into its canopy and eventually brought it to a halt. The cars headlamps flickered then swooped around like giant eyes reversing away, looking for a new way out. As the bike created some distance, the sedan limped forward again and noisily bumped over the glass and kerbside as steam began to gush from beneath the front trim.

Noah guided the bike towards the burning skyline, in the hope that the major or the captain would be somewhere nearby. *'If they had a few armed men accompanying them, that would be bloody bonza too'*, he thought.

The black car soon caught up again and kept pace for a while, trying to bump against the bikes rear wheel whenever it could. Its driver was clearly desperate to stop the riders ahead before they reached civilisation and at any cost.

Noah's only advantage was being able to mount the empty pavements to avoid the demonic cars more determined attacks.

At the next corner everything got a little bit more complicated.

Noah swerved to avoid the fire engine, but when he rode over a fat hosepipe the bike became briefly airborne. It crashed back down then skidded away, ejecting its passengers onto a mound of sandbags before ultimately spinning off into the wet spray.

The sedan driver had been distracted by the ruptured hose and smashed into the corner of the fire truck with a shuddering bang. The car's engine raced for an instant then died amongst a cloud of fog.

'Corporal, Private, are you alright?' The major shouted as he and Justine ran in to help the men out.

They all turned to stare at the burning building that seemed beyond saving now. If anyone was in there, they were cooked.

As Jarli tried to raise his head his wide eyes were filled with fear and reflected flames. He quickly caught his breath then stammered out, 'They gonna fill up that hole Major, they after this too.' He picked up the battered remains of the radio transmitter box and rattled it.

'Say again?' was the most efficient response the major could think of.

Noah nursed a cut on his elbow and stepped out to explain, 'Well Jarli eventually found the tube for the tennis ball messages on a little mound and Sparks wanted to see a ball to go down it when...'

'When, as I lay there ready to drop the ball down, some big shadow blokes appeared all over the clearing,' Jarli said excitedly. 'I watched 'em in the distance, them order up Noah and Sparks from the bunker with this,' he shook the broken radio again. 'Then four of them shadow soldiers went down the hole.'

'Shadow Soldiers?' the major asked.

'Came from nowhere all dressed in dark camo, dropped our blokes like sheep, never heard a shot,' Noah pointed at the crashed sedan, 'Sparks refused to hand over this radio kit and that ugly fellah silenced him soon as.'

Justine looked down sadly at the broken motorcycle, making its own steam as the fire hose shower cooled it down.

'Sorry about yer bike Miss,' Noah apologised then looked at Jarli and carried on the tale. 'Soon-as Sparks collapsed, them shadow men down the bunker called out and there was this commotion. Followed by a really big thud.'

Jackson's eyes widened. 'And did Jarli have something to do with that?' he asked.

'When I seen what was happening, I had an idea an' I dropped something else down that ball tube boss.' Jarli wondered if he had done the right thing.

'Something else?' Jackson and Justine asked together.

'Yes sir, mainly, I stuck a frag inside the ball sir,' the little scout admitted.

'Ah, a fragmentation grenade,' Jackson explained to Justine.

'Yes Miss, nice little round one,' Noah added. 'Then Jarli pinned my bloke down with his rifle while I buggered off with this,' he smiled triumphantly and patted the transmitter.

Jarli nodded, 'I catched him up running down stream, an' we found that bike leaning by a tree.'

'There were more of 'em sir. Big dark wagons and a cement truck waiting near the main track gates. We only just missed 'em when I hit the road,' Noah confessed.

Everyone turned with him as footsteps came pounding closer.

'Major,' Captain Dreyer called out as he ran around the corner with Sergeant Roberts not far behind.

'What did you do to my police station?' Frank Roberts croaked out, grabbing his knees and panting like mad. 'We must empty, the cells,' he snorted urgently.

As the sergeant moved to get closer and Dreyer restrained him, a dozen prisoners ran out of the archway at the side of the police station supervised by Monkey and Mr Stokes. The felons took in the situation quickly, turned on their heels and ran away with no more than a shrug.

Sergeant Roberts counted off the prisoners from his mental list and relaxed a fraction before suddenly pulling him self free from Dreyer's grip and screaming, 'My paperwork!'

'So from your reaction I'm guessing you have no idea how all this started?' Major Jackson enquired with a nod toward the flames.

Dreyer shook his head, 'It was fine when we left. We were planning to be the guests of honour at Shelter Two. Before we got there the air raid siren kicked off so we turned back, saw the fire and ran all the way.'

There were several dull clunks from behind them as someone tried and failed to dramatically slam a twisted sedan door.

'Well well, I thought you would have left by now Major?' Mr Stevenson tilted his hat and moved away from the smouldering car limping badly. 'Hello Miss Page, you look so very tired,'

Justine nodded a quick scornful hello and agreed, 'I am.'

Stevenson made slow movements so that everyone could take in the pistol he was aiming from beneath his coat. 'Please, tell the Corporal to put the transmitter down and step back.'

Jarli shook his head, 'No way mate.'

'A stand off then?' Stevenson responded with an impatient sigh as he took a good look around.

Two firemen were busily swapping over the split hose at the rear of their engine. The water spray and hiss died away as they worked, leaving only the crackle of the fire to drown out any further conversation. The other firemen had moved to a horse drawn pump in the next street. They were all being efficiently oblivious to anything other than their work.

Stevenson calculated how long it would take for his own men to catch up in their slower vehicles and decided to wait. 'Patience is a virtue you know?' he said, looking the major in the eye.

'Who are you exactly?' Captain Dreyer asked.

'My name is not important,' the ministry man replied, raising his hat with flair. 'And neither are you.'

'Mr Stevenson, hello Mr Stevenson,' Councillor Burdock bolted out from the shadow of a street corner pretending to be out of breath from running.

'Shut up you moron,' Stevenson growled. Beneath the hat you could see that his scarred face did not look at all happy, but it never really did.

'I tried to call you at the Ministry. My uncle Wadsworth helped me. It's funny you know, because uncle Wadsy said your whole department were *all* called "Mr Stevenson". Warned me not to bother any of you unless it was very important and that I would need your specific code name?'

'He calls himself the Caretaker, sometimes,' Justine chirped in, triumphantly.

'Blabbermouth,' Stevenson almost growled. Then he turned his attention and said, 'You got what you wanted in the end Burdock. So you can shut up too.' He finally turned back to the major and confirmed, 'All right, my name is sort of Mr Stevenson, but as I said, that is really not important.'

'I stopped them Sir,' Burdock beamed with pride. 'I got the Home Guard to lock most of the towns people and soldiers down the shelters. The rest of them think we are in the middle of an air raid.'

'So you finally got them open then, briefly? Well that is nice.' Stevenson looked pitifully at the faces in front of him. 'Now can we clean up at least some of this mess? Major Jackson, Miss Page, did you find those missing men for me?'

'No,' the major said sternly.

'They might have found us,' Dreyer said very quietly.

Those closest followed the captain's eyes, but saw nothing other than shadows and firemen.

Stevenson snapped his attention back to Jarli with renewed urgency, 'Bring that over here, *Corporal Charlie Jarli,*' he sneered, then backed closer to the car to cover his rear.

'But it's broken,' Noah said when Jarli stayed put. 'No use to anyone mate.'

'Yes well, that is a matter of perspective. Its malfunction makes it all the more valuable. I need to stop this from happening again. I don't want my operators to be found, do I?'

'We've noticed,' Justine let the statement hang.

'I must say I am looking forward to giving a certain boffin back at HQ a damn good hiding over this.' Mr Stevenson chuckled to himself.

'Is that tin box worth shooting Corporal Chambers and our mates over?' Noah asked, stepping forward to cover his friend.

Stevenson abruptly stopped laughing and considered the question briefly before answering, 'Yes.' He took another step back, 'Yes it was, but your *mates* are asleep, not dead, for now. Let's hope the same can be said of my own men after your little scout blew them up.'

'Just asleep?' Jarli asked, stepping forward.

Stevenson smiled and gestured for both of them to move further away. 'My men *were* equipped with tranquillisers not bullets.' He looked accusingly at Jarli, 'Your radio man was given a choice. Now I am going to give you the same one, but with higher stakes. Hand it over or I *will* shoot you.'

'With a dart gun?' Noah asked. 'Good, I could do with a snooze,' he smiled while bobbing and weaving from foot to foot.

From beneath the hat came a snorted laugh, 'My dart gun is on the back seat now dear boy. This powerful little beauty is the real thing.'

'You can't shoot all of us,' Justine said flatly.

The barrel of Stevenson's gun bobbed along the row, counting heads as he did a silent little sum. 'Yes I can,' he confirmed with confidence.

'We have real guns too.' Harry's voice echoed around them as he emerged from the gated archway, flanked by Finn and Edward who fanned out into the street.

A section of floor collapsed inside the burning building sending more glass and flames out of every nearby window. Showing no concern for her own safety Justine ran to Harry and grabbed him so tight he was incapacitated and had to lever her away. With her tucked safely in behind, Harry's team moved in closer.

Finn put down his coal bucket in the centre of the crowd, took a double-handed grip on his machine gun and nodded hello to Sergeant Roberts with a cheeky grin.

'Your sudden appearance saves us all a lot of effort,' Stevenson butted in, 'but where are the other two patriots from your patrol? Not dead yet I hope?'

'Oh they're around,' Harry smiled.

'Booby trapping street lamps and the like are they, or was that you?' Stevenson asked pointedly.

'We did what we were told to do by our superiors. Am I right in guessing that one link in that long chain, is you?' Harry squared up closer to Stevenson's car.

Edward joined him. 'Someone else made the first mistake, ringing the bells. After that, we just did what we were trained to do,' he croaked angrily.

'Yes, that will need some tweaking won't it? Some ideas seem perfect at first, but then...' Stevenson looked sad and distant for a moment. Then he nodded at the burning building and asked, 'And was this, something you think you were told to do?'

'Burdock did that, I saw him running away,' Finn pointed out the councillor who had been trying to silently creep away from them all.

He looked shocked at the accusation and turned back to argue the toss, 'I did nothing of the sort young man. I saw the fire and tried to help, but it had clearly taken hold and I was running to get some assistance.'

'You threw a can of petrol at me you crazy old dick head,' Finn pelted the words back at him fiercely.

'That was you? I mean, I erm...' Mr Burdock went quiet.

'Bet you were after that notebook of yours eh? Must be hard to wrap up a business when someone else is holding your accounts? Search him son.' Dreyer called out to Finn.

'Everyone just stay where you are,' Stevenson turned toward the major, 'Might I ask why none of you have tried to make a move, take out a weapon or do anything heroic?'

'Well she told us not to shoot anyone,' Jackson said looking at Justine, straight faced.

'Patience is a virtue, don't cha know?' Captain Dreyer mocked Stevenson's very British accent.

'I see,' Stevenson nodded, but he clearly didn't see at all. He checked his watch, listened for something on the wind and gestured to Burdock to join the Australians near the bike.

'But I am innocent. Major Jackson is on a vendetta,' Burdock whimpered. 'The things they found were emergency stores for the town.'

'No, no,' Mr Stevenson shook his head. 'I have been looking closely at this council's activity and at your tax records. It seems your team have all been very entrepreneurial with the Kings money. You will all be getting a large bill, very soon. Far more than you can afford to pay, shall we say?'

'You have no evidence,' Burdock looked at the burning police station. 'This is pure theoretical scandal.' He tried to look proud and important, but no one cared.

Stevenson grinned, 'What ever the local constabulary can not prove, my department will be more than happy to supply evidence of.' He looked at Harry and the other officers in turn. If you all help me, I will help you. Even if I do have to be a tad creative.'

A distant rumble was growing around the corner. It made several grunting attempts to get closer then moved away seeking an easier route away from the street of downed poles and cables.

'That sounds like, what was it your little scout called them? Oh yes, my Shadow Soldiers. I like that.' Stevenson moved behind the car door for protection, just in case someone had decided to be brave at the last hurdle.

The rumble soon returned, accompanied by the brightest lights Harry and the others had ever seen. As the two padded out lorries got closer you could just make out one of them was a real giant, the other was a more ancillary vehicle with less cladding. They both pulled up some distance from the fire and dark human shapes appeared instantly beside the aurora of headlamps. It was hard to make out, but there were at least ten of them. Then the engines and lamp beams went off, leaving almost everyone's vision filled with pink and green splodges.

Harry had shut his eyes tight while the lights were on. Now with them off he could see the men were heavily armed in dark fatigues and some sort of body armour. Several of them were injured, limping, soiled and grazed. Behind them he could just make out waves of dark swirling grey camouflage covering both vehicles. Other than that they had no markings at all.

Stevenson took a moment to reassure everyone, 'Please remain calm, my men are here to help.'

'What does the town have to do in return for your help?' Justine asked blinking madly then rubbing at her eyes.

'Nothing more than continue to be oblivious and ignorant to the world around them. Mr Burdock has done the town one favour at least, by keeping the majority of its inhabitants locked out away from all this and by burning most of the evidence' Stevenson checked the time again. 'Harry, you and your men will leave with me. Miss Page will go back to her parents.' Glass cracked around them and shards tinkled down like rain. 'The Major's Company will leave on a boat tomorrow.' Mr Stevenson glanced over at the Fire Men loosing the battle with the spreading flames. 'So, hand over my radio little man and run along. There's a good boy.'

'We should all try to stop this blaze, it's starting to spread,' Captain Dreyer pleaded.

Stevenson shook his head, 'One thing at a time. Give me the radio.'

'No, give me the radio,' Major Jackson ordered without a care for Stevenson or his men. 'Captain, Corporal, take Private Cooper and Sergeant Roberts and see what you can do to help with the fire.'

Jarli handed over the transmitter and moved away with the others to help fight the flames.

'Stay in sight,' was Mr Stevenson's only condition as he sighed and signalled to his men.

The darkly clad soldiers moved closer, forming a suggestive avenue of muzzles that pointed back towards their trucks.

'He can't go, we're having a baby,' Justine looked into her lover's eyes willing him to stay.

'We are?' Harry shouted. 'That's, well I just can't, I, I love you.'

As the couple hugged and kissed, Justine heard a strange sound. It was like a thousand distant people gasping quietly all around the town.

Stevenson's laugh and the fire drowned it out, 'I cannot leave him here can I? None of this can be known about. You are all endangering the project, nationwide.'

'We won't say a word, we'll just get married and have a baby and pretend this never happened.' Justine put her hands together, begging for an alternative with one more word, 'Please.'

Stevenson ignored her, 'The SD base should have been filled in by now. Something similar will be done at your patrol's operational base Sergeant Clark. We will clear out this sector, retrieve your weapons stashes and move out before dawn.'

It was very odd for Justine to hear him calling her boyfriend Sergeant Clark, instead of Harry. She knew Stevenson was trying to manipulate them, convince them that all this was real again. It was like two owners calling a dog in different directions.

'Stay Harry,' she smiled softly.

Stevenson talked over her before Harry could answer, 'Have you hidden the pretty little Irish girl away somewhere too? I hear the merry widow is alone on a mortuary slab, strangled apparently? I bet we can make something of that. If you continue to harbour Mary, she will be hunted down for murder.'

Justine and the major looked at each other, but said nothing.

'It is a shame Sergeant Clark, this *was* one of the best set ups we had. The locations were ready made. You were well-trained, very well equipped, exceptional local knowledge and clearly up for the fight. Which is why I have arranged for your little gang to be sent somewhere that you can be of more use.'

'And what if we refuse?' Harry asked.

Stevenson laughed again.

Before he could answer properly, Justine pulled out her Luger. 'He won't be going anywhere,' she shrieked.

A cacophony of firing bolts were readied by Stevenson's men, all synchronously changing position to face her and Harry.

'You should ask Sergeant Clark what he wants for himself and his men. Let him speak,' Stevenson ignored Justine's gun and addressed Harry directly.

'I did speak,' Harry said before reaching out and lowering Justine's pistol gently down. 'I asked, what happens if we refuse?'

'Do you really want to risk a shoot out and, *if* you survive, remain here fixing cars and washing nappies?' Stevenson frowned. 'When you could all sign up for my special forces and fight for the country your children will grow up in?'

'What happens if we all stay?' Edward persisted, raising his own gun an inch in defiance of the overwhelming odds.

'You keep asking the same questions.' Stevenson decided it was time to push the conversation forward, 'You can not refuse to follow orders. Assassinating the police chief should have been proof enough of that.'

'What?' Edward and Finn said together, looking at Harry for an answer.

'I, I,' Harry couldn't reply.

Stevenson allowed him a moment, then ploughed on, 'So you see, you all need to vanish. One way or another I have to clean this mess up.'

Justine took it as a threat and raised her gun again.

Stevenson called out to his men, 'Hold fire, the girl is bluffing.'

Her first shot took off his hat. Without the brim to hide it, Stevenson's old cheek scar shone orange in the flames. It flowed through his eyebrow and forehead then stopped at a dark Brylcreem hairline that hid the rest of the old wound. 'I see,' he said looking up. 'Maybe you should come along too? I believe your mother is French and it is possible the pregnancy would be a handy disguise.'

'We are not going anywhere with you,' Harry stated firmly.

In the midst of the stand off Major Jackson carefully asked Harry and Mr Stevenson, 'Why Mr Higgins, why did you kill him?'

Harry looked at Justine for sympathy, but found none in her eyes. It was too big a question.

Stevenson answered for him, 'The local Chief of Police was given the task of checking everyone put forward for the patrols and special duties teams in this sector. He vetted the men here, they all knew him and more importantly he knew who they were. It was another oversight in the planning. I came up with a solution.'

Harry rubbed his mouth and explained nervously, 'There were sealed orders at our base. Mission one in an invasion protocol was the assassination of Mr Higgins. I did it for all of us.' He turned to look at his men then back to Justine, 'We thought we were defending our families, the town and the country. I thought I was defending my men and Mary, anyone who was involved. I had to, you can't be sentimental in a war can you?' He shook his head with uncertainty.

'Sometimes you can try,' Justine said moving closer and holding Harry tightly.

There was that strange groaning crowd noise again from the streets all around them. It was getting bigger and closer. This time it sounded clearer too, more like a massive cinema audience reacting to a film.

The major and some of Stevenson's soldiers scanned their heads around the streets and rooftops. They half expected to see where the sound had come from, but everywhere was currently deserted.

Justine was unsure how she felt, being in love with a sanctioned killer. 'You are a father now,' she whispered into his ear. Then she stood away and asked desperately, 'So what if he is ordering you to go, will you do that too?'

Harry's head was shaking, but it wasn't an answer. Finn and Edward looked at their commander and understood the burden that he'd carried for them over the last few days. Family and friends weighed heavily on all their minds.

The silence was broken by the clarifying sound of a thousand feet on cobbles. It grew louder, culminating from every direction as flickering shadows started to appear at the roads distant junctions.

Around the nearest corner the peopled contents of Public Shelter Number Two had arrived. They all carried large buckets, jugs and pales. As they jogged toward the light of the fire their shadows climbed the walls surrounding the square.

'You've started a trend son,' Jackson pointed out to Finn.

As each group arrived Captain Dreyer employed them gladly to join the firemen and empty their loads on to the flames in a series of human chains.

The people of Public Shelter Number Four were the next to fully appear in the opposite direction, behind Stevenson's armour plated wagons. They had no menace about them and no apparent interest in the dark soldiers or their quarrel. All they had were more brimming buckets and sloshing bowls to add to the chain. They swamped past the trucks in ignorance and moved on towards the burning buildings. Once there, they started new lines of defence against the fire, coordinated by Sergeant Robert's and Captain Dreyer.

'Who let them out then?' Major Jackson asked.

'Who cares, they are as blind as sheep in the night,' Stevenson shrugged whilst weighing up his teams best exit route.

Justine looked around at the chains of people near her and remembered seeing the same faces queuing every morning in the town hall foyer and waiting areas. *Yes they had been sheep*, she thought, *but not anymore*. She saw now that behind the flames reflected in their eyes, there were new firestorms sparking within.

She snapped back to gaze in wonder as Albert appeared from a side street on a white horse. He had two more shelters worth of town folk in tow. Justine and Harry watched together, open mouthed as Albert casually trotted over with a pair of bolt cutters resting over his thigh.

So far all the new arrivals had been passive and friendly, but behind them the major's multi coloured wagons and well-armed men began to appear in the cracks. More Australian soldiers leaned out of windows all around the square as Sergeant Sanderson of the Home Guard came into view sat on the roof of the first brightly adorned wagon to fully arrive on scene. He was armed with a service revolver and a crow bar. Filling the cab and riding the running boards were the rest of the Home Guard platoon, the sober ones at least.

As soon as Albert saw Edward he slid off and bolted over to hug him. Edward had to catch the daft old bugger and keep him upright.

'I knew you'd be alright son,' Albert said.

A second out of synch, his words also boomed out of the speakers, which now surrounded the square on the cabs of all the major's vehicles. Then these echoes formed into a high pitched feed back whine that was deafening. Albert let go undeterred and shook Harry and Finn's hands then followed their gaze down to the gun and the awkward smile on Mr Stevenson's face.

'Are these the *arse holes* who've been causing all the trouble?' Albert shouted over the whistling speakers as he stood up to Stevenson and stuck his chin out.

Finn kicked his bucket as the word "arseholes" echoed around the walls followed by a fading "trouble, rouble, uble".

'No dad, that was probably us,' Edward sighed, unnerved at his own voice suddenly being amplified back at him too.

Then as if to confirm their involvement in the recent and reckless activities, something over by the train yards exploded. It sent a mushroom of fire into the sky above the distant buildings.'

'That would be Elijah at the fuel dump, sorry, orry, rry,' Edward sighed over the speaker system.

Two more balls of flame went up from the same spot and several of the firemen hurriedly organised themselves ready to investigate the new threat.

Around this activity the empty paled members of the public began to turn their attention on Mr Stevenson and his men. Still with buckets in hand they began to crowd in menacingly surrounding the dark soldiers and their vehicles.

'All this complicates matters somewhat. Alright I give up.' Stevenson conceded, stepping forward as if to surrender.

As the speakers repeated his words he snatched Mary's broken transmitter away from the distracted major and pressed his weapon hard into Albert's gut.

'Drop your weapons, all of you,' Stevenson ordered.

Harry's team did as they were told immediately. It took a nod from the major before the men under his control put down their weapons on the surrounding windows and wagons.

'I suggest we expedite an exit and worry about the detail later,' Mr Stevenson stepped back into the human corridor his men had previously created. 'Everyone who is not Australian, or holding a bucket needs to go now.' He signalled to pull out and let Albert move a small distance away while still pointing a gun at his midsection. 'Major, it has been a pleasure. I assure you, all that has happened here will be dealt with. I have full written authorisation from Mr Churchill which will guarantee it.'

'Even you can't wipe out a whole town,' the major protested.

Stevenson considered the problem then said, 'Oh I might have to be a bit more creative, but it can be done. Coventry didn't have to happen, but the greater good is always the best way forward.'

Stevenson turned and headed off towards the armoured trucks with two of his shadow soldiers covering his back. The rest of his men began to try and herd Harry's team away.

Around them the town's folk surged forward. As one they put their hands into their seemingly empty bowls and buckets and pulled out carving knives, screwdrivers and hammers.

'Oh very good,' Stevenson said applauding their efforts sarcastically with a slow clap. 'Please step away now *little people.* Or I will order my heavily armed force to open fire without further regard for life.'

At that exact moment Sergeant Robert's safe reached its optimum temperature and the ammunition inside the police station went off. The clatter of shots exploding rattled everyone to duck and dive away. As they all slowly got back upright, a breathless Patrick popped up through the hatch on Stevenson's biggest armour clad lorry. He smiled like a man who was very happy with his work. Mounted on the cab in front of him was an enormous Bren gun. 'Jesus, look at this new truck I've found Harry,' he shouted down, still grinning madly.

Harry's eyes moved away from Pat and gazed with pride at the towns coordinated surge of bravery and his own change of odds. The Australian soldiers had stepped up to the plate too, re-armed themselves and spread out into better positions around the square.

'This is our town and these are our boys,' a woman standing over Finn's bucket yelled to thunderous applause. Her voice and the clapping rolled over them all in quadrophonic clarity.

As the noise began to feedback again, Finn bent down and switched off the radio set. Harry shook his head as Elijah appeared from the direction of the rail yards with a side stitch.

'The whole town heard everything,' Elijah said brushing away a tear from his cheek. 'It was so emotional, someone should write it all down.' He levelled his own gun ready for action and gasped, 'What a palaver.'

333

Stevenson's soldiers were not interested in slaughter, especially their own. Several of them were already in a lot of pain, thanks to Jarli's handiwork. Without waiting for orders they lowered their various weapons then placed them down slowly and put up their hands. Their boss was not as keen to give up.

'This is not your town or theirs,' Stevenson pointed his pistol towards the major then over to the cowering councillor who was still trying to sneak away.

Several large foundry men quickly blocked burdock's path. One of them reached in and pulled out the ledger they had heard about over the speakers. He patted it on the councillors forehead and said smugly, 'Guilty!'

'This town is mine now, I am in charge,' Stevenson continued to rant. 'I have a letter from the Prime Minister which gives me limitless authorisation.' He groped for an envelope in his breast pocket, held it up and said with an air of apprehension, 'Now put down your weapons, or someone is going to get hurt.' All that this achieved was to swell the wall of men and women moving closer.

Harry was one pace ahead of them all. He stepped in towards Mr Stevenson's weapon and with his hands raised he said gently, 'You should give up Sir. These people aren't going to let you go, not if you don't play nicely.'

Stevenson raised his gun up to meet Harry's face and twitched a shaky finger on the trigger.

Justine steadied her arm on Stevenson's car door and fired one timid shot.

Stevenson looked shocked and released his grip until his pistol tumbled free. Then the man fell back like an ironing board and hit the cobbles with an almighty crack. His eyes flickered, staring up at a sea of faces containing all of the people who had brought about his downfall. There was dark blood oozing out from a gash on the back of his head.

Before the lights went out, Stevenson felt compelled to say two final words to them all. 'Toodle, pip...' he slurred.

Chapter Twenty-Seven

There was a new patient at the hospital. He had slept for almost two days, but was currently awake and lost in thought. Sister Teresa helped him to sit up slowly and offered him a beaker to drink from.

'Where am I?' the man asked through dry and split lips.

Sister Teresa said nothing at first, choosing to check his pulse before answering. 'Your in bed so you are,' she said finally. 'And you'll be staying there for a while if you know what's good for you.'

There was a knock on the doorframe and Duncan Greene came in. Fresh shaven and wearing a suit, he no longer resembled the town drunk he had been. Other than his bloodshot eye's and pale demeanour, he was unrecognisable.

Sister Teresa made a note on the clipboard at the end of the bed and left them to it.

'I bought you these,' Duncan said, pulling over a chair from the bay window. In his free hand there was a newspaper and a brown paper bag. 'Yesterdays run of the Express and Herald.'

'Thank you, what's in the bag?' the patient enquired.

'Fruit,' Duncan replied, 'I thought it would be good, for both of us.'

The headline on the paper read, "Volunteers join Major Jackson's Company overseas". The wide image below showed a line of trucks preparing to leave town in a long convoy. Several of them looked very hi-tech and expensive. In the foreground a neat row of Australian officers and soldiers waved at the camera. Behind them a long line of grumpy looking, darkly dressed men stood with their hands behind their backs. They were the only faces in the picture not smiling.

The article described how the brave new volunteers would go to fight in some foreign land after days at sea.

'Why are they going overseas?' the patient asked.

'To fight in the war son,' Duncan answered, leaning forward to get a closer look at the patient's scars.

The man in the bed scrunched up his features and enquired, 'What war?'

Duncan explained briefly, as the man read on.

The second biggest headline was about the Councillors and Captain Cooke's arrest. There seemed to be large amounts of witnesses now willing to come forward and describe every level of their unscrupulous activities. The smaller picture and caption featured Mr Burdock being arrested in front of the smouldering police station. A good-looking WPC looked on behind him, examining a leather-bound notebook with a serious frown.

'Heroes and villains in the news today,' the patient said weakly, 'Do we know any of them?'

Duncan shook his head. 'Only a bit,' he confessed.

'Those men from the council sound like awful rogues.'

Duncan took back the paper and read the last article on the front page out loud. It explained the benevolence of a caretaker. He was apparently organising the rebuilding and improvement of the town. An office had been set up somewhere in the council chambers where residents could request any work they needed doing with no need for forms or delay.

'That man sounds very generous and kind, to give up his time and use his authorisation to get everything done.' The man in the bed closed his eyes.

'You rest son, you look tired.' Duncan folded the paper away and took out an apple for himself.

'Everyone has been very kind to me, the Doctors and that fat police man.'

Duncan took a bite of the apple and munched through his words, 'That police man asked me, if I'd put you up, when you're a bit better? And they have stored all the building supplies at our yard, so I'm a busy man again. I could do with some help, as soon as your fit.'

The patient opened his eyes again briefly and asked, 'Are you a doctor, do I know you?'

'No son, my name's Duncan Greene. I lost my boy in the war you see and so, well I have a spare room and all his clothes and kit just sitting there.'

'That is kind. I don't want to be any trouble to anyone. I banged my head, that's what they told me and there's this.' The man in the bed pulled aside his pyjamas revealing a large bruise with a red mark where Justine's dart had punctured his shoulder.

'Sergeant Roberts said you'd been washed up in town last night, with those soldiers.' Duncan tapped the cover of the newspaper, 'You lost your memory somewhere son.'

The man in the bed turned his eyes towards the window and stared into the distance.

'I know you're not my boy, you're too old, but I can take you in until you feel, human. That would be the right thing to do. Maybe, someone else is doing that for him?' Duncan stared out of the window too, trying to think of something more encouraging to say. 'You can help around the yard if you like and get strong again. Maybe together we can rebuild the Greene empire.'

'That sounds like a nice plan,' Mr Stevenson mumbled as he drifted back off to sleep.

Standing in the centre of the town square, Harry would happily have gone to sleep, if someone had ordered him too. 'Well men, you're all officially on sick leave for a bit,' he said to the dozens of inexperienced Australian soldiers watching his every move. 'So be ready to get a shed load of exercise and a lot of fresh air.'

'We are still going to Africa? With our mates?' a fresh faced eighteen year old asked.

Harry nodded, 'Your major thought you would all benefit from a bit of additional training first. Then we'll get you where you need to be.'

Edward smiled at the unhappy faces and butted in, 'Don't worry we found a few experienced men to fill in for some of you while you're away. And it's all official and sanctioned, by the Prime Minister himself.'

There was a rumble of approval from the men.

'Well sort of...' Harry winced and raised an eyebrow.

Pat walked over with Victoria; he was carrying enough kit to fill a small van. 'Time to go home Ted,' he said before dumping the equipment down in front of the men. He rubbed his hands to get the blood flowing again and turned back to Edward with a big smile, 'Put your feet up and have a rest.'

'Don't blow anything else up while I'm away,' Edward frowned and saluted Harry before leaving with Victoria.

'I only ever cause a minimal amount of precise destruction,' Patrick shouted after him. 'That's Irish professionalism that is.'

'At least he looks better today,' Harry muttered.

'I wish we could have kept that beautiful big truck, it would have made a nice replacement for Minnie,' Patrick said without thinking, then added, 'Not that anything could replace such a fine English vehicle.'

'Victoria is going to give him a hard time about all this isn't she?' Harry speculated.

Patrick took a moment to look along the rows of new men. 'I think he'll be alright,' he said turning back to Harry. 'To be honest after Vicky spoke to Justine about that calendar training manual of ours, well, she hasn't put it down. She was asking me questions all the way down here. Seems to be pretty screwed on. I think she might even be a good stand in for my Mary, until we track her down.'

'I don't think we'll need her or Mary,' Harry looked away. 'The Australians needed some extra supplies, so I filled that big wagon up with most of our weapons caches too. There is just enough left for these boys to do a few weeks hard training.' He tried to get a smile out of the big man, but the news only seemed to make him crosser.

'Then what?' Pat asked.

'I don't know, it depends on how Mr Stevenson takes all this I suppose. Doctor Jones said he might get his memory back pretty soon or maybe never?'

'So it's all over?' Pat said, moving Harry out of the Australian soldiers earshot.

'No, yes, maybe,' Harry sighed deeply. 'We need to do a bloody good job of flattening out all the creases and making it seem like Stevenson did it all. Then if he gets better we might convince him to leave us alone for the price of everyone's continued silence.' Harry knew it could work, but most likely it wouldn't. 'He can't shoot a whole town can he?'

Pat had an idea, 'If I go and look for Mary, you could all come with me?'

'Well we've been invited to Australia after the war too, don't forget.'

'Via a war in Africa first of course,' Pat reminded him.

'Let's just see what happens next eh?' Harry tried to reassure his comrade.

'Won't they miss Mr Stevenson at the office?' Pat asked.

Harry seemed very unsure, 'Not for a while, I hope. His orders were to stay here and sort this mess out until everything was back to normal.'

'I wonder what that looks like?' Patrick speculated as he raised a hand to shade his eyes and peered out across the street.

All around the square men and women were busy rebuilding the town. The additional Royal Engineers that Mr Stevenson had organised to fill in Harry's operational base had arrived before sun up. Stevenson's authorisation and his Prime Minister's letter had turned out to be a plain envelope stuffed with blank government headed papers. Even so, with a mention of his name and a flash of the official envelope, the heavy equipment and man power had been easily redirected to help the town get back on its feet instead. Combined with the equipment from the river tunnel and last night's wagon of cement, previously destined to fill the bunker in the woods, things were moving fast.

Justine and Mrs Clark were busy too, watching one group of engineers who were stripped to their waists on the other side of the town. The two women stood at an upstairs window with their arms around each other and hugged briefly.

'You know Florence started a rumour that you and the major have been, doing, it?' Margaret declared.

'Florence started a lot of rumours last night Marge. Only some of them were true.'

'So you ain't planning on running off to Australia then?' Margaret huffed and went back to rearranging the room's furniture to make space for two new occupants.

Justine turned away and pulled out some sheets from a bottom drawer. 'I don't know what to think any more, if I'm honest. Before the war I was a girl looking to the future, now I feel like my mother, looking back.'

Mrs Clark helped her to unfold the double sheets and thought about everything that had happened. After a minute of contemplation she said, 'I tell you what does surprise me, just how fast the people round 'ere believe the worst in folk.'

'Oh I don't know, they were much happier to believe the truth when they heard it.' Justine threw the sheet up so that it billowed out flat and floated down. 'Seems the boys are almost heroes now, to most people anyway.'

Margaret sighed, unsure of the praises in the face of so much death and destruction. 'What about you and that Australian officer then?' she persisted.

'Well he did give me a really nice kiss goodbye.' Justine blushed. Then as Mrs Clark's eyebrow rose an inch she added reassuringly, 'On the cheek.'

'I bet he had some bloody suave parting words for you then? Something to make yer bits jangle?' Margaret mocked the army with an overly dramatic salute.

'Not really,' Justine tried to remember his exact words. 'He said he already had a girl back home, a daughter my age. He was worried that one day, her generation would travel here like him. And they would come to ask why their fathers had sailed around the world to fight for someone else?'

The old lady seemed almost happy with that. 'Time to settle down then,' she pressed on, tucking in the linen. 'You can make sure you've got somewhere nice for her to stay when she comes.'

Justine decided to be honest; 'He did also suggest that if we ever wanted to, he'd be happy to show *us* around the other side of the world.'

Margaret shot back angrily, 'Not just going to be you and Harry any more is it?' Her face broke into a wry smile, 'I mean there's me too.'

They both laughed and went back over to the window.

Margaret was the first to speak again, 'I remember being stood here, watching the Aussies bring out that first German. I knew it was going to get worse. I could feel it in me water.' She adjusted her pinafore. 'Never thought it would be my boy doing the killing.'

'He was ordered to do it,' Justine said impatiently. 'I saw the official document when he handed it over to Sergeant Roberts this morning.'

Margaret did what she always did and put a brave face on it. 'Well we've all got some changes to get used to I suppose?'

The old lady rolled up a pillow and shoved it under her pinafore. Then while Justine giggled, she paraded around pretending to be her in a few months time. After a minute of that she sat down on the bed exhausted.

The Court House had now become a temporary police station. It had the space, the facilities and three tiny holding cells filled with ex-council officials. Most importantly for Sergeant Roberts it had an empty filing cabinet and a desk in reception. He stood at it drinking tea and looking out of the window trying to make a decision.

'Thank God young Finn stowed my transmitter in that bucket,' he said to Albert. 'I heard that most of the general public were ready to string up the major and Harry's mob, based on Florence's gossip spreading round the shelters.'

'She wasn't the only one. I overheard Burdock selling a similar story at the pub when I was leaving.' Albert looked sad and unsure. 'It's difficult to see the truth; I didn't know what to think at first. I just knew in my heart that our boys would never do all that without a bloody good reason.

'And you knew that Captain Cooke was planning to do wrong with his, sorry, I mean *your* men *Sergeant* Croft?' Roberts smiled at his friend.

'Yes, so I had to sort it out. Like I said, I followed them until they split up on those bikes then I could only follow William.'

Frank patted Albert on the back and said, 'So you saw what he was up to and undid it all, on a horse?'

'Never got the hang of bikes, I'm good with bolt cutters and mules.'

'Then when you'd let everyone out, the fire just pulled them all in before you could think what to do with them next?' Frank Surmised.

Albert was lost for a moment. 'I tried to explain what little I knew to everyone, but it was falling on deaf ears Frank.'

'I was in the second shelter and they were all pretty cross by the time the doors opened up. Even after your little talk they were still angry mate.' PC Grogan commented as he came in for a cuppa. 'Then while we gathered up buckets and pales on the back of the truck, the speakers came back to life again and we could hear everything that was said.'

'I read your report.' Sergeant Roberts pulled out a sheet from the pile in front of him, 'I quote, "There was talk of guns and stuff, corruption, threats and intimidation so everyone went back for something sharp just in case. We heard what the major said, Burdock, Justine, that funny bloke who lost his memory. It was like listening to a drama on the BBC. Then Patrick just stepped out of nowhere and surrendered to me. He had been following us for a while it seems and explained what was really going on. See appendix (B)". English your first language is it Grogan?' Roberts placed the page back in the pile and tidied it neatly with the others.

Grogan shrugged, 'All there ain't it, every word Serge.'

'We were lucky, very lucky indeed.' Albert expected a reply from Frank.

Sergeant Roberts was busy reading something official on the top of his neatly stacked documents.

'What's is it Frank?' Albert asked.

Frank let out a deep sigh, 'The order to kill the Chief. I get it Albert, I really do but,'

'They did what they did because they were sure they had to. They were trying to save us from the worst nightmare any of us could imagine. Just a handful of men against the whole German army. The odds were against them, no matter what happened.'

'But Mr Higgins wouldn't have told anyone who they were,' Roberts protested.

'Our government didn't want to take that risk did they?' Albert leaned over and tapped a finger on the sheet. 'That is the sinister thing about all of this. One of that Mr Stevenson's ideas.'

PC Grogan gave his humble opinion, 'They were prepared to leave their families and loved ones in order to save all of us, to save their town. That's quite a sacrifice if you ask me.'

Albert nodded.

'Do you think things will ever get back to normal?' Grogan asked, and then regretted it.

'Normal,' Sergeant Roberts almost squealed. 'War changes people Constable. Things never go back to normal. You just have to move forward with whoever's left over after the shooting stops.'

'You could make a start by getting the kettle on again, eh?' Albert shrugged and gave Grogan a sympathetic wink.

THE END...

Epilogue - Terror by Night - In appreciation

The British Resistance Army, like the heroes of Bletchley Park, kept their secrets well hidden during and after the war. They sought no recognition for their actions and held onto their memories for so many years that they were almost forgotten. We owe them that recognition now, and forever.

A typical example of the characters involved was Reginald Sennet the commander of the Dengie Auxiliary Patrol Groups. He had waited patiently for over twenty post war years, for the Government to come and collect their weapons. Reginald had been living with the ammunition and explosives since his patrols had deposited them within his milking shed after standing down.

One sunny day he decided it was a better thing to let go of his commitment to the Official Secrets Act and inform the local police of the situation. We can only imagine the amount of similar caches that were never retrieved. When the Bomb Disposal team arrived, they found the items listed here;

- 14,738 rounds of ammunition.
- 1,205 lbs of explosives.
- 3,742 feet of delayed action fusing.
- 930 feet of safety fuse.
- 144 explosive time pencils.
- 1,207 L-Delay switches.
- 1,271 detonators.
- 719 booby-trap switches.
- 314 paraffin bombs.
- 131 fog signals.
- 121 smoke bombs.
- Thirty-six slabs of gun cotton.
- Thirty-three timed booby-traps.
- Some were still attached to made-up charges.

Officially known as the Auxiliary Units (and unofficially as the Scallywags), the men and women who volunteered were to be our last stand when everything else had failed. Amongst their ranks even Clergymen and Doctors were trained to fight the enemy. Several famous names including George Orwell, J B Priestly and Michael Foot were later discovered to have been involved as active members.

Though ultimately no invasion occurred, they were always prepared to fight. If the day did come, they would without question leave their loved ones and move to holes in the ground and transmission stations. By day they would rest and prepare, then at night come up to gather intelligence and create thorns in the side of any invader.

Once the threat of invasion had passed, many signed up to join the Commandos and other forms of special services until the end of the war.

GOD BLESS THEM ALL

Acknowledgements

I would like to thank most of all, my consultant Mr Corridan. Without his help and the expert medical support of New Cross hospital and eye infirmary Wolverhampton, I would have lost all of my sight a decade ago. Also my good friends Paul Hodgson, Richard Martin and my mother Anne (with an 'E'); along with everyone around me who have always been supportive and pushed me to get this book finished and start working on finishing one of my other titles.

I would also like to thank the men and women of the 'British Resistance Archive' and the members of 'Coleshill Auxiliary Research Team (CART)' who have done so much to save the disappearing information about the people and places that made up our last defence in the Second World War. My discussions with them at various events were the inspiration for this book. The list of munitions information on the previous page was found at their informative website at www.coleshillhouse.com

I took a lot of information from the 'Ringing in History Companion' written by Steve Coleman and loaned to me by our local bell ringer Tim Sunter. It has been a most informative title.

A final thanks would go to the people and places of the Black Country that have come together here to create a fictitious world based on the reality of the world around us all.

Find Frank Chamberlain
at www.frankpages.net
or www.facebook.com/frankspages

Printed in Poland
by Amazon Fulfillment
Poland Sp. z o.o., Wrocław